# THE PETROV EFFECT

# BY

# MAC CUSITER

# THE PETROV
# EFFECT

Front Cover Design: Mac Cusiter
Satellite dish © Naratip Sretan | Dreamstime_20961632
Computer screen © Soulart 2012 |Dreamstime_22872841
Model © Anka Lazarova |Dreamstime_26824588
Back Cover Design: Mac Cusiter
Solar flare © Paul Fleet |Dreamstime_17738015

Gurumbi Publishing
ISBN: 978-0-9941582-5-3

Printed in the United States of America

*The author would like to thank his beautiful wife Val, for her enthusiastic encouragement, patience and love*

# THE PETROV EFFECT

# CHAPTER 1

Abigail Brook Saunders arrived unexpectedly in the world on October 16th 1967. Not only was she due a whole two weeks later, but eight and a half months previously her mother, Ivy Adna Saunders, had made another unexpected, and extremely unwelcome discovery. The intervening months had been marked by a continuous and increasing display of histrionics. Despite the fact that her husband Charles Francis and herself were the only ones who could be reasonably held accountable for her condition, the whole household, including that worthy gentleman, were daily accused of being in some way or other involved in a general conspiracy designed to ruin her figure, damage her complexion, and seriously curtail her quintessential goal to be acclaimed socialite of the year, every year. Only once before had she been in this demeaning condition, and once was enough, even though the latter experience had provided her with a son, Peter Francis, who was just turning fifteen. A handsome lad, and she was proud of him, anticipating his potential to wreak havoc amongst the daughters of her lesser bred rivals who, despite their obvious inferiority, were always vying for acceptance amongst the Boston Brahmins. It had been a setback, one from which she was determined to recover rapidly.

She greeted the midwife's suggestion that breastfeeding was not only natural but of enormous benefit to both child and mother, with a look that would have frozen molten lava.

"The child will have the best care available in this country," Ivy informed her. "Take the screaming brat away somewhere and make it happy – if that's possible. I have a headache."

So simply freed from the obligations usually attached to motherhood, Ivy lay back in her bed, pulled the sheets up around her shoulders and began the onerous task of mentally organizing the next few months of her life. The employment of a suitable live-in nanny was high on the list.

Abigail's father was not nearly so dismissive of the news which reached him that morning. So he had a daughter. He rather liked the idea. He determined, despite the Board of Directors meeting that afternoon, the University Senate function that evening, the Shareholders conference tomorrow morning, and lunch following, he would get along to the hospital and have a quiet look at the latest addition to his family before she came home. Soon he would be inundated with sycophantic well-wishers carrying baby clothes which Ivy would burn, toys which Ivy would bundle up for the poor, and cards which would be thrown into the wastepaper basket after his secretary had answered them.

While Democracy generally flourished in Western society, matriarchal dictatorship thrived within the borders of the Saunders domain. In the months after the enormous social success of their wedding it had occurred to Charles that he may have made an unwise choice. No matter, he would be able to set matters right, and happiness would be just around the corner. As the years went by, the happiness he supposed to be just around the corner retreated to the farthest side of the known universe. Charles became convinced the choice he had made in marrying Ivy, far from being unwise, was the most disastrous, soul destroying, life damning choice it was possible for a human being to make. He had always regarded his job as managing director of the merchant bank built by his father as a necessary but unpleasant chore. Now it became the only refuge in an intolerably subservient existence.
In the past he had exercised his professional leadership in wisdom blended with a nice balance of compassionate sensitivity. Now he ruled like a tyrant, dispensing every directive with a generous amount of terror. Company profits soared, investors were delighted. Senior staff drove top of the range Cadillacs to work and swallowed their Prozac on the way. Neither was there any foreseeable end to his servitude. To

divorce his wife was to commit a social solecism from which there would be no return. Ivy was the beautiful queen of her social milieu, and Charles cursed his eyes for being so focussed on her figure and so blind to what lay underneath.

Under the circumstances one might have supposed Abigail Brook would have turned into a sad, spoilt little girl, yet such was not the case. Spared the poisonous role model of her mother, Abigail grew up under the gentle love of Nanny Fletcher. She enjoyed the occasional visit from her father, and endured the more frequent bullying mockery from her brother which she hated, her one blight in an otherwise perfect world. Some children allow abundant materialism to turn their heads, but Abigail, possessed of her father's former gentleness, seemed to take all in her stride without allowing her worldly wealth to turn into conceit. She played with the children in her elite primary school, and she played with the children of the household servants without making any sort of distinction between them. Her mother would have had apoplexy had she known about it. In short Abigail became the young darling of the house, adored by everyone save her brother and her own parents. Her father probably would have adored her if he had taken the time to see her, but now he spent almost all his time sequestered in his refuge, sometimes taking long business trips to Europe where the bank was thinking to expand its activities.

Abigail finished her senior college year with invitations to attend a number of universities including Harvard, but she opted to go to Boston because her father was on the governing body, and much to her credit she had the idea of doing him honour by attending there. In one of the nicest moments of Abigail's life, he had taken her out to dinner and given her a magnificent pearl necklace to celebrate the occasion.

Father had enjoyed the giving of it as much as his daughter the gift.

From the moment of her daughter's birth, seeds of an unnameable disquiet were sown in Ivy's heart, and lately these had grown to maturity and were about to bear their own distasteful fruit. She had watched as Abigail grew from a beautiful baby into a truly lovely little girl and felt no threat, simply because she had attributed every compliment addressed to her daughter as belonging solely to her mother's credit. Of course she was pretty, a reflection of her mother's superb looks. Of course she was good natured, a reflection of that same maternal attribute. Only when Abigail began to be beautiful in form as well as face did her mother's disquiet take on a more sinister expression. She needed no magic mirror to see that her daughter's fresh and ravishing beauty eclipsed her own ageing looks. Believing fundamentally that her daughter was heart and soul a copy of her own nature, she knew it was only a matter of time before her daughter's natural hatred towards her mother would strike and tipple her off her social perch. The fact that she never did so, simply meant the child was deliberately keeping her mother in agonising suspense for her own sadistic enjoyment. This produced the somewhat ironic result that the nicer Abigail was towards the woman who didn't deserve the least kindness, the more that woman hated her for it.

In her twenty first year Abigail graduated with first class honours in physics, a long list of awards, and an even longer list of male admirers to her credit. None of the latter ever succeeded in drawing more than friendship from the girl. She seemed to have the knack of treating all her ardent admirers with an unassuming – and from their point of view incredibly frustrating – sisterly affection and respect. Naïve, some would have said, and there was a certain amount of truth in that assessment. It would have been closer to the mark to have realised that Abby – as she was almost universally called outside her family – was simply in the business of enjoying life and making the most of it without the encumbrance of any romantic attachments.

Her father had taken her out on her graduation as well, the second time in four years. Her mother had been far too busy. Besides, she said, they had paid for her to receive a good education, so it was hardly to her credit that she had benefited by it. A limousine from the bank had picked them up and driven them to L'Espalier, without doubt the finest restaurant Boston could offer. For the second time in four years Charles luxuriated in the pleasant company of his delightful daughter. The entrée came and went to the accompaniment of friendly daddy-daughter banter. How beautiful she looked tonight, how much she enjoyed his company. After the main course, by which time Charles had consumed three times the amount of wine as his guest by his guest's design, the conversation was skilfully steered onto more serious matters.

"Why does mum hate me?" Abigail asked, her eyebrows a question.

"Hate you? Why do you think…?" Charles said, rather startled by the turn of topic.

"Daddy, please don't patronise me. I'm not stupid."

"No, that you're not." Her father shook his head gently. "Perhaps because you outshine her in nearly every department. Sometimes when I look at you I can hardly believe you're her daughter… if I hadn't seen the evidence before my own eyes."

"But why doesn't that make her proud of me?"

"Perhaps she is a little afraid you will take away what she has."

"But again, why?" Abby protested. "She values nothing I desire. Nothing would entice me to be part of her social manipulating."

"I know that, Abigail, but perhaps your mother cannot comprehend that you could be different to her."

"At least you like me, don't you Daddy?"

"I love you very much, Abigail. Your father will always be your friend and ally in any matter connected with your mother."

"Why don't you leave her? Take me with you? She hates you every bit as much as she hates me." Abby squeezed his arm. "You're a very wealthy man. Why spend your entire life finding reasons for not being at home when the key to your freedom lies in your own hand?"

Charles twirled the stem of his wineglass, staring at the candle flame turned ruby in the rich colour of its contents. For a while he was silent. How many times had he contemplated that very question in the sleepless hours of the early morning, lying alone besides his wife.

He gave a great sigh. "It's not as simple as that, Abigail. My position in the bank, on the University Board, in the community itself, relies on my perceived integrity. If I was to do as you suggested I would lose my position on the Board for a start, and perhaps even my position as Chairman of the Bank. This society is somewhat two-faced, you see. Publicly they require chastity and fidelity. Privately they have their mistresses and toy-boys. I have always deplored such behaviour."

"What's more important, Daddy, your position or your happiness?"

"I wish it was such a simple matter, child," her father sighed again. "Look, here's our dessert. Enough of these morbid thoughts. Let's enjoy the few hours we have together."

Abigail gave him one of her loveliest smiles, but inside her heart she felt a pang of disquiet. If the cold war between herself and her mother erupted into open battle, would her father take her side, or nobody's save his own? She hoped that test of his loyalty would never come to pass.

✳ ✳ ✳

Sometime later Abby received a letter from George McReadie, Professor of physics at Boston University. It expressed the wish that Ms. Saunders work as his student towards her doctorate. Plasma research was highly topical and covered an enormous range of uses, from space travel to industrial machinery. Ms. Saunders would find such a qualification of enormous practical value when it came time for her to seek employment. Professor McReadie considered her a brilliant student and would be delighted to stand as referee for her thesis.

The invitation was far longer than Abigail considered necessary. She liked Professor McReadie, but there was something about the way he paid particular attention to her that she found a trifle disconcerting. Perhaps she was reading too much into his kindness. Besides, she had nothing better to do, and she had always enjoyed physics. Her doctorate would make her father proud of her. Why not spend the next three years of her life extending her capabilities? Surely there was no harm in that, was there?

# CHAPTER 2

On the other side of the world some three years before Abigail Brook was born, Katarina Petrov was beginning her doctorate in particle physics at the Australian National University in Canberra, the capital city of that country, under the supervision of a young physicist by the name of Robert Halliday. He was a good teacher, clever in his field and well on the way to becoming senior lecturer in the faculty, but that was not why Katarina had chosen to work there. She was in love with him. He on the other hand had never been in love with anyone other than himself, and if he had possessed a shred of decency he would have told her what all the rest of the world could plainly see, that he was deliberately exploiting her adoration for the pleasure it afforded him in the bedroom. Those who knew something of Katarina's past life labelled him a despicable animal, sometimes to his face, sometimes to hers, all to no avail. Love is blind to all faults, so they say, and Robert Halliday traded heavily on that maxim.

Katarina Petrov was born in 1943, second daughter to Waldemar and Nikita who lived in Kiev. Their first daughter, Lydia, preceded her into the world by some five years, and a troubled world it had become by the time Katarina came to live in it. Mother worked as a doctor, father a lecturer in classics at the Taras Shevchenko National University in that famous city. The darkness of communism lay heavily over all life in those days, and although it provided both children with a good education, the family were never endowed with anything approaching what those in the West would call 'affordable luxuries'.

Winter nights were cold. There was no fire, and both sisters shivered in their one bed glad of each other's warmth.

The trouble had started when Katarina was eight years old. There had been student protests on campus, and these had been put down with an excess of ruthless violence which had done nothing but fuel discontent. Waldemar, a man of high principle and courage, had condemned the harsh reprisals and argued that the students' case should be heard. It was a dangerous stance to take. One terrible evening, three weeks after Katarina's eighth birthday, he had gathered the family together around the table.

There was pain in his eyes as he spoke. "I have heard from a friend of mine in the Party that the next time there is any student protest on campus I am likely to be arrested. This is what you must do. This afternoon I withdrew my life savings. I dare not wait another day. Take this money and travel to Prague. I have friends there who will arrange for you to emigrate to the United States or Australia. It will cost a lot, perhaps all you have, but you must go."

"When are we to go, father?" Lydia asked with sad, frightened eyes.

"Tonight, my love." He stroked her hair tenderly. "There is a train from Southern Station just before midnight. Now go and pack your things."

"I don't want to go." Katarina could see the tears glistening in her father's eyes, running down her mother's cheeks. She clung to her father, wrapping her arms around his waist as he sat in their only armchair, her head on his stomach. "I won't leave you."

"You must, child," her father said sadly. "I will be alright, and as soon as I am able I will come and join you. There is no life for us in this country. We must begin again. You have to be a brave girl, Katarina. It is hard for your mother and sister. They need your help. Come child, do not cling to your father. Go and help your sister pack."

A car driven by Vladimir, their father's friend, drove them to Southern station an hour later. Katarina waved frantically through the back window, watching the ever-diminishing silhouette of her father framed in the doorway of her home.

They never saw him again.

No less alien were the events which followed on from their horrible parting. The night journey to Prague, always fearful some official would come and arrest them, or some thieves would molest them. The furtive hiding in that great city, the extortionate price Nikita had to pay for their passage to Australia, the inhuman conditions endured on a variety of boats until they reached Vienna. Then the anxious waiting for the flight that would take them to a strange and unfriendly land. She endured the mind-numbing helplessness of not being able to communicate their direst need to anyone. They suffered the belittling stares from those who spoke gibberish to them then went away leaving them bereft of comfort. Often they did not know where they would lay their heads that night, or where their next meal was coming from.

The prolonged awfulness of those years deeply affected young Katarina. The long, hard struggle to learn a completely different language, the ostracism of nearly all her contemporaries throughout her education. The demeaning assumption that she was stupid and ignorant, levelled countless numbers of times by most of her teachers, planted a seed of bitterness in her heart. On top of all was the hope-destroying tiredness that came from studying during the day and working as a lowly paid waitress during the night. She suffered the leering stares of the men as they mentally undressed her while she served them, or did her best to understand what they were ordering whilst they mocked her desperate efforts. Her mother suffered no less, finally working as a night cleaner on a miserable pittance. Their home was little more than a mean sized bedroom, its condition beyond description. When it rained water poured down the filthy paint-peeling walls. When it was hot, they sweltered in the putrefying stench rising up from under the floor boards. At night they endured the discordant music of domestic violence which needed no language to comprehend. They all slept together in the only bed, a relic of some charity long donated, with rusty marks showing through where the springs had reached the surface of their paper thin covering.

Before they went to sleep Nikita would pray with her daughters, thanking God for preserving their lives through the past interminably long day, and asking for the strength they would need to endure the next one. Lydia, Katarina could see, was growing in her faith, but her own was dying with every passing day. How could she love a God who allowed them to go through so much suffering? Her father was dead. She knew, somehow she knew. Her mother was likely to die from sheer exhaustion, and what did the future hold? Sometimes she wished she had died that night when they had been forced to leave their father. A quick bullet would have been a severe mercy, but a mercy nonetheless.

As the years passed their living conditions began to improve. Using every dollar they had saved, the family managed to rent a reasonable unit in the northern Sydney suburb of Thornleigh. Nikita, who was really very clever, had mastered enough English to enable her to get a much better job as a secretary in the local medical practice. After naturalisation, the girls were able to receive educational assistance through their senior high school years. Although they had managed to survive the hardships of those first years in poverty, it had not been without cost. Nikita looked old beyond her time, and perhaps worse, the two sisters had become distanced from one another. It had not been the hardship per se, rather Lydia had grown in her Christian faith, and Katarina had totally repudiated hers.

From the time she had made her loss of faith public to the family, Lydia had gone on the attack. How could she reject the God who had sustained them? The God who had sent the blessed Christ to die for their salvation? Katarina had replied that her head told her God did not exist. Even if her head had told her otherwise, her heart had long since learned to hate even the mention of his name. Ever since then they had quarrelled, and the arguments had become more and more heated and passionate as the years passed.

So it was that Katarina, after winning a Commonwealth Scholarship which paid completely for her first University degree, opted to take up her studies in Canberra rather than Sydney. It was a bitter blow to her mother and sister.

"If I stay here Lydia and I would only argue and fight. I love both of you enough not to want that to happen," she had said in reply to every plea for her to remain.

So she had left, bereft of faith and separated from the love and wisdom of her family. It was an understandable but disastrous choice. The years of hardship had taught Katarina the value of self-discipline and hard work, and she was an intellectually gifted young woman. This combination saw her achieve prime position in her student cohort every undergraduate year. It also meant that she had a great deal of time left to enjoy the hitherto unexperienced freedom of student life. These were the sixties, the years of sexual liberation, of making love not war, of acid and transcendental meditation. To Katarina it was the glorious legacy of leaving her faith behind and walking into the sunshine of a brand new day.

So it was she had fallen in love with Robert Halliday, the man who had so eagerly contributed to the newfound richness of her life. With him she discovered the joy of sexual intimacy. Together they enjoyed the occasional ecstatic trip on mescaline or some other psychedelic which did the rounds of the love-ins, held in various student residences not far from campus. More frequently she shared a joint with friends, its illegality adding somehow to its enjoyment. Most of all she revelled in the repudiation of her former legalistic lifestyle with its rules and religion. All you needed was love.

Then she became pregnant.

It's hard to enjoy your acid and love making when you're throwing up all the time. The day she told Robert Halliday the good news marked the last turning point in her life.

"Robert, we're going to have a child," she said excitedly.

The object of this revelation looked up from the journal he had been studying as though someone had told him he had just days to live.

"You're the one having the baby – not me." He gave her a patronising smile. "Never mind Angel Face, I know just the right guy to get rid of it.

Friend of mine in the biochemistry department, qualified doctor as it turns out, owes me a—"

"What do you mean get rid of it?" Katarina said sharply.

"Well, I assumed you'd want to keep having fun. Can't do that if you have a kid to look after."

"You want to kill your own child, Robert? Is this what you're saying to me?" Katarina's eyes blazed.

"It's your kid, Angel Face. I never shagged you to get one. I don't want it. I can't have a kid around here. You want to keep it, keep it somewhere else."

It took a full minute for the deep, overt compassion conveyed by those words to sink in. In that instant of epiphany the first image which flooded Katarina's mind was her father standing in the doorway of their home in Kiev, sending everyone he loved away for their own safety, remaining to cover their escape at the cost of his own life. She saw her mother preparing their evening meal, exhausted from a long days labour, serving most of it to her children and saying she wasn't hungry. She remembered Lydia's wise words and the unselfish sisterly care she had always bestowed on her ever since she was old enough to remember.

And she had forgotten. How could she have forgotten?

She remembered that life was sacrosanct, to be protected even though it meant the death of someone you love. Here was this creature valuing the living child inside her as nothing more than a piece of worthless trash to be torn asunder and thrown away for the sake of convenience. In that moment Robert Halliday turned from a lover into a monster, an enemy, a foul, self-serving fiend. She sucked the inside of her cheeks until her mouth was full of saliva, stood up and spat the lot into his face. A torrent of foul, uncouth language poured from his wet mouth, and she thought he was going to strike her. Let him try. A woman she may be, but one whose body had become toughened through more hard work than this toad had ever done in his life. He advanced a pace towards her, quickly read the fury in her eyes, then turned away towards the bedroom.

"Get out," he snarled.

"Willingly," Katarina screamed.

But where was she to go? Her life had taken an unexpected turn into uncertainty. Most of her hippie university friends were far too much into peace and love to actually want to show any. After several phone calls from the public call box at the end of the street, Annabelle, who hated Halliday for some reason, said she could stay at her pad for a short while 'until she could make other arrangements.' Her initial reaction was to return to Lydia and her mum in Sydney, but an overpowering sense of shame prevented her. What would they think? How could she face them? No, she would not add a further burden to their lives when they had already borne so much.

Her honours degree had to count for something, and indeed it did. Within the space of three short weeks she had obtained a job in a Standards Laboratory in Melbourne. The pay was reasonable, and she was able to rent a small one bedroom unit in Carlton. For the first couple of months life was as enjoyable as life can be when you feel ill most of the time, but now there was at least hope for the future.

Then her supervisor noticed her slowly changing shape.

Being a chivalrous man, he immediately reported it to senior management, who were quite unaware of her condition for the simple reason that Katarina had neglected to tell them. Over lunch that day they considered the implications of this news, the cost of predictable sick leave, the possibility of medical compensation. Perhaps they might be forced to consider maternity leave of some sort. Surely there was a husband? No, she was a woman of loose morals who had become pregnant through promiscuity, a fine example to set as an employee of such a respectable company, etc., etc. By the end of their meal they were in complete agreement. The only decent thing to do under the circumstances was to terminate her services immediately.

Now Katarina's situation degenerated from hopeful to desperate. The rent was due at the end of the month and she had no ability to pay. There was not another friend in sight, and the pathway home remained blocked by guilt. She spent her days applying for practically any job advertised. It was always the same result. Those requiring her higher qualifications were enthusiastic right up to the time they saw her. From then on each interview went the same way.

"Why are you looking for work when your husband can support you while you take care of your child?"

"I have no husband. Is that a problem for you?" Katarina would raise her eyebrows, already knowing it was.

"Of course not," her potential employer would lie, "but how do you expect to be able to work for us and take care of your child at the same time?"

"I give you my word I will work for every hour you pay me," Katarina would assure them.

"Thank you Miss Petrov," would come the response. "We will let you know in due course how you have fared at interview. I must remind you we have many other applicants."

Sometimes they actually took the trouble to mail their rejection to her, mostly she never heard from them again.

Ironically, considering the excellence of her qualifications, those positions requiring relatively unskilled workers rejected her as well, but not on the grounds that she was pregnant. There was a pattern in each of those interviews too.

"So you studied Physics," her prospective employer would say, wrinkling his nose as he scanned her CV. "Never liked physics. You must be very clever. We don't require qualifications like that. Have you ever made hamburgers before?"

"Yes." Katarina would reply with feeling.

"How old are you?"

"Twenty three."

"Thank you Miss?"

"Petrov."

"We will call you if we need you to start. We do have a lot of other applicants for the position you know."

Younger applicants, Katarina thought to herself, who come cheaper. Nobody ever rang her back.

The rent ran out the following week, and the landlord told her to get her stuff out by Friday or he would bring in some people to move it out into the street, and she wouldn't like the way they did it.

It was a desperate woman who made her way down to the Women's Refuge on Thursday evening, clutching all she possessed in two large striped plastic bags. Even then the man in charge didn't seem to believe her.

"How long have you been an addict?" he said, harshly.

"I'm not an addict," Katarina replied, trying to keep her voice level.

"Did you get pregnant while you were on acid?" His hand rested on the doorhandle.

"No"

"We don't usually take unmarried mothers."

"I have nowhere else to go," Katarina pleaded. "Please don't make me beg. I can help you. I'm good at preparing food, cleaning up. I could work for you here—"

"An unmarried mother on staff? This is a Christian organisation."

"Yes, I can see that now," Katarina said, doing her best to supress the cynicism she was feeling.

"If we were to accept your help in exchange for food and lodging, it could only be until your confinement. We cannot take responsibility for new born babies here. Do you understand?"

"Yes, only too well."

They took her in, three skimpy meals in turn for what really amounted to slave labour. Katarina would be up at five in the morning and tumble into her bunk bed amidst the snoring and occasional weeping of the other women in the dormitory at eleven at night, sometimes later. Still, she was being fed and she had a place to lay her head. Life had returned to the daily hardship it was before, without certainty of tomorrow. Her former endurance gave her heart where most others would have given up. She began to make friends amongst the other women whose circumstances were often as dire as her own. Real friendships, with none of the empty superficiality of her former acid-soaked libertarians.

It was one of these friendships which began the closing chapters of her life. Her name was Susanna, and she came to work in the refuge every other Thursday night, a pleasant, good looking woman in her mid-thirties.

One evening, just before Katarina was due to retire for the night, she came over to her with a small scrap of paper in her hand. "Sweetheart, you're due pretty soon, aren't you?" she asked gently.

Katarina wrung out the dishcloth and draped it over the sink. "Four weeks, maybe three."

"Things can be pretty rough around here for a young unmarried mother." She smiled and touched her cheek. "Look, I know you've got what it takes to make it on your own, but just in case you have trouble you're always welcome to stay with me."

She handed Katarina the little piece of paper. On it was scribbled an address and a phone number.

"Thank you." Katarina took the paper and placed it in her pocket. "Do you know I was the top graduate in physics at ANU? Look at me. No one would give me a job. It's so unfair. They take one look at me and think "whore", or else I'll be too occupied with my baby to do their job properly," she said bitterly.
"Either that or I'm too old. They have to pay more for an adult, and they don't want to. I can read it in their faces. Even the communists let you work if you were qualified." The anger in her voice reflected in her face.

"They were all men, weren't they, the ones who rejected you?" Susanna gave a wry smile.

"Yes, they were," Katarina agreed. "Men have the power in this society – they always have the power."

"They are not always more powerful, Katarina," Susanna said softly. "One day, perhaps I can show you how to reclaim your power over men – and make them pay for the privilege."

"That would be nice," Katarina sighed heavily.

"Tomorrow, child." Susanna stretched out her arm and rubbed Katarina's shoulder. "Tonight you must rest. You look done in."

"The baby makes me tired," Katarina said, struggling to stop the tears.

"It does that, sweetheart. I'll see you in a fortnight if you're still here. Don't lose that paper, will you?"

# CHAPTER 3

I n the red desert centre of Australia, where the Todd river runs through a gap in the MacDonnell ranges, lies a town called Alice Springs. It is the largest town in the Northern Territory.  Amongst other things the town is famous for its spring regatta on the Todd river, called the Henley-on-Todd, after the well-known royal regatta on the Thames in England. It is the only regatta to be cancelled because of wet weather. The 'boats' are made from metal frames carried by the 'rowers' as they race along the sands of the dry river bed, making it the only dry river regatta in the world.  The British are not amused.

In nineteen sixty six, just four years after the commencement of this historic event, Australia, inspired by American paranoia concerning the spread of communism, together with its own fear of nuclear annihilation, entered into an agreement with the United States to establish a top-secret base on its own soil. It was the middle of the cold war.

The base was to be named a 'Joint Defence Space Research Facility'. Just how 'joint' the facility would be was somewhat ambiguous, since the Americans didn't care to divulge exactly what the base would be for. Australians were assured it would play a strategic role in stopping the spread of deadly communism, without making the country a nuclear target. Whether this dubious piece of spin convinced many Australians was extremely doubtful. Some politicians said they believed it, and others simply agreed to it for political convenience.

In December of the same year, the Minister of External Affairs, Paul Hasluck, signed an agreement between the Australian and US governments to locate the base just eighteen kilometres south west of Alice Springs, on a large property known as Temple Bar Station, owned by cattleman Jim Bullen.

He reacted with patriotic generosity.

"If it's pure Australian defence you can have it for nothing," he said, "but if it's just American the answer is no. If it's joint, the answer's still no."

The Australian government listened carefully to his objections, then resumed his land anyhow. Over the next thirteen years Pine Gap grew to become one of the largest satellite ground facilities in the world. By the early seventies the eighth huge radome had mushroomed out of the red desert soil. Its presence in Australia was seen by some as attracting a nuclear threat. Many regarded it as an example of arrogant American imperialism on good old Aussie soil. Others described it as a desecration of Aboriginal land, and a threat to World peace. Australians, especially those who lived in the outback where openness and honesty have greater value than they do in the cities, intensely dislike activities being conducted on their own turf which are so secret nobody is allowed to find out what is going on there. While they may not have known exactly what the four hundred or so Americans on the base were up to, it was a pretty fair guess they weren't counting the stars at night, despite being officially told the base was purely used for space research.

In 1979 the Alice Springs Peace group was formed principally to organise protests against the base. These had been taking place sporadically ever since the first clod of earth was turned on the site. Early on, some gung-ho lads with more enthusiasm than brains had ridden their bicycles out onto the runway in front of a huge America Galaxy aircraft as it was attempting to land. They were arrested and charged.

In 1983 over seven hundred women gathered outside the base to protest, including twelve women from the Federal Labour Party. The rally also had the backing of the then Prime Minister, Bob Hawke. Other protests followed. In October 1987 the Alice Springs group organised a

"Close the Gap" demonstration, in which three hundred people were arrested.

The Cold War finished in 1989.

The protests continued on into the next millennium, but political support for them dwindled. Like everything else associated with Pine Gap, the reason was not abundantly clear.

In fact, the end of the Cold War saw the largest single increase in staff at the facility, from the initial four hundred to at least one thousand as it stands today.

The activities which go on in Pine Gap have grown with the staff as one would expect.

Familiarity breeds contempt, however. Now most Australians have come to accept the little state of America in the heart of their continent. After all, their kids watch American TV shows, go to American movies, drink American soft drinks and listen to American songs most of the time. Some of them even speak like Americans. What harm can a little American base do?

# CHAPTER 4

S usanna rang the Woman's Refuge on Thursday afternoon to say she had extra clients that night and would not be able to come. One week later Katarina caught the bus to hospital while she was having contractions. The hospital, she discovered, had a special maternity ward for unmarried mothers with specially selected staff who saw their job as a God-given opportunity to bring sinful young women to repentance. They insisted, loudly and often, that the very best thing a sinful young mother could do for their baby was to allow it to be adopted into a good Christian home and removed from its mother's shameful presence. They seemed to regard pain in childbirth as a fitting punishment for the sin of fornication, and the more pain the better. Katarina had a long labour, begun, continued and concluded under a tirade of sanctimonious moralising admonition, its only benefit being to make its recipient work all the harder to shorten its duration. Katarina held her little boy against her breast with smouldering eyes that defied anyone, saint or angel, to take him away from her.

The next day she was presented with adoption papers.

"Sign these," the sister informed her, "and you can stay until the baby's new parents come to pick up your child. If you refuse to sign you have to leave tomorrow."

Katarina refused to sign.

So it was that Katarina, clutching a small new-born boy wrapped up in one of her own woollen jumpers, walked out of that hell hole with her head held high. Feeling very sore and tired, she began the long journey to the address Susanna had given her.

She travelled up St. Kilda road to Bentleigh, got off the bus and slowly walked another kilometre along a pleasant street until she came to a lovely old home set well back from the road, its huge house number painted on a sign near the gate. By the time she arrived, Katarina was well-nigh exhausted. She found herself praying to a God she really didn't believe in that Susanna would be home. She was. The lady herself answered the door clad in a rather revealing dressing gown and threw her arms around the pair of them.

"Come in, you must be so tired," she said in a warm, welcoming voice. "So this is your baby. Boy or girl?"

"His name is David," Katarina stammered. "This is so kind of you." She burst into tears.

Susanna was good to her word. In a few minutes Katarina found herself in a comfortable bed with a crib beside it. A bowl of hot soup and some delicious sandwiches followed. Katarina accepted them with tears flowing down her cheeks. Even though she had borne the heartless treatment of her tormentors in hospital without a tear, this stranger's kindness overcame her completely. Susanna fetched a brush from her bedside table, and kneeling up behind her on the bed, began to brush her hair. The river flowing down her cheeks subsided into a trickle, then the trickle to a single drop or two, as Susanna's therapy took effect. Her benefactor waited until every last drop of soup had gone along with every crumb. She kissed her on the forehead and left the room.

For the first time in so many months, Katarina allowed herself to relax, to feel her own pain and exhaustion. She lay back on the pillow, and in less time than it takes to tell she was fast asleep. David woke her up a few hours later in the same compelling manner that all babies use to wake their mothers. Even after such a short sleep she felt so very much better.

She was delighted to find herself able to feed him without assistance. On the shelf under the crib were a pile of cloth nappies which her host had provided.

*How kind of her*, Katarina thought to herself as she made a pretty good first attempt at folding one of them around her son's loins. *I wonder what she does for a living? How come she can stay at home during the day?* Susanna had never mentioned a husband. In fact Katarina had gathered from several previous conversations, that the lady was not at all inclined towards marriage, for the simple reason she was quite uninspired by men in general. Whatever job she had certainly enabled her to live in a beautiful home, far larger than any Katarina had ever stayed in before. She laid David back in his crib and returned to bed, drawing the soft blanket up around her chin. How long had it been since she slept in a bed like this? Never, if you didn't count the nights she slept with Halliday.

She shuddered at the recollection. *I'm never going back to that*, she thought, bundling all the horrible experiences of her life together. *My son deserves better. He's not going to grow up in poverty without his mother because she's slaving her guts out all day at some menial task. He's not going to do without proper food and a decent place to live.* Then and there she silently made him that promise. "No matter what it takes," she said to herself, "no matter what it takes."

It was evening before David woke her again. While she was feeding him she heard voices coming from outside her window. With the child still on her breast, she went over and peered down through the fine material of the curtain liner. Her bedroom was upstairs, and afforded a good view of what was happening on the forecourt below. Susanna was saying good-bye to some man, and the way she was doing it gave Katarina cause for pause. Surely she could not have misunderstood the tenor of several past conversations? The man went through the front gate, down the street a short distance, got into his car and drove off. Katarina kept watching, for Susanna had made no move to go inside. Not ten minutes had passed when another man, alighting from an expensive vehicle, came in through the gate to be greeted in much the same manner as the last one had been farewelled. Katarina shrank back behind the curtain, certain she had unwittingly discovered the answer to both her unspoken questions. With David fed and changed she decided it was time to explore her surroundings. Besides she was hungry.

Outside her bedroom there was a long passage which led past other doors in one direction, and towards a staircase in the other. Katarina chose the latter, walked down the stairs, and turned into the first large room which led off from the lower corridor to the right. It was a spacious lounge room, and on the opposite wall another door. She crossed the room and went through, finding herself in a modern kitchen. On the opposite wall was a large refrigerator, and next to it a small door leading into a walk-in pantry. Katarina went in and emerged with a cheese and a packet of biscuits. Going over to the refrigerator, she extracted a bottle of milk. All the time an idea was growing in her head. Yes, this was the way forward. It wasn't what she would have chosen had she the choice, but one would be totally stupid to knock back an opportunity that fate had provided, a means of securing the promises she had made to her son. Half an hour or so later she heard voices coming down the stairs. The front door opened and shut, and a short time later Susanna appeared in the kitchen doorway. She paused at the sight of Katarina sitting there with an almost empty glass of milk in her hand.

"What are you doing down here? You should be resting," she said anxiously.

"Teach me." Katarina put down the glass.

"I beg your pardon?" Susanna asked, raising her eyebrows.

"Teach me," Katarina repeated in a determined voice. "At the refuge you said you'd tell me how to regain my power over men. I'm ready to learn. Teach me."

Susanna studied the young woman for a long time. *Yes, she thought. Rhiannon was ill and unlikely to get better in the short term. This girl could replace her perhaps. Fate was like that. Do something kind for someone and you are often rewarded.*

"Are you sure you want to do this?" Susanna frowned her concern.

"This house, is it yours? Do you earn enough to be able to live like this or did you inherit it from someone else?" Katarina asked.

"I bought it outright a couple of years ago," Susanna said. "A lot of hard work went in before I could do that, though." She frowned again. "This profession is not like finding treasure in the backyard."

"How long did you work before you came here?" Katarina continued to question.

"Ten years or so, but the first three were for someone else who took most of the profits."

"That's hardly any time. My parents—"

She brushed all thought of her parents aside. No matter how destitute they were, they would never have resorted to this. No matter, she had chosen her course when she had said goodbye, and now she had to travel her own road. At least her son would never know the deprivation she had been accustomed to.

"Your parents?" Susanna raised an eyebrow.

"I have no parents," Katarina replied tersely. "I have nothing to lose."

# CHAPTER 5

For the first six years of his life, David Petrov grew up in that big house with his mother and Aunt Susanna. Never for one moment did he think it strange that so many men came and went at odd times of the day and night. Uncles and friends they had told him, and knowing no better he had taken them at their word. He was a well-cared for young lad, and wanted nothing in the way of clothes or food or attention. He had gone to the best kindergarten and had been enrolled for a private primary school since he was six months old. Katarina had been unwell on his fifth birthday, but she had said it was just a cold, and the two had gone into Melbourne for the day to see the sights. Just a cold it might be, but it took a full month before she was well again.

As the days began to shorten towards the end of autumn the following year, she became ill again, a hacking cough that would not go away. With the coming of winter she grew worse, and David spent much of his time after school with her in her bedroom, which was something he had never done while her friends were visiting her regularly. Now all that had stopped, but even though he enjoyed a prolonged time with his mother, it distressed his young heart to hear her cough so badly and for so long. Not once did she complain, but a six year old is quite perceptive enough to read the exhaustion in his mother's eyes, and hear her laboured breathing as she spoke to him. Aunt Susanna was kind and thoughtful as usual. The doctor came and went on a regular basis, and if anything could be bought or done to make his mother feel better, Susanna would buy or do it.

One particular night her coughing was so bad David could not sleep. At some early hour in the morning he got out of bed and tiptoed into his mother's room. She was sitting up in bed looking quite dreadful, her breath coming in wheezing gasps. He pulled himself up beside her and began to rub her back with his small hands. After a while her breathing seemed a little easier.

"David," she gasped. "There is some medicine in the bathroom cupboard, a bottle with a blue label. Could you bring it to Mummy with a medicine glass, please?"

The boy hastened to fetch the bottle and the glass. He returned to the bedside and watched as his mother measured out a dose and drank. She turned to David and motioned him to come up on the bed next to her.

"You mustn't worry about me, dearest, it's nothing more than a nasty infection in mummy's lungs," she said quietly. "It will be completely gone by spring. I'm thinking it might be better for Mummy if we went up north to stay with your aunt for a while. It's warmer in New South Wales than down in Victoria."

"Will any of my uncles be there too?" David asked innocently.

"No, dearest, I don't think so. Your aunt lives with your grandmother. You'll like them."

"Not as much as you," he protested gently.

She reached out her hand and grasped her son's small one in her own. He could feel her shaking slightly, and placed his other hand over hers by way of comfort. He didn't let go until his mother had lain back on the pillow and drifted into a rather rattly sleep. He detached himself gently, slid very carefully off the bed and went back into his own room. He was tired, so tired that he slept right through the alarm, and as a consequence was going to be late for class. He buttered some bread, included a slice of cheese for a sandwich, filled his water bottle with juice from the refrigerator, and placed them both in his small school case. Checking to make sure he had his homework folder and exercise book, he bolted out the door and ran all the way to school. By the time he had reached his classroom the teacher had already begun the first lesson. He opened the door and went in.

The teacher paused in her delivery and turned towards him. "Hello, David. Why are you late to my class today?" she asked, not unkindly.

"My mother was very sick last night and I was up with her until very late," David explained.

"Your mother's a whore!"

The outburst came from the mouth of one Billy Thornton who, being almost a year older than David, knew what a whore was. David had no idea what a whore was, but he recognised an insult when he heard it. To make matters worse the whole class was laughing, and the teacher's face had gone a funny shade of pink.

Undeterred, Billy repeated his jibe: "Your mother's a—"

He didn't get any further, because David's school case hit him fair in the face. He fell out of his chair with blood streaming down his nose, but David wasn't finished yet. He thought of his dear mother being so brave and so sick, and here was this boy insulting her in front of all the class. His feet bore down heavily on Billy's stomach, and the boy let out a scream. By this time the classroom was in uproar, and he could feel his teacher's arms around him, trying to pull him off, her voice in his ears telling him to stop. She sounded very upset, even scared.

David did not stop.

Billy was trying to hide under his desk away from the feet that were kicking him solidly, but there were still bits of him sticking out, and David aimed a kick squarely on each one of them. Half the class were egging him on, because Billy had bullied many of them, the others were just screaming. He heard the classroom door open, followed by a sort of hush, then strong arms were pulling him off his wailing victim. The Headmaster lifted the boy clear and set him down on his feet.

His face was like thunder. "David Petrov, just what has got into you?" he asked in an incredibly self-controlled voice. "Do you realise you are in serious trouble?"

"He called my mother a whore!" David shouted, pointing to the bedraggled mess cringing under the desk.

"Come into my office, David," the Headmaster commanded. "Now."

David followed Mr. Griffith out of the classroom. He might be feeling a little nervous, but there was not one trace of repentance in his heart. There would never be, no matter what the Headmaster said to him, no matter what the punishment was. Mr Griffith told his secretary he was not to be disturbed. He ushered David into his office and told him to sit down on a chair opposite his large desk.

"Explain to me exactly what happened," he said quietly. "You may start at whatever place you want."

"Yes, Sir. It happened because I was late, I suppose," David began, a little nervously.

"And why were you late, David?"

So the whole story came out, and the Headmaster allowed him to finish it without comment.

"Do you know what a whore is, David?" Mr. Griffith asked in the same quiet voice.

"No, Sir, but it's a dirty word. He called my mother a dirty word," David said indignantly.

"I believe you, David," Mr. Griffith said, nodding his head. "Now this is what I want you to do. Go back into the classroom and tell Miss Taylor that you are sorry for causing such a disturbance in her class. Then I want you to say sorry to Billy Thornton for hitting him."

"Sir, I'm not sorry at all," David objected, fire in his eyes.

"We cannot go around hitting people who insult the ones we love, David," Mr. Griffith said firmly. "Society would be a terrible place to live if we all took the law into our own hands. I'm not excusing what Billy Thornton said to you, but you responded in anger. You must learn to control that anger, David. Now go and do as I have told you."

David returned to the classroom. As soon as he entered the room a complete hush descended on all present. He went to Miss Taylor and made his apology. Gritting his teeth he searched round for Billy Thornton, but the latter had been taken to sick bay. David sat down very much relieved. When he saw Billy again he might apologise, but then he might not.

The Headmaster's secretary came into his office. "What are you going to do?" she asked in a worried voice. "Thornton is a bully but he was telling the truth. I feel so sorry for David. What a terrible home for a nice little boy to grow up in."

"Do?" Mr. Griffith frowned. "I'm going to ring Mrs. Thornton and tell her what has happened."

"She will want to take it further if I know Mrs. Thornton," his secretary grimaced.

"Then she will have to do it herself," Mr. Griffith sighed. "The boy does not know what his mother does. Do you think Mrs. Thornton will want to be the first one to tell him? I doubt that even she would sink so low."

❊ ❊ ❊

David returned to find his mother sitting up in the kitchen with Aunt Susanna. They smiled at him as he came into the room. Katarina held out her arms and David ran into them.

"Have you had a nice day at school darling?" she asked, a little breathlessly.

"No," David complained. "Billy Thornton called you a whore, and I bashed him until his face was all bloody and he was yelling his head off."

His face was buried in his mother's arms or he would have seen the expression of distress on her face, the glance that passed between her and Susanna.

"There, you see?" Susanna said quietly. "Confirms your decision, doesn't it? You have to go, Sweetheart. I will manage, and it's for the best, for the boy."

Her mother nodded, almost imperceptibly, and held David closer in her arms. "David, do you remember how I wanted to go north to visit your aunt and your grandmother?" she said softly. "Well, we're going to leave tomorrow. Aunt Susanna is taking us to the big train station in Melbourne, and we're going to catch a fast express train to Sydney that travels all through the night. Won't that be exciting?"

"How long will we be staying there, Mummy?" David extracted his face from her arms.

"I'm not sure David dearest," Katarina smiled. "Perhaps until Mummy gets better. I know you will miss aunt Susanna but it's all for the best. You'll like aunt Lydia and Grandmother Nikita. They are really lovely people."

Despite her encouraging words David remained far from convinced. He had met many uncles and had been impressed with none of them. Apart from aunt Susanna he imagined any extra aunts would fall into the same category as uncles did, strangers who seemed preoccupied with something, certainly not him. They left that afternoon. Susanna had tears in her eyes when she said 'goodbye'. David had never seen her cry before, and this, more than anything else, deepened the premonition growing in his mind that all was far, far from well.

The train was called the Southern Aurora, and the long journey would have been exciting were it not for his mother's shocking cough. They had a sleeper all to themselves which was very nice. His mother did not wish to go to the dining car, so a simple meal was brought to the cabin by the steward, a bowl of soup for mum and a pie and chips for him.

The morning saw them travelling through rolling hills, then more and more houses, and more railway lines travelling in the same direction. The closer they came to their destination, the dingier and dirtier the houses passing closer and closer to the railway line became. Finally they stopped on number one platform Central Railway Station. David waited for their luggage to be brought by the porter, and they came out of the end of the platform into a huge area covered with a high curved roof. A helpful stranger carried their bag down one flight of steps and up another. They boarded another train which stopped at a lot more stations. After what seemed an awfully long time, they reached a station called 'Thornleigh'. Disembarking, they climbed slowly up the steep steps and down to the street that ran on the other side of the platform. No one came to their aid. By the time they reached the street his mother was gasping for breath. They plodded slowly along for quite a distance, until they came to a gate and a path leading down the side of a block of units. His mother stopped opposite a door marked number four and knocked.

Footsteps echoed down the hall and the door opened wide. A woman who looked a little like his mother stood in the doorway and stared at the two of them as though she couldn't believe her eyes. Her face darkened. She spoke several words in a language David could not understand and began to shut the door. All at once he saw his mother fall to her knees, her hands held out in front of her in a gesture of helpless supplication. Tears streamed down her cheeks.

"Lydia, have mercy I beg you," she cried out loudly to the woman behind the steadily closing door. "If you have no mercy for me, then in God's Name, have pity on my son. Let me speak to mother. I need to speak to mother."

Not a word could David understand, for his mother had replied to her sister in Russian. The door began to open a little, and the woman appeared again, her face hard and angry.

"Our mother died a month ago," the woman replied tersely in Russian. "I do not wish to speak to you. You were the one who left our lives, remember? Go back to your own."

Katarina bowed her head onto her knees, coughing and struggling to breathe, hugging herself and sobbing, inconsolable in grief. The sight of her in this deplorable condition kindled that same swift anger in David's heart, a small child's rage at the heartless, foul creature who stood in the doorway, whose words had struck his mother down in anguish. He bounded up to the half-open door and aimed a savage kick at the creature standing there. He missed, but his foot struck the door with such force that a piece of wood split off the side. He never glanced up at the object of his wrath to see the startled expression on her face, but he felt her restraining hands come down hard on his shoulders. He struggled to free himself, staring furiously into her face at last.

"You're horrible!" he screamed angrily. "Mummy said you were nice, but you're not. I hate you. You've hurt Mummy, and she's so sick. I hate you."

He struggled free from her grasp, hitting out wildly at the arms that attempted to restrain him, and ran back to the weeping figure on the pavement. With both arms he struggled to lift her up onto her feet. Katarina rose slowly, hardly finding the strength to stand. Grasping her son's shoulder for support, she turned away from her sister in the doorway.

"Come on, Mummy," he said manfully. "Let's go home away from the nasty person. I'll help you, Mummy."

Together they shuffled down the street, an angry, hurt little boy and a grieving woman, their arms wrapped around one another. They did not turn back or they would have seen Lydia at the doorway staring after them, seen the tears in her eyes, the uncertainty on her face. A full minute passed. The door slammed shut.

The next train to Melbourne left later that evening, and after catching the local train back to Central Station, mother and son went into the Railway Café and bought some food. Katarina said nothing, and although she had stopped crying she looked very pale and exhausted. Her cough had returned with a vengeance. Watching her, David began to feel a cold hand of fear rise up and grip his young heart. She looked so ill, as if she was... He shut the thought out of his mind. He had never seen death, but he was not unable to sense its presence, to fear it. They booked their luggage though and left it in the luggage office on platform one, ready to be loaded on the train when it arrived.

It had grown cold. David huddled close to his mother for warmth, yet even as he did so he could feel her shaking. A sense of the rank injustice of life threatened to overpower his young mind, and he sat staring sightlessly out into the distance, trying to come to grips with all the foreign and terrible events of the day. The train came into the platform, and after what seemed an age, they heard an announcement through the loudspeaker system telling them they could board. Picking up the few belongings they had decided to take onto the train with them, they began to walk towards the end of the platform, searching for car number eight. Now they had reached it. Katarina gripped the stainless steel handrail, her foot on the first step.

"Katarina , ostanovites'!"[1] The voice behind them in the crowd was almost hysterical.

"Katarina Mne ochen' zhal. Pozhaluĭsta, ne popast' na etot poezd."[2]

David saw his mother turn around with a loud sob. The dreaded tyrant of the morning rushed out from amongst the crowd. The two women flung their arms around one another and clung together as though their lives depended upon the strength of their embrace. Both were weeping loudly. The crowd, embarrassed by this public display of emotion, were giving them a wide berth. David was even more angry and confused than before. How could his mother embrace the creature? What were they saying to one another? He felt very alone and rejected, worse, betrayed. He stood there, a small boy near two weeping women crying gibberish to one another. A porter came up and politely asked if Mrs. Petrov would be boarding the train.

---

[1] Katarina, Stop!
[2] Katarina I'm sorry. Please don't get on that train.

For the first time the evil woman said something that he could understand, even if the message was horribly unwelcome. "No, my sister won't be travelling to Melbourne. She's staying with me instead. Can you tell us how she can retrieve her luggage? I would appreciate it very much if you could offload it quickly, because I have a taxi waiting."

The luggage was brought, and the two women moved off towards the taxi rank with David following, a sullen, angry little boy. This was the last straw. His world had now completely disintegrated, because his mother hardly seemed to notice him, and the two of them were speaking gibberish again, cutting him out. They scrambled into the back of the taxi, offering him the seat between them. David shrugged his shoulders and opted to sit in the front with the driver. Right now he didn't much care for the company of either woman, although somewhere deep down in his heart he knew that this horrible creature had made his mother happy. The gaunt, pale look had disappeared from her face, and there was a smile behind her tears and a shining in her eyes that had been so dull and lifeless just minutes before. Not that he could feel any gratitude towards this so-called aunt. No, he was still too angry for that, but if she treated his mother well he might be prepared to consider her in a different light.

Perhaps. Perhaps not.

Three quarters of an hour later they arrived back at the unit in Thornleigh, and the evil aunt ushered them both inside. The living room was warm and comfortable. Rather than sit down his mother went straight to a photo on the mantelpiece and held it against her breast. She had begun to cry again.

"How did she die?" Katarina stammered through her tears.

"About five years ago she had a stroke which left her paralysed down one side," Lydia replied quietly. "She couldn't work anymore and needed constant care. My firm allowed me to do my programming at home a couple of days a week, provided I came into the office and ran it on the machines on the weekend. They were very good to me, but it was a hard life. With the coming of winter she became ill with pneumonia and died in her bed while I sat with her. She called out for you before she died. I told her it was you beside her bed."

Katarina made a soft moaning sound and collapsed onto the floor. David ran to her side, and Lydia, stricken in horror, rushed to the phone and rang the doctor. She returned to find Katarina still unconscious, with David kneeling beside her, stroking her hair and looking scared. Lydia knelt down beside her and felt her forehead.

She turned to the boy. "Go into the bathroom and fill the bath half-full of cool water. Can you do that?"

"Why?" David asked defiantly.

"Because your mother is burning up with some sort of fever. We must cool her down. Hurry."

Glaring at her whilst recognising the tone of command in her voice, David ran out of the room. He had hardly done as she asked when Lydia came through the bathroom door carrying his mother in her arms like a baby. *She must be pretty strong*, he thought to himself. Doubtless he would have thought other less complimentary things, but he wasn't given the chance.

The evil aunt had more commands for him. "Take off her shoes. Never mind her clothes. Help me lower her into the bath."

Katarina gave a shudder as the cool water surrounded her, and opened her eyes. There was fear in them. Lydia felt the temperature of the bath, picked up a flannel and began to wash her face.

"You are burning up, Katarina," she said. "Do you know what is wrong with you? Have you been sick like this before? I've called for the doctor. David, bring me the thermometer in that cupboard, on the second shelf. Stand on a chair, child."

Lydia stuck the thermometer in Katarina's mouth and kept bathing her face and hair. His mother was visibly shaking now, and her teeth were chattering.

42

# THE PETROV EFFECT

"You're making her worse," David objected loudly.

"Your mother is very ill, child," Lydia said firmly. "If I cannot get her temperature down she will die. Pour some more cold water into the bath. You have to trust me. Alright, if you won't do as you're told, then stay out of the way."

The expression on David's face would have frozen molten steel. He stood his ground unmoving, but he didn't try to stop the evil aunt from doing what she wished. In the middle of all this the front door bell rang.

"That will be the doctor," Lydia said. "Go and let him in."

David ran down the corridor and opened the front door. A tallish man stood there, holding a black bag in his hand.

"My mummy is very sick and my aunt is making her worse," he said with feeling.

The doctor pushed him aside and strode down the hall in the direction of the bathroom. He glanced briefly at Lydia, bent down and felt Katarina's forehead, then opened his bag and injected something into her arm.

"Help me take her out of the bath," he instructed. "Her temperature will come down now. I need to see if I can locate the source of this infection. Where is her bedroom?"

They pushed David out of the room, and the two of them lifted Katarina out of the bath. They removed her soaking clothes, and wrapping a towel around her, carried her to the bedroom which had been her mother's.

The doctor spent a long time examining her closely, then he turned to Lydia. "You see this purple mark on her back? Her bra strap catch must have made that. This is where the infection began. Why her body has been so unable to fight it I do not know at present. The infection has spread to her lungs and she is verging on pneumonia. I have prescribed her some very strong antibiotics. You must get them made up immediately. There is an all-night chemist on the other side of the railway line. Here's the prescription. Please go now. Is that her son?" Indicating David standing in the doorway, "take him with you."

When the door had closed behind them the doctor went back to examining Katarina, this time concentrating on some areas he had not examined so closely before.

"Mrs. Petrov," he said gently. "I would like you to answer some very direct questions. I did not want your sister or son to hear them, which is one of the reasons why I sent them away. I hardly need the answers in any case. The condition of your body is suggestive of a disease which affects your immune system. It would be helpful if you could confirm my diagnosis, however."

Katarina laid her head back on the pillow and told him all he wanted to know. They were deep in conversation when the front door opened once again.

"I believe you should tell your sister the truth," he said softly.

"She will hate me," Katarina choked. "I could not live with that." She shuddered and shut her eyes.

"Perhaps you do not know her well enough then," the doctor replied. "She and I go to the same church in the city. I do not know what you believe yourself, but your sister is a woman of strong Christian faith. It will be hard for her to hear, but as for hating you, I do not believe she is capable of it. Do you not know why she came back for you this evening? She loves you. You hurt her very much, but she still loves you. You must trust all to that love, and I do not think it will fail you. I will say nothing, however, other than to instruct her how to care for you."

Katarina nodded. "Will you tell her the other news – your prognosis? I think she could bear it better if it came from you."

"I will do that," he said quietly. "Now you must rest. There has been a lot of stress in your life today, and this has not helped your body fight the disease. I will come again tomorrow and see how the antibiotics are working. Goodnight."

He went through the door and closed it.

Lydia came down the hall towards him. "Geoff, how is she? She will be alright, won't she? I know she is—"

"Lydia, can I have a word with you in private, please?" Geoff turned towards the child. "David, it is David, isn't it? David, you can go in to your mother now. She's resting quietly and I have given her something to help her sleep, but I'm sure she would like to see you."

The boy flew through the door and shut it behind him.

Geoff turned to Lydia who had gone very pale. "Your sister is dying, Lydia, and there is nothing you or I can do about it except pray, and although I believe in God as you do, I do not think we will see her healed. With careful nursing she may live for a month or so, perhaps, maybe more."

"What is she dying of?" Lydia stammered. "I thought she had just picked up some sort of fever—"

"I don't know what she will die of in the end," Geoff said sadly. "That's not the problem. It's her immune system. It's been compromised by a virus, and for this disease there is no cure. Eventually she will pick up some bug or other, even a common cold, and her immune system will fail completely. You cannot prevent it."

Lydia stared hard at her friend, her eyes questioning him as eloquently as her voice would have done.

"You must ask her, and I think she will tell you Lydia." Geoff squeezed her arm gently. "She has made some terrible mistakes in her life, but she loves you dearly. In her own words she would rather die than lose your love. She knows what she has done, and does not seek to defend it. I think your forgiveness would mean everything to her if you were able to give it from the heart."

He squeezed her arm again, picked up his bag and moved towards the door. "I will be back tomorrow, sooner if you need me. If there is anything else I can do, please let me know."

With that he let himself out. Lydia went into the kitchen and made herself a cup of tea. Her hands were unsteady as she grasped the cup, a mixture of anger and grief mingled on her face.

"Dear God," she said to herself, "I'm not strong enough for this. You could have let her die alone, but you sent her back. I know why you sent her back. I know what I have to do, what half of me wants to do, but the other half is still so angry with her. Where was she when we needed her so badly? Now she has destroyed her life, and what of this child? Where is his father? Who is his father? What am I to do? Help me."

Lydia had never ever heard anything like the voice of God in her head, and even then she could not have sworn He had spoken to her, yet words came unexpectedly into her mind that she would remember forever. "Love the boy, Lydia, love the boy." She threw the remains of her tea into the sink and went to her sister's bedside.

Katarina was lying back on the pillow looking very pale, with David lying beside her. He turned towards Lydia with an expression that said in just about every possible way "I'm looking after Mum, go away."

"David, your mother needs to sleep now, and so do you," Lydia said gently. "Come with me and I will show you where your bedroom is."

David refused to budge.

Katarina opened her eyes and rubbed his back. "David, go with aunt Lydia. Please. Mummy will be alright, she needs to sleep. I'll see you in the morning. There's no school tomorrow."

With great reluctance David followed the evil aunt out of the room and down the corridor.

"Here you are, David," she said when they arrived. "I have put your pyjamas out on the pillow with your toothbrush. When you have cleaned your teeth hop into bed. Would you like some help?"

"No."

The walls of hostility were far from fallen, nonetheless David took note that the evil aunt had given up her own bed for him. Lydia went back into Katarina's room and saw that she was asleep, breathing somewhat noisily. She turned out the light and went into the lounge room, lay down on the sofa and threw a rug on top. Try as she might sleep did not come for a long time. In the early hours of the morning she woke to the sound of terrible coughing coming down the hallway. The light was on when she came into Katarina's room, her sister sitting up in bed and writing something on a note pad she had found in the bedside table. She looked dreadful.

Lydia came to her side. "Is there something you want, little sister? What are you doing?"

Katarina folded the single sheet of paper in half and wrote David's name on the outside, then shut her eyes for a second as if the effort of writing had exhausted her. "Lydia, I have to … tell… you," she gasped painfully.

"Tomorrow, little sister," Lydia said gently.

"No. It must be now," Katarina insisted, her voice tinged with desperation. "I turned my back on everything good, Lydia, you, God. I have thrown away my life and now it nears the end. You must hear what I have become."

For a long while Lydia sat on the bed while her sister struggled to pour out the story of her life since the day she left home. Many times she had to stop for breath, many times to wipe the tears that were streaming down her face, and they were not the only ones being shed. Visions of Katarina as a happy young girl flashed before Lydia's eyes, of the family together in Kiev before the terrible days came, of Nikita praying with them all after a long, difficult day. She looked at the suffering woman in the bed beside her, and felt her own heart to break. All the anger was dead, pity and grief had taken its place.

"I have made confession, Lydia," Katarina struggled for breath. "I have asked God to forgive me. Now I am asking you to forgive me. If you cannot, I understand. I do not deserve to be your sister anymore."

Lydia wrapped her arms around the sick woman. "You will always be my sister, dear one. I forgive you, but my heart is very sad. How I wish you had never left us."

"I wish that too." Katarina reached out her thin arms and wrapped them around her sister's neck. For a long time neither spoke, for no words could ever convey the joy and sorrow of that reconciliation.

"You must rest now, little sister, we have all tomorrow to enjoy together," Lydia said softly.

"Lydia!" Katarina's eyes suddenly burned with fire. "I beg you, don't hate David. He is the only good thing to come out of my dreadful life. When I am gone, please love the boy."

"*Love the boy?*" Lydia choked, shocked at her sister's words and appearance.

"He is your flesh and blood," Katarina pleaded. "He has no one else." Suddenly she was holding Lydia by the shoulders, her fingers whitening in a vice like grip. "Please. I beg you."

There was something in the tone of Katarina's voice that filled her sister with fear. Her bare arms were so thin and shaking, her eyes were burning with fire.

"I will take care of David, Katarina... I will do my best to love the boy the way you do."

"Then give him my letter... when he is old enough." She reached up and wrapped her arms around her sister's neck again. Her voice was soft and sad. "Bless you dearest Lydia. I love you so very much."

48

Lydia felt her sister's body relax, and laid her gently back on the pillow. It was only then she realised that she had stopped breathing.

David was wakened by the sound of sobbing. He made his way fearfully towards the source and found the evil aunt kneeling with her arms wrapped round his mother who was lying very still and quiet on the bed. Instinctively he knew what had happened, saw the terrible grief, knew that this woman must have really loved her. Timidly he approached, for he was in the obscene presence of death, and he felt its chilling power. He reached the sobbing woman and laid his head on her shoulder, felt her arms wrap around him, her tears pouring unashamedly down his neck. It was the beginning of a new and different life for both of them.

❈ ❈ ❈

In the years that followed, Lydia Petrov married doctor Geoffrey Burkitt. They bought a home in Petersham and settled down to live with David, who in a remarkably short time became like a son to them. David, on his part, came to love them too, appreciating what it was like to have a father as well as a mother. He never forgot Katarina, and each year when he was older, he would make a private pilgrimage to her graveside in Rookwood cemetery with a small bunch of flowers in his hand. He entertained no superstition that her soul was somehow especially present with him as he knelt beside the unadorned tombstone. It was simply a moment of memory, of respect for a mother who had loved him to the end.

It always puzzled him as to why Lydia had been so angry with her the first time they had met, especially as the more he had come to know her, the more he realised what a lovely person she was. He was honest enough to discern qualities in her that he knew were lacking in his own mother. There was a certain steadiness, and in particular, her compelling trust in the God whom he himself had come to believe in. Often he had asked Lydia about it, especially in the early years, and she had taken him on her knee and told him he should be thankful that God had given him a loving mother who had done everything for him. It wasn't really an answer, but he appreciated it. Somehow he felt that Lydia could have added details which would not have cast his mother in any good light, and her reticence to provide them was in keeping with the love she had for her sister.

Then one morning, after his eighteenth birthday, Lydia came into his room carrying a small piece of paper with his name written on it. She was looking sad and a little apprehensive, and the hand that held it out to him was not entirely steady.

"David," she said, "I am giving you this because your mother made me promise to. Before you read it I want to tell you a story about two sisters who began their happy childhood lives in Kiev. I want you to know what happened to us, what we went through, because it will help you understand why your mother did what she did. It's a long story, David, and you have become part of it."

The telling took a long time, for David wished to know every detail of their young lives, their flight into the free world, the hard years in Australia. Some of it he knew, but most was a revelation to him, and although it made him sad, it also grew his love and admiration for its narrator. At the end he put his arms silently around her shoulders, for he could think of nothing to say that did not sound trite. Now he understood the answer to his long question, and he felt himself somewhat in awe of the woman who, after being the brunt of nothing but a small boy's angry rejection, had opened her heart and her home to him.

"Lydia, you're awesome," he struggled with the words. "I don't know what else to say."

Lydia held him close. "Now you must read your mother's last letter. She wrote it just before she died. Do not think too badly of her, David."

Lydia left the room, and David picked up the note. Only a page of writing, yet it left him in tears, half sad, half angry, and as a young man he very rarely cried. He sat thinking about its contents for a long time, and eventually went to see Lydia, praying that he would find her alone. Searching the house, he eventually found her in the garden, abstractedly drowning a shrub in a sea of mud. She saw him coming and turned off the hose.

"Why?" David stammered. "She was your sister. She knew better. Why?"

"Because she was tired of suffering, David. She wanted a better life for herself, for you. She thought she had found a way to achieve it. One bad choice often leads to another, and starts a whole downward spiral."

"She asks me to forgive her. I'm so confused. I loved her, but I never thought… How can things that are bad ever lead to ends that are good?"

"Nothing can turn something that is wrong into something that is right, David, yet God is able to rescue good things out of the most dreadful human rebellion. Look at yourself. Geoff and I do not seem to be able to have children, but God in His grace gave you to us instead."

"I loved and respected her," David said, "now I learn what she was doing all my life… I can't respect that. How do I think of her now?"

"Just as you have always thought of her, David, as the mother who loved you to the very end. You must forgive her, just as I have forgiven her."

"I'm afraid, Lydia. My mother started off so differently, and she came to this. I am her son. Perhaps I will come to the same godless end."

"You do not have to fear, David," Lydia said quietly. She reached out and gripped his arm. "Katarina made her terrible mistake while she was still living with us, not after she left. Everything else when wrong after that."

"And that was?"

"She became angry with God, David, and decided to reject Him. After she had made that decision she found more and more reasons not to believe in Him. She deliberately walked away from a life lived under His love and lordship and called it freedom. Now you have seen where that freedom leads. You do not have to follow that path. You are Katarina's son, not Katarina."

David wrapped his arms around Lydia. Once again he could feel tears running down his face. "I love you so very much," were the only words he could say.

# CHAPTER 6

In the years that followed David went to Sydney University and studied a combined degree of Electrical Engineering and Science with the intention of becoming a computer engineer. In his long summer holidays he worked for a firm of computer systems designers, and it was they who, quite unintentionally, determined the future course of his life.

For two years he put up with his immediate supervisor stealing all his ideas and using them to further his kudos within the company. In his third year he decided he had had enough. That summer he had designed a small pocket device which wirelessly talked to the owner's computer and encrypted its hard drive with a constantly changing key. Provided the device was in the vicinity, the computer worked as though nothing was happening. As soon as it was moved away, the encryption on the hard drive became suddenly apparent. It would take a very long time to decrypt any of its data without that magic little pocket device, so long in fact that nobody would ever bother trying. He trialled his invention and managed to get it working perfectly, much to the satisfaction of his supervisor, who could see promotion skyrocketing around the corner.

David was not possessed of a vindictive nature, but he had really had enough.

The final design he gave Alfred Pinnock one Thursday afternoon was not quite the same as the working version, and if Pinnock had gone to the trouble of testing it before claiming it as his own invention, he would have found that out. But he didn't. The company manufactured five thousand of the units before they discovered that far from encrypting the information on the drive, all it did was turn every piece of data into the phrase 'Alfred Pinnock is a thief' repeated countless numbers of times. Needless to say the company did not retain David's services after that. There was a great deal of unpleasantness as they tried to get him to divulge the correct design, because the honourable Alfred, despite claiming it was his own, was apparently suffering from inconvenient amnesia.

The upshot of it all was that David decided to change his direction and do honours in Physics rather than continue in computer technology.

Each Physics honours student was required to attend lectures on advanced quantum mechanics, and David found, as he entered the lecture room, that he had about fifty fellow students. He took his seat and waited. A door on the other side of the lecture theatre opened, and in walked the most beautiful woman David had ever seen. She wore a rather shapeless laboratory coat, but this did little to hide her superb figure, the elegant shape of her neck, her perfectly oval face, shapely lips, huge blue eyes with long dark brown eyebrows above them. Her golden hair cascaded in glorious waves down her back, adding the finishing touch, despite the attempt to diminish its beauty by clamping it in a common rubber band at the back of her head. The sight of her would have put Venus off her lunch, and it produced an entirely predictable reaction from a room full of lusty male honours students.

Bill Norton, sitting next to David, loudly remarked that he would rather be doing chemistry with her than physics. The student next to him gave a wolf whistle. Several others in the row behind made loud and pointed comments as to their preferred method of interaction with Professor Cole, and it had little to do with quantum mechanics. A lad in the front row made some comparison in which the latest fashion model came off a poor second, while the rest of the lecture group simply stared at her. Professor Cole gave her admirers a look which told them instantly what she thought of them, and launched into the most erudite lecture on quantum mechanics David had ever heard, his pleasure only diminished by the reaction of his colleagues to every movement of the stunning creature giving it.

By the end of the lecture his embarrassment had grown to the point where he felt he must apologise to her in person, and he made his way up to her room when he had summoned the courage. His resolve was somewhat lessened on arrival by the sounds of another lecture taking place behind her office door. The good Professor was telling one of her colleagues what she thought of the group she had just had the misfortune to teach. Hearing it, David reflected that the erudition and passion of this present lecture far outweighed those qualities in the first. He knocked nervously on the door only to have it flung open in his face.

"Yes?" It was the lady herself.

"Professor Cole," David stammered, "on behalf of my fellow students I wish to offer my sincere apology for our demeaning behaviour during your lecture. I am ashamed of it."

"David Petrov, can you explain to me why you have the authority to offer apology on behalf of those who have not sent you to apologise?"

"No, Professor. I should have said, I wish to offer apology for my own impertinence."

"As I recall, David Petrov, you remained silent during my lecture. The only communication I received from you was a slight colouring of your face when John Thompson metaphorically expressed his desire to have sex with me, rather than to listen to my thoughts on quantum mechanics," Sarah Cole said evenly.

David turned the colour of a ripe tomato. This was the first time Professor Cole had met with this group, yet she knew every name, every face, and worse, could recall every comment, every expression. He stood there silently, his embarrassment now grown to epic proportions.

The good Professor continued. "Nonetheless, David Petrov, I note your displeasure at the behaviour of your colleagues. Allow me to tell you that by the end of the course there will be fewer of them, so your embarrassment will be proportionally less. Now I'm going to have my lunch with my colleague Doctor Caruthers, so I hope you will excuse me."

She shut the door.

David slunk away feeling wretched, not knowing how important that short encounter would prove to be in his future academic career. True to her word, within six months the number of his colleagues had reduced to half, and those remaining admitted that their original description had been inadequate and misguided. Now she had become the beautiful dark angel from hell, sent to torture them with totally impossible assignments, who took delight in destroying their self-confidence and male pride in every possible way at every possible moment. David, on the other hand, had come to be included in the very small circle of those towards whom Professor Sarah Cole was actually friendly.

Initiation to that select group had begun the second time he had knocked on her door, nervously seeking enlightenment on a particularly nasty problem in one of her assignments. This time she had invited him in, and the conversation had taken an unexpected turn.

"Tell me about yourself, David Petrov," she asked quietly. "I am interested to discover why you are quantitatively different from the other students I have the misfortune to teach. You don't ogle me. Why?"

David turned a deep shade of pink. "I've had a rather atypical childhood education, Professor." He shuffled self-consciously on his feet. "Besides, I'm a follower of the Way. That may seem a most inadequate explanation, but it's the best I can offer. I hold you in far too much respect to wish to indulge in the behaviour of my fellow students, besides—"

"Besides?" Professor Cole raised her eyebrows.

"I fear you will think me impolite, Professor."

"Tell me anyway," she asked, not unkindly.

"You are so incandescently brilliant... I feel rather like a knave in the presence of royalty, and I do belong in the palace at all."

Sarah actually laughed. "I'm not royalty David, just different. In one thing we are the same, however. I too am a follower of the Way. Now sit down and tell me about your atypical childhood."

David sat down and smiled at her. Try as he would, he found he could not take his eyes away. If he believed in fairies he would have said he had come under her spell, yet it was of a deeper kind than he had imagined possible. Almost as if she had silently commanded him, he began. Sarah Cole's eyes never left him, and at times he felt as though those eyes were questioning him, checking the integrity of his story, urging him to continue, sizing him up. He told her everything, which in retrospect amazed him. Yet for some inexplicable reason he knew she would not think ill of him. Somehow he knew that these very private and personal details were completely safe with her, that she would understand. Throughout the whole tale Sarah never spoke, and Elizabeth Caruthers, who had come in during the last few minutes of it, stood quietly in the doorway with her mouth open. Never, in all her time with Sarah, had she ever witnessed anything like this.

"Come in Elizabeth," Sarah called to the figure in the doorway without turning her head. "Stop standing in the doorway like a stunned mullet. David has been telling me the story of his life. It is a rather sad tale, yet it has made him the young man he is today. Perhaps with his permission I will tell you some day."

David, mesmerised by Professor Cole's face, had not heard any other sounds. He looked up quickly and found they had company. This latest demonstration of Professor Cole's uncanny abilities added weight to his growing conviction that the good Professor was far more than an intellectual genius. If she had confessed to being able to read his mind he would have believed it. She smiled at him. Elizabeth's mouth remained in the same food receptive position.

"David," Sarah said with a smile, "if you complete your honours year with a first, I would like you to consider going on with your doctorate under my supervision. There is some interesting physics I believe you could research."

The recipient of this unexpected offer was not the only one in the room who was totally stunned. David was completely lost for words at first. "I would count it an honour, Professor," he stammered at length.

"We will speak again, David Petrov. Keep trusting in our God and you will have nothing to fear," Sarah said with a smile.

He left the room on cloud twelve that morning.

# CHAPTER 7

Sydney is one of the fortunate cities in the world to be served by a fairly good railway system. It is nothing like the Metro in Paris or London or Hong Kong, but it has served its commuters faithfully if not always reliably for an awfully long time. Since the original network was installed there have been no less than seventeen subsequent proposals to construct new railway lines in addition to the present ones, and of the seventeen, only one has to this date been successfully completed. The other proposals have served a variety of different functions, from distracting the public who were whingeing about State Rail, to distracting the public who were whingeing about the State Government. As the list of unsuccessful proposals continued to grow, public gullibility continued to decline. The proposal for 'Sydney Metro' in two thousand and eight didn't even complete the investigative stage before it was ridiculed out of court together with the government who proposed it.

Each proposal involved some sort of geological survey, and each geological survey involved, among other things, digging holes. There was no harm in digging a hole, you could always fill it in again, and both processes improved unemployment statistics.

In nineteen ninety the State Rail Authority opened up yet another proposal, to construct a new underground line along the western edge of the central business district between Redfern and Wynyard to be known as MetroWest. There would be several new underground stations constructed, and some unused platforms on existing stations brought back into service. To make sure the whole proposal was geologically feasible, they did what they always did. They began to dig holes in the various streets above the proposed route.

Wild Bore Services was hardly the best qualified company to be given the job, but they were certainly the cheapest, and boasted the fastest response time. At least the latter claim was true. Tell them to bore down somewhere and that's exactly what they did, pronto, as fast as their drilling equipment would let them. This contract had been a lifesaver for the company. It was about to go into liquidation. They had been told to fetch core samples at intervals under Redfern Avenue, and that particular morning had set off to begin the task. Parking along the street was pretty scarce, and the drilling rig had to travel a good way down before it found a place to pull off the road and set up its drill head. Within half an hour they had brought up their first core sample, which contained a little extra something sandwiched between the layers of clay and Sydney sandstone. At the same time Sydney Telephone Exchange lost every single connection west of the city, telephones, mobile, data, the lot. In less time than you can say "Oh shit," subscribers on the eastern side of the exchange were bleating loud and long.

For example, "the bank has lost contact with its central computer. Every single customer transaction is down. What do you think that will do to our business? We're talking millions in compensation."

Or another, "Aircraft Search and Rescue Watch cannot contact its western monitoring stations. We have lost the location of about one hundred light planes. Do you think you might be able to …?"

This was followed by a very earthy description of what the telephone company ought to do in the next two minutes, or they would possibly be responsible for loss of life. There were thousands of other complaints as well, and these amounted to exactly half the people who wanted to complain, because the other half were on the other side of the break.

You may think it would be a simple matter to determine the cause of the problem because it was such a big problem, but in fact the exact opposite was the case. The main optical data cable west of the city had obviously been severed. The question was, where? The foreman on the job with Wild Bore Services had a vague inkling they may have cut through something important. It wasn't his fault in any case. He was doing what they had paid him to do. After spending a whole five minutes trying to call his superiors, he shrugged his shoulders, moved the rig to where another parking spot had become available, and sent down the drill for another sample.

Same result.

It took the full morning before a police car on siren came round the corner, and screeched to a halt in front of the rig. The police officer shouted through the open window something about a cable being cut, and had they found any bits and pieces of it in the drill cores? From then on matters were much clearer on all sides. The police radioed the location, Wild Bore Services were sent on their way to hell, and a small team of telephone technicians with very worried faces arrived on the scene. It's one thing to repair the damage when you cut through your own telephone cable with a spade, it's quite another to repair a large core carrying twenty thousand optic cables which cannot be joined by twisting them together again.

By the end of the afternoon a very large hole had taken the place of the core drill, and an even larger team of contractors were digging furiously. When it was nearly dark enough to turn on the portable lighting which had been erected around the hole, one of the bulldozer operators severed a water main. In a remarkably short time the very large hole became a very deep lake with water squirting up in the middle. The rather soothing sound of the water splashing down was in marked contrast to the colourful language filing the air around the edges of the lake. The bulldozer operator was swearing he couldn't see where he was digging, and besides that, nobody had told him anything about a water main. All he had been told was to get his machine up here pronto and start digging. The discussion went on until the lights had been well and truly lit, and a medium sized crowd was gathering around the perimeter to watch the fun. It was well into the early hours of the morning before the water had been turned off, the hole pumped out and extended, and its bottom, top and sides lined with concrete slabs which were now in the process of being stuck together, forming a dry pit where work on the cable could be performed.

The next morning, two Telecom technicians whose expertise lay in joining optic fibres, climbed down the wooden ladder into the freshly prepared pit to begin the herculean task. George carried with him a huge pile of computer printouts which told him what to join with what, complete with some corrections pencilled over the original numbers. Neither was this just a straight join-up-the-ends affair either. Wild Bore Services had lived up to their name and severed the cable in not one, but two places, leaving a whole section ruined, which meant a completely new section of cable had to be added. To make matters worse, those who had dug and lined the pit had not taken into consideration the fact that George and Harry were rather large men. George wore braces to keep his trousers on, and Harry was fast getting to the same point. Both men were squeezed together as tight as it was possible to work on an exacting and delicate job and breathe at the same time.

After eleven days and five hours of backbreaking work, they had joined all the cables except two, and therein lay the problem. There was apparently only one cable to join them on to. By this time they had already received several visits from irate supervisors who impressed them with the urgency of the whole situation, using short words of a metaphorical nature.

"We have to start again on that group over there," Harry groaned.

"Not bloody likely," George growled. "If we have to go through all that again we'll be here another bloody week. Look, bring me that splitter, will you?"

"What for?"

"We're gonna feed these two lines into this one, see?" George demonstrated with his hands. "The one that's a different colour. I've been monitoring it, see, and there's nothing on it. My guess it's a spare. It can easily carry the additional traffic – that's if there is any. There's a lot of spare capacity on this loom, and in any case they can sort it out at the other end. Come on, I've had a complete gutful of working down this hole, and fair dinkum, if you keep having that salami with your lunch I'm asking for another team."

An hour later two very weary men crawled out of the pit. A steel plate was fastened over the hole, and life went back the way it was. Wild Bore Services were handed a bill of fifty thousand dollars which they refused to pay, so the telephone company successfully took them to court for five times that amount. Wild Bore Services dug their final hole by sending a ridiculously exorbitant invoice to the State Rail Authority which they also refused to pay. This time the court action found in favour of the Rail Authority and a bankrupt Wild Bore services bored off into the sunset.

# CHAPTER 8

Abby completed her doctorate in the usual three years. Although she could have taken less time there was nothing else she particularly wanted to do except maybe travel, but then there would be plenty of opportunity to do that. Her relationship with Professor George McReadie had been the only aspect of the last three years that troubled her. A married man in his late forties, quite overweight and greying around the temples, he had been nothing but helpful, sometimes too helpful. Abby found herself having to tell him, more than once, that she would prefer a little less help and a little more freedom to make her own mistakes. Nonetheless two years and eight months from beginning her plasma research she had begun writing up, and today, with three copies of her hard work under her arm, she made her way to McReadie's study to hand in and say 'good-bye'. Next month she planned to be in Switzerland for some skiing, then perhaps she would try for a job in Paris with a company that made industrial plasma cutting equipment. It would have been hard to find a happier woman in all of Boston.

It is an unavoidable consequence of the human condition that no life on this broken planet can endure from the cradle to grave without encountering its share of suffering. Some are born into it as a way of life. For others it sends word of its imminent arrival so its recipients can steel themselves for the onslaught. But in Abby's case, it was though her entire world had been suspended on a thin sheet of glass, which in an instant of time shattered into fragments like a car windscreen, leaving her falling into a new and undreamed of existence. Ironically, the stone which caused the initial fracture was nothing more than a pathetic, overweight pebble.

McReadie knew of her coming that day and realised this would be his last chance to open his heart to her. His own marriage, he knew, would be over the minute he did so, but that would be no loss. He had spent all night filling his mind with visions of Abby throwing herself into his arms and moaning that she couldn't wait another minute to have him. His fantasy had moved from the ridiculous to the erotic, and before the alarm had summoned him from bed, he had succeeded in fantasising several different but equally revolting scenarios as the result of his irresistible advances. He arrived at his office almost panting with anticipation.

Abby, of course, had absolutely no idea as to what she was walking into that morning. Their conversation began pleasantly enough, although she detected an unusual tension in the air. McReadie praised her on the quality of her work and told her its acceptance would be a mere formality. She thanked him and was about to walk out the door when the music moved suddenly into the minor key.

"Abby," McReadie said, breathing hard, "there's something else I must tell you before you leave. In fact I hope it may change your plans completely. I must not, cannot let you go without telling you how I feel about you. You are the most beautiful woman I have ever seen. I desire you passionately. I can't sleep at night for wanting you. I believe you might feel the same way. Let's not fight our desires, Abby. I have to have you."

This revelation caused Abby to freeze. She could feel the blood rushing into her face in horror. *So this is why he wanted me to work with him,* she thought. She turned around, furious.

"Professor McReadie, I have never given you the slightest indication I felt anything other than respect towards you. This nonsense is purely the product of your sad imagination. I beg you to say no more. I'm going now."

"No!" McReadie shouted. "We were made for each other."

With these words the good Professor leapt from behind his desk, grabbed Abby by one arm, then tried to grab the other. No doubt he intended to kiss her senseless, believing that having experienced the ardour of his passion she would respond the same way she had done in every version of his personal fantasies. In attempting to free herself from this uncalled for assault on her person, Abby stepped backwards and tripped over the leg of McReadie's desk, sending her flying to the floor with various items raining down on her. McReadie, still gripping the arm which was slipping away from him, tumbled down on top of her as well, striking his head on the side of his desk as he fell. The blow rendered him temporarily senseless. He was aware only that he had fallen on something soft. He stretched out his arms to raise his considerable weight and realised the soft material underneath his hands were Abby's breasts, and the expression on her face didn't fit at all with any of his erotic fantasies.

From her supine position on the floor, squashed by McReadie's large bulk and flattened by his hands pushing himself up on her breasts, Abby jumped to the very reasonable conclusion that the monster on top of her was preparing to satisfy his dastardly desire. By now she was truly frightened, and in desperation she felt around for some sort of weapon within reach. Her fingers finally alighted on a copy of her thesis which had fallen from the desk when it moved. Grasping her only weapon with all her might, she swung it hard and fast into McReadie's face. There was a sickening crunch, and McReadie collapsed like a sack of potatoes on top of her again, squashing her so completely she had difficulty breathing. Not at all comprehending his semiconscious condition, Abby took this to be his method of subduing her to his will, and applied the thesis repeatedly to the top of his head until she felt his weight sag even more. Using all her strength she managed to wiggle out from underneath him. He lay there on the floor with blood streaming from his nose and mouth. There was blood all over her top, blood all over her thesis. She scrambled to her feet, grabbed hold of her handbag and fled from the room, shaking like a leaf.

She didn't stop running until she had reached the main administration building, and there took refuge in the women's toilet. What was she to do? She had to report the incident to the dean of the faculty, surely. How many other girls had fallen foul of McReadie's lust? Now the danger was over the tears came. How could she have been such a fool? Perhaps her work was not as good as she thought, for McReadie's praise was hollow and worthless now. Still shaking, she left the toilet and made her way to the dean's office which was located on the floor above.

Miss Primrose Collison, secretary to the dean, understood her job as gatekeeper of the dean's privacy only too well. Even members of the faculty had trouble getting past her unless they were on a select list of the dean's personal friends. George McReadie's name was on that list. She glanced up as the door burst open, stared at the dishevelled blood stained girl in the doorway and jumped to her feet in surprise.

"My dear," she exclaimed, "what on earth has happened to you?"

Abby burst into tears. "Someone tried to rape me. I hit him with a book and he bled all over the place. I want to report him to the dean."

The shocking nature of this revelation was not lost on Miss Primrose Collison. She gasped in horror, and taking the girl by the hand led her to a comfortable chair in the office. "Of course you have to. Would you like a cup of tea? Who was this animal who assaulted you?"

"Professor McReadie."

"WHAT?"

"I went to hand in my thesis and he said he wanted to have sex with me. Then he grabbed me and pushed me on the floor with him on top of me and then—"

"Enough." Miss Collison exclaimed in horror. "This is terrible. I must speak to the dean. Please stay there Miss?"

"Saunders, Abigail Saunders."

She disappeared through the door on the other side of the reception desk and did not reappear for quite a while. When she did there was a notable change in her manner.

"You may go in, Miss Saunders," she said standoffishly. "The dean has been appalled by the seriousness of your accusations. I hope you realise how serious they are? They could get you expelled from the University."

"I thought the man who assaulted me would be the one expelled from the University, not his victim, or does the faculty condone rape?" Abby replied angrily.

"I would advise you not to take that attitude when talking with the dean, Miss Saunders."

Suddenly Abby was struck with a horrible realisation. It would always be McReadie's word against hers, and she began to doubt that she had acted wisely in bringing the incident to senior university staff. She found the dean seated behind his desk, and he was not looking happy. He made Abby describe in great and embarrassing detail everything that had happened. By the end of it the girl very much wished she had taken no action at all. Far better it would have been to let matters lie, to have waited until tomorrow then rung McReadie threatening exposure if he did not treat her thesis fairly.

Now it was too late.

"I can assure you Miss Saunders," the dean said coldly. "I will investigate the matter with the utmost urgency, and if these accusations prove to be true professor McReadie has a serious case to answer. If it transpires you are simply creating scandal, then I can assure you the university will be forced to take another course of action."

He paged Miss Primrose and asked her to escort Miss Saunders from the room. There would be a hearing the following Monday, and would Miss Saunders please attend. There would be no need for Miss Saunders to repeat any details of the affair to anyone in the meantime. Abby arrived home that night feeling more apprehensive than she had ever done in her life. It was Wednesday, and the hearing was in five agonisingly slow days' time. She thought of confiding her fears to her father, but decided not to because she dreaded the possibility the whole affair might escalate into something truly horrible if it ever became public knowledge.

Monday morning saw a very nervous Abigail once again facing Miss Primrose Collison. She was told to wait, and the expression on the woman's face was the antithesis of friendly and understanding. Abby's heart sank. She was eventually ushered into the Dean's office. Four men were seated there, the dean, the deputy vice chancellor, someone from the University board, and a man from the senior administrative services department.

The Dean began. "Miss Abigail Saunders, I have carefully and meticulously investigated the statements you made last Wednesday concerning professor McReadie, and I have found them to be completely false and seditious. Indeed, professor McReadie came and spoke to me himself concerning you when he was released from hospital on Thursday afternoon. He tells a very different story. Apparently he had told you many times that your research was worthless, and that he would not consider accepting your thesis unless you took his advice and conducted your research to a standard acceptable to this University—"

"He's lying!" Abby shouted. "He complimented me nearly every day. He said my research was—"

"I would ask you to be quiet until I have finished, Miss Saunders," the dean said coldly. "He told me what actually happened that morning. You arrived with your thesis as you said. Professor McReadie, seeing as you had taken none of his advice, refused to accept it. You pleaded with him, but he told you certain standards had to be maintained, and you had failed to meet them. When he told you this you offered to sleep with him if he would change his mind. He naturally refused. You then removed your shoes, jeans and underwear and sought to force yourself on the Professor. He was appalled at your flagrant promiscuity and eventually was forced to push you away. You were furious to find your attempted seduction had failed, and began to physically attack the professor, using your thesis as a weapon. You knocked him to the floor and then attempted to have intercourse with him. He fought you off, and that is when you smashed his face with your thesis until he was unconscious. Perhaps by then you realised your strategy had failed and decided by way of revenge to destroy his integrity, his marriage, and have him kicked out of the faculty. That attempt has also failed, Miss Saunders."

For a full minute Abby sat there in stunned silence, overwhelmed by the litany of lies that had been told about her. How could they believe such things? How to answer?

"It's all lies," she stammered. "Can you really imagine I would have taken no notice of McReadie if he had told me my thesis would not be accepted in the end? For a whole two and a half years? What would be the point of my continuing? Why bother going to the expense and effort of writing up if I knew there was no chance of being awarded my doctorate? Your secretary saw the condition I was in when I arrived at this office, you saw yourself, Dean. Did I look like a woman spreading lies? Could you not tell? It's only his word against mine, why do you believe him and not me?"

"I'm afraid it is far more than that, Miss Saunders." The dean regarded her with a disgusted expression on his face.

"What do you mean?" Abby cried in protest. "No one else saw what happened in McReadie's office."

"We spoke to your parents."

"My parents?" Abby started so violently the handbag on her lap fell to the floor.

"Your mother, actually. Your father was out of town on business." The dean's voice hardened. "Your mother told us she has despaired of your profligate sexual activity for years. She said you were a daughter to break any parent's heart. Apparently this is not the first time you have seduced men to your advantage, although it may have been your first unsuccessful attempt."

This speech left Abby reeling. She tried to say something but the words kept getting stuck in her throat. Her lips felt dry, her heart was pounding, a cold sweat was beading on her forehead.

"My mother hates me," she finally stammered out. "She's telling lies. I have never had sexual relations with anyone. It's all a lie," she cried loudly, "a horrible, vindictive lie. Ask my father. Go on, ask my father."

"You say your own mother hates you?" The dean raised an eyebrow. "Gentlemen, I believe that alone gives us insight into the character of this young woman." He turned towards Abby again. "We managed to contact your father only this morning. While he would not comment on your sexual mores, he was in no way opposed to the action we plan now to take. You are expelled from this University forthwith. Your thesis will not be sent to any referees. I warn you against attempting to gain candidature for your doctorate in any other reputable University in this land. We intend to take steps to ensure that. You are free to go, Miss Saunders."

Abby left the room in a state of shock. She knew her mother hated her, but until now she had never felt that hatred's vindictive, piercing bitterness. Surely her father would not have endorsed such an action. Why was everyone telling lies about her? She walked over to the Physics laboratory to collect the few personal items that remained there, but halfway across the foyer she encountered McReadie coming the other way. His face was covered with black and blue patches, and his nose had some sort of splint attached, but his eyes glowered at her with a look of pure, seething hatred. Abby felt as though she had been struck a physical blow. She turned on her heel and headed out the doorway. Her personal effects would have to remain there, she was never going near that building again.

The remainder of the day vanished into a haze of furtive movement, avoiding any place where anyone might recognise her. By this time Mrs. Ivy Saunders, pinnacle of propriety, would be slandering her own daughter's character from the rooftops, her disgusting lies reeking with sanctimonious shame and false piety. By now she would be the talk of the Brahmins, all of them tut-tutting and dear-dear-ing, sharpening their hypocritical claws for the kill. Soon her reputation as a common slut would be firmly established on nothing, and worse, the men she had always managed to avoid would come sniffing around her once again with heightened expectations.

Under cover of darkness she arrived home at last. The remainder of the family had just sat down for the evening meal when Abby came into the room. Three heads turned in her direction, her mother, an expression of undisguised triumph on her face, her father, looking as though he would rather be on some distant galaxy, and her brother, his face contorted with a cynical leer.

He fired the first salvo. "Hi Sis. Hear you tried to do McReadie. Appalling taste. You should have done the dean first," he laughed loudly.

"Hello, Father," Abby said, her voice like ice. "I was told you were in favour of the University council expelling me from my degree. Is that true?"

Her father regarded her with something approaching dread in his eyes, but whatever he was going to say was cut short by his wife.

"What else could he have done?" Ivy snapped indignantly. "George McReadie's brother is chairman of the University board. Your behaviour placed your father in an impossible position. If he had said anything else he may have lost his place. You have no one to blame except yourself Abigail. I despair of your flagrantly immoral behaviour. Fancy trying to seduce such a decent married man like a common slut. You're a disgrace to this family. Have you any idea how much I have *suffered* because of you today?"

"I pity you father," Abby sneered, "too spineless even to defend the virtue of your own daughter."

"Get out." Her mother's eyes blazed with hatred. "How dare you speak to your own father like that. Get out!" she screamed.

"Willingly," Abby hissed, fire in her eyes. "May I burn in hell before I cross the threshold of this stinking house again."

"Don't worry Sis," her brother laughed, "all whores eventually burn in hell anyway."

The leer on her brother's face said it all. Abby moved towards the door, but as she passed him she flattened her hand and struck him a resounding blow across the face. You could have heard the sound of that slap on the other side of the road. Her brother leapt towards her, one hand on his cheek, but now Abby was brandishing a silver candlestick she had snatched off the table by the door.

"Why don't you try, brother dear?" Her voice was dangerously soft. "Care to find out how good I am?"

Her brother glowered at her, but made no attempt to discover how good she was. There was a look in his sister's face which he had not seen before, and it gave him cause for pause. Abby left the room feeling completely numb. Somehow her world had collapsed. What had she done to deserve this? *How ironic*, she thought, *if I had done what McReadie wanted I would be graduating with my doctorate in a few months.*

She shuddered at the thought.

Reaching her bedroom, she pulled a travelling suitcase from the top of a wardrobe and began to fill it with essentials. The last item to go in was her bloodstained thesis. She wasn't quite sure why she wanted to take it. Perhaps it was the only remaining evidence of her academic integrity, and she was not willing to let the past three years count for absolutely nothing. Some other university would surely allow her to continue her studies. She zipped up the case, rang for a taxi and went out to the front gate to wait for it. Next stop, Los Angeles, on the other side of the continent.

# CHAPTER 9

Abby was by no means penniless, for her father had made sure she was paid a generous allowance, and using this she had rented a small unit in Bunker Hill. It wasn't the sort of accommodation she was used to, but at least it was her own. Over the next six months she applied to every university she could think of in the United States as well as Oxford and Cambridge in the UK. Always the result was the same. Each institution showed initial interest based on her previous academic record, but after a week or so they informed her – or not – that they had contacted her previous referees and consequently considered her to be an unsuitable candidate. Abby cited numerous people as referees, but they all had one thing in common – they lived in Boston. Obviously her name had become a byword for immorality and vice, a bane and a danger to any reputable department. By now her initial funds were running low, and abandoning the attempt to further her studies she began applying for jobs. Exactly the same thing happened, initial enthusiasm followed by rejection. No matter how hard she tried to shake herself free, all roads led at some point back to Boston, and that was where they ended.

The sum total of this continuous and unjustified rejection began to tell on Abby's usually sunny personality, and day by day she found herself becoming more and more depressed. Several times she thought about going back to Boston and murdering her mother. Such a course of action was out of the question, even though the thought of her mother lying dead in a pool of her own blood was very appealing. Eventually, with her funds dwindled to nearly nothing and still no sign of a decent job on the horizon, Abby was forced to look to what eight months ago she would have called demeaning employment. Even then she had to lower her age by five years before anyone would look at her. In the end she managed to get a job serving hamburgers at a cheap eatery in Chinatown, a depressed and angry young woman. Her only recreation was every other Friday night when she would go down to the pub at the end of her street and enjoy a cooked meal and a glass of cheap wine.

One evening, when she was feeling particularly low, a young man came up and sat down at her table. He was reasonably good looking, and seemed gentle enough, so Abby allowed him to stay and the two fell into conversation.

"You seem so unhappy, Pamela," he said. Abby never gave strangers her real name.

"I've had some unlucky breaks," Abby confessed. "How about you?"

The lad shrugged his shoulders. "Got kicked out of university for smoking pot on campus. Parents broke up, Mum took another lover who hated me so I left home. I've grabbed any job I could since then."

"Really?" Abby smiled at him. "That's a lot like what happened to me, although I've never smoked pot before."

"I don't smoke it now – not very much," he laughed. "Doesn't do a lot for me and there are better ways to feel okay. I use this now."

He pulled a small white packet out of his pocket. "Ever been on coke?"

"No, never." Abby wrinkled her forehead. "What's it like?"

"Only one way to find out." He ripped the corner of the packet and spread a thin line of powder on the surface of the table. Taking a straw from its receptacle he broke it in half and offered one half to Abby.

"What am I supposed to do with this?" Abby asked.

"You put one end up a nostril and sniff up the stuff on the table with the other. In a little while I'll put some more down and you do it with the other nostril, then you wait a while and you'll feel great."

Abby, feeling a little apprehensive, followed his instructions to the letter. Initially there didn't seem to be much change, but then, slowly, gloriously, her head began to clear. Every sense seemed to be heightened. Now she knew there was a way out of all her troubles. The door of the cage had swung open and the rich sun-drenched savannah stretched out towards the blue horizon. She looked across at the boy and smiled.

"Thank you. I feel – relaxed, cool. Are you going to have some too?" Suddenly, irrationally, she wanted him in her bed. "Kiss me," she ordered.

Billy kissed her gently then followed suit with another package. The bartender looked over in their direction a few times but made no attempt to stop them. After a few minutes Billy turned and pressed his lips against hers in a long passionate kiss, his arms drawing her hard against him.

Abby's whole body tingled with pleasure. "Come on quickly," she panted. "I'll show you where I live."

She was nearly dragging Billy out the door. It wasn't very far to her unit, but the journey was periodically interrupted by another passionate embrace. They reached her unit, tumbled through the front door, and slammed it behind them. By the time they reached the bedroom both of them were stark naked.

❋ ❋ ❋

The next morning Abby woke up with the light streaming through the window. One look at the state of the bedclothes was sufficient evidence to convince her she had voluntarily surrendered to a complete stranger what she had previously been so zealous to protect. She looked around the room. She was alone, but a small packet of white powder was on the bedside table, Billy's way of saying "thank you" for the sex. Another man had taken advantage of her, drugged her, taken what she could only give once. Tears of rage cascaded down her face. What a bastard. She felt cheap, cheaper than she had ever felt in her life. The accusing words of her mother came ringing back in her ears, and as they did so her very self-identity crumbled into nothing.

Was she pregnant?

That was a very real possibility. She would throw herself off the building if she was. How could she have possibly sunk so low? She was trembling, her mind was muddled, desperately unhappy. The world was crushing her to death. Kicking off the last of the sheets she rummaged round to find her purse, and extracted the broken-off straw. Making a line of white powder from the packet, she sniffed it up one nostril then another. In a short time the terrible feeling of depression and rage had evaporated, and the clarity she desired had returned. Now she knew what to do. The packet was empty, and she knew the effect would not last forever. This time she would be more controlled. Perhaps there were ways to make the euphoria last longer. First things first, she had to find a steady source of coke. Her brain sang with clarity. This was being alive, alive like she had never been before. First the coke, then she had to see a doctor.

※ ※ ※

The next six weeks saw Abby becoming more and more addicted to the drug that enabled her to cope with life. First it was coke, then crack, cocaine's more lethal form. The ever-helpful bartender had an endless supply apparently, but the cost of her addiction was spiralling out of control. Now she was working seven days a week and six nights, yet her income was still insufficient to cope with demand. Crack could be smoked and injected, but although the effect was absolutely fantastic it didn't last very long. Far better to sniff it or swallow the dose in a shot of Bourbon. Now the search for more lucrative employment became a dire necessity. Any sort of job was acceptable, as long as it paid the appropriate amount of cash. Melissa, a fellow addict who she had become friends with at the bar on Friday nights, suggested where she might find it.

Susanna ran an escort service for discerning clients in, of all places, Hollywood.

She took one look at Abby standing in her waiting room and grunted loudly. "You're pretty enough. Have you ever done this sort of work before?"

Abby shook her head.

 "No," Susanna smiled. "Sorry. My clients always demand experienced girls. I can recommend..."

"Please," Abby appealed, "I'm desperate. You pay more than the other places. Melissa told me."

"Melissa is a common whore," Susanna sniffed. "We don't deal with their type. We supply companions to discerning gentlemen." She frowned. "Wait a minute. You really want to try your hand at this?"

"I have to."

"Very well. We have one client who is a little demanding. If you manage to make him happy then I will take you on. You get thirty percent, which means five hundred dollars in your pocket by tomorrow. Interested?"

"I'll do it," Abby said eagerly. "Give me the address."

Susanna's willingness to take Abby into her exclusive agency was not motivated by any sort of philanthropy but rather the exact opposite. Dominic's tastes were such that several girls had returned in poor states of health, and three had not returned at all. Their bodies had been found a week or so later, but no evidence had linked their deaths to Dominic. Besides, he paid extremely well, and his father was the head of one of the Families. Susanna's life would not be worth a dime if she failed to provide the service he had paid her for.

That evening Abby found herself knocking on the door of a large Italian style manor in Hollywood Hills. Half an hour later she was escaping through a bathroom window and running for her life. She had been so revolted by the suggested evening's activities her stomach had threatened to discolour the shag pile carpet which lined Dominic's bedroom floor. She had felt strongly that this would not be included in the list of Dominic's pleasures, and had begged to be excused for a moment while she went to the bathroom to prepare for the evening's debauchery. She had squeezed herself out of the window, and fallen a whole storey to the ground. Totally destroying the unfortunate shrub growing below, she had raced across the lawn through the sprinkler system, and thrown herself over the back wall. By now her clothing was practically shredded, and her shoes were still in Dominic's bedroom. She didn't bother to return to Susanna after that. If this was what an escort companion did she didn't want anything to do with it. After changing her clothes and putting on her last pair of shoes, she came back to the pub for a nerve settling drink – and another packet.

In the space of one hour her life would change forever.

# CHAPTER 10

The bartender's eyes flickered towards the door. His whole expression morphed into one of abject terror. Abby, noticing the ashen colour of his face and the direction of his eyes, turned towards the door and dropped her glass on the floor. Dominic stood there with another older man, and both were staring in her direction. Dominic, a sadistic leer on his face, seated himself at a table near the door with a third man, and the older visitor came and sat by her at the bar. The bartender had vaporised into thin air. Abby could feel sweat breaking out on her forehead. Never in her life had she felt so terrified.

"Miss Louise, I believe." He spoke with a soft, cultured voice that added significantly to the aura of terror which emanated from his presence.

"So who wants to know?" Abby snapped back. It was bravado, and he knew it.

"My dear Miss Louise", the voice went on, "please do not presume to patronise me. I believe you know my son, Dominic?" He indicated the man by the door.

"We met briefly."

"Too briefly. My son paid your employer a considerable sum for a service you chose not to provide. This necessitated a visit to her premises. In the end Miss Susanna was most happy to extend your services to my son indefinitely and even waive her fee. She sends you this small token of her bona fides. You will recognise her earring I'm sure."

He produced a small plastic bag and pulled one of Susanna's earrings out of it. The ear was still attached. Abby felt faint in the head and fought to retain control. To pass out in the presence of these animals was to wake up in hell itself. Right then, the third man who was sitting beside Dominic came over and spoke quietly into the older man's ear. The latter nodded, and turned to 'Louise' again.

"My son and I have to attend to a small matter of business in the alley," he murmured. "When we return you will come with us, won't you, and you will give my son the satisfaction he wants for as long as he wants it. Please say yes, or does there have to be some unpleasantness to make you change your mind?"

"Yes," Abby stammered, her mind full of loathing and terror.

The three men left the room via the back exit into the alley behind. What poor creature was about to meet his end there Abby didn't know, but unless some sort of miracle happened she knew she was going to be next.

It was then she noticed the third man had returned through the backdoor and was coming slowly towards her. With every step of his approach she could feel her heart hammering, the skin prickling around her neck, the sweat actually running down her arms. This was it. *God*, she thought, *make him shoot me through the head*. The man went behind the bar, took an expensive bottle of wine off the shelf, opened it, filled a glass and returned to sit beside her. Abby could feel herself shaking.

"Miss Saunders," he said evenly, "I believe you are having some difficulties with the couple of gentlemen who were here a few minutes ago. Would you care for this glass of wine?"

Abby's face reflected the terror she felt. What was coming next? The stranger placed the glass beside her arm.

"I assure you, Miss Saunders, I mean you no harm," the stranger continued. "In fact I can offer you a means of escape from your present distressing circumstances, and believe you me you need it."

"I don't need help from you," Abby stammered.

"I believe you do." The stranger poured out some wine into another glass. "The man who has bought your services is unlikely to be very satisfied with them, seeing as you have never prostituted yourself in your life."

"Tell that to my family in Boston," Abby snapped at him.

"Ah, yes, your scandal-mongering friends in Boston. No, Miss Saunders, you have never worked the streets, and therefore it's most unlikely your client, Mr. Dominic Calderone, would find you equipped to meet his perverted requirements. He is most demanding. Allow me to show you a picture of the last girl who failed to come up to expectations."

He extracted a postcard sized photo from his coat pocket and handed it to Abby. She took one look at the pile of human carnage and promptly threw up all over the bar.

The stranger pulled a handful of paper napkins from a dispenser and handed them to her. "Just so. That was Jackie. I have two other photos if you like, one of Francine and one of Suzie. Would you like to see them?"

"Next time I throw up all over you," Abby croaked, her throat burning.

"Please don't. How do you feel like being the fourth example of the gentle Dominic's handiwork? Very thorough, isn't he?"

"Who are you?" Abby muttered shakily.

"We will come to that. Now as I said, I offer you a choice. I can make this problem go away. You should know that Dominic's father, Cesare

Calderone, makes Dominic look like a saint. I don't have any pictures of his victims, but I can produce them if you wish."

The terror in Abby's face told him most eloquently she didn't wish at all. "How can I believe a single thing you say?" Abby hissed at him.

"Assuming I can convince you, would you be prepared to listen to what else I have to offer?"

"That I become your personal sex slave?" Abby spat bitterly.

"Nothing so unpleasant, I assure you." The stranger smiled encouragingly. "We would take you and train you to do the job we believe you can do. If you succeed at your training – and I'm sure you will, Abigail Saunders, because you are a very clever young woman – we will offer you a job which pays a much higher salary than you could possibly hope to earn working for Susana, lying in intensive care in LA Central. At the same time you would be serving your country. What do you say?"

"I think you're full of bullshit," Abby muttered.

"But if I can convince you that I'm not?"

"I'll think about it."

"I'm afraid that's not good enough, Miss Saunders," the stranger sighed. "Now my offer is about to expire, and your two friends will walk back into the room. They will not be happy. I'm afraid the next time we meet will be in the city morgue when I identify the remains of your attractive body."

"You piece of shit," Abby hissed defiantly. "What sort of choice is that?"

"Considering the circumstances I'd say it was the offer of the year. Look, here's a picture of Suzie."

Abby glanced at the photo and shut her eyes. Her face was white and her arms were trembling visibly. "Oh God," she shuddered. "What do I do?"

"Please follow me out the back door," the stranger said, standing up. "I can assure you no harm will come to you."

Abby, her feet barely obeying her ragged mind, followed the stranger out of the bar, down the corridor and out the rear door into the alley behind the pub. To her surprise it was relatively crowded. Cesare and Dominic were standing against the wall on the other side of the street, their hands reaching high above their heads. Cesare was quietly muttering a continuous stream of filthy language, but Dominic looked pale and frightened.

Seeing her arrive in the alley, Cesare turned in her direction and spat on the ground. "You filthy little bitch," he hissed. "I'll cut your body apart piece by piece. You'll beg to die—"

No doubt there would have been a lot more, but the stranger nodded to the men who were holding the silenced Glock pistols. There was a number of soft plopping sounds. Blood spurted from the chests of father and son and both fell face down on the street. The men fired off a couple more rounds into the bodies just to make sure, then calmly pocketed their weapons and walked off towards the corner.

Abby bent over and emptied the remainder of her stomach into the kerb.

"I trust you are satisfied, Miss Saunders?" The stranger asked, quite unperturbed.

All Abby could do was nod.

"Then please accompany me and my men to the cars parked down the main street. It would be foolish to remain here. When Cesare's friends find the bodies they will be very annoyed and dangerous. We will let the LAPD deal with them."

"Who *are* you?" Abby demanded.

"Later, Miss Saunders. There are some topics of conversation which need greater privacy than we have on a public street. Now here are the cars. Please, in the back seat."

Abby got into the back of the car and found herself sandwiched between the stranger and another man. What was going to happen now? Had she traded one demon for the prince of demons himself?

"Congratulations, Miss Saunders," the stranger said finally. "You have made a wise decision. You will not be returning to your flat. I have had one of my men collect your personal effects. You must be hungry. Is there anything we can give you?"

"You can give me a fix," Abby muttered. "I need a fix."

"Ah yes, another little packet." The stranger said smiling. "Your friend the barman was not being very nice to you either, mixing your crack with heroine. He mixes it with other things too, especially for the occasion. Your boyfriend Billy ordered a special mix. Tends to lower one's inhibitions, I gather. You may be pleased to learn that Frank the barman is going to be handed over to the drug squad later tomorrow, after he has given us a little more information. Now, it was a fix you wanted? Gordon, can you oblige?"

The man on the other side of Abby took an odd looking gun out of a small case and shot her in the neck.

※ ※ ※

Abby woke up in a room devoid of all furniture save a bed and a toilet. Her first thought was that she needed another packet, and she needed it now. Near the pillow on the bed was a plastic bottle of water. Florescent lamps burned continually in the ceiling, and as far as she could see there was no switch to turn them off. She was wearing different clothes, by what process she could not imagine. Her light blue top and short matching slacks had been replaced by a soft grey tracksuit. Her feet were covered with socks of the same colour, and there were no shoes to be seen. On closer inspection Abby could see the cameras installed in each corner, no doubt placed to cover every inch of the room. So much for a girl's privacy. On the opposite wall to the toilet there was a door. Abby went over and tried it. It was locked. She banged on it with both hands.

"Hey!" She screamed in protest. "I need some food. I need a fix. Open this bloody door."

There was absolutely no response, yet Abby had not the slightest doubt that they – whoever 'they' were – could probably hear her breathing. By now the desire for another little packet of white powder was becoming painful. She had to have a fix.

First to command their attention. Abby ran over to the bed. Ripping the clothing onto the floor, she pulled the mattress off. Unfortunately the bed itself was made of welded steel, and resisted every effort she made to wrench the structure apart. No chance of a weapon from there. Taking the top off the plastic water bottle, she went over to one of the cameras and squirted the lot all over it. Cameras didn't like water. She had found that out one day when she had accidentally dropped hers into the swimming pool.

Absolutely nothing happened.

By now she was feeling thirsty. She went over to the toilet and flushed it, filling the bottle from the bowl. So what if it made her sick. Her watch had been removed as well, so she had no idea of time, yet with every passing second the craving to have another dose of cocaine - heroine mixture became steadily worse and worse. She began to feel incredibly agitated, angry. How dare they do this to her. She took one of the bed sheets and stuffed it down the toilet, then pressed the flush lever continuously. Water rose up in the bowl and spilled down the outside onto the floor. Now there was a flood, but the muscles of her arm were aching so badly she had to relinquish her hold on the lever. She switched to the other arm until the pain in that became unbearable too, then she did it with her feet, one after the other. By now the room had turned into a shallow swimming pool, and water was obviously running out under the door. She hoped it was doing a great deal of damage.

Suddenly she had to go to the toilet herself. How incredibly demeaning. She yanked the sheet out, just as cramps tightened around her stomach. Her tracksuit pants were soaking wet, and the water had soaked halfway up her tracksuit top. She began to feel cold, but she was sweating. Once again the cramps tightened around her stomach and she cried out in pain. Eventually the entire contents of her gastrointestinal system had been delivered one way or other into the bowl, and still the cramps persisted. Every time she tried to stand up the room began to sway in a nauseating manner, and she would end up retching again. She felt desperately tired but not at all sleepy. It was as though she had managed to contract a double dose of the 'flu together with food poisoning.

Still no one came.

After a while she managed to crawl back to the bed, but she couldn't manage to lift the mattress back on. Besides, all her bedding was soaking wet. She lay down on the sodden mattress, pulled a dripping blanket over her shivering body and felt as though she was going to die.

Eventually a small team of men and one woman entered the room. Another mattress was placed on the bed. She was lifted, stripped, dried off with towels as if she were a piece of furniture, stuffed into another tracksuit, thrown on the bed and strapped down. A blanket was thrown on top of her. The sole woman, who must have specialised in spearing elephants, jammed a cannula into her arm and connected it to a bag of fluid. Abby struggled against the straps pinning her limbs to the bed. Not one word did they speak to her.

"I have to pee," she screamed, wrenching her arms against the straps. "I tell you, I have to pee! I'll soak your precious mattress again. Watch me."

The same gentle woman dragged down her tracksuit pants as though she was skinning a tiger, and thrust a stainless steel bed pan under her bare backside.

"Pee away, sweetie," she said.

They all left the room.

There are no words in the English language to describe the agony that Abby endured for the next forty eight hours, the excruciating cramps, the diarrhoea, the suicidal feelings, the nausea. For hours on end her skin would be covered with goose bumps and she would shiver uncontrollably. Her mind was playing tricks on her. They were killing her, torturing her for information she could not give them. She fought and fought against the restraints holding her fast to the bed. Her muscles were screaming in pain. Over and over she begged her captors to free her legs, to massage her cramps, but no one came. Sometimes she would scream out at the sadistic swine who were doubtless enjoying the spectacle of her intense suffering with the full range of expression her tortured mind was capable of. When the exhaustion set in she would babble nonsense with the same intent as the words.

After what seemed an eternity she fell asleep, but then the nightmares began. The only human contact was the monster of a nurse who would come in and change the bag of fluid and the stinking pan wedged under her derriere, the nurse who offered not one syllable of comfort or reassurance. For a whole nine days this dreadful treatment continued, although Abby was unconscious of the passing of time. Slowly, slowly the cramps became less and less. Her stomach settled down, her tortured muscles simply ached rather than going into spasm, and the sweating stopped. Eventually, exhausted beyond measure, Abby fell into a deep untroubled sleep. The nurse came and removed the bedpan, extracted the drip from her arm and drew the blankets around her shoulders. Abby never stirred.

When she awoke there had been a change. A single table had been added to the furniture, and on the table was a bowl of cereal, some fruit and a jug of milk. Picking up the single plastic spoon, Abby devoured the entire contents in a manner which would have appalled her family back home. As soon as she had finished, the door opened and another woman whom she had never seen entered, carrying a pair of running shoes.

"Go to the toilet then put these on," she ordered.

The woman watched as Abby, who had begun to feel her natural self-consciousness returning, performed each duty as demanded.

"Come," the stranger barked.

She followed the woman out of the room, down a corridor and into a large area which had been set up as a gym. What followed was a workout that left Abby's muscles screaming for mercy again. She had run further than she had ever run, lifted weights she had never lifted before, lay down on machines programmed to find every muscle in her body and torture them individually. Once, only once had she stopped and told the woman she couldn't do any more. The monster had pressed a small device into her leg, and Abby had spent the next five minutes squirming in pain on the floor. After the morning's exercise she was conducted back to her room. The table had been laid with another meal. A short break, and the physical torture began again, then dinner, then bed. The lights remained full on, but that didn't stop her sleeping like a baby.

This treatment continued day after day for a whole month. Although she hated the routine, she couldn't help noticing that her physical condition was improving. Not only her physical condition, but her mind was also returning to its former awareness, enabling her to take stock of her situation. Now she realised what was being done to her and why. Her job, whatever it was, required her to be totally cured of her addiction as well as being physically fit. Well, it was working, and Abby, despite the things she muttered to her trainers, was grateful to them.

Just as she thought she was beginning to master the whole exercise routine she acquired a new trainer, a sadist who delighted in torturing her. Abby had never worked so hard, suffered so much verbal abuse, been so threatened with another burst of 'my little electric encourager' as she had been that day. Lunch had been replaced with a drink of water. When she finally arrived back in her cell at the end of the day, there it was, a small white packet sitting on the table.

There was no other food.

Beside the packet lay a bottle of Vodka, some straws and a syringe, all that was needed to administer the contents of the package in whatever manner she chose. It was a terrible temptation, and Abby felt some of her old responses returning, the prickling of her skin, her muscles feeling sorer than they had a minute ago, her head muzzy and needing the clarity the drug would give her in minutes. She also remembered her first weeks in this hole of hell. She stared at the table, only too aware of what her captors were doing and why they were doing it. Gritting her teeth, she took the packet in her hands, and deliberately not thinking too much about what she was doing, flushed the entire contents down the toilet.

The Vodka would have been nice, but not on an empty stomach, so she flushed that down too, followed by the syringe without its needle. The needle she stuck into a little hole in the brickwork that she suspected of being a microphone. She hoped it had given some eavesdropping little creep a few moments of unpleasantness.

If she thought her act of courage would have brought a healthier meal she was mistaken. That night she went hungry, but the breakfast the next day was much more substantial, superbly cooked steak and fried eggs, salad and cereal with fresh fruit. Gym that day was conducted by another trainer who was polite as pie. Her exercise program had been reduced, good coffee was served at morning and afternoon tea time with French pastries, and she was even given lunch – turkey and cranberry sauce with double cream brie on German rye bread. Returning to her room there was another packet on the table. This time it was easier to flush it down the toilet than before.

The next day was pure hell, Spartan breakfast followed by torture at the gym. The usual packet would be waiting for her instead of her longed-for evening meal. This sort of treatment went on for nearly two weeks. Never once did Abby resort to the fix of cocaine – or whatever was in the packet.

The treatment to cure her of her addiction had been successful, but there was a side effect its designers did not foresee. It aroused in Abby a fierce desire to get the better of her captors, not just impress them with her progress, but to give them a taste of the hell they had put her through.

In truth it was the beginning of a paradigm which would control her life over the next years, the desire to overpower men and destroy the empires they imagined they controlled. To this list she added the occasional woman, case in point her two torturers whom she hated so much their sex was irrelevant.

The extent of her transformation was revealed by her very first act of defiance, showing how much she had changed from the essentially modest young woman of six months ago. It took place exactly twelve days after the first packet had arrived. Ignoring the latest offering on the table, she dragged the bed into a corner until it was end on and close to one of the cameras. She took the packet and placed it on her pillow, conveniently within reach at any time during the night. Beside it she placed the short straw which had also been provided. No doubt by this time whoever was on the other end of that camera would be taking particular notice. Let them. Next she slowly and seductively removed every item of clothing, and lying on the bed, arranged her body in the most erotically provocative configuration she could think of. *Let them stare at that all night*, she thought to herself. *Come on boys, you've had power over me all this time, now let's see what power I can exert over you.*

✻ ✻ ✻

The training centre controller was alerted at twenty fifteen hours that evening, unusual traffic into the observation rooms. He decided to investigate. Down one floor, he swiped his card through the reader and pressed his hand against the panel. The door opened silently. The darkened room was packed full of men, ogling at the erotic image of the beautiful naked woman appearing on every screen, and making comments in keeping with their lust. The controller ordered the room cleared.

He picked up a small communications device. "Sally get your arse up here pronto, and bring Mary with you."

Sally appeared two minutes later with another woman in tow.

"What do you think of that?" He pointed to the large monitor screen. Abby had just rearranged herself into another seductive pose.

"What's she doing that for?" Sally asked, surprised.

"She's fighting back," the controller grunted, "giving her tormentors a problem in their pants. No men are to be allowed on duty up here tonight. Tomorrow I want Miss Saunders removed from holding cell nine and relocated to her suite on level four. Make an appointment with her to see me at ten hours tomorrow."

Abigail Saunders' new life had begun.

# THE PETROV EFFECT

✳ ✳ ✳

The next morning Abby was awakened by another complete stranger. Sally came into the room bearing a totally different set of clothes, an expensive skirt with a top to match, both in an attractive shade of blue, and more importantly, new shoes.

"Good morning Miss Saunders," she greeted the naked woman in a friendly voice. "I have brought you some clothes which you may prefer to that stained tracksuit. Underwear is in the bag. You will find other essentials in your suite on level four of this training facility. If you will come with me I can show you where you can have breakfast. Should there be anything else you require, please let me know on this internal number." She handed Abby a small card.

Abby got out of bed, weighed the advantages of remaining naked, then decided to slip into the clothes provided. She had been a trifle on the cold side last night, but by the look of it her strategy had been quite effective. She would remember that. An hour later, after a decent breakfast in what appeared to be some sort of staff canteen, she was escorted upstairs to the controller's office.

The latter gentleman waved his arm towards a comfortable armchair. "Please sit down Miss Saunders," he said. "First, may I congratulate you on your recovery. We are most impressed." He gave a fleeting smile. "May I also compliment you on your attempt to seduce your observation staff. It necessitated a rescheduling of personnel, which for someone in your situation was quite an achievement."

"I always do my best to please." Abby teased a curl around her finger.

"Just so," the controller continued. "Now I would like tell you a little more about the job we have recruited you to do. We are the CIA, Miss Saunders. Our operations cover a wide variety of fields as you can imagine. The increasing frequency and scale of terrorist acts against the United States has forced us to employ some very specialised operatives. We wish to train you as one of these. Your targets will be men whom we suspect of conducting anti-American or pro-terrorist activities, men who have resisted our best efforts to obtain data on their operations. You will be our secret weapon, Miss Saunders. You will get to know your target, inveigle yourself into their lives, their affections, gain their trust. Your brief is to accumulate the evidence we are seeking, that is all. You will not be trained as an assassin. Your job is not to curtail their activities, simply to acquire evidence they are taking place. How you do it is up to you. The rest you will leave up to us."

"Why me?" Abby frowned.

"You fit a certain profile, Miss Saunders," the controller explained. "An extremely attractive young woman, academically competent – in your case, highly competent – who has been, through certain circumstances, severed from your family, friends and connections, that sort of thing. We began to be interested in you after that business at Boston University. When the scandal followed, our interest intensified. We were a little slow in implementing our decision to recruit, and as a result you have had to go through some rather unpleasant experiences. I take it you intend to remain in our employ?"

"What else is an orphaned girl to do?" Abby conceded with large, innocent eyes.

"I am glad to hear your say it. Your training will commence next week. In the meantime we would like you to settle in here, feel at home. You have a suite on level four, but you can leave the building at any time. There's a shopping centre down the road which you may care to visit. The next phase of your training will not be so physically demanding."

"My training?" Abby laughed. "On how to seduce men? That would be the world's shortest course."

"Why so?"

"All you do is look at them and they're seduced. Can't we skip that? What's to learn?"

"My dear Miss Saunders," the controller assured her, "we are not training you to become a whore. You may, in fact it's highly probable, that you will end up sleeping with your target, but such an activity is not a mission imperative. The object of the exercise is not to get into their bed, but into their confidence. If you can do the latter without the former then it means nothing to us. I should add that in doing your job you will be performing an essential service for your country. I know it may not mean a lot to you, but it does mean a lot to a few billion people."

"If you say so," Abby grunted. "You said something about shopping? I was a crackhead, remember. I take it the sort of people you're talking about are not given to confiding their covert business to destitute females?"

"We will always provide the appropriate level of cover, Miss Saunders. However, you have a point. If you go down to level one and see George, he will provide you with a new credit card which has somewhat flexible limits. I believe you will find that ten thousand dollars have been already deposited into a bank account in your name. Please do not read this as a licence to spend. George will supply all the details."

Abby to raised her eyebrows. "Ten thousand? Already?"

"As you say, Miss Saunders, the men we wish you to associate with need to feel you are of a certain financial and social status. As for the rest, it's up to you." He picked up some papers on his desk, paused, turned to face her again. "I must say you come across with a certain angelic innocence. Don't lose that, Miss Saunders. Keep your angelic face, even if your heart feels as dark as the devil himself." He turned back to the work on his desk.

A new and powerful Abigail Saunders had been unleashed on the world.

# CHAPTER 11

D avid Petrov completed his doctorate with some twenty five papers to his credit, or rather to the credit of his mentor Sarah Cole who guided his research in productive directions. Their relationship had grown over those three years, not to the point where David ever felt totally comfortable in her presence, nor to the point where Sarah regarded him as exceptionally clever. He was simply a hard working young man who shared a common faith with her, a young man whose life and love for his Lord had produced a character Sarah had grown fond of. That in itself was a superlative recommendation, for the only other person in the same category was her colleague and close friend Elizabeth Caruthers, whom Sarah held in deep affection. The two women shared a flat together which was enough to make some of their colleagues believe they were gay. Such was not the case, although neither of them had managed to find the right man. Elizabeth had an attractive face and a pair of eyes which laughed most of the time, but she was not what you would call stunning. Now in her thirtieth year, most of the young men she would have been interested in were married, some of them happily.

Sarah, who was heart thumpingly beautiful, had men of all ages constantly begging for her attention, and she despised them all. She was quite lonely at heart, and often cursed her own appearance which had made her life so very difficult. One day, perhaps, she would find the man who she could look up to, but as yet she looked down on all of them from a very great height. David, who never interacted with her on that level, never felt the crushing weight of her distain. The absence of her customary censure caused some of her colleagues to conclude – without any justification - that they were lovers.

Not long after David had completed his doctorate, a vacancy occurred on the Physics staff for a junior lecturer, and encouraged by his mentor, David applied. To secure such a position so early in his career was almost unheard of.

Sarah deliberately absented herself from the interview committee so that no one could point an accusing finger at the selection process.

She did however, write a private note to the dean in which she suggested that doctor Petrov was an excellent choice for the position, and that she would regard his rejection as a sign that the administration of this University was blatantly incompetent. Such incompetence might even make her consider relocating to a position overseas.

It was, as the dean put it to his secretary, barefaced blackmail. Professor Cole brought the department glory, honour, and even more importantly, large sums of money, on a regular basis. Anything which caused her to think of leaving was not to be entertained for a second. As a result the interviewing committee were so impressed with their young applicant they offered him the job.

Not all the staff were excited by their choice.

Despite this initial controversy, doctor David Petrov soon distinguished himself as a superb lecturer who cared for his students. The dean, reading the latest accolade from one of these, tossed the letter back on his desk and reflected that despite the interference of Professor Cole, the interviewing committee had made a sound choice. David's own colleagues were forced to agree.

※ ※ ※

The problem began when David decided, as his personal research project, to study the structure of the ionosphere.

Everyone knows the ionosphere is the outer layer of earth's atmosphere, extending up to two hundred and fifty kilometres from the planet's surface. It is important, not because of the gaseous material within it - because there isn't much - but because of the interaction between those gaseous atoms and the solar wind. This stream of energetic particles and radiation from the sun ionises the neutral atoms in the region, turning them into positive ions and electrons. It is these free electrons which make the ionosphere significant.

Almost since the beginning of radio it became clear that there was a layer of atmosphere which, to differing degrees depending on the time or day of the year, acted like a poor sort of mirror. The imperfect reflection caused radio waves below a certain frequency to bounce back towards the earth and so travel over the horizon. In those early days this enabled people to communicate by radio with others on the opposite sides of the globe. The layer became known as the Kennelly – Heaviside layer, named after the scientists who predicted its existence in nineteen hundred and two. Nowadays it is known as the E region in the ionosphere. With long range radio broadcasting becoming a thing of the past, this particular function of the ionosphere is not nearly as important as it used to be, although amateur radio operators still find it helpful. By nineteen sixty, as a result of more research, the region had been further subdivided into D, and F layers, and some fine structure proposed in one of these.

David had no wish to duplicate any of these findings, but he was interested to know exactly how the solar wind interacted with the layer, how the amount of ionisation could be measured and perhaps predicted. The degree of ionisation affected earth – satellite communications. David's particular focus was the data transmissions from satellites involved in the Global Navigation Satellite System developed by the USA. Even though it was at present used for only military purposes, David thought it very possible the service would one day be made available for use by civilian aircraft, shipping, and possibly motor transport. The ionosphere affected different components of these satellite transmissions, slowing some of them down. This would produce data errors which, in the case of navigation signals, would result in an incorrect absolute grid reference. How large these errors would be he did not know, but in most military and certain civilian applications, even a small error could be very serious indeed. Aircraft locating their runway in bad weather, and ships navigating through reefs would be two excellent examples.

Apart from these practical applications his study would add knowledge to the exact manner in which the solar wind caused changes in the height and electron density within the ionosphere. Other important research might follow.

With these thoughts in mind he had run his project past his mentor Sarah, who gave him her approval. It wasn't a project which inspired her personal interest, but the results might turn out to be useful. Besides, it was completely safe. She had once before endorsed a project against her better judgement which had turned out to be anything but safe, and she would regret it forever[3].

❋ ❋ ❋

To work out how many free electrons there are in the Ionosphere, their temperature, speed and distance, David intended to employ an existing technique which was nearly equivalent to conventional radar. He proposed to send a pulse of energy up into the ionosphere and detect the energy reflected by the free electrons there, a phenomenon known in the world of Physics as Thompson scattering. The electrons in the ionosphere are completely random in their configuration, so the phase of the reflected signal is random as well. For this reason the process is referred to as Incoherent Scattering.

At the time when David proposed his experiments there were few such studies being conducted. The enormous dish at Arecibo, Puerto Rico, measuring three hundred and five metres in diameter, strung over an underlying karst sinkhole, had been sending megawatt pulses of energy at four hundred and sixty megahertz into the ionosphere since nineteen sixty two using its Levinthal transmitter. The Millstone Hill observatory at Westford, Massachusetts had been involved in similar experiments.

---

[3] See The Breach by Mac Cusiter

David knew he neither had the funds to build such a powerful transmitter nor the space to erect an enormous dish receiver, so his challenge would be to succeed in making the same sort of measurements without them. Relying on his expertise gained through four years of an electronic engineering degree, he planned to manufacture a different sort of antenna. It was a long tube-like arrangement, with the transmitter located at one end. If designed correctly, it would project a much narrower beam of energy into the ionosphere. Because it was narrower he could get away with less power, perhaps as low as one hundred kilowatts, and achieve the same beam density as that produced by those overseas. Having the whole transmitter and antenna in one package avoided the costly use of long, expensive waveguides. David hoped it would also minimise stray radiation problems. In addition he planned to transmit at roughly three times the frequency used at Arecibo, which would carry three times the amount of energy.

The receiving antenna would have to be a large dish, but there he had been lucky. A Sydney television station had just replaced their large satellite receiving dish with a newer and larger model. The old one was sitting in the backyard of their studios at North Sydney. David was welcome to it for nothing, if he could arrange his own transport. The dish was far too large for any transport within David's meagre budget, but this was no obstacle. Over the next two weeks he spent much of his free time laboriously taking it apart piece by piece, and transporting the pieces to a cordoned – off area at the back of the Physics building.

The Dean had given him permission to reassemble the whole lot on the roof of the Physics building along with a small shed to house the power supply and control equipment. David was extremely grateful. Bill Hawthorn, who ran the heliostat with its array of antennae pointing towards the sun, was less than thrilled at having some other transmitter on the same roof as his sensitive receiving equipment, but he held his peace.

Over the next six months David managed to build the actual transmitter using a power supply borrowed from electrical engineering, and a couple of high power klystrons which he had managed to secure from a firm that made industrial microwave ovens. All in all the little box on the roof was capable of delivering a one hundred kilowatt pulse – not a bad effort from something constructed mostly from other department's junk. The majority of his research grant money was spent on the low noise head amplifier for the receiving dish. The receiver itself was a particularly sensitive one which David had borrowed from the Australian Commonwealth Scientific and Industrial Research Organisation (CSIRO) on the understanding he keep them in the loop as far as his measurements went.

The longest phase of the project was the laborious task of obtaining data on all satellites whose orbits might have crossed within reach of the beam with the tube antenna and receiving dish pointed vertically into the sky. Any satellite in the path of his powerful transmitter beam could well be damaged, and he didn't want to be landed with an expensive law suit from its owner. He managed to find the orbit information of the GNSS satellites without very much trouble, which confirmed his prediction that the whole system would become public in the not too distant future. Other commercial companies were somewhat loathe to divulge just where their satellites were and what they were doing. A whole six months crawled by before he was certain he had a complete list. Not one geostationary satellite was anywhere near the beam, and none of the others passed even close. David was very excited.

※ ※ ※

On the twentieth of August nineteen ninety five David powered up his equipment for the first time and fired a series of narrow beam, one hundred kilowatt pulses straight up into the ionosphere. Joy oh joy, he was also able to receive incoherent scatter coming back into the receiving dish. Bill Hawthorne was not quite as joyful, because his heliostat receivers went off-line for a good five minutes afterwards, and when they came back on-line they were not working as well as they had just before. Bill was livid. First he went to the dean and told him to get Petrov's rubbish off the roof or he would personally boot it off himself. Then he went to David's room and told him the same thing, using far more expressive and colourful language. Next he went and complained to every other member of staff until he had pretty well run out of fresh expletives. Then he went home in disgust.

The upshot was that doctor Petrov was told to henceforth remove his transmitter to another location. It was a severe blow.

The other location proved somewhat of a problem. Not all buildings had flat roofs, and those that did were quite unanimous in rejecting the notion of a powerful transmitter sitting on top of them. What havoc could such power create? The other faculty heads seemed to know. The School of Business said one pulse would make you sterile. Pharmacology told him that it would cause cancers, Biochemical Science that it would initiate genetic mutation, Mathematics that it would cause computer malfunctions. The list went on and on. If David had been at all gullible, he would have reached the conclusion it would be safer to perform nuclear fission experiments with his bare hands.

After nearly despairing he would ever find a home for his equipment he had a breakthrough.

There was a flat-roofed building on the other side of City road, the Edwards building, which had once been used for offices before it was bought by the University. At present it was occupied by the faculty of Travel and Tourism, together with some lecturers from Psychology who could not be accommodated in their usual premises. Lately, part of the faculty of Music had also been added to the number of occupants. Several rooms had been converted into music practice studios. The musical instruments in these turned out to be mostly of the percussion variety. The lack of funding - or administrative bungling - had left the studios without any acoustic insulation, and the sound of would-be rock drummers doing their thing for long periods sent the travel lecturers, whose offices were adjacent to the noise, nearly barking mad. Even the psychology lecturers lodged complaints, though they were on the far side of the building.

The music lecturers responded to the growing discontent by suggesting that their critics wore earplugs, which would ensure they neither heard the drummers nor their own bleating colleagues. They were even happy to provide said earplugs from their own funds. The travel lecturers, who were by this stage well on the way to taking daily sedatives, retaliated by making sound recordings of the students while they practiced, then playing them back very much louder while the musicians were having their own lectures.

The culmination of this friendly banter was a free-for-all punch up, during which several expensive drum kits and a set of Bose speakers became damaged beyond repair. In the final upshot the music lecturers were relocated to a temporary home in an industrial technology park on the other side of the railway line at Redfern. In order to quash any possibility that they might return, the faculty of Travel and Tourism offered doctor Petrov two adjacent offices and as much roof space as he wanted. If he wished to store equipment in the empty practice studios he was welcome to do that too.

Being fried by radar was presumably a silent process.

It was February nineteen ninety six before David was able to fire his first pulse into the ionosphere from the new location. Thankfully he already had all the satellite data, and the relocation did nothing to change the vertical orientation of his antennas. Unfortunately Bill Hawthorn claimed his receivers hiccupped badly every time David pressed the button. In order to avoid unnecessary bloodshed, David agreed to perform his initial experiments after the sun went down, and Bill agreed to turn his receivers off at some times during the day so that David could take measurements when the sun was up.

One further small problem had to be overcome before David could actually analyse his results. There was a fair amount of computing power required, and to do the calculations he needed the large mainframe computer that was located in the basement of the Physics building. To send the data in real time, which was the much preferred option, a fast link was required between the Edwards building and the Physics building on the other side of City Road. In this he was fortunate. The building already had a dedicated optic fibre line to the same computer, which was used by the other departments for their own research. If David conducted his experiments in the evening after they had finished work, he was welcome to use its full capacity.

On the sixteenth of February he began to collect data in earnest.

# CHAPTER 12

Following on from her rehabilitation, Abby revelled in six months of intensive training. The gentle art of making herself the indispensable object of her target's desire was not the only skill she acquired. She learned how to infiltrate and monitor personal computers. They gave her techniques to remember the combinations of safes and passwords after only one exposure. They taught her the art of observing behaviour patterns which might contain clues as to her target's covert activities. Her training instilled methods of passing on her information to her contact, strategies of knowing when to bail out and how to do it. She attended speech therapy classes so she could speak without that tell-tale Boston accent. She learned how to steer every conversation in a useful direction. A great deal of her training had been supervised by her controller Harry O'Callaghan. He had conditioned her to be dispassionate, to focus only on her assignment, caring about no one and nothing else. The speed with which she had come to adopt these attitudes had surprised him no end.

Abby, who preceded her training with the secret desire to send men to hell, realised that these new techniques would be excellent tools in the pursuit of that goal. Becoming a femme fatale appealed to her. Using her warmth as a weapon excited her, something which Harry never really understood. In his own mind he believed he was the one responsible for hardening her heart against anything that wore pants, and the more he became attracted to her, the more he despised himself for doing it. Towards the end of her training her initial respect for him began to wear thin, especially when he suggested she would benefit by honing her sexual skills in his bed, something he did with monotonous and infuriating regularity.

Her first assignment involved one Senator Frank Amaretto whom the CIA suspected was laundering large sums of money from somewhere – they suspected drug sales – and using the profits from this activity to further his political career. It was arranged that Abby should attend a political fundraiser in the company of her 'partner', Harry O'Callaghan.

The day before the fundraiser, Abby was sitting at her desk, carefully going over the brief she had been given, when there was a knock at the door. Harry came in, wearing an unusually solemn expression.

"What's wrong?" Abby said, placing the brief down on her desk. "Unlike you to look so serious, Harry. Claudia in cryptography given you the cold shoulder again, has she?"

Ignoring the jibe completely, Harry sat down. He took a small plastic envelope out of his pocket and held it up. Inside was a red capsule. "There's something I have to give you," he said seriously. "Every agent gets one of these. Please don't take it the wrong way."

"What's in the capsule, Harry?" Abby asked, a frown wrinkling her face. "I don't do drugs anymore, just in case you've forgotten."

"This isn't drugs. It's a way out," Harry muttered, his eyes on the floor.

"Way out of what?" Abby said, her annoyance rising.

"Way out of life," Harry said softly.

"A suicide pill?" Abby asked incredulously. "I'm not planning to die. What aren't you telling me? I thought this was a routine assignment. Is my life in so much danger? Nice of you to let me know the day before the sacrifice."

"Will you listen?" Harry sighed. "Every agent gets one of these. Just in case. Look, Abby, the characters we deal with aren't big on mercy. All they care about is making money."

He balled his fist. "They don't mind if their weapons slaughter the innocent. They don't care if their drugs kill young kids. If they ever think you've betrayed them your life isn't going to be worth a dime, and you had better believe it."

Abby stared at the capsule. "So when do I use this?" she asked. "When the CIA wants to reuse my office space?"

"This isn't funny, Abby," Harry growled. "You use it when every aspect of going on living is worse than dying, when there's no way out. I pray it never happens to you." He handed her the small plastic envelope. "Keep it somewhere on you all the time. Believe me, when you need it, you'll know. You can keep it in your mouth indefinitely, even swallow the damn thing and nothing will happen. Bite on it and you end up shaking hands with St. Peter."

Abby took the small capsule from Harry's hand. "I didn't think you were so religious, Harry," she laughed. "I don't think St. Peter is going to too pleased with me. Just as well I don't believe any of that rubbish." She changed the subject. "Wait until you see what I'm going to wear tomorrow night," she laughed again. "I'll have Amaretto panting after me in minutes."

※ ※ ※

Abby's prediction was no understatement. Her revealing evening gown caught the good Senator's immediate attention, along with nearly every other man in the room. It gave Abby a thrill of pleasure to see wives and girlfriends tugging their partner's heads away from her direction. As planned, Harry staged a small incident at the appropriate time, an argument with his beautiful partner. It was loud enough to reach the Senator's ears, and quiet enough to keep other knights in shining armour out of the game. The Senator, hearing angry words being flung at the iridescent beauty standing nearby and seeing her obvious distress, came over to intervene. Harry fired a couple of parting shots and left in a huff. Abby looked as if she was about to cry.

Ten minutes later she was being guided on the Senator's arm to his very own table. Conversation went brilliantly, and before the evening was over he asked her if she would like to come home for a drink. She refused. Would she do him the honour of lunch the following day? She was busy. How about Wednesday? Abby accepted with one of her angelic smiles.

It took only three months to complete the assignment, and for two of them Abby had been making Frank very happy every night. She had memorised his password by waiting until he was about to log on, then approaching from behind and nibbling his ear. Senator Frank logged on, manfully mastering the distraction. Out of the corner of his eye he noticed his partner was completely naked, and for that sort of persuasion he had no adequate defence. With the help of a little piece of hardware, Abby successfully managed to copy some very interesting files when he finally went out, leaving her lying in his bed. She slipped the tiny disc to her contact at the local supermarket. Two days later she memorised the combination of his safe because she was draped around his shoulders while he opened it, so complete was his trust in the beauty who had become such an essential part of his life. Later on that day, while the Senator had been detained on some matter at the office, a CIA team raided his house and collected a great deal of information from that safe. The Senator's activities in the office must have been incredibly strenuous. Driving home in the evening he fell asleep at the wheel and drove his Lincoln into a wall.

The electorate mourned, so did a number of drug lords who found themselves suddenly bereft of funds. Several of these ended up very dead a few weeks later. Abby remembered her terrifying experience with Cesare and Dominic Calderone and felt a thrill of triumph ripple down her spine. Serve the swine right. She ran her fingers around her ears, feeling the diamond earrings Frank had given her. Should she declare them? No. That was part of her reward, a little icing on the cake, a tribute to her excellence as an operative.

From then on it was success after brilliant success. George McAllister in New York providing weapons for the IRA, Francis Poulenc in Washington selling state secrets to his murky friends in Berlin, Senator Bret Munroe selling CIA information to MI6 in Britain, John Standish, arms dealer in LA selling weapons to terrorist cells in Iraq. One by one they went down in remarkably short spaces of time, Abby collecting the hard evidence that put each one of them away. In each case the CIA went to some length to protect the woman's identity, even if it meant the death of her target. If their demise worried Abby she gave no sign of it, and every indication she enjoyed sending another male to meet his maker.

Her controllers nicknamed her 'D.A.' which stood for Deadly Angel, and it seemed that no target was immune to her techniques. It would be doing Abby an injustice to assume her success was due to her expertise in the bedroom. It was her angel-faced innocence coupled with her astute brain that did the trick. Her targets no doubt enjoyed her in the bedroom as well, but there were other women who could serve them in the same manner, and probably had from time to time. No other operative possessed the sweet faced naivety which engendered their fatal trust so quickly. Over the next twelve months a total of nine targets went down, and Abby travelled all over the world enjoying her newly discovered power and revelling in the praise of her superiors.

Her tenth assignment gave her controller some cause for concern. After only a month she told her contact the man was guilty of doing what they suspected him of doing, namely leaking secrets from a company which made high tech missile guidance systems to his contact in North Korea. The problem was that Abby had made the call on practically no hard evidence at all. There was the odd suspicious meeting, an abnormal amount of security around his home, a refusal to elaborate on certain topics, nothing like the usual hard evidence she had so far been able to unearth.

"He's doing it," Abby insisted, her face serious with certainty. "A woman knows when a man's hiding information from her, and this one does it whenever I get near the truth. He'll become suspicious if I keep poking around – I think he's beginning to suspect something anyway. You want him, you take him now. He's as guilty as all hell."

The CIA had been very anxious to plug the leak and very unsuccessful in doing it, so they had acted on Abby's sixth sense and brought the gentleman in for interrogation. After some time they were able to confirm Abby's accusations, and the assignment ended well.

Her section leader called Harry into his office a week after the file on Martin Tench had been closed.

"What are we looking at here, Harry?" he demanded. "A woman with an extraordinary sixth sense, or a woman who hates men and will do anything to send them to hell?"

"Perhaps a bit of both." Harry lit another cigarette. "Don't forget she was right. Tench was a very hard nut to crack, and he was suspicious of everybody. We didn't have any luck with the other two operatives, remember? Perhaps we shouldn't have sent the D.A. in so soon after John. We know what happened to him. Why did we send her in so soon afterwards?"

"Orders from way upstairs," the section leader grunted. "I take your point, Harry, but a woman with a vendetta against half the human race is a menace, and if we find out that's the way it is, well, you know what has to be done."

Harry knew what that meant, and it was the last thing in the world he wanted to do. Unknown to his boss his own career was in jeopardy too. He had become far too attracted to a certain beautiful operative, one whom he knew did not return any of his feelings to the slightest degree. To the contrary, her heart had grown colder, a steel trap for any man foolish enough to wander near. He cursed himself for being the one who had helped to spring it.

# CHAPTER 13

Over the previous fifteen months the project had gone extremely well. David began to build his database of knowledge on the behaviour of the ionosphere. The plots of data from each experiment were very nearly those which the theory would have predicted. Almost, but not quite. A small spike, located at exactly the transmitter frequency, was present in every plot. It was obviously a reflection of some kind, but David had not been able to track down its source, much to his annoyance.

One morning in March he had arrived to find his favourite parking spot occupied by a large builder's skip, and approaching some workmen dressed in yellow overalls, he politely requested them to move it.

"No chance, mate," one of them laughed good naturedly. "That skip's gonna be there for a while."

"Why?" David grumbled, casting his eyes over the pile of scaffolding which the workmen were offloading from a truck. "What's all the scaffolding for? How long is the skip going to be here? I don't want it interfering with my delicate experiments."

"Sorry, mate," the man in yellow overalls replied sympathetically, "but the building's got concrete cancer, see? Water has got in along the steel reinforcing. The steel is rusting and it's starting to split the concrete off. We have to replace all the windows and cut the rotten concrete out. It'll take months. We'll try to keep the scaffolding off your end if you like, but it's got to get there eventually."

"Okay, thanks," David said politely, supressing his annoyance.

Accepting the inevitable, David parked his van in another space closer to the building and a bit harder to get into. Over the next few weeks, despite the frustrating and inexplicable reflection, he continued to collect excellent data. Patterns were beginning to emerge between the height of the ionosphere and the number of free electrons floating around in every square metre. The patterns linked in with the information Bill Hawthorn was able to provide from his heliostat, and the two had begun, despite initial problems, to cooperate professionally. Bill could evaluate the magnitude of sunspots, and David could see the increase in the velocity of the solar wind. The sun had begun to be particularly active, and David was anxious to collect as much data as he could on the behaviour of the ionosphere over the next few weeks.

❋ ❋ ❋

Murphy's Law of Maximum Perversity is one of the most detested and frequently experienced laws in the universe. Stated simply, it says "something will always foul your experiment up when you least expect it," or words to that effect.

Tonight that law was about to make its presence felt once again.

David readied the main computer in the Physics building to receive his scattering data. The prompt on his laptop screen told him the mainframe was on line, and David activated his transmitter. The whole experiment ran under computer control from that point on. The transmitter would fire a burst of energy up into the ionosphere, then the receiver attached to the large dish would scan a small band of frequencies on either side of the one transmitted, sending data down the line to be analysed. David watched the hexadecimal numbers stream across the screen.

Suddenly the laptop beeped.

The mainframe had rejected the data he was sending. He tried again, same result. As he watched, the screen began to fill up with characters that weren't coming from his satellite receiver. Even one extraneous character would corrupt his data and signal an error from the program running on the mainframe. He watched the screen carefully. The spurious stream of characters had stopped. He pressed the transmit button again. New data from the dish receiver streamed across the screen.

The laptop beeped again.

He watched as more spurious characters appeared amongst his data, then once again, all was quiet. Once more he pressed the 'transmit' button.

Once again spurious data appeared mixed up with his own.

After a short while the mysterious flow of data ceased. Each time he sent a pulse from the transmitter he would see the same thing happen. If he didn't activate the transmitter the line was quiet, but each time he did, some spurious rubbish would corrupt his own data. This went on for half an hour before he was finally able to send sets of complete uncorrupted data to the mainframe in the Physics building. Where the other rubbish had come from he had no idea. Tomorrow he would check every connection to the receiver. Perhaps something had wiggled loose and caused a problem. Perhaps a piece of shielding had failed and he was picking up local TV or something. What a pest, he thought. Half the night wasted.

The next day he went over every single module of the receiver, every connection, tested everything which was possible to test, and found no problem whatsoever. He wasn't able to test the receiver after a transmitted pulse, because Bill was running heliostat experiments all day. To complete the tests he would have to wait until the sun went down.

The simplest explanation was that someone else in tourism or psychology was using the line at night when they weren't supposed to be. He would speak to the department heads if the problem persisted.

By five o'clock his stomach was reminding him rather pointedly that he had missed out on lunch, so he jogged across the patch of ground separating the Edwards building from the walkway which crossed over City road, and called in at the Wentworth café for a sausage roll and an apple. He noticed that the concrete cancer contractors had erected more scaffolding, and the large builder's skip, which had been parked so annoyingly in his parking space on the edge of the car park near the grassy slope, had begun to fill up with rubbish. He hoped the scaffolding wouldn't come any closer to his equipment on the roof. True to their word they had begun at the other end of the building.

Half an hour later he was back in the lab and ready to perform the first test of the evening. He powered up the equipment, initiated his program on the mainframe and the software on his laptop, and sent a pulse skyward. The receiver responded with data, the link conveyed it to the mainframe, all went well.

He fired another pulse.

Just as he began to think he had cured the problem once and for all, the laptop beeped with the same error message. Before his eyes a stream of foreign hexadecimal data appeared on the screen:

96BD98A5EDF4AB886104FD95AB5ACDBA97AFD7EC83
FD543719DA3BCD98DEACD3E48FE1AC4ADBA5CD7E4F2C265CDADCD76
29C2A0BDAFD3A8B5F31876C4A6FDCB448A9FS4BFEA43910AB9A1FCD
6B3F2A7C3FF
BDCA998619AFBE76EDAF54BBA8ED8710A0FD
CDADEA56719876543910ABA5C7D7F3FDACBA4D913BAA98C4D7B3D0A
4CDB23AC7F4DD986F3FD592B36AF4D9CCD5EFCEA8F4D09AFDACBE4
A3CB6FDAFF
>
>
BE776ADEABCD93BE66DFDA674EABDFC910A6FDA9761BCEA7DC
A0D76310B5D0FDC3EA9FDBC64D2B9AFEBCA5C9AA

By this time David had had quite enough. Someone in travel and tourism or psychology must be working back late and sending data of some sort down the line, the line he had been promised sole use of after six o'clock at night. He checked his watch, it was six forty five. Well, someone was going to get a little problem in return.

He highlighted the spurious hexadecimal data and sent a copy of it back down the line.

That should tell someone he had gone online, and would they please get off. Just for good measure he danced his fingers all over the keyboard until the whole screen had been filled with garbage. Now he would try again. Success. Not a single spurious character appeared on his screen for the rest of the evening.

# CHAPTER 14

Everyone has heard of Pine Gap, but it is doubtful if any Australian citizen, and few in the Federal Government, know about Nuralungunya. The radomes of Pine Gap spring up like oversized white mushrooms above the red desert sands, but you could have walked right over the top of Nuralungunya without even realising it was there – not that you could, actually. A high barbwire topped fence with its periodically placed metal signs which read 'Dingo Proof Conservation Area - Keep Out' would have given you cause for pause. Even so, the barren ground with its stunted desert Oaks and clusters of Spinifex gave no clue to the huge facility which existed two hundred feet below them. Connected to Pine Gap and integral to its purpose, Nuralungunya was the USA's command centre for strategic nuclear weapons deployment – or one of them. If all hell broke loose at home, the entire US military machine could be controlled from here.

The date in Washington was March the fifteenth nineteen ninety seven, the time, four fifteen a.m. Buried deep in the operational heart of Nuralungunya at this precise moment, Commander J. Rogers Jnr. US Navy, sat alongside his counterpart from the US Air Force, Commander William Abernathy. The room was hardly spacious, the lighting subdued but efficient, the quietness interrupted only by the constant murmur of fans circulating air through the ceiling vents. Behind them was a single steel door with an eye scan device, swipe card and keypad. In front of them was a large console with a central keyboard, two keypads, two card readers, several banks of switches and illuminated panels. In the centre stood a large screen, completely black save a blinking asterisk in the top left hand corner. A single speaker, covered by a grill, and a microphone extending from the panel on a black gooseneck, completed the picture. Each wall, with the exception of the one with the door was devoid of any openings whatsoever.

This was the ultimate command centre, the room from which executive decisions were translated into action at the highest level, commands which would, in milliseconds, be conveyed by the network of geostationary satellites and triple encoded, fire-walled data links to those appointed to carry them out without question.

Operation Phoenix was about to reach its climax.

Phoenix was the ultimate test of the system designed to launch a pre-emptive strike in the event of a nuclear threat to the United States. The command which would be issued in exactly fifteen minutes would go to the captain of the Ohio class nuclear submarine US Michigan. It would provide the launch capabilities of that vessel with their most exacting trial to date.

Fourteen minutes.

The vessel, having reached its exact coordinates, would be calling its crew to action stations, readying missile tube one and its occupant, a Trident C4 UMG-96A carrying a single nuclear warhead, for activation and deployment on command. On receipt of the correct instruction and launch codes, the missile guidance systems would be readied and programmed. The safety locks on its solid fuel propulsion engines would be removed, and the explosive charge necessary to create the enormous pressure of steam required to thrust the missile above the surface, would be placed in standby mode. Just thirty seconds later the vessel would be shaken by that mighty blast, and within two minutes the missile would be cruising in low earth orbit at a velocity of nearly twenty two thousand kilometres per hour.

Just because the cold war had ended some seven years ago was not sufficient reason to discard vigilance. Communism was, and would ever be a threat. Yesterday the communist bloc, today North Korea and its allies. For years the USA had been attempting to come to some agreement with Pyongyang. Millions of dollars had been given in humanitarian aid, and yet they remained an implacable brooding enemy, ready to take the advantage if any opportunity presented itself.

Commander Rogers Jnr. withdrew a small card from his pocket and swiped it through the reader on the console near his right arm. Following his action, Commander Abernathy did likewise. A single pair of green lights blinked momentarily and then went out. No one without the exact knowledge of protocol and procedure would have had the slightest chance of initiating anything from this room. Commanders Rogers and Abernathy possessed that exact knowledge.

Commander Rogers turned his card over. On this side were a list of numbers. "Forth down, 138609643876". He keyed this number into the pad on the console.

"Seventh down, 998765108735." Abernathy keyed his number into the keypad next to his right hand. The green lights on the console were now on permanently and the asterisk had been replaced by:

>command

"You remember how this goes?" Rogers said tersely.

"Sure," Abernathy replied. "We have just selected the Michigan. The data link to the vessel is now open on secure satellite feed alpha-037. You know the choice of destination? I simply ask to confirm protocol."

"Pyongyang," Rogers grunted. "Little commie bastards are going to get it. Only wish they were. It'd make for a better world. Go ahead."

Using the keyboard under the single screen, Commander Abernathy keyed in the command:

Missile TC4UMG-96A Activate

The screen responded:

>enter access codes
>code A:

To activate the missile required a thirty digit code from each commander. Both men produced sealed envelopes from their coat pockets and tore them open. Abernathy typed into the keypad:

975743933876351986537619762358

The screen responded with another prompt:

>code B:

Rogers typed the second activation code into the machine using the keyboard:

kjrNHgerogAPkirhywmFtYgnrwoHHe

The screen responded with:

>access codes accepted
>enter command

"We go for it," Abernathy grimaced. "I bet the captain of the Michigan is pissing in his pants right now."

"Probably," Rogers growled. "You ready with the abort sequence?"

"Go ahead and launch the bloody thing," Abernathy replied nervously.

Rogers typed the words into the keyboard. His hand was not completely steady.

Missile TC4UMG-96A launch

>enter launch codes
>code B

Abernathy was about to type a number into the keypad when Rogers grabbed his arm. "It's asking for my code first this time. You have to be more careful."

"Glad you noticed. Go ahead." Abernathy wiped his forehead.

Rogers keyed his code into the keyboard.

WWWimhGbdmhYYtrnHbfdgHrpOkinjy

>*code accepted*
>*code A*

Abernathy followed suit. He looked steady as a rock, although a heart monitor might have told a different story.

9864837629649165395391630228 65

The screen responded.

>*missile launch sequence initiated – launch in 30 seconds*
>*command*

There were beads of sweat on Roger's forehead. He waited all of six seconds before typing on the keyboard.

Missile TC4UMG-96A abort launch

>*enter abort code*

This code was only twenty characters in length, and either man could have entered it. Roger's hands had never left the keyboard, however. He glanced at his envelope and entered the numbers written in bold type at the bottom.

Mp876387HHH543KKK888

>*missile launch aborted*
>*enter command*

Rogers wiped the sweat off his forehead and leaned back in his chair. For a moment or two neither man spoke.

Abernathy turned to his fellow commander with a smile on his face. "Glad that's over, aren't you? I'll bet the captain of the Michigan is handing around the Bourbon right now."

"Speaking of Bourbon, I think it's time we adjourned to the mess," Rogers said with a sigh. "Nothing like starting a nuclear war to work up a man's thirst."

"Okay. Swipe and shut down. I can feel it gurgling round my tonsils already." Abernathy placed the sealed orders back in the envelope and began to shred them into little pieces.

"Me too," Rogers muttered. "Two swipes and we're—"

He didn't finish his sentence, for some more writing appeared on the screen.

>enter command
Missile TC4UMG-96A Activate
>enter access codes
>code A
9757439338763519865376197623 58
>code B
kjrNHgerogAPkirhywmFtYgnrwoHHe

"What the bloody hell is going on?" Rogers stared at the screen. Abernathy, who had begun to get up, fell over the leg of his chair. The writing continued.

>access codes accepted
>enter command
Missile TC4UMG-96A launch
>enter launch codes
>code B
WWWimhGbdmhYYtrnHbfdgHrpOkinjy
>code accepted

>code A
98648376296449165395391630228655
>missile launch sequence initiated – launch in 30 seconds
>command

"Shit! It's launching the bloody missile." Rogers stared in disbelief at the words on the screen. "It must be some sort of operations test. The bastards. They could have told us about—"

"Shut up and type in the abort command!" Abernathy shouted, staring at the shredded paper in his hand. If Rogers had done the same thing...

Rogers whipped the contents of his envelope out of his pocket. His hand lurched towards the keypad. But the screen hadn't finished with them yet.

>command
lsiohbnnoloweub2349nb24u7m3 2ui2ib 3,l,3u3opopo2n 3ym ,lw2304ubn aql,an la89y7nbk ,
>unauthorised internal security breach detected
>isolating all communications

"What the bloody hell?" Rogers shouted.

"Shit!" Abernathy screamed in horror. "The missile. It's going to launch. For God's sake, the abort code. Type in the bloody abort code!"

Rogers keyed in the code with a shaking hand.

This time the panel light flashed red. Abernathy keyed his seventh number down as he had at the beginning in an attempt to regain access to command. The red light came permanently on. The silence was shattered by the scream of a piercing siren.

"God help us!" Abernathy could feel sweat pouring down his forehead.

The door behind them flew open. Two marines burst into the room with firearms levelled. "Commanders, step away from the console," one of them ordered. "Now. Marines, prepare to disable the commanders."

Both men turned round and lifted their hands in the air. Rogers was deathly pale.

"For God's sake," he stammered in terror. "There's been a malfunction in the command security. Someone has launched a nuclear missile from the Michigan. The bloody thing is going to detonate in sixteen minutes if we don't—"

"Commanders, step away from the console," the marine repeated. "Immediately, or I will give the order to incapacitate you both."

Abernathy and Rogers stepped away from the console. The armed men frogmarched them through the door and along the corridor into the operations monitoring room, in what Commander Rogers regarded as an unnecessarily undignified manner. It was relatively crowded in contrast to the secure command station, although the apprehension on the faces of its occupants was pretty much the same. Large screens around the room were black save for the single message:

>internal security breach. Communications isolated

"Just what the Sam Henry is going on?" General Harry Claydon bellowed at the top of his voice. "Abernathy, what the hell have you done?"

Beads of sweat were running down Abernathy's forehead. He shook himself free from the two marines who had grabbed him by the arms.

"We did nothing," he protested. "We were following protocol. We readied a Trident from the Michigan then aborted the launch as instructed. We were about to leave when we saw that someone else had launched the missile. We thought it was part of the exercise, but when we went to log back on the system shut us out."

"It's shut everyone out," Claydon roared. "What was the last known status of the Trident?"

"It was proceeding to launch mode. The warhead was armed," Rogers stammered.

"It's target?" Claydon barked.

"Pyongyang North Korea."

"Dear God," Claydon groaned. "Get me the captain of the Michigan."

"General Claydon, Sir, we can't contact anyone." A pale-faced operator cried loudly from her console. "All secure lines to Pine Gap have been shut down."

"Claydon swore loudly. "There must be some emergency override. Get off your arse, woman. How long before the missile reaches Pyongyang?"

"It deploys its warhead from low orbit in fourteen minutes," Rogers stammered. "North Korea claim ninety kilometres from their coastline as their own. The damn thing will be over them in thirteen. Then it's just a matter of two minutes before the warhead hits the capital."

"Genocide," Claydon groaned. "My God. Marines, remove the security cards from Commanders Abernathy and Rogers and escort them to the secure room. Make sure they stay there. Use force if necessary."

"General Claydon," Rogers pleaded loudly. "We are the only ones who have command authorisation to the captain of the Michigan. If you imprison us you will not be able to—"

"Marines?" Claydon shouted. "Do I have to repeat my orders? Are you hard of hearing, or do I put you in there with them?" Claydon reached for his sidearm.

The marines frogmarched the two protesting commanders out of the room.

Claydon turned to the lieutenant in charge of communications systems. "Well?" he barked. "Where's my bloody line to the Michigan, lieutenant? I'll—"

"General Claydon, Sir, the security override has disabled all systems. I can't even log on." The lieutenant bleated in great distress.

"So we just sit here wait until World War Three begins?" Claydon bellowed. "Isn't there someone in this God forsaken hole who can shut the ------ computer down?" You, Andersen, you're the brains of this outfit. Disable the ------ thing. Pull the bloody power cord! Take a bloody axe to it."

"Sir, there might be a telephone line still available," the pale-faced station officer spluttered in a shaking voice.

"Telephone? Telephone?" Claydon roared. "Speak sense or so help me I'll knock some into you."

"When this place was built there were standard telephone lines installed," the station officer stammered. "I believe there's a civilian phone in the head of section's office – or his secretary's."

General Claydon was not a small man, yet the speed with which he moved out of that room, down the corridor, up three flights of stairs and along to the head of section's office, amazed those who were following. The others remained seated at their consoles as if someone had sprayed paralysing aerosol all over the room. Reaching the specified office Claydon flung open the door with enough force to dent the wall behind it.

On the other side of the desk was a young lieutenant by the name of Sally Lyons. Sally disliked her job, disliked being ordered around all the time, disliked it when men barged into her office and demanded instant service, disliked men in general.

"Give me the telephone!" Claydon roared.

"And you would be?" Sally snapped defiantly.

"General Harry Claydon, and unless you want to be a cleaning toilets for the rest of your life, find me a bloody telephone. Now."

"All our secure—"

"I know that you fool of a woman," Claydon roared again. "An ordinary civilian telephone. Where is it?"

Sally's natural dislike of large men who railroaded her was now at maximum, yet there was a look in this madman's eyes that caused her to suppress her natural reaction, which would have been to get up, demand higher authorisation, and slam the door in his face. This man was very afraid.

"Sir," she said, "I think there was one, but it hasn't been used for ages. It used to plug in to a socket somewhere. It was behind that filing cabinet, at least I think that's where it was."

The General took two paces towards the said item of furniture and hurled it over onto the floor. There behind it was a humble telephone plug. Sally Lyons sprung to her feet, partly out of fear, partly out of protest.

"Look, there it is, and see, there's the old speaker phone, fallen out of the filing cabinet you just lost your temper with."

Without another word the General snatched up the instrument, plugged it in and dialled a number.

'Beep, beep, beep … A recorded woman's voice spoke. "The number dialled is invalid or discontinued. Please check the number and dial again."

General Claydon swore, long and hard, glaring at the defiant expression on Sally Lyons face.

"If the General would mind me saying," she shouted over the tirade, "you have to dial double zero then the country code, then the area code, then—"

"Shut up woman," Claydon shouted.

He took her advice, nonetheless. In a few seconds there was another voice over the telephone line.

"This is a secure government facility. All correspondence should be forwarded to the minister of internal security. You do not have permission to—"

"This is General Harry Claydon," he said, struggling for control. "Please give me head of section. His name is Michael Oran. Do it now, or by God I'll have you sacked within twenty four hours!"

"I'm transferring this call to our security division," the voice replied. "I advise you to hang up before heavy penalties are imposed. We are able to trace the calls from cranks and fanatics."

The General's face clouded black with rage, but somehow, by the using every molecule of his self-control he managed to speak softly, even gently to the irate receptionist on the other end of the line. "I am stationed inside Nuralungunya at present. We have a crisis. All our usual secure lines are down. I beg you, please put Michael on the phone. He knows my voice. It is of the utmost importance that I speak to him in the next few seconds. If you doubt me, please trace this call."

There were a few small beeps on the line, then silence for a good thirty seconds. General Claydon looked as though he were going to kill someone.

Finally an angry male voice answered on the other end of the line. "Oran here. What the devil is all this? Who are you?"

"Michael, this is Harry. I'm speaking on a civilian telephone line because all our secure comms are down. Michael, we have a Def Con One emergency on our hands here."

"Harry? What's going on?" Oran demanded. "We can't raise Nuralungunya. You seem to have dropped off the planet."

"Michael, we have a Trident nuclear missile launch from US Michigan and we can't abort or self-destruct it. We can't speak to anyone, let alone issue commands. The bloody thing is headed for Pyongyang and we've got about eight minutes left."

There was silence at the other end of the line. A shaken Michael Oran eventually replied. "We were monitoring a launch detection here. The Captain of the Michigan has confirmed launch as well. What were you thinking of?"

"I don't know what happened," the General groaned. "The missile is already in orbit. We must abort warhead deployment – blow the damn thing up. Can you do that from there?"

"Missile destruct codes are held by the joint Chiefs, and they will only release them on orders from the President," Oran said in an unsteady voice.

Claydon groaned. Sally Lyons, overhearing the conversation on the old speaker phone choked on her breath and sat down shaking like a leaf.

"Michael, you're our only hope," Claydon continued. "If you can't stop it then it's World War three. The States will never recover from this. We would be guilty of murdering millions of innocent civilians without provocation. I'm bloody begging you Michael."

"I'll have to contact the President. I'll call you on this line as soon as I can. Hang tight."

With that the line went dead. General Claydon sat down heavily on the side of the filing cabinet. Sally Lyons stared at him as though he was the devil incarnate.

Within seconds of speaking to Harry Claydon, Oran was on an emergency secure line to the White House. It was barely five a.m. in Washington, and the President was where you would have expected him to be at that time in the morning, in bed with his wife. Just three minutes later he was in the Situation Room still wearing his pyjamas. The only other person there was Trudy Wilson, the CIA liaison officer, and Commander Brett Dyer, Whitehouse Military Advisor to the President. Both looked ashen. In less than one minute they had briefed the man with the state of the nation, or rather what would be the state of the nation in about five minutes time.

"The North Koreans have detected our launch and are preparing countermeasures. There may be worse news, but it's not confirmed at this time," Trudy said, putting down the phone.

The President's face had gone a rather bright shade of red, but much to his credit, considering the hour, his lack of breakfast, and the fact that that he had been rudely awakened from a particularly pleasant dream mere minutes ago, he managed to speak without giving vent to his rapidly escalating rage. "Where are our Chiefs at the moment?"

"General Claydon is in Nuralungunya, General Corbett is on the destroyer Hermes and General Norris is on his way here by helicopter. Corbett and Norris have been briefed and concur to release the codes. They are standing by. You can speak to them now if you want to confirm." Trudy picked up the instrument.

"Then for heaven's sake release the codes and destroy the thing before it gets any closer to its target," the president implored her.

"There might be a problem, Mr. President," Trudy said, battling to keep the rising panic out of her voice. "We are trying to reach General Claydon."

"Who cares a shit about Claydon?" The President bellowed. "I order you to release the codes to Oran at Pine Gap."

A truly frightened Trudy gripped the pen in her hand so tightly that it snapped in two. "That's just the problem, Mr. President, Sir. Due to the nature of this present operation, Claydon is the only one who has them."

The President found his rational faculties slipping somewhat, and he fought desperately to regain control of them. His voice, when he finally spoke, sounded as though he had spent the last twenty four hours screaming his head off. "Then get Claydon on the horn. Why haven't you done that already?"

"Because it's a public international call, Mr. President, and we're having some trouble getting through. We've managed to contact the overseas exchange in Sydney. We're through to operators in Adelaide and Darwin and they're attempting to raise the number, but whenever they ring there's a message saying it's been discontinued. Oran is listening to whatever comes in here, and as soon as we establish contact he will—"

"You have public telephone operators involved?" The President rasped. "Is this what you are saying?"

"There is no other way, Mr. President. We have less than four minutes left before the Trident deploys its re-entry warhead. I thought—"

"I am going to obtain missile abort codes – highest security classification - by public telephone via some little chit of an operator with big ears and an even bigger mouth? Is this what you're saying? Is this what the United States military security has been reduced to? I tell you, woman…"

There followed a somewhat metaphorical description of how the President would like to see certain delicate parts of his CIA chief simmering on a plate within easy reach.

"Mr President—"

Trudy was mercifully interrupted, because the speaker on the conference table in front of the President had sprung into life.

"This is Marg Courtney, Darwin exchange here. I've managed to get through to that number, mister, who am I speaking to?"

"A company in the United States, Marg," Trudy said. "Could you put me through, please."

At least Trudy had managed to keep the panic out of her voice. One glance at the President was all it took to see he was well and truly beyond the power of speech. There was a beep or two and then Claydon's voice came over the line.

"General Claydon. Is that you, Mr. President?"

"General Claydon," Trudy replied, "we have Presidential clearance to communicate the abort codes to Oran. It would seem at the moment that you are the only Chief who has them."

"I don't have them. Rogers and Abernathy have them. Hello, are you there?"

There was another beep and Marg's voice came over the speaker.

"Listen love, I've lost the connection. Would you like me to try again?"

"Please." Trudy's hands were visibly shaking, and her face was ashen grey. There was a long pause then Marg's voice returned.

"Sorry, love. I can talk to the gentleman but whenever I try to connect to you the line drops out. Is there any message you want me to send him? I'm due to go off my shift any moment now so can you make it quick?"

"Could you ask Gen... ah... Mr. Claydon for the invoice number on the termination contract, please?" Trudy said, forcing herself to speak without screaming.

"What contract was that? The termite contract?" Marg said sharply.

"Yes, and when he gives them to you, could you write them down so you don't get them wrong?"

"Listen missy, I may not be all that smart but I have a good memory, and I'll thank you to remember that."

Trudy pressed one hand on top of the other to stop them shaking. "Marg, I'm sure you do. Now would you ask him, please?"

There was a pause then Marg's irate voice came through again. "He says he's not a bloody pest control company. Look, I'm fed up with being sworn at, so if you want to talk to him you can connect yourself."

"Marg!" The President had found his voice at last. "Marg, I'm sorry for whatever Mr. Claydon said to you, but this means a lot to us. Would you do us the honour of trying again, please?"

"I suppose so. Hold on a minute."

The President ran his hand over his face. Minutes were exactly what they didn't have enough of. The recipient of Marg's chagrin was currently sitting on an overturned filing cabinet with a telephone handset belonging to the sixties on his lap, surrounded by the station officer, Sally, and a number of other top operations staff, including one commander Rogers, handcuffed to the two marines standing beside him. The station officer looked at his watch for the twentieth time in the last few minutes. He felt physically ill.

Commander Rogers bellowed at Claydon. "What the hell is happening? What the blazes are you doing?"

General Claydon smiled at him sweetly. "I'm talking to some long distance operator about an invoice for exterminating pests, what do you think I'd be bloody well doing? Hello, What? Oh, Wait..." Then to Rogers, "Hand me the abort code."

"Operator?" Claydon spoke into the phone, "Here it is and... what you say? You won't need to write it down? For pity's... no, I'm grateful, I apologise, please get it right... no, it's not as though the world will end if you make a mistake, but try to imagine that's exactly what will happen... no, I'm not trying to be smart, and I know you're trying to help."

"Two minutes." The station officer was sweating profusely. Sally Lyons was quietly crying, her shaking hand covering her mouth, and several others looked as though they were about to collapse onto the floor.

General Claydon took the card he had obtained from Rogers and read. "Capital M small case p... okay, you call it lower case, okay... lower case p, no, 'p' as in Peter. There's a bit more... numbers 876387 no, three, eight seven... upper case H for Hotel and then upper case H... you're going to write it down anyway?"

"One minute. God help us." The ashen faced station officer looked as though he was going to throw up.

"Alright, Marg," Claydon continued, "Upper case M for Mike then lower case p for Peter then numbers 876387 capital H for Hotel three times then numbers 543 capital K for Kilo three times then the number 8 three times."

"Was that 83 or 888?"

"888. Marge, could you read that back?"

"Sounds like a bloody funny invoice number to me. Are you on the level?"

"The invoice number, Marg, please."

"OK. Mp876387HHH543KKK888 is that right?"

"Perfect, Marge. Could you send it on? Of course you're going to. Look thanks for your help. I really appreciate it. Hello? Line's dead again."

"May God help us, thirty seconds," Rogers croaked.

Claydon put down the receiver on its cradle and placed it carefully on the side of the filing cabinet. He took out a handkerchief and mopped his brow.

The station officer had slumped down on the floor. "We've got a gnat's chance in hell, don't we?" he laughed hysterically, "and we can't even tell if it's happening. Here we are in the world's most sophisticated command centre and we don't even know if its World War three out there. It's just a farce, isn't it, a bloody useless farce."

In the Whitehouse Situation room Marg's recitation of the number had gone straight to Oran and he was now in the process of sending it via satellite to the Trident. General Norris had arrived, been briefed, and was talking to General Corbett on the Hermes. The line to Nuralungunya had gone dead again, and nothing further was coming verbally from Pine Gap. Screens around the room indicated the position of the Trident. It was obviously travelling over North Korean territorial waters. Other screens showed activity around known North Korean launch sites, heat blooms in ships stationed at Haeji and Tasa-ri, in short the perfectly predictable reaction of a nation which believes, with excellent reason, that it is about to be nuked out of existence. The President wiped his hands over his eyes.

"It's too late," he groaned. "The Trident will have offloaded its warhead by now…"

The screen opposite the President suddenly displayed a red cross in the trajectory of the Trident. A message appeared underneath.

**Trident C4 UGM – 96A destruct confirmed. Warhead deployed**

"What's that supposed to mean?" The President stuttered. "What—"

"Oran here. Mr. President, we confirm destruction of the Trident, but it occurred at nearly the same time at which the warhead was deployed. We do not believe the warhead was armed. We are attempting to trace the trajectory, but at present we cannot rule out impact on North Korean soil. There is little risk of detonation, but a high risk of radioactive contamination over a wide area. We are sending you data on our secure satellite feed."

"That would be the same secure satellite feed that was compromised a short time ago?"

"We are not certain of anything, Mr. President. The spurious launch commands came from Nuralungunya to us. A reasonable assumption is that someone sent them from there. That area has been locked out by its own security, as I have no need to remind you."

Norris took out a florid handkerchief and mopped his brow with it. Trudy sat staring at the screen as though someone had glued her eyeballs to it. The President lay slumped back in his chair, his face black with fury. Norris applied his damp handkerchief to the previous area which was now just as damp as before. He was about to speak again when the screen which had been displaying the weapon's trajectory changed to a satellite view of the Sea of Japan. The North Korean coastline appeared in the top left, and a red circle somewhat to the right of it.

Oran's voice filled the silent room. "We are able to confirm no land impact. Warhead splashed down within the area designated on the screen. The radius of that circle is about five nautical miles."

 "Thank God it's over. Close call, that was," Norris said with a sigh.

"Over? Over? Are you insane?" The President spluttered. "Do you think for a second the North Koreans don't know what we know? Corbett, are you there?"

"Mr. President?"

"I'm going to get our friends in Seoul to send some unusually fast fishing boats out into North Korean waters. How soon can you rendezvous? You have detection equipment and divers aboard? Make sure the rendezvous is nowhere near the North Koreans. This must no look like what it is. Understand?"

"Yes, Mr. President."

"Corbett, there are almost certain to be other players on the scene. On no account provoke an incident with them. Just get the bloody thing."

"Yes, Mr. President," Corbett affirmed as confidently as he knew how.

The President wiped the sweat off his brow, reached out and poured himself a long glass of water from a jug on the table. He looked across at Trudy, who was still as white a sheet.

"Have a Boeing pick up Claydon. Send an NSA team with it to begin interrogations at Nuralungunya. Get your boss in here, pronto, and the head of the NSA. Someone is going to be very, very sorry they did this. Now get me Pyongyang on the horn."

"What will you tell them?" Trudy rasped, trying to clear her constricted throat.

"That one of our GNSS satellite launches went completely awry. It went into low Earth orbit and we managed to destroy it before it passed over any other country. Simple precaution, really, there was never any danger."

"You think they will believe that?" Trudy rasped again

"Of course they won't," the President growled angrily, "which is why we have to find the warhead. They may be somewhat reticent to believe the Unites States would nuke twenty two million people just because we were pissed off with their leaders. That's what I would have believed an hour ago. I want those people in this room at twelve hundred hours tomorrow. If they aren't here so help me I'll have them shot!"

Half an hour later a very worried President left the Situation room. Trudy was right, Pyongyang didn't believe it, but they weren't quite prepared to believe the truth, either. *They're waiting for some hard evidence,* he thought to himself, and he prayed they would never find it. Nonetheless he knew the United States had already lost an enormous amount of political ground, which Pyongyang would be quick to capitalise on. He groaned audibly as he made his way back to the bedroom to change out of his pyjamas. Right now he wished he had never set foot in the Whitehouse.

# CHAPTER 15

*Washington, January 1997*

Dupont Circle is always full of traffic, but inside the Obelisk Italian restaurant its roar had been reduced to a mere murmur, hardly discernible above the accomplished quartet that played Italian operatic numbers on a raised dais at one end of the crowded room. On a table for two, Abigail Charles sat opposite an older man with a rather handsome face whose name was Henry Makin, managing director of Makin Industrial, a large engineering firm whose services had been employed all over the States. Just recently he had expanded his activities to Dubai for the construction of a luxury hotel complex not far from the airport. Makin was speaking softly, his blue eyes transfixed on the Beauty who sat opposite him. Never, he thought, had he seen her looking so lovely. A black satin evening gown adorned her perfect shoulders, wrapped tastefully around her shapely breasts and disappeared below the table cloth where, if one could see, it was tied around her slender waist with a sash of the same colour. Her long arms were extended towards him, and her soft blue eyes looking into his. It had been a superb meal, and now all that was left on the table were two glasses of wine, their ruby redness reflecting the candlelight. He reached out and touched one of the hands extended, feeling her long shapely fingers curl over his own.

"Abigail, you look breathtaking tonight, my love. Sometimes I cannot believe my luck. Just eight weeks ago I was a lonely man. Fiona left me without the confidence to begin again, and I was so convinced I would never fall in love with another woman, but I have, and what a beautiful woman."

"Henry, you exaggerate," Abigail said softly, squeezing his hand.

"No, I do not. You've changed my life, Abigail. You're intelligent, beautiful, a superb lover, and you're so interested in my life. Fiona couldn't have cared less."

"Your life is a success story, Henry. Anyone would be interested, particularly since you have expanded your interests into the Middle East. I know you've landed some large contract there, even though you're being so secretive about it, aren't you, my love? Don't you know I want to share your entire world, Henry?"

"I do. It's to that end that I wanted to give you this."

He reached inside his coat pocket and produced a small box. Opening it he took out a magnificent diamond ring, its facets refracting the candlelight into a million sparkles which danced on the table cloth and across Abigail's face.

He took her left hand in his own and placed the gem on her third finger. "Marry me, Abigail, and I swear I will devote my life to making you the happiest woman in the world."

Abigail's face lit up with an angelic smile, and lifting his hand drew it softly to her lips. "Of course Henry, but I'm afraid our nuptials may have to be delayed slightly."

"Why is that, my love?" His eyes held her tenderly, although there was a question in them. "I thought seeing as how we are already sharing the one bed we should get married next month, or just as soon as we can arrange a suitable venue."

"Not for that reason," Abigail smiled tenderly. "It's because those men who are coming towards us want to talk to you about your work in the Middle East, Henry, and I'm afraid they might interfere with our wedding plans somewhat."

An astonished expression crossed Henry's face. He glanced around. Four men were approaching their table.

"Abigail," he said, totally confused, "what are you talking about? Who are these men? What—"

Henry suddenly slumped in his chair, and if it wasn't for the men who just happened to be passing he would have fallen to the floor.

Abigail was on her feet, terribly distressed. "Waiter, my fiancée has collapsed," she called loudly. "Please send for an ambulance." She glanced quickly around the restaurant. "Is there a doctor here?"

The strangers lifted Henry's limp body out of his chair and laid him gently down on the floor. By now a small crowd had gathered.

One of the other men came over and laid his arm gently on Abigail's shoulder. "It's alright, Miss. I'm sure he'd going to be okay. The ambulance will be here directly. Can I get you anything to drink?"

Abigail shook her head miserably. Her hands were shaking. She knelt down beside her fiancée's unconscious body and lifted his head gently into her lap. Just then two paramedics came over with a stretcher, together with the waiter who had rung for them.

"Miss Charles," the waiter said, "the ambulance was only a few streets away when I rang. Please do not distress yourself. I'm sure Mr. Henry will be in the best of care in a matter of minutes."

Abigail nodded in reply. The paramedics lifted Henry onto the stretcher and prepared to leave the room.

One of them turned to her. "Would you care to accompany us, Ms? There's room in the ambulance."

For answer Abigail snatched up her handbag and shawl and followed them out of the room. The rear door of the ambulance was open, and Abigail stepped inside after the stretcher had been secured. The door closed, and the machine tore off down the road with its siren blaring.

"Well, that went smoothly." Abby turned to Harry who was sitting beside her next to the unconscious body of Henry on the stretcher. She removed the diamond ring from her left hand and repositioned it on her right, stretching out her fingers to admire the effect. "What do you think?" she asked. "Suits me, doesn't it?"

Harry shook his head. "You're a cold hearted bitch, Abby."

"Why thank you Harry," Abby laughed cynically. "You don't usually hand out compliments so early in the evening. Got a date with Claudia in cryptography, have we?"

"I couldn't care less about Claudia and you know it," Harry said defensively. "What are you doing this weekend? Would the grieving fiancé care to seek comfort at my place in the country? Just a few hours' drive and we would be able to enjoy a weekend of quiet relaxation together. You can't have another assignment on so soon."

Abby reached out her arm and tenderly stroked his cheek. "Now, Harry," she soothed, "how many times do I have to tell you I only have sex with men I hate? Do you want me to hate you too, Harry?"

"No," Harry sighed. "Cold hearted bitch."

"That's much better. In any case I'm going up to Boston to see my father this weekend."

Harry's eyes widened. "Your father? I always understood you didn't exactly get on with him."

"I don't, Harry dear." She gave a cynical laugh. "The man's in hospital, heart attack or something, not expected to live much longer. I just couldn't bear to have him pass away without a smile from his loving daughter."

"How did you know he was there?" Harry muttered, his disinterest showing.

"Message came through my cover company, Fletcher and Sons Consulting Services. Don't know how he got on to that, but he's not without influence you know. Must be worth millions."

"And his loving daughter is going to make sure her hat is in the ring when the will is read," Harry grimaced.

Abby gave him a mocking smile. "Why Harry, that's unkind of you. My mother will have already made certain she gets every cent, she and my foul apology for a brother. You think I would want any of my father's money? You don't know how much I despise him."

"Cold hearted bitch."

Abby ignored the comment. "Could you ask Trevor if he would mind dropping me off a block from my hotel? It's a pleasant evening and I could do with a walk."

Harry conveyed her request and spent the rest of the journey saying nothing at all. He would have liked to have said a great deal, but he knew the second he opened his mouth the words would be twisted back in his face. He had trained her so effectively, told her too many times that to be an operative was to be alone, cold, untouchable by love, unmoved by affection. How bitterly he regretted the lessons she had learned so well.

✳ ✳ ✳

Abby arrived at Boston General the next evening, having ascertained the ward and room number occupied by her father. She waited until visiting hours had finished, not wishing to run into her mother or brother, although she felt the likelihood of that happening was remote. No, her mother would be too busy broadcasting her anxiety to her sycophantic followers than to actually feel any. Then she would play the role of the grieving widow, publicly distraught, privately jubilant. Now all that wonderful property would be legally in her own hands. No more sniffing around father when she wanted a particularly lavish gift. She exited the lift and smiled at the nurse on duty as though she had every right to be where she was. Gathering her handbag strap around her shoulder, she made her way with determined confidence to her father's room.

He was awake when she entered, and the sight of his emaciated form lying on the bed staring vacantly at the ceiling, brought a momentary pang of conscience to her heart. For a fleeting instant the memories of them enjoying each other's company over a fine meal flashed through her mind, the warmth in his face as he looked into hers. Then she remembered the empty promise he had given her on one such occasion, his cruel refusal to take her side and fight for the virtue of his own daughter. Her resolve hardened like concrete. He was aware of her now, his head turned towards the door, his eyes alight and shining with joy.

"Abigail, oh Abigail!" he cried in a voice which sounded stronger than he looked. "I never thought you would come. I cannot tell you how I have longed to see you, Abigail."

There were tears in his eyes. Abigail mentally shut them out of her vision. She came over to the bedside, gave her father an angelic smile, bent down and kissed him on the forehead. His skin felt paper dry and thin, making her want to wipe her lips clean of his touch, but instead she sat down on the bed close to him.

"How are you, Father? You're looking well."

"Don't waste these moments with cheap lies Abigail. I'm dying. Your mother is delighted, and the world couldn't care less. Please don't offer me platitudes. For once in my life I don't want to hear them."

"Of course, Father," she said consolingly. "How stupid of me. You look like a shadow. I thought it was a heart attack."

"No, bowel cancer. I haven't eaten in so many days now. No point really. Enough about me. Tell me about yourself. I can see by the way you're dressed that life has been good to you."

"It has indeed, Father, and it's all due to you," Abby beamed.

"To me? How could that be possible?" He frowned. "I haven't heard from you since the day you left. It took me some time to find out where you were, but the bank has been helpful. A consultant, I believe. What do you do?"

"Consultant?" Abby laughed. "No, Father dear, that's just a cover for my real job. I'm a whore, and a very well paid one. Don't you remember, father? Everyone was calling me a whore, and you must have seen my potential, because you never said a word in disagreement."

Her father shut his eyes, and tears spilled down his upturned face. He made a soft groaning noise. Abby patted his hand.

"Don't stress yourself Father. You see you were right," she laughed. "I've had so many men since then, and I've found my job the perfect way to express my hatred towards them. Not you, of course, Father dear. I've had such a successful career, how could I be cross with you?" She patted his hand again. "Bet you didn't realise I was a drug addict on the streets less than twelve months after I left home? Of course you didn't, you never tried to find me. But I didn't stay there. No way."

Her father was lying very still, his eyes shut, tear streaks down his face.

She patted his hand reassuringly again. "You mustn't think I'm an ordinary whore, Father. My employer pays me handsomely for every client I seduce. Sometimes they've even killed them for me afterwards. Do you know, I never felt a second's remorse." She laughed, "just last night I even had one of them propose marriage, and all it took was six weeks of sex. I'm pretty good at it, you see. Look at the ring he gave me. Couldn't refuse that sparkler, could I?" She gave her father's hand a gentle shake. "Look at it Daddy, come on, open your eyes and admire it."

Only then was she aware of the beeping coming from the monitor on the other side of the bed. The line on the screen was completely flat, and even now her father's face was beginning to display the colour of death. Abby gathered up her handbag and left the room. Soon the nurse would arrive, and she didn't want to be found in the presence of the dead man. How lucky she had been. Another hour and she would have been deprived of the opportunity to tell her father how much ... But for some reason she couldn't finish the thought. Ever since she had heard of his illness she had been savouring the moment of revenge, but now it was done, it had left a surprisingly bitter taste in her mouth, its pleasure empty and hollow. How much had he heard before he died?

She found herself wishing he had been spared every single word.

What was happening to her? From somewhere deep within she felt the stabbing pain of a wounded conscience screaming its disgust. What had she achieved? Perhaps he had indeed heard, perhaps the revelation had killed him. Killed her own father? The thought shocked her profoundly. What had she become?

# CHAPTER 16

Twenty kilometres east of the South Korean coast and thirty kilometres south of the Northern Limit Line, the Arleigh Burke class destroyer, USS Hermes, sat waiting in the early hours of the morning to rendezvous with a Pohang class Corvette from the South Korean navy. High above them a P3 Orion reconnaissance aircraft was keeping watch on the activities of fifteen North Korean fishing boats and three naval vessels, probably patrol boats, all well above the Northern Limit Line. So far there had been nothing abnormal to report. The Corvette duly arrived, its captain came aboard the larger vessel, and was ushered into the ship's secure operations room. The briefing took only fifteen minutes, and while it was in progress several US Navy frogmen and some specialised equipment including a sensitive gamma ray detector, were loaded aboard his boat.

The captain of the destroyer concluded their briefing. "To repeat, on no account provoke an incident with the North Koreans. I take it the men on the specially prepared Fast Boat are well briefed as to the situation?"

"To anyone else it looks like a dilapidated fishing vessel, and all the crew know how to be convincing." The captain of the Corvette replaced his cap on his head. "I will keep the Corvette five to ten kilometres south of the Northern Limit Line and they will go ahead. When they find any local increase in gamma radiation from the seabed they will stop and your frogmen can take over the recovery of your communications satellite –

or what's left of it. Just why are you using gamma detectors for that job?"

"The satellite has a plutonium power supply," the destroyer captain said. "The rest is classified."

"Just so." The captain of the Corvette did not add that prior to his joining the South Korean navy he had taken an honours degree in physics. Plutonium based power supplies did not emit gamma rays. Still, it did not do to question operational orders like these, originating as they did from the very top of his chain of command.

He turned to face the other man as he stepped into the passageway. "What happens if the fishing boat is challenged and they have divers down?"

"They stall as long as they can," he replied. "Recall the divers immediately. It takes time for them to come up, so that's where your men will have to use delaying tactics – get the nets tangled, or a winch problem, anything. We may have a chance to revisit the area the following night. On no account provoke an incident. If there's trouble, the boat should leave quietly without a fuss. Only cross the Corvette over the line if it absolutely cannot be avoided. If they continue to follow your boat south of the line then okay, but otherwise, don't blow your cover. Pyongyang must not be led to believe there's anything out of the ordinary going on. I want to stress that a great deal depends on your ability to complete this mission. The Orion will keep us informed if there's any activity up north, and if there is, abort and return below the line before any confrontation takes place. Is that clear?"

"Crystal clear, captain. I will take my leave, Sir."

Minutes later the Corvette pulled away from the destroyer, the latter heading south east, the former heading nearly due west. Some five miles from the South Korean coast it reached its rendezvous with the specially prepared fishing boat, and the men and equipment were transferred. As the dawn was breaking, both vessels headed north until they reached a position five kilometres south of the Limit Line.

The captain of the Corvette radioed his counterpart on the fishing vessel. "I leave you here. The Orion is still giving us the all clear. You have the target circle on you scopes. The slightest trouble, get back."

"Understood, captain."

The fishing vessel moved north. On deck its carefully trained crew began to ready their fishing nets. Below deck, several officers from the South Korean Navy studied the screens and readouts from the detection gear as the frogmen checked their equipment.

"We're entering the target area now," the captain reported. "Orion reports no activity. Gamma levels normal. Conducting first sweep to the North."

"Carry on," the captain of the Corvette replied, one hand on the mike, the other holding a pair of powerful binoculars. Reaching the northern extremity of the area, the fishing boat turned west then south and began another sweep. Nothing. Reaching the southern extremity they turned west for a short distance then north and prepared to sweep again. Suddenly one of the officers manning the scanning detector reached up and made some adjustments to the instrument.

"We're getting a local increase in activity," he said. "Tell the Captain to slow down. Ten degrees to port, slow, slow, gamma increasing, no, now we're past it. Stop. This is worth a look-see."

On cue the frogmen and their equipment slipped over the southern rail of the boat, and the fishermen began to launch their nets into the sea from the other side. The Orion, circling high above, reported the small fleet of fishing boats were moving north and the naval vessels stationary.

Deep below the surface, US Navy frogman Stevens urged his submersible further down towards the seabed. The gamma monitor attached to his diving suit had indicated a rise in radiation levels, and he was carefully following its directions. Visibility on the ocean floor was becoming poor. He switched on the bank of powerful lamps on the front of the submersible. Now there could be no mistake, he was looking at debris of some kind. He reported in.

# THE PETROV EFFECT

All hell broke loose.

The patrol plane commander of the Orion was the first to notice. He pressed his intercom switch. "MiGs! Two of them. Coming in off the coast. Damn and blast them. Where the blazes were you, radar? Didn't you see them?"

The patrol plane second pilot automatically restarted the number one engine which they had shut down to conserve fuel. It was standard practice, but it took valuable seconds. Meanwhile the patrol plane commander had turned the Orion onto a south-westerly course. With number one engine operational he opened the throttles wide. The tactical coordinator shouted into the intercom. "Movement below. Three boats heading south towards our target. Dam, that's no patrol boat – one of them is a torpedo boat. Two PT-381 patrols, and a blasted torpedo boat."

"Radar reports two MiG's closing rapidly." Radar reported, belatedly tracking the incoming.

A series of holes appeared in the side of the Orion as one of the MiGs opened up with its canon. The radar operator lay slumped amongst the ruins of his equipment. The plane commander banked hard over to starboard. Another pattern of holes appeared in the forward fuselage, The tactical commander jerked and lay still, blood spattered all over the cabin. All the pilots could do was to maintain course south, completely at the mercy of the attacking aircraft.

The plane commander turned to his number two. "Why don't they finish us? What game of cat and mouse do you suppose they're playing?"

"They just want us out of the way," the man replied. "We're losing hydraulic pressure. Navigator, get us a course to Yokota Air Base. Engineer, what's our status? Can we make it? We're south of the Limit Line now, damn it. Why don't they lay off? Open comms to our mates down there."

"All secure comms are down Sir," a frightened in-flight technician replied.

Number two engine died. Smoke began to pour from its cowling. Both MiGs turned and headed for home. Three quarters of an hour later the Orion came to rest on Japanese soil, two of its crew dead, three wounded. They were lucky to have landed at all.

Deprived of his intel from the sky the captain of the Corvette had no idea what was happening to the North of him, and for exactly the same reason the first hint the captain of the disguised fast boat had of trouble was the appearance of a North Korean torpedo boat on the horizon.

"All divers recall immediately," he bellowed.

"We need more time," shouted his number two. "Stevens is on to something. He will take time to resurface in any case."

"Head for the boat now. That's an—"

He didn't get to say anything else, because a Scrubbrush anti-ship missile struck the boat amidships, and the vessel disappeared from view in one huge ball of fire. The untimely end of the fishing boat did not go unnoticed by the captain of the Corvette. He gunned his engines and headed south for home. The United States navy were not going to like this one little bit. He hoped that no divers were down when the boat exploded. Pity the poor devils if they were.

❈ ❈ ❈

Within ten minutes of the incident the White House received an urgent wire communication from Pyongyang concerning a flagrant violation by the United States of airspace belonging to the Democratic People's Republic of Korea. On this occasion, and this occasion only, the North had shown mercy. Next infringement would result in the plane destroyed by the excellent skill of the People's Air Force.

There followed several pages of white hot rhetoric as to what the United States could do with itself, concluding that under the circumstances the Democratic People's Republic of Korea had no alternative than to withdraw from the Nuclear Non Proliferation treaty it had previously assented to.

Minutes later another and even more vitriolic wire was received from the same source. It reported a violation of North Korean waters by vessels belonging to the South. When asked to withdraw to beyond the Northern Limit Line, the fast boat had opened fire. Fire had been returned, and the South Korean vessel had sunk after its fuel tanks had been hit. The remainder of the wire was also filled with white hot rhetoric as to what the United States could do with their support for the South, followed by a dire warning as to the result if further infringements were detected. The People's navy had been alerted and would be watching. Woe to those crossing the Northern Limit Line.

The President read both of these love letters handed him by the White House military advisor, and spent the next ten minutes delivering a very metaphorical description of General Corbett's ability to plan his way out of a wet paper bag. The meeting scheduled at twelve hundred hours in the Situation room was going to be memorable indeed, and right then the White House military advisor would have given a great deal to be absent from it. Only a few days ago his wife had suggested a vacation to Australia.

The woman must be psychic.

# CHAPTER 17

At precisely twelve hundred hours the President strode into the Situation room accompanied by Trudy Wilson and Brett Dyer. Seated around the table were General Claydon, US air force, General Corbett, US navy, and General Norris US armed forces, all sitting on a different side of the table to one another. Dianne Collins, director of the NSA, whom the President had once called the toughest bitch on the planet – within her hearing, sat by herself opposite Corbett. Norman Harding, director of the CIA, Peter Lawson, his offsider, and two other communications specialists, George Russell and Clive Harris, both from the CIA, made up the number. The air of dread and foreboding was reflected on every face except Norman Harding, who always wore the same completely impassive expression.

The President sat down at the head of the table, and his face was anything but impassive. His opening salvo was directed at Corbett.

"I would like to have you sacked, Corbett," he growled, "but I can't with Pyongyang breathing down my neck. Hear this, as far as I'm concerned your career is hanging by a thread."

He turned to the rest of those assembled and wagged his finger at them. It might have been funny in any other setting. "As for the rest of you, if there is one squeak, one hint, the tiniest suggestion in the media of what has been going on, then I promise you a long time in a US federal prison. Do I make myself clear?"

There was silence. Finally Dianne spoke, her acidic voice grating on every other ear in the room.

"The NSA has nothing to do with the operational bungling of other sections around this table. You need to paint with a more delicate brush, Mr. President. Why don't you begin by asking Claydon why he tried to begin World War three? I would be interested in his reason."

Claydon shot to his feet like a Trident missile. The last twenty four hours had reduced his patience and tolerance level way down to zero.

"That remark is typical of the sexist rhetoric you swill over everyone, Collins," he roared. "Put your money where your mouth is or shut it. Come on, give me one piece of hard evidence that I had anything to do with this brouhaha. If it wasn't for me you'd all be quivering like mice in your bunker two miles under this building."

Collins looked at him in much the same way a mother might look at a naughty child caught stealing from her purse.

"We have interrogated the entire staff at Nuralungunya including your two Commanders," she said matter-of-factly. "Abernathy has had a breakdown. We are confident neither man is able to explain the spurious commands issued to the Michigan. They are being held in a secure facility for their safety. You have a mole in your show, Norman. Better flush him out before he manages to fire a missile at the White House."

Norman Harding's face registered nothing. He turned politely to Dianne as he replied. "Or a mole in the NSA, dear Dianne. The NSA are responsible for security at Nuralungunya. What happened? Some little hiccup with the computer? Picks up the launch codes from Abernathy and Rogers, then goes ahead and does the job itself. Who programmed it to do that? One of your disaffected sisters? The commands came from Nuralungunya – I have records as to the exact digital sequence from the secure comms operator at Pine Gap. Apparently your investigation has stalled through incompetence, Dianne."

"The CIA was responsible for the initial design specifications for that site, so we are back to your department, Norman," Dianne retaliated. "Don't try to flush your own incompetence all over me."

"For God's sake, stop this bloody bickering." Norris shouted, his stress escalating. "The whole secure communications network has been compromised. Can't any of you get that through your heads?" he screeched in a shaking voice. "What happened in the Sea of Japan? Corbett's operation was ratted."

"Corbett's operation was a shambles," Claydon roared, his face livid. "We lost good men because he botched the job. The Orion was badly shot up. How did the Corvette communicate with your fishing boat, Corbett? Marine band radio?"

"No, messenger seagulls," Corbett roared back. "How the hell do I know how the little commie bastards found out? Norris is right. Someone's reading our secure traffic like the morning newspaper."

"With great respect, gentlemen, that's completely impossible." George Russell looked as nervous as he sounded. "The US secure satellite network uses the most complex encryption algorithms on the planet. None of the satellites are registered on any civilian database. No one knows they're there at all. The network is impregnable, and if, and I say if, just one of those satellites is compromised in any way, the secure signal is re-routed so that its recipients would not even realise there had been a break in communications."

The President held up his hand to quash further comment while he addressed the young man. "Russell, was there any such problem with the signal from Nuralungunya to the Michigan?"

"Pine Gap operations centre received the signal from Nuralungunya, and so did the Michigan," Russell reported. "There could not have been a problem. Only two satellites are required to convey that data. One lies over the eastern seaboard of Australia, the other mid Pacific. If either went down the message would have been re-routed to other satellites over the Indian Ocean. It wasn't, so both these satellites must have functioned perfectly."

"You have checked those two satellites?" The President queried.

"Not yet, Mr. President," Russell replied. "There was no need. As I told you, the data went through, and that in itself tells us the satellites continued to function normally."

"So, can anyone tell me what happened?" The President asked, manfully controlling his temper. "Do we have a computer hacker, a communist spy, or a mole at the very highest level?" He pointed round the table. "Perhaps one of you."

More silence. The President continued, his voice slowly rising in pitch and volume. "You can't tell me, can you? The collective heads of our whole National Security and Defence Forces can't tell me how come they almost nuked twenty two million innocent people. I assembled you here for answers, and what do you give me? A whole heap of horseshit and departmental bickering."

He slammed his fist repeatedly into the table.

"So help me," he roared, "if you can't do better I'll have your resignations now. Now! That means you too, Dianne. You hear me? Now talk bloody sense or shut up. The first person who gives me one more piece of bullshit is going down." He glared at the assembled company around the table. "So, what happened?"

The silence, which lasted for a good five minutes this time, was broken by a single word from Harding. "Terrorists."

"Terrorists? What do you mean, terrorists?" The President barked, his eyes blazing at Harding.

"Since the end of the Cold War the Communists don't have the infrastructure to mount anything like this," Harding explained in a very level voice. "Corbett's operation was compromised because he lost intel from the Orion. They bungled the job. It's not much of a long shot to believe the North Koreans were monitoring traffic from our vessels – after all, they were already on high alert." Harding toyed with the pencil in his hand. "They knew we would try and recover whatever it was that landed in their territorial waters, and we underestimated their vigilance. If some communist cell had hacked into our secure network, why would they launch a missile at their own people? Surely you must see that."

The silence remained unbroken.

Harding put the pencil he had been toying with down on the table and continued. "So we have to look elsewhere. A mole, you say? Working for whom? Pyongyang? Once again, the same argument applies. Why launch against themselves? There was no guarantee we would be able to destroy the Trident once it was in orbit. Nobody takes such a risk with their own people. So what do we have left? Terrorists. Some terrorist cell with massive comms infrastructure has managed to get into our secure satellite network, despite what Russell says."

Russell looked as though he was about to object, but seeing thirteen pairs of unfriendly eyes turned upon him he remained silent. Satellites could not be interfered with like that. The data they sent on was the data they received. He wasn't prepared to defend the obvious at that point however.

"Terrorists?" The President asked. "Do we have any idea as to who? And how?"

"Not at this time, Mr. President, but I'm convinced that this is the direction we must pursue. There is one other possibility, albeit a somewhat farfetched one."

"And that would be?" The President queried.

"The computer at Nuralungunya actually went berserk. Oran says it's impossible, but I don't trust my laptop, let alone a machine of that complexity. If it hadn't locked everyone out we wouldn't have had this crisis on our hands." Harding watched the fire kindling in Dianne's eyes.

"Speaking of crisis," the President went on in a dangerously quiet voice, "whose idea was it to test our first strike capabilities by actually readying a live missile for launch?"

"It was my idea." Claydon could feel the sweat around his collar. "The decision was taken in discussion with my commanding officers. We felt this was the only way to really test the complete readiness of our defences."

"And who was it decided Pyongyang would be the target?"

"I must take responsibility for that, Mr. President," Claydon confessed. "Besides, those commie bastards have been a right pain in our arse for the last six years."

"You are relieved of command." The President smashed his fist down on the table. "Commander Albright will take command of our Air Force while you take a long holiday. You will return when I decide it's safe to accept your resignation. Once again, if there is a whisper of this to the press in any country, I will permanently retire the lot of you." He turned towards Harding. "That is an interesting proposition, Norman. How do you propose to locate this terrorist and his organisation?"

"I would like Dianne to get her people checking the computer installation at Nuralungunya," Harding replied casually. "I will do some checking at Pine Gap. Are you convinced Abernathy and Rogers didn't initiate this? They were in a perfect position to do so. The simplest explanation is more often than not the—"

"What did I tell you?" Dianne said sharply, her eyes narrowing as she glared at Harding. "We have already interrogated Abernathy and Rogers. They do not fit the usual terrorist profile. Besides, if they were guilty, how would they expect to get away with such a kamikaze act? People who do kamikaze acts nearly always boast about them. You can interrogate them if you think you can do any better, Norman."

"Not at all, Dianne," Harding replied evenly. "I'm sure your people did a very thorough job. I'm surprised they're still alive."

Claydon glared at Dianne Collins as though he would have enjoyed stretching her on the rack. "I tell you my men are innocent," he said, breathing heavily, "it says something of their courage that they have stuck to their guns under such duress."

"Your turn will come soon, General." Diane turned towards him and smiled. "We have not completely dismissed the possibility that you yourself are involved."

Claydon launched out of his chair, murder in his eyes. George Russel and Clive Harris, the two men who were sitting on either side, grabbed Claydon and urged him back into his seat. He glared towards Dianne, breathing heavily and saying nothing. His career was already finished. What was a murder or two after the humiliation that would inevitably follow when the public got wind of the debacle? Someone would blow their cover, they always did.

The President turned again to Harding. "Do you have any other suggestions Mr. Harding? Apart from keeping Claydon away from my chief of NSA. I want that man restrained in a secure facility."

"I do, Mr. President," Harding answered. "After Dianne and I have completed our investigations, I believe we should reload the software – after every line has been checked, of course – reload the software into the computer at Nuralungunya and run exactly the same test again."

"You can't be serious?" The President gripped the sides of his chair.

"Not with a live missile, Mr. President," Harding assured him in the same level voice. "Some software will be installed on the Michigan to make it look as though we are addressing a real missile, whereas we will be doing no such thing. This gives our terrorist friends another opportunity to test their prowess. It also gives us another opportunity to discover who they are."

"Approved," The President grunted. "We will schedule a re-run when you can both agree we are ready to do so. Any developments, keep me completely and instantly informed."

The meeting broke up after that. Two plain clothes men from Dianne's department took Claydon to a waiting car. Harding flew to Pine Gap aboard the CIA's Boeing with George and Clive, and Dianne headed back to her office.

# CHAPTER 18

Abigail Saunders returned to Langley on the following Monday afternoon. Harry, as he sometimes did, was sitting in her chair when she arrived at the office. This time there was an expression on his face she hadn't seen before.

"Our section controller wants to see you," he said evenly. "You had better get going. Oh, how about a coffee before you do?"

"Nice to see you too, Harry." She studied his face for a moment. "Yes, coffee would be nice. Staff canteen?"

"No, Roger's down the street. They make better coffee."

Now Abby knew something was wrong. The coffee they served at the diner on the corner was the worst she had ever tasted, and Harry knew it. They strolled out of the building together without saying a word.

As they reached the footpath Harry spoke softly. "It's time to activate that exit strategy I've told you about. Get ready. Do it well."

"What in heaven's name for?" Abby said, shaken. "I haven't—"

"Henry Makin was innocent," Harry cut her off. "There's one hell of a stink going on."

"He's was guilty as all hell," Abby protested.

"No, Abby." Harry stopped and swung round to face the woman. "Admit it, you only had a hunch, didn't you? Like Martin Tench, only this time you were wrong. They got the wrong man, Abby. For goodness sake listen to me. Our section controller has had the guts kicked out of him and he's angry as all hell. I think they're going to do something with you today. They might schedule you for retraining. You know what that means."

"He was guilty, Harry. A woman knows," Abby said defensively. There was fear in her eyes.

"You're a fool, Abby, but you'd better stick to that line like glue. Here, you'll need this." He palmed a small pill into her hand. "Just before you go up, crunch that. Ten minutes after and you can watch your mother being fed into a chipper and feel nothing. Remember, Abby, an agent who gets emotionally involved is no longer an agent. I think they're going to test that this afternoon, and you had better show them you don't give a damn or you won't have time to put your exit strategy into operation."

"Why are you doing this, Harry?" Abby frowned.

"You mean you don't know? Perhaps there wasn't any need for that pill after all." He shrugged. "It only works for about half an hour, then you feel lousy. Tell them you have a hangover, because it sure feels like one."

"I've already got another passport," Abby said, half to herself. "Most of my cash is in a bank in Zurich they don't know about and can't get to anyway. I've got a stash of stuff in a locker and some more in a safe deposit box. Thanks, Harry. I'll skip the coffee and go face the music."

Harry walked into the diner and Abby returned to the building. She went to the ladies toilet to take her pill and make up her face, then caught the lift up two floors to her controller's office.

Martin Freeman opened the door and waved towards a chair. "Henry Makin was cheating on you with another woman, wasn't he?"

"No," Abby said offhandedly. "If he was I didn't know about it."

"But you hated him enough to want him dead." There was fire in the controller's eyes.

"I do my job. The man is guilty. Haven't you broken him yet?"

"Not exactly," the controller gave a sarcastic smile. "That's where we need your help. I'm sending you down to level zero."

"I don't do torture."

"Ah, but you're very persuasive. As you say, we can't break him, but perhaps you will have more success." His voice hardened. "I'll see you to the lift." He rose from his desk and grabbed Abby lightly around the arm.

Abby could feel the pill taking effect. She would have been terrified at the prospect of seeing what they were doing to her target, but right now she couldn't have cared less.

"Suits me." Abby pulled her arm away from Freeman's grip. "I can see my own way there."

"I insist, just in case you get lost. It's a long way down to level zero."

Grabbing her arm again he escorted her out of the office, along the corridor. Reaching the lift he pushed her inside, swiped a card through the reader, pushed the 'basement' button three times and stepped clear. The lift doors closed leaving Abby descending inside. Eventually the lift stopped and Abby walked out into a bare corridor lit with florescent lamps behind steel bars sunk into its walls. It reminded her of the time she had spent in rehabilitation cell nine. One door at the end of the corridor was open, and Abby went through. The sight that met her eyes would have made her instantly sick, but the pill was doing its job.

Henry Makin was strapped into a steel chair with steel bands around his wrists, naked from the waist up. There was blood all over his hands where he had struggled against his restraints. Marks of various sorts criss-crossed his chest, but his face – she would never forget that face. The eyes were haggard, shrunken in their sockets, the face of a man who had endured beyond what was possible for a human being to endure. His breath was coming in gasps from his dry, open mouth. A cannula needle protruded out of one arm. He turned his head as Abby entered the room. The two men who were conducting the interrogation hardly seemed to notice. One of them held a hypodermic in his right hand, the other was saying something to the prisoner, but Abby didn't register the words because Makin screamed at her.

"Curse you, bitch! I'll see you in hell. I want to hear you scream—"

He didn't say anymore because the other man had hit him across the face. "Miss Saunders," he said, as though he was asking her preference in chocolates, "do you have anything to say to Mr. Makin before he leaves this world? We have not been able to secure any cooperation from him at all. Perhaps you could assist?"

Even under the influence of the drug Abby could feel herself shaking, and only her voice remained steady. She walked over to the tortured man until she was facing him. "Tell them what they want to know, Henry, and you'll die easy. No more pain, Henry. Just tell them what they want to know. I promise you—"

"Curse you to hell bitch," Makin screamed. "I'll be there. I'll give you so much pain... forever... So much pain..."

A gurgling, insane laughter came out of his open mouth, a horrible sound that made Abby wince despite the effect of the pill.

"Do I have to hear any more of this nonsense?" she snapped.

"No, Miss Saunders," the man with the syringe replied. "Perhaps you would like to administer the lethal injection yourself?"

"I don't kill people."

"Oh, but you do."

He plunged the hypodermic into his victim's arm. Makin gave a hideous scream: "Bitch!" then died. The man withdrew the needle and threw it into a container as though nothing had happened.

"Better go and tell the controller we couldn't break him," he said. "Perhaps we will have the pleasure of your company in this chair one day. Must say it would be a lot more interesting than he's been. There's a lot of special things you can do with a woman before she dies."

"I'll tell the controller what you said." Abby sneered at them both, turned and walked through the door, down the corridor, into the lift, up from the hell of level zero into the light of the normal world. Reaching the level of her own office she went into the ladies toilet and threw up. The effect of the pill was wearing off. She must see her controller before it wore off completely.

Taking the lift up two more floors, she strode brazenly into his office without knocking on the door. "I've a message from those zombies you employ on level zero," she said in an offhanded voice. "Makin is dead. They couldn't break him. By the time I'd got there it was too late anyway. He was already insane with the cocktails they were giving him. I don't know what you wanted me there for anyway. Oh, and your zombies threatened to torture me if they saw me again. If I were you I'd send them for retraining before they do some more damage."

The controller smiled at her in a manner Abby didn't much care for. "I'll bear that in mind Miss Saunders. I take it you are still adamant the man was guilty?"

"Of course he was," Abby said with conviction. She raised her eyebrows. "Do you think I send innocent men to their deaths?"

"I was of that opinion," the controller said evenly. "Perhaps I was wrong. Go and have a rest. You look ill."

"I'm coming down with the 'flu," Abby explained. "Must have caught it in Boston. My father died while I was talking to him and it's made me feel a bit out of sorts."

"I'm sure it would have, Miss Saunders. Take the rest of the day off."

Abby went out of the office, down the lift, out of the building and into her car. Arriving at her own apartment she headed straight for the bathroom and threw up again. Wrapping her dressing gown around her, she came back and sat on the settee, shivering in horror, trying to wipe the ghastly images from her mind. Suddenly she lurched towards the bathroom but didn't make it. The next few minutes were spent wiping the carpet clean, or as clean as she could when her hands were shaking so much. Deep down in her heart she knew without doubt that she was wrong, that an innocent man had died. Did that make her a murderer? Yes it did, a double murderer if you included her own father.

Inside her head she could still hear Makin screaming "see you in hell, bitch." Hell? She was already in hell, in jeopardy of her life, not sure that she wanted to live, knowing she didn't want to die. Perhaps Makin was right, and hell was endless, screaming agony. That's where she was going, and she knew it. She went into the kitchen and drank a long glass of water which only served to make her feel more nauseous. She wondered what would happen if Harry hadn't given her that pill. Perhaps she would have been the next one in the chair. She vomited violently in the sink. "Mustn't think like that," she said to herself.

❊ ❊ ❊

The controller completed the report he was compiling, and signed his name at the end. Abigail Saunders was to be removed from the active duty list pending further investigation as to her mental condition. If it proved to be unsatisfactory, she would be sent to a retraining facility and then redeployed only if she managed to convince her trainers she had become impartial to both men and women. Pity, she seemed so talented. Such a beautiful woman, too. Still business was business. He was the last line of defence for his country, and nothing was of higher priority than that.

❊ ❊ ❊

Abby stayed up as late as she possibly could that night, watching drivel on television until her eyes were closing from fatigue. She dragged herself into bed and turned out the light. The bed was soft and warm and comforting. She fell asleep. Somewhere in the night she came to consciousness. She was in terrible pain. Someone was thrusting a red hot needle through the length of her body. It had penetrated her uterus, now her bowels, and she screamed in agony. Now it was perforating her stomach. She writhed from side to side, unable to move or defend herself. The needle had missed her heart and lungs and was ascending her oesophagus, its fire burning her with unbearable pain. She tried to call out, but the needle had skewered her vocal chords. Now it was in her mouth, still rising, now her brain was punctured, her thoughts becoming muddled, flashes of light and strange sounds in her ears. It was through the top of her head, and now a hand was drawing it out, pulling it through, leaving her body screaming and broken. She looked up, and there was Henry Makin. In his withered, fleshless hands he held a long, red hot needle. There was a hideous smile on his cadaverous face.

He laughed, long and hard. "Did you enjoy that, bitch? I'm going to pierce every cell in your body. Not your heart, that's dead already. When I'm done I'm going to do it all over again. And again. And again, all through eternity. Where now? Your pretty eye, that's it. Right through your eye and your brain and out the back of your head. Here it comes."

She saw the burning needle approaching, felt the heat from its ghastly point. With one massive thrust, using every sinew of her mind and strength that remained, she managed to skew herself out of its way. Now she was falling into black nothingness, falling, falling. Her whole body smashed into something hard. Sight had gone, and she was conscious only of the carpet against her face. Carpet? With a shaking hand she reached up, found the cord of her bed lamp and switched it on. The room flooded with glorious, warm, white, cleansing, holy light. Abby covered her face with her hands and sobbed. Not a single tear could she summon to her eyes, yet she was shaking like a leaf. She went over to the wall and turned on the main bedroom light.

Light, she needed light.


Never, never would she sleep again. Such horrors were waiting for her in the darkness, horrors that terrified her to the depth of her very being. She went out into the living room, turned on every light in the house and then the television.

The morning saw her still hunched up semi-conscious on the settee, the television still blaring discordantly.

# CHAPTER 19

The Boeing was due to land at Pine Gap in an hour. Harding stared out the window at the barren wasteland passing below the aircraft, and reflected on the past twenty four hours. He felt tired, but not a trace of it showed on his face. Struck with a sudden thought, he turned to George Russell who happened to be sitting next to him. "George, when we get down I want you to check out those satellites. Explain to me again exactly what the setup is with our secure satellite communications."

"All the secure digital intel from Nuralungunya and the Gap is sent out via our satellite network," George explained. "If it's target is in the Pacific region, it goes out through geostationary satellite twenty nine, which is on the eastern seaboard, then to satellite fifty two which is over the Pacific. Either that or to one of three orbiting satellites which pass roughly east to west in higher orbit. Satellite twenty nine must be okay because as we know the data reached the Michigan via that route."

"Nonetheless, check it out, will you?" Harding asked. "I want to know if it so much as hiccupped before it sent the data on. Check it thoroughly, George. Do it yourself. I know my arrival will put the cat amongst the pigeons, so just go about your business while everyone else is flapping and trying to cover their backsides."

"I'll do that, Sir. I think it's a dead end, but I'll check every response that twenty nine made during the incident. It will all be stored on the mainframe. Then I'll check fifty two. Is that our only lead?"

Harding rubbed his hand over his face. "I said I didn't trust the computer at Nuralungunya. If there's anything odd there I have no doubt Dianne will winkle it out in her ever so loving way."

George shuddered. One experience with the woman was enough to convince him he didn't want another. "You still think it's terrorists?"

"I do. It's the only thing that makes sense." Harding stretched himself in his seat. "There were a lot of dissidents left over when communism collapsed in the USSR. Could be some of them are thinking to get their own back in cahoots with our little Islamic fanatics in the Middle East. There are some nasty people around, George. I think we are up against some very clever nasty people."

The aircraft landed some forty minutes later, and George went about his business. The tension on the base was worse than he had predicted. The Head of the CIA was here. Heads would roll at the slightest provocation. Harding was a man to be feared, as many apocryphal tales could testify. Those whom Harding found guilty of unsatisfactory performance seldom came back to tell everyone else what had happened to them.

※ ※ ※

It was a very apprehensive George who knocked on Harding's door the next morning. He had spent most of the previous afternoon and all of the previous night checking the data, trying to make sense of what was essentially nonsense. Nonsense it may be, but it put him in a very uncomfortable position.

He entered the room at Harding's bidding and sat down on the proffered chair. "I've checked the satellite data as you requested, Sir," he said, trying hard to keep his voice steady.
"And?" Harding's face held the suggestion of curiosity.

"It makes no sense whatsoever," George blustered. "According to the data we received, geostationary satellite twenty nine faulted for the entire duration of the secure data transfer."

"What exactly does that mean?" Harding put down the coffee he was drinking.

"This is where it makes no sense," George said, wiping his brow with his handkerchief. "The error codes received indicate that the satellite was off the air all the time we were trying to send data to it. According to these codes the satellite did not receive any data, and it didn't pass any data on to geostationary satellite fifty two or any of the satellites orbiting over the Pacific at the time." He shook his head. "This can't be true, of course, because the Michigan received the signals, and the only way it could have done that is via geostationary satellite twenty nine."

"So the satellite sends back spurious codes whilst the transmission in question is being sent?" Harding frowned.

"It would appear so, Sir."

"How can someone interfere with a satellite, George?" Harding slowly picked up his coffee again.

"Well, Sir, if another satellite was somewhere in the vicinity it might be possible, but otherwise it's totally impossible." George squirmed in his chair. "Satellite twenty nine has two antenna horns, one is pointing towards Pine Gap with a very narrow footprint."

"Footprint?"

"The projected area on the Earth's surface which the satellite can receive data from or send data to. The other antenna on the satellite is not directed towards Earth at all, it's directed high over the Pacific, so that geostationary fifty two or some other satellite in higher orbit can pick it up."

"So if someone wanted to knock the satellite out they would have to be somewhere within that footprint?" Harding's eyes narrowed into slits.

"Either that or they would have to have a massively high powered transmitter," George agreed. "Even if they did, and they could override the directional horn on the satellite, any data they sent would conflict with the genuine data we were sending, and we would get a different error message. In that case, the satellite wouldn't send anything to the Pacific satellites. As we know, the Michigan received the data all right, too much of it."

Harding lifted his cup to his lips, replaced it slowly in its saucer. "Could someone have forced the satellite to send spurious data by simply swamping the signals we were sending it?"

"Any satellite could in theory be knocked out by an incredibly strong signal," George explained. "But if that were the case it would never have sent any data on to fifty two. Besides, nobody could intercept the data that Nuralungunya was sending to the satellite. The only way such a transmission could be intercepted, would be from another satellite in close proximity to satellite twenty nine, and there isn't one." George gesticulated with his hands.

"I would like to get confirmation of that, George," Harding said thoughtfully. "How would I go about it?"

"You could re-task some other satellite to go have a look and send back pictures. I think only the President could authorise that, probably through NASA."

"Thank you George, you have been most helpful. Could you maintain the closest watch on satellite twenty nine? I'm going to contact Peter and ask if he could do a little investigation as to who has the potential to transmit data to satellites. Over what part of the eastern seaboard is satellite twenty nine located?"

"It's almost directly over the city of Sydney, Sir."

"I was afraid you were going to tell me that." Harding said levelly.
"You've done well, George. I would appreciate it if you kept our conversation and your careful observation of satellite twenty nine completely between ourselves." Harding stared into the bottom of his

empty cup. "No one, and I mean no one, George, is to even suspect what you are doing. Do you get my drift? There are nasty people around, George, and we don't know how far they have penetrated our organisation. All I can tell you is when I get my hands on the person who did this, I'm personally going to rip every organ out of his body."

George nodded in complete understanding. If he stuffed up it was his organs which would be ripped out first, let alone any terrorist. He almost felt sorry for him, whoever he was. First things first, he would log on to the central computer and erase any trace of his recent activities. Next he would create a small application which would log the satellite's error codes into a file which only he could access. All the time he kept trying to reconcile the failure of the satellite with its apparently successful transmission of data. The most reasonable explanation was that its own internal communications software had been tampered with. It was possible of course, but if a terrorist had done that successfully, they were to be greatly feared. What you could do to one satellite, you could do to another. He shuddered at the possibility.

❋ ❋ ❋

Three days passed without incident, which was hardly surprising, since absolutely no satellite traffic was being sent to or received from Nuralungunya or Pine Gap. Dianne Collins and Norm Harding were doing their thing. Neither of them had come one millimetre closer to discovering the terrorist, or uncovering the slightest trace of the infrastructure he must have used to accomplish the impossible. On the fourth day Cassie Watson, Secretary to the President, came into the Oval Office carrying a small package.

"Mr. President," Cassie announced, "there is a trade delegation from North Korea waiting to see you. I told them they would have to proceed through the normal channels, and they didn't seem too pleased. They wanted to give you this – it's a sample of their manufacturing know-how or something. It's been thoroughly checked by security. I have no idea what it is. They left this card as well."
"A trade delegation? We don't trade with Pyongyang," the President muttered. "What the devil are they doing here? What's this?"

# THE PETROV EFFECT

The President opened the small ornate wooden box. Inside was a shiny square of black material, several millimetres thick. He took the square out of its container and felt it in the palm of his hand. It was surprisingly light.

"Get Brett in here, will you?" he barked.

Cassie disappeared, and moments later the presidential military advisor walked into the room.

"What do you make of this?" The President handed him the small square of material.

"Where did you get this, Mr. President?" Dyer asked, frowning heavily.

"There's something odd going on, Mr. Dyer," the President growled. "This was given to me by a so-called trade delegation from Pyongyang. Considering our present relationship I find that bizarre. This is a sample of their manufacturing processes, or so they claim. I fancy it might be something completely different."

Brett Dyer turned the small square over in his hand, weighing it as he did so. He tried to bend it gently between his thumb and forefinger. He smelt it. He held the surface up to the light, then placed it carefully and slowly on the table next to the President. His face was far from happy. "I will have to get confirmation, but I'm nearly sure. Are the members of this trade delegation still in the White House? I would suggest we keep them here."

"I believe they've gone but they left their card," the President sighed loudly. Tell me the worst."

"This is a sample of advanced carbon fibre, strengthened by these small internal ribs, see? It's part of the Trident warhead casing." Dyer paused, wiped his brow. "They've found the blasted thing."

The President gave a groan, and mechanically pressed the intercom. Seconds later Cassie re-entered the room.

"Cassie, ring this number and make an appointment with this delegation. Get me Wilson, head of foreign aid on the horn. I want to see the following people in my office within the hour."

He made a list and handed it to her with the card.

Cassie's eyes widened somewhat. "You have appointments with the secretary of state and there's that—"

"Cancel them. Cassie, I want those people in here within the hour," the President said grimly. "Tell them I'll have their jobs if there's the slightest protest." The President's fists were clenching and unclenching, and his voice left no room for argument.

"Yes, Mr. President." Cassie ran out of the room.

The President ran his hand across his face. "It's the end of this administration. They've got us by the balls and they know it. I wonder they didn't try to nuke us in return."

"I don't think there was much chance of that, Mr. President." Dyer replaced the small sample back in its box. "Pyongyang must realise that something went wrong. If we had wanted to nuke them we wouldn't have aborted the missile and tried to recover the warhead. They know that, and they're going to capitalise on it. The trade delegation gives us a legitimate public method of meeting their demands. Besides, the whole incident must have shown them how vulnerable they are, and they're not going to provoke us into having another go, one which we won't abort. No, it's humble pie washed down with billions of dollars of aid if we want to keep our jobs."

"I fear you're right," the President growled, resuming his seat.
"May heaven help the terrorist that did this. I want him and his accomplices eviscerated. Eviscerated, you hear me?" he shouted, smashing his fist repeatedly on the table. "If Harding and Collins don't come through, I swear they'll be spending the rest of their lives sweeping streets." He shook his head miserably from side to side. "We have been brought low, Dyer. The entire United States had been brought low."

Two days later the trade delegation met with the President under the tightest security that has ever been imposed on a foreign delegation entering the White House. It was a long meeting. In the end the public would learn that the United States, in a humanitarian effort to ease the suffering in North Korea would send, over the next two years, a little over four billion dollars in aid. The United States would build the North Koreans three light water nuclear reactors if Pyongyang would allow independent investigators from the United Nations to inspect all their nuclear facilities to ensure they were not manufacturing weapons grade plutonium. The United States would remove economic sanctions against the Democratic People's Republic and provide trade incentives, technology and equipment. The United States would consider importing manufactured goods, the list went on and on. In exchange, North Korea's ability to manufacture a certain type of advanced carbon fibre would remain confidential and private between the two governments.

Congress would not be happy, but then Harding could deal with them. When it came to persuading reluctant Congressmen, Harding and Collins were without peer. Nonetheless he sent a secure message to Peter Lawson at Langley to the effect that the CIA had better come through and quickly if they knew what was good for them. The CIA might be masters of their own business, but the President of the United States could cut off their funding like turning off a tap. It wasn't even a veiled threat, and Lawson knew it.

# CHAPTER 20

The Australian Security Intelligence Organisation began in nineteen forty nine at the directive of the then Prime Minister, Ben Chifley. In those days it worked closely with its British counterpart MI5. The partnership dominated the fifties in an operation which became known as "The Case". This resulted in the destruction of a spy ring operating out of the Russian Embassy in Canberra, with links to the government at the time. Relations with their USA counterpart, the CIA, was also, in the words of the then Director "a very personal one", and the two organisations worked closely together through the sixties. In the seventies, however, the personal relationship degenerated somewhat when the CIA discovered that ASIO had been penetrated by a KGB mole, and in this condition was not to be trusted with any sensitive information. Try as they might, ASIO was never able to locate the mole. In two thousand and four the former KGB Major-General Oleg Kalugin boasted publicly on the Australian Broadcasting Corporation's Four Corner's program that they had infiltrated the security organisation for over ten years until the early eighties.

Being treated as a mushroom - kept in the dark and fed on manure - did nothing to improve ASIO's love for their friends on the other side of the Pacific who made them feel very much the underdog in the business of national security. To make matters worse, ASIO made the unfortunate mistake of casting several Labour politicians in a politically unfavourable light, with the result that the organisation became the object of a Royal Commission and a Parliamentary Committee inquiry. In nineteen seventy three their office in Melbourne was raided by the Commonwealth police on the instigation of one of those irate Labour Party politicians.

Small wonder they were resentful towards those who regarded them as incompetent. Despite the political backlash, the organisation had continued to expand its charter through the eighties and nineties, but the CIA still regarded them as vulnerable players in the game, an attitude which the current Director-General, one Brian Hill, detested with a vengeance.

That particular day in nineteen ninety seven, the same gentleman picked up the unsecured phone in his office and found, much to his astonishment, that none other than the then Director General of the CIA, one Norm Harding, was on the other end of it. To make matters doubly infuriating, it was a local call, and Hill didn't even know he was in the country. How could that have happened? All airports were monitored carefully. He would have a word with that fluffy twit Trudy in the immigrations department, more than one. Hill ground his teeth, silently. No wonder they were the laughing stock of the Americans. He listened as Harding rattled on for fifteen minutes about the way the CIA valued its close and personal ties with their Australian friends, making the occasional grunt whenever the American paused for breath, which wasn't very often. Hill knew the length of the sucking up was roughly proportional to the magnitude of the request which would follow, and fifteen minutes meant a right royal pain in the backside was coming up.

After exactly seventeen and a half minutes Harding came to the point. There was a dangerous terrorist cell known to be operating on Australian soil, and the CIA would value the cooperation, relied on the cooperation, of their friends in the urgent task of neutralising it. He glossed over the fact that the Australians had no inkling of this cell's existence, and gave no hint as to how the CIA had gleaned its information. Rather he laid great emphasis on teamwork and mutual benefit to both countries when the cell's activities were terminated. Just what the cell did and how it did it was also notably absent from the conversation. In response to Hill's request for further enlightenment, he was simply told the cell was extremely dangerous, so dangerous its existence imperilled both their great nations. So urgent was the need, the CIA would be happy to supply manpower, infrastructure and expertise to assist in bringing the perpetrators of this unnamed terror to book. They would be happy to provide guidance, relying on the stalwart reputation of the Australians for thoroughness.

Hill took that last piece of flattery in the very worst possible way.

Having dispensed with the camaraderie, Harding eventually told Hill exactly how this wonderful cooperation would commence, and Hill committed every word to his photographic memory.

He put the phone down and turned to his friend and Deputy Director Noel Clark. "Do you know who I've had on the phone?" he said, "the Director of the CIA, no less. Phoning from some local number. What's he doing over here? Takes a tidal wave to get him out of his office in Foggy Bottom. Something big is in the air."

"How did he get here?" Noel put down the sandwich he was enjoying. "Our monitors would have picked him up if he had come through any airport. Must have come through the RAAF."

"No he didn't – we monitor them too," Hill grimaced. "Nothing changes with the CIA. I'm sick of them. It's the mushroom approach all over again. They want to muscle in on our show in the name of cooperation and take over. Do they tell us what it's all about? Of course not. They wouldn't trust us to ferret out a crocodile in a koala park."

"What did they want?" Noel Clark asked, a bemused expression on his face.

"Apparently there's some super terrorist cell operating somewhere in Sydney." He laughed scornfully, "threatening the entire existence of the free world, yadda, yadda, yadda. Then there was a heap of rubbish about friendly cooperation. Empty rhetoric. Whatever they're really doing is far too hush-hush for the likes of us."

Hill threw a pen towards a receptacle on his desk. "All they want us to do is to collect some data. They want to know the location of every satellite dish within a twenty kilometre radius of Darling Harbour, whether it's capable of transmitting data to a satellite and if so, what's the radiation pattern. The usual pain-in-the-butt boring, labour intensive stuff. Not only that, they want us to go and overfly the entire area with some special detection gear, just to check our findings. Trust, you see."

Hill picked up the biro from the floor and had another shot. "Oh, and they would like to have one of their people on the flight deck of the aircraft. More trust. They want it yesterday too. Typical. Who knows what the blazes is going on? One thing sure we never will."

"Are you going to do it?" Noel grabbed the biro before its next flight and replaced it carefully in a jar containing several others.

"I've got no flaming choice," Brian Hill said gloomily. "Somehow Harding's got the prime minister in on the act. Being the nice cooperative gentleman that our P.M. is, he's guaranteed to give them all the assistance they need." He shook his head, sadly. "I tell you, Noel, this job is becoming the high wire act in a circus. One little slip and it's straight into the mouths of the lions below."

"You want me to handle initial collection of data?" Noel sighed. "I guess it will take a while for them to get this special gear out to us."

"Not on your Nellie. It arrives tomorrow morning by special flight into Richmond RAAF Base – and thanks. You had better get moving on it."

❄ ❄ ❄

Four days and a lot of man hours later, three men, Noel, Brian, and no less than Norm Harding himself, were pouring over pages and pages of data, photographs and printouts from the equipment they had flown all over the Sydney metropolitan area, much to the annoyance of air traffic control at Kingsford Smith International airport.

Brian had the floor. "What is the problem?" he asked again. "Our flight data confirms what we already know. The only dishes which uplink to satellites are the Overseas Telecommunications dishes at Belrose which fire out across the Pacific, the Australian Broadcasting Commission's dish in Harris Street on top of their building, a dish on Redfern Mail Centre, and the other television station dishes that are used to exchange program material via various satellites, all of which are known. There are countless small satellite TV dishes scattered throughout the metropolitan area, but they are easily identified."

Harding replaced a large sheet of data on top of the pile. "There are no other dishes capable of up-linking to satellites, capable of transmitting anything at all?"

"Apart from those already mentioned, all the others are receiving dishes," Hill explained. "You can see by the way the dishes are pointing which satellites they're obtaining data from." He ferreted around until he found the set of aerial photographs. "I tell you, whatever you're looking for isn't here. We've located no less than fifteen amateur satellite dishes in the designated area. Seven of them belong to radio hams, and the other eight to television DX'ers, plugging in to overseas television channels. The radio hams communicate to their own satellite in both directions. All the others are only receiving data. We have profiles on every single one of them in any case, and you've read them."

He threw the photographs on the table and lay back in his chair. "Do you fancy your super spy is among them? Personally, I think you're paranoid if you do – unless there's anything else you want to put on the table, like exactly what the blazes is going on?"

Harding put down the photograph he had been studying. "This dish on top of the building there – it's pointing straight up. What satellite is that communicating with?"

"Which one is that?" Brian leant forward. "The one not too far from City Road? That belongs to the University of Sydney Physics department."

"This dish is a transmitting dish? These experiments involve transmissions?" Harding queried.

"The dish is purely a receiving dish," Hill said, ferreting for more paper. "I have it here from the dean of the Physics department, wait a second, no, the other pile, Noel, thanks." He took the folder from Noel's hand, opened it and began to read.

"The dean writes – 'there are two devices used to collect sky data associated with the Physics department, a phased array of Yagi antennae which form part of the heliostat experiments run by doctor Bill Hawthorne, and a large aperture dish which doctor David Petrov uses to collect data from the ionosphere as part of his research."

"Petrov?" Harding's eyebrows went up. "That's interesting. Didn't you once have some dealings with a guy called Petrov? Soviet spy, wasn't he?" Harding turned his head towards Hill, his brow wrinkled as though trying to recall a memory.

Hill slowly replaced the folder in the pile on the table before replying.

"As I was saying, the dish is used for receiving purposes only. We thought you would be interested in that one, so we overflew it with your gear every single day. Not a skerrick of radiation coming up from it. Took a photo each time. They're in the file with the time of day they were taken. We even had a technician come and take a covert look over Petrov's setup, on the excuse of trying to fix a problem he and some others were having with their optic fibre connection to the main campus. I've got his report pinned to the back of the dean's letter. He says—"

Hill picked up the letter, turned it over and read. "The head amplifier on the dish is connected directly to a sensitive multi-band receiver, capable of tuning signals from one point zero Gigahertz to two point five Gigahertz. No transmitting device is attached to the dish. There's more technical stuff, but I can tell you that dish isn't transmitting a thing."

"Looks like we're back to square one then." Harding scratched his ear.

"Whatever that means," Hill said. "Norm, why don't you tell us what's going on and we may be able to give you better assistance. You know, in the interests of all this cooperation you've been rabbiting on about."

"At the moment that's classified." Harding's face wore a patronising smile.

"I know it's hard on you guys, but this work you've done for us, hey, it's been a great help already. We've just got to look elsewhere. Perhaps there's someone operating offshore. Could I stretch a favour and ask you to monitor the location of all reasonable sized vessels? Ones that could poke a decent sized satellite dish skywards – within a fifteen kilometre radius from the coast from, say Mona Vale to Port Hacking? Could you do that?"

Trying to keep the anger out of his voice Brian Hill replied. "I'd have to check with our friends in the Maritime Services and the Coastguard. Even so, I don't think they take note of which vessels have satellite dishes. Perhaps you could re- task one of your special satellites, you know, one with an earth pointing telescope."

"Thank you for the suggestion," Harding said. "In the meantime, I want this whole business sown up tighter than a clam's buttocks. No mention to anyone other than those who were directly involved in the data collection. Get them together and scare the hell out of them if they so much as breathe a word. I don't even want them talking to their pet cat."

"Can do," Hill said, mimicking Harding's patronising tone. "I take it you know the P.M. has told us to cooperate with you as if our lives depended on it."

"Believe me, they depend on it," Harding said grimly. "Now I'll take my leave, gentlemen. Right now I'm stationed at Pine Gap. Your info will enable us to put phase two of our operation into effect. I'm grateful. America is grateful."

Harding left the room and joined the two marines who were waiting outside to take him to Richmond RAAF base. Hill gathered up the mess of paperwork which was strewn all over the table, and threw it into a box with a good deal more force than was necessary.

"So that's how he got into the country," Hill muttered. "Direct flight to Pine Gap. No wonder we didn't spot him. Glad he told us, I was going to blast Trudy. Did you hear that last bit? America is grateful. America is grateful is it? I'll bet you a million dollars America doesn't give a rat's arse about it. What's this all about, Noel? Did you get any clues?"

"Something or somebody has been interfering with their secure satellite communications, that's for sure," Noel said, walking towards the drinks cabinet. "Probably stuffed up something pretty important, I'd say, and our little Foggy Bottom friends are worried about it. Did you pick that up?"

"That they're worried?" Hill laughed. "You bet they are. The Director meeting with us like this? There's a cat in with the pigeons and it's making its presence felt. You heard that barb about our thoroughness? Oh, and he couldn't remember about Petrov – some sort of spy or other. Like blazes he couldn't remember. They speak with forked tongue, Noel. Trust them as much as you'd trust a sleeping crock."

"What was the business with Petrov all about?" Noel asked. "Some joint operation?"

"Nothing like that," Hill grunted. "It was long before your time with us, nineteen fifty one to be exact. We were cultivating a spy by the name of Vladimir Mikhaylovich Petrov, who worked in the Soviet Embassy. Went like a charm, and the old boy was sending carefully doctored intel back to the Kremlin for about three years before they got wise. We had to spirit him out to a safe house pretty damn quick, but they got his wife Evdokia, and shoved her on a plane back home. They told her Vladimir had already taken off for Moscow. The plane had to refuel in Darwin, and we managed to talk to her via the pilot. He told us the KGB – or former KGB - agents were packing guns illegally, and we used that to bundle the whole lot of them off the plane when it landed, along with Evdokia. After she'd spoken with her husband and found he was very much alive and wanting asylum, she agreed to return to Sydney. They stayed in hiding for a while at a place in Palm Beach, I think it was. Real coup, and the press recorded every word. We dug up some embarrassing links between the Labour party and the Communists too, real juicy stuff. They've hated us ever since."

"The Communists?" Noel searched around for a clean glass.

"No, you nit," Hill laughed, "the Australian Labour Party. They hate our guts. Surely you remember that raid down in Melbourne. They were behind it. Went bad for them in the end, but any opportunity and they have another go."

He paused in thought for a minute. "Noel, I want you to dig up all the stuff you can about Petrov, not Vladimir, but the bloke who's running the ionospheric stuff at Sydney University. Just a long shot, really."

"Why? You think he's the ultimate terrorist? It's just a receiving dish, or so the dean said. He couldn't have stuffed up their satellite."

"It has nothing to do with their satellite," Hill explained. "His name, Petrov, that's the problem. The Yanks are twitchy, and when they're twitchy they're even more paranoid than they usually are, and that's saying something. If Petrov is innocent I want him protected from their grubby little hands, and if he isn't, then we've got a lead that might beat the CIA at their own game. I'd like to see their faces if we did. Check him out. I want to know if there's any connection between his family and Vladimir Petrov, if he's ever been in trouble with the law, that sort of thing. Shouldn't be hard."

"No worries, boss," Noel said, grinning. "I take it we don't share this stuff with our tight lipped friends?"

"Not until they show us more of their hand, or unless we're forced to. How about a decent lunch, Noel? I'm sick of this café bar coffee."

"Now you're talking."

The two men walked out of the room and headed for the restaurant at the end of the street. Mancini's made awesome pizza.

❄ ❄ ❄

At that very time Norm Harding was boarding a private plane for Canberra. He had an appointment with the P.M. that afternoon. The meeting with Hill had crystallised the line he was going to take when he got there. Hill was cynical, and liable to ask too many questions which they could not risk answering. ASIO had been penetrated once before.

Who was to know if it hadn't been penetrated again? Yet if they kept Hill in the dark they would lose his cooperation, which could make their mission difficult. No, Hill had to be forced to cooperate whether he wanted to or not, cooperate no matter how much or how little he knew. A specialised Australian Anti-terrorist Unit, that was it, to which ASIO would be responsible. American expertise guiding Australian enthusiasm, that was the way he would sell the concept. Hill would hate it like poison, but once the unit was established he would have no choice but to work with it. He smiled as he imagined the look on Hill's face when he found out he was working for the CIA.

# CHAPTER 21

Abigail Saunders stared out the window of her apartment in Washington DC at the rain pouring down on the Potomac river. Somehow it described her mood over the last two weeks perfectly. The clouds were black and threatening, and it was cold, perfect metaphors of her future with the CIA. No one had contacted her, even Harry, and that could only mean one thing, she had been removed from the 'active' list. Heaven help her if she was scheduled for retraining. Not that she had been idle. Her exit strategy was all but complete, and her employer's lack of interest had helped.

At first Abby had been incredibly careful, expecting to be shadowed wherever she went, but try as she would she couldn't detect a single tail on her activities, a single watcher, a single bug in her apartment. Mind you she had taken no chances at all. It didn't pay to take chances, especially when you are engaged in the activities Abby had been engaged in. Three different passports, unknown to the CIA, clothes and medical supplies at various train station lockers, money in a number of different currencies, wigs, contact lenses, the lot. One hint of trouble and she was gone, as far away and as fast as possible. Australia, she thought. Backwater of the world, but a comfortable backwater. Harry would not let her down. He would find a way of warning her of danger. Harry was in love with her, or whatever he called the lust she often read in his eyes.

She had never taken advantage of it, never shown him anything but grudging respect, not even friendship. Friend? In all her world there was no one she could address by that title. How life had changed from those happy, carefree days in Boston, when she waltzed through the world with so many friends. Friends? No, people who believed lies about you weren't friends.

Putting on her Armani coat, she took an umbrella off the stand near the door and caught the lift down to the foyer, her destination the post office and her private mailbox which was several blocks away. She caught a taxi outside the apartment and headed in the opposite direction, carefully watching behind her in case she was being followed. No, apparently not. Getting out of the taxi, she walked another block before catching the next one which dropped her off two blocks from the post office. Another quick journey, a turn of her key, and she was holding a small bundle of letters in her hand. Moving quickly away from the post office, she caught a third taxi to a small café on the other side of the city, one which lay in a quiet suburban street. Not too private so a stranger would be noticed, but private enough.

Sitting down with a coffee she began to open her mail. The third letter was from a law firm in Boston: Chambers, Chambers and Marsden. She tore it open. Inside were two envelopes, one bearing an official seal, and the other her name in a writing which she immediately recognised as belonging to her father. A small shudder ran down her spine as she remembered her final encounter with him. At first she thought of tearing the whole lot up, for there was nothing he could say to her that mattered, be he alive or dead, nothing she wanted to hear anyway. Only a morbid sense of curiosity made her rip the envelope open. She began to read.

> *My dearest Abigail,*
> *I know when you receive this letter I will have left the world forever, and I have little hope that the eternity to which I go will be better than the life I have managed to lead on this Earth. I know you no longer hold me in any affection, and I do not blame you in the least. In the bitter years which followed on from that terrible evening when you left us forever, I have learned to regret the single most despicable act in my life. At the time I believed my public duty*

*to the University and the Bank was of more importance than my own daughter's virtue, a righteous cloak for my own utter selfishness and desperation to cling to the two remaining pillars in a life of rubble.*

*I have no right to ask for a forgiveness I do not deserve, and which you are justifiably right to withhold, yet I would beg you to believe these words I have written. Each year since that deplorable evening I have set aside a little money in an account which one day would become yours. It does me no credit, for I have already forfeited the one and only lovely thing in my life, and I am not attempting to buy back something which is beyond price. My only hope is that it may help to provide you with the comfort you deserve, dearest Abigail, and in some small way assist in releasing the joy I know still lives inside you.*

*With all my love, dearest Abigail,*
*Father.*

Abby put the letter down on the table with an unsteady hand. This would have been the time for tears, but try as she would she could not command her eyes to shed a single drop of moisture. Conflicting emotions raged through her mind. One moment her hatred would gain the upper hand, then her sorrow and regret would wrench its mastery from her heart. Her father was a miser, and in any case her mother and her foul brother would have made sure that all the estate went in their direction. A hundred thousand dollars – if it were even so much – would not assuage the pain of that terrible evening, the public distain and humiliation, the silence of her father. Barely mastering the desire to burn the lot, she opened the seal on the other envelope and read.

Dear Ms. Saunders,
We write to you on the matter concerning the estate of the late Charles Francis Saunders which was granted probate recently. The will of the said Charles Francis was contested by two other beneficiaries, but their court action was unsuccessful. Therefore, in accordance with the aforesaid Last Will and Testament of the deceased Charles Francis Saunders we are able to transfer from that estate the sum bequeathed to Abigail Brook Saunders by her father the late Charles Francis by means of Bank Transfer to the full amount of eighteen million five hundred thousand nine

hundred and fifty dollars being the sum originally deposited with our Executors Trust Fund whilst the will was contestate plus interest earned. The transfer will be conducted as soon as you are able to furnish our offices with your personal banking details.
Sincerely,
Harold Marsden for Chambers, Chambers and Marsden.

Abby put down the letter with a shaking hand. She felt sick, cold. Lifting her coffee to her lips she took a sip, but it tasted like medicine. It was blood money, she the murderess, this her spoils. A shudder passed all the way down her spine, and beads of cold sweat formed on her forehead. A passing waiter was about to ask if she wanted a refill, but one glance at that face was enough to send him scurrying to other patrons on the far side of the room. Once again her stomach threatened to distribute its contents on the floor, but with a desperate effort she managed to control the spasm. The rain poured remorselessly down outside the window, but the storm in her own heart rendered her oblivious to all else. A millionairess without a dollar's worth of happiness to call her own. She glanced at the envelopes with an expression that was close to loathing. Not one cent would she spend, but she couldn't bring herself to give it all away either. No, transfer it to her account in Zurich, leave it there. The CIA would try to get their hands on it if they knew. One day, one day perhaps, her heart might recover enough for her to care about something, and that something was likely to become a very well-endowed something. Not now, there were no feelings of that sort left inside her. Was it depression that made her wish she was back inside her mother's womb? Safe inside that hateful home until the day she was born? It would have been better to have died before then, before some unthinking doctor drew her bodily out of her place of safety into this sickeningly awful world.

Sick, she was sick.

Anyone else who had just been given eighteen and a half million dollars would be dancing on the table, not trying desperately to avoid throwing up on the floor. Gritting her teeth she dropped a fifty dollar note on the table and left the restaurant.

# CHAPTER 22

I t was 4:45a.m. Washington time. Two men sat at the console in the dimly lit Supreme Command centre at Nuralungunya. Commander Norton withdrew a small card from his pocket and swiped it through the reader near his right arm, and Commander Richards followed suit with his, both men keying in their respective numbers. Over their shoulders Norm Harding watched the winking asterisk on the large screen in front of them. The single pair of green lights blinked their acceptance momentarily then remained steady. The asterisk changed to a ">" indicating that the command centre was in communication with the captain of the Michigan. Richards spoke.

"Confirming destination?"

"You don't have to do that. Destination has been set in the sealed orders given the Captain of the Michigan. You don't know where the missile is targeted," Harding said tersely.

Norton keyed the first command into the console.

>Missile TC4UMG-96A Activate

The screen responded:

>enter access codes

>code A:

The commanders entered their access codes one after the other. The screen responded.

>access codes accepted
>enter command

Norton typed the words into the keyboard. His hand was not completely steady.

>Missile TC4UMG-96A launch

>enter launch codes
>code A

The commanders entered their respective codes. The tension in the room could be felt. Neither commander was aware that this was only a simulation.
The screen responded.

>missile launch sequence initiated – launch in 30 seconds
>command

There were beads of sweat on Richards' forehead. His fingers moved deliberately and carefully on the keyboard. This was not the time to make a typing mistake. He had heard rumours that something catastrophic had happened the last time this exercise was performed. It wasn't going to be repeated on his watch, no way.

Missile TC4UMG-96A abort launch

>enter abort code

This time Norton's hands typed carefully, ever so carefully on the keyboard. The screen responded.

>missile launch aborted
>enter command

Norton wiped the sweat off his forehead. "I take it we shut down now?"

"No. Wait." Harding had laid his hand on Norton's shoulder. "Touch nothing. Nothing. Wait until I tell you to log off." He picked up the phone that lay further along the console. "Get me the Captain of the Michigan. Captain? Harding here. No, this is an ultra-secure line. Okay at your end? Good. There is a number on your screen. Please tell me what it is. Thank you."

He leaned over the console and typed:

>XXVUYT987KLt

The screen responded:

>mission completed
>command

"What was all that about?" Richards said, angrily. *What the blazes is going on?* He thought. There had been no changes to protocol in his briefing. Very specific it had been, and Richards had dreaded every second of it.

"Just a little security precaution, gentlemen." Harding waved towards the keyboard. "Now you may log off. Thank you for your cooperation."

"Do we ever get to know what part of the world we almost vaporised?" Richards complained bitterly. "I can tell you, neither Norton or myself appreciate being placed in this position. We're here because we're following orders, not because we in any way approve of this insane testing process." He stood up from the console. "Unless you purposely keep your commanders in the dark, but then, why bother with us? Why don't you go and start world war three all by yourselves?"

"I think it would be wise to keep those opinions to yourselves, gentlemen." Harding's tone should have given Richards cause for pause.

"What is the CIA doing in this room?" Norton was standing, gripping the back of his chair with white knuckles. "Who authorised your presence? The President? I thought the whole purpose of your outfit was to prevent nuclear war, not precipitate it. Strange how you can get these things wrong."

"It is indeed," Harding said evenly. "Please accompany me to the debriefing room."

Three men walked out of the room, and only one of them was remotely happy. So it had apparently gone well this time, the very thing Harding had not anticipated, especially as the target was Beijing. That information had been conveyed earlier to the Michigan by the same secure satellite communications system as the rest of the simulated launch-abort launch commands. Surely he would have provoked a reaction? Even if the terrorists had found the target unbelievable, why not interfere as before? Perhaps change the target and nuke Nuralungunya instead? Pour more scorn on the dear old US of A. Maybe it was a software bug after all, and sweet Dianne had not updated him as to the state of the nation in that department. How typical of her. Well, the debrief was in the Situation Room in the Whitehouse at twelve hundred hours, and it would be a long trip. The Boeing was waiting at Pine Gap.

# CHAPTER 23

At twelve hundred hours the Situation Room was crowded with the usual participants. The President sat at the head of the table, looking like any President would when he has been forced to spend ten billion dollars on his enemies because of the incompetence of his own staff. Trudy Wilson, who had borne the brunt of his ire since the very first meeting was pale and tired. Brett Dyer looked worried. Generals Albright, Corbett and Norris seemed as comfortable as men sitting on an unexploded bomb. George Russell the communications specialist, shone with the false attentiveness of a sleep-deprived man pumped full of caffeine. Norman Harding looked, as he always did, completely impassive and slightly bored. Only Dianne Collins, Director of the NSA seemed happy, which would have given any observant being cause for pause.

No one was at all anxious to ignite the fuse.

"How are you feeling today, Mr. President?" Dianne broke the steely silence, that same infuriating smile on her face.

"Cut the small talk, Dianne," the President snapped. "You were never any good at it. Alright, somebody tell me something I would like to hear."

"As far as we can tell the simulation went perfectly, Mr. President." Harding pushed himself back in his chair with an air of confidence. "I was personally in the Supreme Command centre when the exercise was conducted. I spoke via secure comms to the Captain of the Michigan. The simulation software on board worked exactly as expected. There was only one small hiccup and George has been looking into that."

"Do tell us, Doctor Russell. This small hitch?" The President leaned forward in Russell's direction.

"Secure satellite twenty nine appeared to fault again, Mr. President," Russell said nervously. "We now believe this is due to some problem within the satellite itself, and we are attempting a solution with some new software. So far we have not had any success, but we are working around the clock on it."

"This was the same satellite which faulted before, the one which transfers the data from Nuralungunya to our fleet in the Pacific, is it not?" the President asked, a slight tremor in his voice.

"That is correct, Mr. President. The satellite works perfectly even though it sends back error codes sometimes," Russell answered, doing his best to keep his voice from wavering.

"So, all the naughty fairies have gone back to Disneyland and we can dance and be happy," the President said, his voice growing in volume and trembling with rage. "Except I can't, because the taxpayers of this country have been forced to spend ten billion dollars on the communists. You hear that sum?" he shouted. "Ten billion dollars!" The President smashed his fist down on the table. "Do you think the naughty fairies might return for another giggle? Perhaps we should just nuke Disneyland to make sure they don't."

No one even smiled, with the exception of Dianne who was doing it all the time, blast her.

Norm Harding stopped doodling on a pad near his hand. "We haven't had a complete report yet, Mr. President," he soothed evenly. "Perhaps Dianne has uncovered some software glitch in the computer at Nuralungunya. She seems to be simply bursting with good news. Why don't you tell us what you've found, Dianne? Dazzle us all."

Dianne smiled at him. A look of mild astonishment crossed Harding's face.

"Of course, Norman," she said. "No, there was nothing wrong with the computer at Nuralungunya. We checked every line of code, recompiled and reloaded the whole lot. We ran exhaustive tests. It's working perfectly."

"So back to the fairies then," Harding smiled back.

"Not quite, Norman. I wonder if you would be good enough to check that these are the missile launch codes you used in the last simulation?"

She passed a scrap of paper across the table to an astonished Harding. He glanced at it briefly then handed it back.

"That is so very far above your pay grade, Dianne," he said reprovingly. "May I ask how you managed to acquire these? If it was from one of my staff I can assure you they have a most unpleasant and extremely short future ahead of them."

"Just what's going down here?" The President interrupted, sitting on the edge of his chair.

"Dianne has handed me a copy of the launch codes we used in the latest simulation launch – abort launch operation, Mr. President," Harding said, trying to keep the astonishment out of his voice. "So, Dianne, your moment of glory has arrived. We're all panting with anticipation. Tell us where you got them."

"From a chat room on the internet," Dianne beamed.

There was stunned silence.

The President's face contorted in apoplectic rage. "WHAT?" he bellowed, shattering the silence.

Even Harding's completely passive face had morphed into an expression of shocked disbelief. Trudy Wilson had abstractedly stuffed her hand in her mouth, and George Russel looked as though he was going to faint. The three Generals had gone a funny pale colour and Brett Dyer stared as though someone had just removed his kidneys without asking him first.

"That's completely impossible." Russell croaked out the words. He could see his job, and probably his life were about to pass into history.

Dianne, with a smile which told Harding she was savouring every second continued. "We studied all the lovely information our friends in ASIO collected – you remember, the satellite dishes and all that stuff. We plotted the location of satellite twenty nine on top of a map of Sydney. Do you realise there's a dish directly under the thing? Now as you know, Norman, we run your ultra-secure decryption algorithms over a large sample of internet traffic just to see if anyone has got wise, and it always results in gobbledegook. But when we ran it over some of the stuff the owner of that dish has been posting on the internet, we came up with some real numbers – all of the right length to be launch codes which you have confirmed they are." She smiled again. "Oh, and you may be interested to know the caption which preceded this little revelation? I have it here – 'who belongs to this rubbish?' Sort of rubbing salt in the wound, isn't it?"

The silence that followed on from those words was deafening. From the appearance of the President's face he was going to require medical attention any second.

"I suppose you know the identity of the individual who sent us this poisoned barb?" Harding asked, evenly.

"But naturally, Norman," Dianne cooed. "His name is Doctor Petrov, a lecturer in Physics at the University of Sydney."

"Petrov?" Harding exclaimed. "I don't suppose you've done anything so stupid as to pay him a friendly visit, have you Dianne?"

"Pay him a friendly visit?" The President exploded. "I want him eviscerated. Get him and eviscerate him. I want him and all his foul organisation eviscerated. That's an order."

"Begging your pardon, Mr. President, but that would be the most ludicrous order you have ever given. I trust you're not serious," Harding said evenly.

If looks could kill Harding would have been lying dead on the floor. It was several seconds before the President was capable of reply. He drew a glass of water to his lips with a shaking hand, and taking a gulp or two, returned it slowly to its place on the table as he fought to regain the power of speech.

He turned towards Dianne. "Thank you, Dianne. It would appear you alone, out of all the other company in this room, have retained your wits." He fixed the CIA director with a piercing stare. "You had better have something to say, Harding, because of now your job – and your whole department – is teetering on the brink of extinction. I suggest you weigh your words with more than your usual care."

"Think about it for a minute." There was an edge to Harding's voice. "This terrorist organisation we're up against is no amateur player in the game. They can even afford to tell us the name of one of their operatives, to show their hand. You can't do that unless you have a watertight way of protecting yourself. If we went in and took Petrov apart we would learn precisely nothing, and they know it. All it would do is tell them that once again we had swallowed the bait. Can't you see? This is sheer provocation, sheer bravado. They have us by the balls and they know it. They want us to know it. They would love us to react. Once again we would look the fools we are. Besides, they might be tempted to do something in return, like launch a nuclear missile into the Whitehouse."

"So true, Norman dear." Dianne smiled at him. "You seem to be grasping the situation with admirable clarity. Perhaps there is something else you haven't got round to appreciating just yet. The location of these ultra-secure satellites, what classification does it carry?"

"It's classification one, and you know it, top secret," Harding replied, his control teetering slightly. "Only the President and I have access to that information."

"Wrong, my dear Norman," Dianne goaded. "The terrorists have it too. They build a satellite dish right under one of them. It's a reasonable assumption they must know the location of all the others. Who knows what they're up to? Right now every secure satellite has probably got some nice little dish sitting underneath it, using technology that we haven't heard of to read every piece of secure traffic we're sending, ready to start whatever they want to. Nice thought, isn't it Norman?"

"Shut it down." The President gripped the sides of the table with both hands, his knuckles whitening.

"I beg your pardon, Mr. President. Shut what down?" Brett Dyer stammered.

"Shut the whole thing down," The President shouted. "Every military satellite, every secure communications link."

"But, Mr. President, that would mean—" General Corbett began.

"Can any of you great security experts guarantee, carte blanche, that this terrorist group can't read our secure communications anytime they want to?" The President fixed them one by one with fire in his eyes. "Can you Russell? Can you Dianne? Can any of you lot?" He waved his arm in the direction of the three Generals. "And of course Harding doesn't even know it when they do. They read our launch codes like the morning paper. Anyone want to stake their life on the integrity of future communications?"

There was absolute silence, broken at last by Dianne.

"We are not able to guarantee the integrity of the network at this time, Mr. President."

"Then shut it down. I want it shut down. Now. Is that clear?" the President bellowed.
"But Mr. President," Albright objected, horrified. "If there was a situation, a clear and present danger to the United States, Sir, how would you communicate with your commanders?"

The President shot to his feet, kicking his chair out from behind him. His face was suffused with blood, his hands shaking with rage.

"You want to know that, do you, Albright? Well, I'll tell you. Since our highly classified channels are as secure as the evening news, I'll go out onto the Whitehouse lawn and launch a carrier pigeon! What else? The entire United States brought to its knees. Defenceless. Order the commanders to remain on standby and maintain complete digital silence. Not a beep out of them. If they want anything they have to come here in person, here, you understand?"

He pointed his finger at Harding.

"And as for you, I give you twenty four hours. If you haven't got a strategy in place to deal with this Petrov, it's you I'm going to eviscerate, and I'm going to enjoy doing it." He turned, strode a couple of paces towards the door, and turned again. "What in hell are you waiting for?" he bellowed. "Get out of my sight."

"Before you go, Mr. President," Harding said in the same even voice.

Dianne looked startled. Harding must have a death wish. The President whirled around on his heel and transfixed Norman Harding with a stare that teetered on the brink of madness. His voice, when replying, was dangerously soft. "You wish to waste more of my time, Mr. Harding?"

"I do, Mr. President. In order to carry out your instructions I need the cooperation of ASIO. More than that, I need to be able to direct ASIO in this matter, that is unless you want them to know just what has happened and how incredibly vulnerable we are as a nation right now. I want your approval to set up an Anti-Terrorist unit in Australia, one to which ASIO is responsible. It would have to come from you, Mr. President, in consultation with the Australian Prime Minister."

The President considered this request for a full ten seconds. "Done," He barked, turned on his heel and strode through the door. Trudy Wilson went after him, leaving a room full of very unhappy people behind.

Harding turned to George Russel who was slumped in his chair abstractedly chewing his tie. "George, you told me that this sort of thing was impossible. I am so very annoyed with you, George."

"I'm still telling you it's impossible," George stammered. "Why doesn't anyone believe me?"

"I think the presence of our launch codes – and the dialogue between them – on that little piece of paper in Dianne's hand makes you look pretty much the fool, George, unless you can give me an excellent reason why, despite all this evidence it remains impossible."

"Let's say that this organisation has an incredibly powerful transmitter," Russell began, sitting up in his chair. "This Petrov blasts the receiving gear on the satellite to smithereens. Okay, that's possible. That would generate the error codes we're getting. If he doesn't keep it up the receiver eventually settles down – provided it's not damaged – and the satellite sends us a code that says its back in business – like it does on each of these occasions."

He mopped his forehead and continued.

"What Petrov can't do is intercept the signals we've sent to the satellite. That's what's impossible. He could possibly make the satellite's receiver think that the stuff he was up-linking was genuine, swamp our signal. In which case it would send his stuff on out into the Pacific." He took out his handkerchief and mopped his brow again. "But, and I say it again, unless there are other satellites we don't know of up there, he has no way of obtaining the transmission from Pine Gap in the first place."

"Then how does he get these codes, George?"

"I don't know," Russell muttered.

"I tell you what, George. Find out. If you're right then I want to be the first to know. If you're wrong George, then I fear your career may have run into a snag. Now go find out. Is that clear?"

George said it was clear as crystal and left the room as though the devil himself were behind him. Harding picked up a phone from the table and dialled through to Peter Lawson.

"Peter, Norm here. I want thorough intel on one Doctor David Petrov, lecturer in Physics at Sydney University. Get everyone busy on it. Now. No, I mean drop everything else. I want to know when this guy blows his nose. I want to know who his parents were, who their parents were, and in particular if he's any relation to Vladimir Mikhaylovich Petrov. No surveillance. No one is to go within a hundred miles of him. Twenty four hours, Peter. Not one minute more."

He put the phone down. Even Dianne was surprised at the grim expression on his face.

❋ ❋ ❋

Peter Lawson digested the urgent request from his Superior thoughtfully. It was clear as crystal that Harding had taken the bit between his teeth with a vengeance. The Petrov affair was ancient history. Surely Harding didn't imagine this present brouhaha had anything to do with that? He spent the next ten minutes in deep thought, then rang George Russell on his mobile phone. George had been in the meeting with the President, and he was anxious to obtain another man's perspective on what had really happened before his boss delivered his own personally edited version, that's if he bothered to tell him at all.

"Let me get this clear, Russell," Lawson said after receiving George's reluctant recitation of the furore. "Despite all this evidence you're still sticking to your guns that it's impossible to interfere with a satellite the way Dianne and company are assuming?"

"Sir, I don't think it's technologically possible," George said nervously. "I'm prepared to accept that this so-called terrorist group may have done something quite brilliant, but physics is still physics. For this scenario to work there would have to be another satellite involved, one which can receive signals from Pine Gap. Mr. Harding is checking that. If there is one, then it can't be a matter of some small terrorist group anyway. A few individuals don't have the infrastructure to launch a satellite."

George mopped his forehead again. "He thinks I'm a complete fool," he added.

"A fool doesn't become the head of our top level satellite communications," Lawson countered. "Russell, I want to ask you a favour. If and when you find out how all this is happening, I would like you to tell me personally. I want you to tell me first."

"Sir, you know any such correspondence would not be sanctioned. It would have to go through official channels, and Mr. Harding would be certain to find out and take punitive action. I really suggest you come to arrangement with him, Sir," George said, his forehead budding with fresh sweat.

"I would never ask you to put yourself in any such risk," Lawson countered. "I am going to give you the address of a company which makes satellite guidance systems. If they receive anything from a doctor Samuel Townsend they will pass it on to me instantly. No one else will be the wiser. We all have our little secrets, Russell. Just send a copy of your report there by mail courier from a public post office. Only when you're certain. Just as a safeguard, Russell. You know it's always a good idea to have a backup. Some messages can go seriously awry."

George didn't like the idea at all, but Lawson was his superior too. With a deep sigh he added the address to the contacts on his mobile phone.

※ ※ ※

The Prime Minister of Australia looked less than happy as he put down the phone. He had agreed out of political necessity, but that was not to say he liked the standover tactics to which he had just been subjected. A great many other matters seemed to be bound up with his willingness to allow the CIA to establish an anti-terrorist unit on Australian soil. Trade agreements for Australian wool, import tariffs removed on a whole raft of products, as well as other things which seemed equally unrelated to terrorists. There was a note in the US President's voice he didn't much care for, hadn't heard before. He had asked if there was any actual evidence of terrorist activity in his country, and the President had replied he thought there might be, and sure as hell there would be in the not too distant future, the way things were shaping up in the world. It was all for Australia's benefit anyway, and – he stressed this bit – America would underwrite any costs incurred.

"Kept in the dark," the P.M. muttered to himself. He picked up the phone.

Brian Hill snatched the handset from its cradle. "Yes?" he barked.

"P.M. here, Brian."

"Sorry," Brian muttered, "it's been a bad day."

"It's about to get worse," the P.M. sighed. "I've been talking to the President of guess where?"

"No guessing needed," Brian sighed again. "You may be interested to know we had a visit from the director of their super intelligence agency a couple of days ago. Right here in my office. I take it you were never informed? Arrived in Oz via Pine Gap, bypassing our oh-so-tedious immigration procedures."

"The devil he did!" the P.M. exploded. "What do they think this is, another state of the Union?"

"There's something big afoot. What's happened your end?" Brian asked.

"Apparently Australia is about to become the breeding ground for world terrorism," the P.M. grunted. "No details. The whole thing was vague as a politician's promise. The President of the USA wants to set up an anti-terrorist unit to which ASIO will be responsible. They want it so bad they're willing to throw in a bunch of trade incentives and goodness knows what else just to get it up and running yesterday. I had no choice but to agree. Standover tactics, that's what it was."

Hill gave a soft whistle. "There's a crock in their chicken coup all right. I don't like being treated like a mushroom, and Harding knew it. Never thought he'd stoop to this though."

# THE PETROV EFFECT

"I tell you, Brian, I don't like it either," the P.M. said earnestly. "We may have to cooperate with the blighters to begin with, but you give me something I can take back to their big boss and believe me I will. Tell you what, why don't you give our mutual friend Robin Naylor a call? Put him in the loop as much as you can and get him to watch out for violations of Australian law. It you can nail them with an offence you can boot them."

"A good idea. Let me know how this develops, will you?" Brian put down the phone and swore. He thought of leaking the story to the Australian newspaper. Perhaps Harding would have a heart attack.

❋ ❋ ❋

Robin Naylor was Chief Commissioner of police, a very clever and capable man. There were a lot of criminals who had laughed at his softly spoken voice, and now they were behind bars, some for a very long time. He listened to what Brian had to say in silence. "I'll keep my eyes open," he assured him. "There are a few boys I can trust with this, and I'll brief them tonight. Petrov, you say? Do you want any help digging stuff up on him?"

"No, it's all been done at our end. I've got a meeting with Noel Clark my number two in minute or so, and if I need anything more I'll give you a call. It's all a bit fluid right now, but I appreciate your help, and I'll call if anything more comes up."

Brian Hill rang off and went upstairs where Noel was waiting for him in the briefing room with several other staff.

He slumped into a chair and took the lemon lime and bitters from his secretary's elegant hand. "Thank you everyone," he said. "I know you've worked hard to get this stuff. Over to you, Noel. Annette, can I have another one of these?"

Annette headed for the drinks cabinet, and Noel pressed some keys on his laptop. The large screen in front of them came to life.

"David Petrov," Noel sighed. "Sad story, really. Born to Katarina Petrov and one Doctor Robert Halliday."

"Yet he takes his mother's Russian name." Hill took the second glass from Annette's outstretched hand. "Out of loyalty to his homeland, perhaps?"

"For a much better reason, Noel said. "Halliday was a lecturer in Physics at the Australian University in the ACT. Katarina Petrov was his Ph.D. student, and he got her pregnant. He managed to get several other girls pregnant too, and the University put the heavies on him. Eventually he left and went to Byron Bay to join some commune or other. He died in nineteen seventy – overdosed on some psychedelic, and good riddance. Apparently he was heavily into the stuff even while he was at the University."

He took a coffee from Annette and smiled his appreciation. "Now we come to the sad part. Katarina Petrov wandered around looking for a job, but being pregnant and unmarried was not socially acceptable in those days. Prospective employers didn't much like the idea of having a single mother on their staff – probably for financial as well as social reasons. In any case she didn't manage to get a decent job and ended up slaving for a pittance in this womens' refuge in Melbourne. She worked there right up to the birth of her child in nineteen sixty eight."

A Picture flashed up on the screen. The building looked even more dilapidated than it had when Katarina had worked there.

"You've done well, Noel," Brian complimented. "I can see what you mean about a sad life. Dissidents were made from such beginnings however."

"Worse is to come," Noel said grimly. "After the birth Katarina Petrov went to work for a well-known prostitute by the name of Susanna Gordon. It was good money in those days, and I guess she was sick of the poverty. In any case a few years later she became ill, moved to her sister's place in Thornleigh NSW, died there. That would have been in nineteen seventy four." Another slide flashed up. "Her sister's name is Lydia Petrov, now married to a medical doctor by the name of Geoffrey Burkitt. They live in Petersham."

"Is this Lydia Burkitt or her husband active on any political front?" Brian queried.

"Not at all. They're highly respected members of some church – let me see – St. Andrew's Cathedral in Sydney."

"Do we have any prior history on the Petrovs before they came to Australia?" Hill placed his empty glass on the table.

"We do, but its patchy. They were born in Kiev to one Waldemar Petrov and his wife Nikita who was a medical doctor. Waldemar was Professor of history or languages – that's not clear - at the Taras Shevchenko National University in Kiev."

"Ah, now that is interesting," Brian nodded. "Any links to our Vladimir Mikhaylovich Petrov?"

"None that we can discover," Noel said, finishing his coffee in a gulp. "Katarina was born in nineteen forty three, and Lydia some five years earlier. In nineteen fifty one Professor Petrov was involved in some student unrest on campus, on the side of the students one would gather, and it appears he sent his family away. A couple of weeks later he was arrested and we have no idea what happened to him after that."

"A man who sees trouble coming and takes care of his family, by all accounts," Brian mused softly.

"Appears that way," Noel agreed. "Not exactly the background for a super spy, is it?"

"Not really, unless David Petrov was bitter about the treatment of his father in Kiev and opted to take some sort of revenge. What happened to Nikita Petrov?"

Noel flashed another slide up on the screen. "After coming to Australia she worked in menial jobs, mostly, then as a medical receptionist. All in all a pretty hard life. Suffered a stroke and her daughter Lydia nursed her until she died. Everything indicates that she's a very decent human being.

She brought up David, remember. Not likely to infuse him with terrorist ideology, do you think?"

"No, I don't. Pray continue Noel. I'm sorry I interrupted."

"As I said, David Petrov stays with his aunt and her husband. He also becomes active in Christian circles. He begins a double degree in Electrical Engineering and Science at Sydney University. Apparently he's a very bright lad." A copy of his academic record flashed up on the screen.

"Any signs of rebellious behaviour?" Hill asked.

"One," Noel chuckled. "He trained as a computer engineer and worked part time for a company called Control Data Solutions." Another slide flashed up on the screen. Noel continued. "Apparently they booted him after two years. There was an incident involving his supervisor. We spoke to another employee who was around at the time it happened, and their take on the matter is that Petrov's supervisor was ripping off his intellectual property. Petrov apparently served him a dose of his own medicine. The source we spoke to thought it was very funny."

"So he can look after himself. Is that all? No police record? No affiliation with politically active groups on campus?"

"He was a member of something called the Evangelical Union," Noel said.

"Sounds highly subversive to me," Hill laughed. "It's a Christian group, no political agenda. Now he's a lecturer. That's unusual, isn't it?"

"Slightly. He has a mentor on staff, one Professor Sarah Cole, resident genius from all accounts."

A slide of the good Professor appeared on screen. It was taken at the International Symposium on Superconductors at the Hague in Belgium, and she was wearing an evening dress. It was the only one of its kind in existence, and quite famous for that very reason.

Annette whipped her head around and gave Noel a withering stare. "You men. Always throwing in some distraction. Just where did you get the photo, Noel? One of your private collection?"

Noel pretended to look wounded and Brian laughed.

"I'm afraid I have to defend Noel at this point," he laughed. "That is indeed a picture of our Sarah Cole, toted behind her back to be the most beautiful woman in the world. Stunning, isn't she?"

"You know her?" Annette turned her surprised face towards her boss.

"Quite well. So does Ross Baker from MI6. We've had dealings with the good Professor. She has been incredibly helpful on more than one occasion. I don't believe our American friends have had the privilege though. The chances of her being a terrorist are none and Buckley's."

"He's her lover, then," Annette retorted, staring at the picture.

"Err, most unlikely," Brian said, a smile lingering on his face. "I'm afraid the good Professor is somewhat disparaging of our male kind. Straight laced as a metre rule. Won't tolerate the slightest bad behaviour amongst her students, hates it when people gawk at her, like you're doing now."

Annette deliberately turned away from the screen. "Then why is she so nice to him?"

Brian stroked his chin with his hand. "I'm guessing, but perhaps because both of them are Christians. I imagine there's not many others in the Physics department. Perhaps she's learned about his past and felt sorry for him. Just because she's a genius doesn't mean she's heartless."
Brian nodded to himself. "And it's very hard to fool her. She has an ability to see through people which is quite uncanny. What do you conclude, Noel? Super terrorist or decent human being?"

"The man's as innocent as the driven snow," Noel answered with a sigh.

"I agree with you." Brian picked up his glass from the table and drank. Annette looked down at her pager, took one more quick glance at Sarah Cole, shook her head and left the room.

Brian swivelled his chair towards Noel, the smile still lingering on his face. "Anything else?"

"Our American friends are interested in Petrov too," Noel said grimly. "We have had a formal request to provide a dossier on him within a very short timeframe." He picked up his coffee mug, realised it was empty and returned it to the table. "I think they're also conducting independent research as well, blast them. A couple of our sources said they had already been approached by someone asking the same questions. What should we do about it?"

"Dilute the facts with tons of useless information," Brian said, frowning. "Delaying tactics. See if you can spot their agents and make their lives a little more interesting. Perhaps their cars won't start or their hotel rooms get the once over. Use your imagination. Like their hide to run their own covert stuff in our backyard and then ask us to do the same job. I'm even more concerned with our friend David Petrov than I was before. I want a couple of our boys to shadow him very carefully. Tell them to check for American visitors or anything out of the ordinary. Mustn't let our little friends know we're doing it. With any luck this whole business will come back to bite them."

Annette, returning to the room, visited the drinks cabinet and came over towards them holding a couple of glasses which didn't smell like lemon lime and bitters.

"I thought you would appreciate this," she said. "I've a feeling you're going to need it."

"Why is that, Annette?" Noel took a glass from her hand.

"While you've been briefing I've had a call from the P.M. He says the director of some new department is coming to talk to you tomorrow about what he expects us to do for them. Know anything about that? I thought you were the Director of covert operations around here."

"Not any more, apparently." Brian sighed and took a sip of the golden liquid. "I had a word with the P.M. before I came up here."

"Well, I'm taking my orders from you and Noel." Annette marched out of the room leaving both men smiling at each other. No one was going to tell Annette what to do, and they knew it.

Brian took a long sip from his whiskey and groaned. "So it's started. That was quick. You were right, Noel. I don't think that's a cat amongst their pigeons, it's more like a dingo on acid. I've never known our little friends to react so smartly to anything. Wonder what Petrov is supposed to have done? All this is only an excuse for conducting their own game over here without telling us what the blazes has happened. Go and make life hell for their agents before we're officially told to cooperate with them."

Noel swallowed the rest of his whiskey in one gulp, got up from his chair and placed his glass down gently on the table. "It will be a pleasure." He turned and walked out of the room leaving Brian alone with his thoughts, and they weren't good company.

# CHAPTER 24

Exactly two days after that briefing ended, another briefing took place between a very frustrated Norman Harding, a very twitchy Peter Lawson and a much larger team of frenetic if-not-so-eager beavers who had been ferreting out information for the past forty eight hours without very much sleep. It had taken them hours and hours to sift through the huge pile of rubbish their colleagues in ASIO had been sending them almost constantly since they had been ordered to. They not only knew where Lydia Burkitt lived, they knew the colour of the house, the ground plan, when it was built, and by whom. They knew when the milk was delivered, what quantity, and how much the Burkitts paid for it. They knew when Lydia Petrov went shopping, what she bought, where she bought it. They knew David Petrov's favourite colour in socks and where he bought them, too, and a great deal more they knew, reams and reams of it.

Then there had also been those inexplicable problems with their own operatives in the field. Sam Harrows had his laptop stolen just before he was to email his report. George Morgan was taking covert pictures of Geoffrey Burkitt's surgery from the vantage point of the restaurant on the other side of the road, when a waiter had bumped his arm and sent his special camera diving to the bottom of his beer. There had been some mistaken identity thing with Sally Perkins, which had ended up rather badly when the police discovered she had entered the country under an assumed name. Australia was a country where everything went wrong, it would appear. Thank goodness they were going to sort those simple minded people out.

One of those tired, not-so-eager beavers dimmed the lights and the projector burst into life with a picture of Taras Shevchenko National University in Kiev surrounded by protesting students. An older man holding a banner was circled in red.

One of the beavers began. "This is Waldemar Petrov on the campus of the National University in Kiev, nineteen fifty one. As you can see he is part of the student protest."

"Or orchestrating it." Lawson rubbed his chin. "In which case he's an MGB operative."

"I hadn't thought of that." Harding, his face bearing its usual state of impassiveness stared at the screen. "What about his wife?"

"Nikita and the two children Katarina and Lydia left Kiev a couple of weeks later. We don't know what happened to Waldemar."

"Interesting. How old were the children?"

The not-so-eager beaver continued. "Lydia was thirteen and Katarina eight. Bit young for them to be operatives in training."

"You don't know our friends," Lawson grimaced. "What happened to them when they eventually came to Australia?"

"Nikita worked on menial tasks for a while before becoming secretary to a medical practice. She—"

"I suppose they were his children," Harding interrupted.

"What makes you think they could be someone else's?" The not-so-eager beaver asked.

"I'm beginning to see something ugly here," Harding said slowly. He turned towards Lawson. "Let us suppose for a minute that Waldemar is a MGB operative, and a high ranking one. He does the job on campus, then probably gets a promotion and a new name for his trouble. Now his wife leaves the country – or perhaps she wasn't his wife. Perhaps we are looking at a long game here, gentlemen. The KGB – or former MGB - are known to have had children in training camps that they eventually released in various locations in the West. They grow up in Western society, they plug themselves into key positions and then, when the time is right they strike. Let us suppose that Nikita is another MGB operative. She takes the children to Australia and trains them carefully, all the time building infrastructure that will eventually strike a blow against the enemies of communism. Tell me more about what happened in Australia."

"They seemed a rather poor family—"

"Poor is always good cover," Harding interrupted. "Go on."

"Then when Katarina was nineteen she left home, that would be in nineteen sixty two."

"Interesting. What did she do?" Lawson asked.

"She went to the Australian National University in Canberra and studied Physics, got pregnant to her Ph. D. supervisor. Her life seems to have gone downhill from there. The woman became a prostitute, and died of AIDS when her son was six."

"Pursuing our scenario a little further," Harding mused out loud, "let us suppose an ideological fricassee develops in the family. By this stage Lydia and Nikita are getting their network together, but suddenly Katarina decides it's not for her. She wants out, and the others throw her to the wolves. They cut off all ties with her. Does that fit the facts?"

The not-so-eager beaver was beginning to get some of his eagerness back. "It does, rather," he said. "We haven't been able to dig up one piece of correspondence between Lydia and Katarina until nineteen seventy four when she takes the six year old boy back to Lydia and dies the same day."

"She takes him back?" A smile flickered across Harding's impassive face. "She knows she's dying and goes back to offer her son as sort of payment for her failures. Makes sense. And Lydia takes the boy?"

"She does," the beaver said. "I guess that fits the pattern. She gets married to a medical doctor, one Geoffrey Burkitt. Don't have a picture, sorry."

"Perfect cover for her. And Nikita?"

"Nikita died of a stroke a year before Katarina returned. David Petrov grows up with them and eventually goes to Sydney studying a combined degree of advanced computer technology and Physics. A good combination if you want to get involved in something nasty."

"Indeed," Harding agreed. "Lydia trains him, encourages him to adopt communist ideologies, uses him in the original plan. But it all goes wrong, doesn't it? Communism collapses and they're left high and dry with no support and nothing to do anymore. What a waste of an organisation which took so many years to build. But they don't waste it. They decide to put it to another use." Harding pressed his lips together in a grimace.

"Terrorism?" The beaver was becoming more eager by the second.

"No, of course not." Harding looked disgusted. "These people are old school communists. Communism failed in their home country, but not with them. No, they're going to make it work. The only thing missing was the genius. You said Petrov was smart, but they needed more than smart. They needed someone who could figure out how to break into our secure satellite comms and stuff them up – and they found him, somewhere. Communism never died for them. With the right help they believe they can win, strike a crippling blow to the West."

"I think we might have found your genius, Mr. Harding." The beaver was positively exuding enthusiasm. The same slide of Professor Cole flashed up on the screen, accompanied by predictable comments from all the men present.

"This is Professor Cole who also works in the Physics department at Sydney, and who, by the way, is reported to hate everyone except Petrov," the beaver explained. "She's the University's resident genius, apparently incandescent in the field of superconductors. Up until now we couldn't figure out how she fitted into the picture. Petrov did his Ph.D. under her, and on her recommendation was appointed onto their lecturing staff."

"Obviously her lover. I take it she has others?" Harding was sitting bolt upright in his chair.

"Not to our knowledge, which we find exceptionally strange," the beaver continued. "I think it's fair to say her lovers are well hidden from view, probably individuals who have been very helpful in establishing this network of horror. I mean, with a body like that she's sure to have made use of it somewhere in the cause of communism."

Harding pinched his nose between his thumb and forefinger, shut his eyes, and after a moment of silence began to speak slowly. "So this Professor Cole becomes part of the organisation. She gets Petrov into the right place at the right time. By now there's a web of nasty little people in the right place at the right time. It all begins to fit, Lydia and David Petrov with Cole providing the brains. Of course there are others, and the fact that we can't find them only makes me certain we're on the right track."

Harding opened his eyes. "Diabolical, isn't it? A communist spy group turned into a monster. No wonder they can afford to show their hand. Not only do they think they can win, they think they've won. I wonder what their next move will be? It explains why they didn't mind nuking Pyongyang. It would have served their purposes perfectly. They don't like their brand of Communism, and they would have turned the dear old US of A into the arsehole of the world. Was there any other stuff we should know about?"

# THE PETROV EFFECT

The excited eager beaver pointed to a huge pile of paper on the table with a disgusted expression. "ASIO sent us heaps of other stuff but it's all rubbish. They just don't get it, do they? Can't distinguish quality intel from garbage. In case you want to know Petrov only changes his socks once a week, and he's got three pairs."

Norman Harding stood up and stretched. He was feeling a great deal more confident than he had on that dreadful day in the Whitehouse where he had been tipped well and truly on his backside by Dianne. Now they knew the game, knew the principal players. ASIO would soon discover how they were accomplishing the impossible, and it would all be over within the month.

By the look on his face Lawson didn't share his optimism.

"What do we do?" another beaver asked. "Get hold of Cole? Our boys might have fun getting her to talk."

"Don't go within a hundred miles of Cole," Harding warned. "If anyone is going to watch her it's going to be the Australians under my orders. When all this is over Cole might be extremely useful to us. I don't want her damaged in any way. I don't want Petrov suspecting anything at all, and believe you me, he will expect us to grab him. We don't want to play his game. Remember there are other players around as well, and besides, we want to know how he does what he does. I feel it would be useful knowledge. There are a few satellites up there which we would like to, let's say, influence a little. No, ladies and gentlemen, we establish our beach head in ASIO and go to work. What do you think, Peter?"

Lawson shifted awkwardly in his chair. "He could be completely innocent, and we could be barking right up the wrong tree. Waldemar Petrov could have been on the side of the students, and none of the other stuff could be true either. It's conjecture, too much conjecture, not enough fact."

A frown crossed Norman Harding's usually impassive face. Turning to Lawson he spoke quietly. "You better hope we have got it right, Peter, because if we haven't, the demon group is still out there, and next time they strike I promise you we will all be sweeping streets."

He paused in thought. "Alright, go get me a special operative, one we can put in Petrov's little world without him suspecting a thing, one who can winkle out what's going on. I'm willing to bet you your job I'm right, but we do need to make sure. Besides, we need to know how this damn thing works anyway. Can you get me an operative, Peter?"

Lawson nodded slowly. "I can get you an operative, Norman."

With these few words Lawson left the room. He strolled thoughtfully down two floors until he came to his office, went in and carefully closed the door after him. Opening his desk draw he took out a small notebook and dialled a number. Martin Freeman answered.

"Freeman? This is Lawson here. I need an operative, Freeman, a very special operative. I want you to select one for me and we will brief them over here... No, that's classified. Let me tell you what we want. The target is a lecturer in Physics at Sydney University, one David Petrov. We suspect he's probably one of the smartest operators we've ever come up against, a very nasty piece of work and exceptionally dangerous. At the moment he looks as clean as a preacher's sheets. What? No, that's classified again. We want to know how he does what he does and who's doing it with him."

He paused, deciding on how to frame his next request.

"Oh, and Freeman, there's a chance that this guy is innocent, and if he is we're in deep trouble. For now he has to be guilty as all hell, and that's what the evidence is going to show. We need some breathing space up here or the whole organisation is going down. That includes you, Freeman."

Freeman's reaction to this gentle threat could be heard over the other side of the room. Lawson waited until the man's rational facilities had reinstated themselves and continued.

"Let me clarify," he said sternly. "You're not getting my drift. In the short term it's imperative we find some evidence, Freeman. Later on we might be able to revise our assessment. One more thing. If we're right, he's almost certainly expecting us to try something, so this operative of yours has to look so perfectly innocent he won't make a connection to us."

He cleared his throat and spoke as forcefully as he could. "This is classification one, Freeman. Stuff it up, I will personally see you're retired. If you can't think of an appropriate operative tell me, because it's better we send no one rather than the wrong one. Have I made myself clear? Oh, and we want that operative in place within a week or less. No, I'm not joking. Get busy."

He paused, pressed the phone to his ear. "And one more thing, Freeman. This conversation never took place."

He slammed down the phone. The whole operation was hanging on a thread, and he didn't like the gauge of the cotton. Harding could be a monster when he had the bit between his teeth, and he was fighting for his life. Pity help anyone who got in his way.

❋ ❋ ❋

Freeman put down the phone with a troubled expression on his face. He was no fool, and he knew if he stuffed this up he would need to implement his exit strategy before someone exited him permanently from everything. He shut his eyes and pressed his fingers against one another. Did he know of such an operative?

But yes, but no.

There was an operative who fitted the bill in one respect, but not in another. She was almost certain to find the required evidence, even if it didn't exist. A hazard in normal circumstances, but in this case perhaps an asset. He was going to send her to the retraining department for target practice, but this might be a better way of removing a loose cannon. If this Petrov was as good as they implied, he would almost certainly spot her as an agent and take care of her permanently. One problem off his shoulders. Then he could bleat that he had lost a crack operative and needed to have her replaced with another one who didn't have a psychopathic hatred for anything in pants. Two problems off his shoulders. He phoned Harry O'Callaghan.

# CHAPTER 25

The time was up. Without word from anyone including Harry, Abby had reached the inevitable conclusion she was about to trek down retraining alley. Her exit strategy was complete and waiting only for her to initiate the carefully planned series of events which would, she hoped, end up with a Miss Fenwick attending some post graduate course in some Australian university, it didn't matter which. She never intended to disappear into idleness, no, just a welcome sea change from one active life for another. Who knows, one day she might actually fall in love and get married? No, that wasn't going to happen, but her days of prostituting herself for the sake of an insane organisation were over too.

It would be a long road back to an ordinary life, and Abby had no confidence that the scars of the past would not prevent the dream from ever becoming a reality. There was always the final way out. Laced carefully into her bra strap was that small red capsule which Harry had given her the day before her first assignment. She remembered his words. "If you ever get to the point where living is worse than dying, bite on this." Hopefully her life would never come to that horrendous place.

It was five a.m. Her toilet completed, she dressed quickly and began to tick off items from her mental 'to do' list. The note on the telephone pad which contained a phone number in Boston, heavily underlined together with a flight time, a note from her milliner saying the dress could be picked up Tuesday with a pencil scribble on top to the effect that she planned to go there in the morning. Tickets for a weekend in Hawaii next month carefully placed in the kitchen cupboard, top drawer, a bill for garbage services with 'pay Wed.' scribbled on it. Little things, but important. No one must get the idea she had left the country. First stop, a cheap hotel not far from the airport, where she would change the colour and style of her hair to match the one in her passport.

Breakfast completed, she put on her cream leather Armani coat and trotted out into the corridor, slamming the door behind her. She left a small note on the milk delivery box saying 'no milk for two days' and she was gone, descending the elevator to the foyer. She had a planned casual conversation with the concierge about her friend in Boston becoming ill, and her intention to visit her today. That small task completed, she hailed a taxi to the domestic terminal.

A large black limousine pulled in front of the taxi which was coming into the kerb. Before Abby could run, two men jumped out of the back and grabbed her. One of them fired a tranquiliser into her neck, and they dragged her into the back of the limousine like a piece of boned fish.

It was a very frightened and very groggy Abby who came to consciousness on a bed she immediately recognised as belonging to the rest room not very far from the office where she and Harry worked. The presence of the latter gentleman on the end of the bed only served to turn her fear into seething rage.

She sat up far too quickly, thought she was going to be sick, and flopped back down on the bed again. "You bastard," she hissed.

"Such politeness towards someone who has just saved your scrawny neck." Harry smiled at her.

"Bastard," Abby muttered, trying not to throw up.

"You were on your way out, weren't you?" Harry grinned. "You wouldn't have made it. Freeman has had you under constant surveillance for weeks, just waiting, wanting you to make a break for it, so he could schedule you for the meat processor. Told me I was going in too if I made the slightest attempt to contact you, then the swine had me tailed as well. Yesterday something new turned up, and Freeman called his dogs off. I still figured you'd be ready to make a run for it, so I picked up where they left off."

"How'd you know I was getting out this morning?" Abby groaned. "Have Freeman's team of perverts been watching me in the shower? Sick, that's what you are, a sick lot of voyeurs."

"I don't know how Freeman's operatives have been keeping you under surveillance, but they were, and what's worse, you didn't twig to it," Harry said grimly. "How did I know this was the big exit? Simple. My team were watching the lights in your room. When you got up at five in the morning they knew. You never get up before nine."

"Nosey bastard," Abby groaned, shutting her eyes and laying back on the pillow.

"Better be thankful I am, because right now you might be heading down to level zero," Harry said pointedly.

For answer Abby turned her head over the edge of the bed and threw up. Harry dropped a towel over the mess and came back with a glass of water.

"Sorry. Shouldn't have said that. Listen, I told Freeman I called in and found you were sick. You came with me but had to go the restroom in a hurry. He's expecting you in an hour, and you had better stick to that story."

Abby wiped her face on the bedclothes and stood up. It didn't work all that well and she flopped down on the bed again. After a while she reached out and squeezed Harry's arm. "If I still want to get out will you get me a corridor?"

Harry moved his face closer and spoke softly. "Don't rely on it, Abby. If it was up to me you could disappear tomorrow, but you know how this place works. Everyone spying on everyone else. The stench of paranoia, can't you smell it as soon as you get through the front door?"

"I guess so," Abby shrugged. "The only way I'm going to get out is get dead, isn't it? Do you know, sometimes I wish I was."

"Listen, some new operation has come up," Harry whispered earnestly. "It might be just what you need to lift your flagging ego. Why don't you see what it's all about before you go thinking about pushing the button on yourself? I don't like it when you talk like that. Not like you to give up."

"Thanks, Harry. I owe you." She smiled towards him.

"I can think of a nice way you can say thank you."

"I don't do that with friends, remember?" She gave him a wry smile. "I'm your own handiwork. Can't cry, can't love any more. I know what you want, but you killed it in me, Harry, and I helped you do it. Now you've got to live with the stone statue you've sculpted. I'm your reward and your punishment. Can't love you, don't hate you either. Best I can do."

"Yeah I know." He sat there silently, contemplating her words. She was right, but she never realised just how much he hated himself for what he had done. Trying not to look too closely at her lying there on the bed looking pale and a little frightened, he got up and went over to the door. "Sam from the pharmacy is coming in a few minutes with a cocktail to make you feel better. There's another dress in your locker. No, I haven't been peeking, you showed me when you were last here. Go change and then go up to see Freeman."

He left the room without further comment, and a in a few minutes Sam came in, her usual bubbly self, with a glass of something fizzing in her hand.

"Drink this, doll," she said, "and then suck on one of these." She produced a couple of pills encased in a blister pack. Abby drank the white fizzy stuff, made a face and put one of the tablets in her mouth.

"If I stand up I throw up," she said. "Can you fix that?"

"Already have, doll. Sit there for a minute or two then go get changed."

Half an hour later Abby was knocking on Freeman's door, looking a good deal more confident than she felt. She entered on Freeman's command, feeling as though she was walking into the lion's den. The gentleman was seated behind his desk with a leer on his face, the closest approximation he could manage to a smile.

"Good to see you, Abby," he said. "Glad to know you weren't planning to go without saying goodbye"

"Why would I ever want to say goodbye when you've done so much to make my life enjoyable?" Abby hoped he couldn't read the bitterness on her face.

"Glad to hear you say it," Freeman leered back. "I'm putting you back on the active service list. More than that, I'm giving you a top category assignment just to show how much we value you sticking around. This is the biggest thing of the decade. Come through on this one and you can write your own ticket to anywhere."

"And why do I get chosen for this great honour?" Abby said sourly. "I take it the chance of coming back alive is so close to zero you can reuse my office space as soon as I'm in the field."

"So unkind," Freeman murmured. "No, I genuinely mean it. This comes from director Harding himself. This is the single most critical assignment we've ever had, and you had better believe it."

"What's involved?" Abby raised an eyebrow.

"Above my pay grade," Freeman said bitterly. "You get briefed by the aforementioned director at ten hundred hours tomorrow. I take it you aren't thinking of saying no?"

Abby gave him a patronising smile. She ran the fingers of her right hand through her long hair and shook it out from her neck. "You know I'm a girl who can never say no, Controller. What man in the world is about to become intimate with the Deadly Angel?"

"He's in sunny Australia – Sydney, I think."

218

"Australia. Now that's ironic." She turned towards the door. "Okay, I'll report tomorrow at ten hundred. Oh, and if you want to continue wasting your time, just tell your dogs to keep following me around. I've had such fun leading them on a wild goose chase. Why not put a camera in my shower while you're at it? I can do some stuff they would really enjoy."

She tossed her hair over her head and sauntered out of the office leaving Freeman suitably unhappy. He had underestimated her skill for one thing, and one of his team, the one who had been so careless as to give his game away, was scheduled for extensive retraining. He would find out who it was.

He would have been even more unhappy had he been able to read Abby's thoughts as she caught a taxi back to her apartment. Her resolve to stay for tomorrow's briefing was teetering on the edge. No one, even Harry, would expect her to pull the plug and disappear right now, so now was the ideal time. Once again she heard Harry's advice ringing in her head, "wait, see what it's about." Okay, she'd wait. Perhaps this assignment in Australia would provide an even better jumping off place. Once an operative was on assignment they couldn't monitor their activities as closely for fear of blowing their cover. This wisdom prevailed by such a narrow margin she was even surprised with herself as she knocked on the Director's door at ten hundred hours the next morning.

❋ ❋ ❋

Harding had never seen Abigail Saunders before, so he was suitably impressed when she walked into his room dressed in a revealing black outfit from Pierre Cardin with matching Gucci shoes. Abby sat down on the proffered chair and crossed her shapely legs, watching the direction of the man's eyes. Yes, the dress was working. More power to her. Harding, consciously lifting his gaze from her thighs, stared into her face. She was a beauty all right, and there was a brain behind that exquisite face as well, so Freeman had said. He had better be right. He hated Freeman, but the man did get the job done, usually.

"Ms. Saunders," Harding began, "There is a Physics lecturer at Sydney University by the name of David Petrov—"

There was a sudden change in Abby's appearance. For a second, only a second, the self-assured powerful woman had been replaced by another, but it was gone so quickly that Harding could not tell whether it had been fear or loathing which had crossed her pretty face.

He continued as though nothing had happened. "We believe this man is part of what was once a communist subversion cell operating in Australia. With the collapse of communism in their home country, this cell has morphed itself into something far more dangerous, far more deadly. They are self-proclaimed enemies of the United States, Ms. Saunders, and I regret to tell you they have struck this free world a crushing blow already. The detail is classified, but I can tell you that right now they have a stranglehold over our secure communications systems. Contemplate that."

He paused so she could register the gravity of his words.

"The President is gravely concerned," he continued. "You have been assigned this operation on no less than his authority."

He watched carefully to gauge her reaction. There was none.

"These people are incredibly smart," he said. "They have utter confidence in their ability to throw us off the scent, but they must not succeed. We need to know who the other members of this cell are, and how they are doing what they are doing. We need incriminating evidence against this David Petrov. Until we get it we're helpless. I have been told you are somewhat of an expert in finding evidence, Ms. Saunders. This is your assignment. You must not fail."

"What exactly is this demon terrorist supposed to be doing?" Abby asked in a level voice.

"Did I say terrorist?" Harding raised an eyebrow momentarily. "No matter. I take it you know what the word 'classified' means. Your controller O'Callaghan has more intel which he can release to you on a need-to-know basis. You are right about one thing, Ms. Saunders, this man is the devil incarnate."

"And how do you propose to drop me into his world?" Abby asked, frowning. "If he's as good as you say then he'll see straight through my cover and treat me accordingly. If you think I want to play sacrificial lamb for the CIA you've got another think coming."

"Well, I must say you've got guts," Harding grunted. "No, we've thought of a plan. This Doctor Petrov has requested a Ph.D. student to assist him with his research into the ionosphere. You will be that student, Ms. Saunders. I believe you were a Ph.D. student once, so you can fit into the role perfectly."

The strange expression crossed Abby's face once more, only this time it lingered a little longer. So she was to be a Ph.D. student again, only this time she would be the one doing the seducing, the seducing and the destroying. Suddenly she couldn't wait. The sweet savour of revenge began to bud in her mouth. Oh, she would be good. She would be extraordinarily good. She would have this man begging for more in her bed within forty eight hours, maybe less. Perhaps she would take him on the floor of his own office after their first introduction, how perfect would that be? Evidence? She would find all the evidence they wanted. This time she would go down to level zero and push the needles in herself. Harry was right to make her wait. In an instant all the self-doubt, the fear, the wanting to disappear, had evaporated in one explosion of revengeful desire. The Director was speaking, and she was hardly aware of his voice.

"Your cover must be perfect," Harding said. "You will have to brush up your physics, Ms. Saunders. Any lack of knowledge in that area would almost certainly be your undoing. Doctor Petrov must be convinced it's worth taking you on. I have managed to get you some academic help, and you if you agree, we will start your briefing this afternoon. Your superlative academic record has been retrieved from Boston University, and we have added some extra stuff which explains what you have been doing since you decided leave University and travel. I'm aware there were some problems with your Boston referees, so we've constructed some others for you. When they're contacted by email they'll sing your praises to the rooftops. There's a lot of work involved on your part before you set foot in another physics lab, and it must be done quickly. These maniacs are likely to strike again."

He paused, studying her face. Yes, there had been a change. Cynicism had been replaced by a certain inexplicable eagerness. He narrowed his eyes slightly. "There is something else you must understand before you go into the field. These people will expect us to be involved, in fact they have practically requested it, although I cannot go into details. They will suspect you from day one, Ms Saunders. If they conclude you are an operative they will terminate you, probably in a most unpleasant manner. Are you willing to undertake this assignment under these circumstances?"

"I'd beg you to let me go." Abby's eyes were burning with fire.

"Such enthusiasm?" Harding smiled. "I can see Freeman has made a good choice for once in his life. That was the bad news, now here is some better. We're sending a whole support team in with you. They will report to a new department called the Australian Anti-Terrorist Unit, headquarters in Canberra, an extension of our activities in that country. ASIO – our Australian counterpart – will be working under their direction, although they will not be told anything about you or your support group. From the public's point of view they will be a company of engineers who deal in specialised construction projects, and you will be working part time with them as a consulting physicist. Indirectly we can assist you in any way you wish, but when you are with Petrov or anyone connected with him you are on your own. If you get into trouble we will not interfere. I want that crystal clear, Ms. Saunders. Do you still want to go?"

"Try to stop me." The same passionate expression.

"Very well. There's a car waiting to take you to your Physics tutors. They will be pretty brutal, but their purpose is to save your life. There is one other piece of good news, or I take it you will be pleased. Harry O'Callaghan will be your controller while you are on this mission."

"Thank you, Director. Mr. O'Callaghan is a very capable man." Abby gave him a genuine smile.

"I'm sure you know. Thank you, Ms. Saunders. Our country thanks you." Harding's face became grim. "I'm counting on you to succeed, Ms.

Saunders. Should you make a mess of this assignment I will personally tear you apart piece by piece. Please do not for a moment think I'm joking, Ms. Saunders. That would be a grave miscalculation. Oh, and good luck. If you come through I guarantee you will be suitably rewarded. Goodbye, Ms. Saunders."

The expression on his face made Abby shudder. So the stakes were high. She tossed her hair over the back of her neck and strode out of the room. Next stop would be her high-powered Physics tutorial, and she couldn't wait to start. There was something cathartic about studying Physics, something clean, rewarding, invigorating. How long had it been since she was forced to use her brain in such an enjoyable pursuit? She hoped it wouldn't take long to retrieve the acuity she once possessed.

# CHAPTER 26

David Petrov had been surprised by the swift response to his request for a post graduate student, considering he had only published it on the University's website. Boston, too, not exactly local. He scanned the academic record in front of him. Impressive, not one subject with less than a high distinction. It crossed his mind as unusual that such a gifted student had not immediately transitioned into a doctorate, and her reference from the head of the medical physics department at Cornell was almost overdone in its praise of her thoroughness, her quick inventive mind, her delightful personality. So she had been travelling the world, and wanted to return to her favourite discipline. A veritable academic angel, by all accounts.

He tried to picture the woman described by these accolades and found it didn't seem to work. A brilliant student with an excellent position in Cornell, who instead of returning and completing her aspirations in the department which obviously thought so highly of her, decides instead to fulfil her burning desire for further study with an unknown researcher in a small department of a University on the other side of the planet. Still, she was the only applicant. Seeing as she was already in Sydney and due to fly out in a week if unsuccessful in her application, he felt the only decent thing would be to give her an interview. He scheduled an appointment for the following Monday at ten o'clock.

At precisely that very hour on the day appointed there was a knock on the door. The enigma walked into his office wearing a pair of pale yellow designer jeans and a loose fitting low-cut lemon T-shirt. Her hair looked as though she had spent the last few hours with a professional hairdresser, who had teased every flounce and curl into perfection. David, despite his natural modesty, found himself staring at her shapely figure for longer than he deemed polite. He offered her a chair on the other side of his desk, and produced her C.V. from a folder in his top drawer. Abby smiled at him like an angel. In truth she was surprised at how young he was, and what a pleasant face he had.

"This is very good of you, professor Petrov," the Angel said with a beautiful smile. "I know it must sound strange that someone from the other side of the world would want to study here when they had opportunities at home, but the truth is I have fallen in love with this country. I'm thinking of becoming an Australian citizen and remaining permanently. I can only do that if I'm accepted into this post-graduate degree, but please believe me, it's not the reason for my application. I'm fascinated with your ionospheric research. If you doubt me, please ask any question you wish."

The laughing lilt to her voice rang pleasantly in David's ears, and he imagined he could enjoy hearing a lot more of it. She was around his age, her head about his shoulder height, incredibly pretty, and … He forced his mind back on to the job.

"Ms. Saunders," he began. "Can I check one or two details of your academic record? After you obtained your honours degree from Boston you went to work with professor Blaney at Cornell in the field of medical nuclear magnetic Imaging studies. Is that correct?"

"Yes it is. Professor Blaney wrote me a reference as well. It's on the next page. Can I show you?" She stood up and leant over him deliberately, turning the page in her folder. "Yes, there it is. Have you read that?"

David lifted his eyes from the printed page and found himself staring close-up at a pair of shapely naked breasts dangling suspended above Ms. Saunder's loosely hanging T-shirt. Abby watched his eyes come to rest exactly where she expected them to, saw colour flood into his face. *More power to me*, she thought. *You're going down, Petrov.*

But what was this?

The doomed doctor Petrov had shut his eyes, and there was something in his face which told Abby he was immediately aware that she had engineered the whole incident to her own ends. This was disastrous. No target ever responded usefully when they knew they were being seduced. Now the target was rising out of his chair, his face turned somewhat away from her.

Abby was right. There was no doubt whatsoever in David's mind that he had been the target of a cheap seduction attempt, just as there was no doubt about the lovely form of her body. His initial scepticism concerning her perfectly tailored C.V. came flooding back. Neither could he pretend he hadn't been impressed, but any woman who attempted to use her sexual prowess to lure him to her will, reminded him of his own mother who had put her own to such use with other men, and a wave of revulsion swept over him.

He turned deliberately towards the window. "Miss Saunders," he said, still averting his eyes, "I can see from your academic record that we are roughly the same age, and you being a woman, I think it would be inappropriate for me to conduct this interview further."

She had blown it, but why? Something was missing in the brief she had been given. Not only had he read her intention, he had been repulsed by it. Perhaps he was gay. She was going to have a word with Harry when she got back, and they could take this assignment and stick it... Then she remembered Harding's parting words and began to feel afraid. If Petrov was as deadly as he had said she would be wise to get out now, but if she got out another dreadful fate awaited her at the hands of her own employer. How could she be expected to succeed when she had been improperly briefed? Yet succeed she must.

A quick attempt at recovery had to be made.

"On the contrary," Abby smiled desperately. "You are the one I will be working for. I would think that gives you the perfect right to ask me any question you wish."

She had also risen from her chair so there was no possibility of a second glance at the assets he obviously found so offensive.

David replied, his face still towards the window. "Nonetheless I do. If you would be so good as to wait here I will speak to my own boss, professor Cole. She is leaving to go on a lecture tour in Europe tomorrow, so it will have to be today sometime. I cannot promise you within the next ten minutes however."

"Please, I really don't mind," Abby protested. "I would much prefer—"

But doctor Petrov had left the room. Still, it hadn't been a total disaster. This professor Cole was a woman, and woman to woman Abby was sure to find an ally in her cause. A full fifteen minutes passed before David returned. Using her most angelic smile she enquired, using polite and careful words, if the good professor had been willing to do her the honour of an interview.

"As a matter of fact she has," David answered, "and if you would like to go to room one hundred and eighteen down the corridor, she will see you now. I will act on professor Cole's recommendation without reserve. If it is favourable I will be asking you to start on Wednesday. Good morning, Ms. Saunders."

"Good morning, professor Petrov, and thank you for your kindness. In retrospect I can see that you are being very fair and decent towards me. I appreciate it."

*Appreciate it? I'd like to tear your throat out*, she thought. *Smile, Abby. You're good with women. Ten minutes, she and I will be like sisters in a common cause.*

She knew exactly how to play it. Being an academic, this professor Cole was likely to be a spinster, gifted in the brain department, but somewhat deficient in looks. She would flatter her, make her feel like a princess, pretend to be overawed by her intellectual brilliance. Piece of cake. She left the room with David Petrov staring out the window in the opposite direction. No matter, he was still going down. Once she had made sure he wasn't gay, she would play the shy, gentle angel who could not help herself but be captivated by the sheer force of his powerful manhood. Piece of cake. She reached room one hundred and eighteen. The first knock produced no response so she knocked again. A woman opened the door, a pleasant looking woman with an unexpectedly attractive face, although she was wearing a dress which reminded Abby of an oversized gunny sack.

"Professor Cole, so incredibly kind of your to take—"

"I'm not professor Cole. My name is doctor Caruthers. Professor Cole is through that door. Please go in, she's expecting you."

There was a frosty note in her voice. No matter, thought Abby, give me ten minutes with this professor Cole person and she'll be purring like a kitten. She opened the door and froze. Seated behind a desk was the most beautiful creature Abby had ever seen. A discarded laboratory coat hung over the back of a chair. The woman herself was wearing a light blue designer top and a fashionable matching skirt, both hastily borrowed from Elizabeth Caruthers, who was now wearing all Sarah's clothes, and didn't think much of her appearance in them.

Abby stood there transfixed, her heart sinking by the second. Compared to this stunning beauty she was deficient in every department. Not only that, but Abby knew she already looked older. How could that be possible? Surely this woman was more advanced in years than she, yet not a day of it on her face. The creature turned. Huge luminous deep blue eyes shone out under long, dark, perfectly shaped eyebrows, eyes that seemed to pierce into her very heart.

"Ms. Saunders, please sit down in this chair." She indicated the one on the other side of her desk. "I have read your dossier. No, please do not speak, there are one or two small matters that require my attention. Please remain seated in silence. I take it you can do that?"

"Of course," Abby stammered, still reeling in shock.

Of course? Yet with every passing second Abby began to feel less and less comfortable. Try as she might she could not turn her eyes from the creature who appeared to be ignoring her, yet somehow seemed to have taken hold of her mind. Xenophobia, and it was growing by the minute, a sensation Abby had never experienced before and never wanted to experience again. The minutes ticked by, and professor Cole made not the slightest attempt to engage her in conversation. From time to time she typed on the keyboard in front of her, or wrote on a small note pad. Abby began to feel an irrational indignation rising up inside her. How dare she be treated with such contempt. She cleared her throat noisily. The creature took no notice.

Eventually she could stand it no longer. "Professor Cole," she said indignantly. "I didn't come here to be ignored in front of your desk."

*What had prompted her to say such a stupid thing?* Abby felt the colour rising on her face. She had blown her chances again without a word being said. What was happening to her? The creature looked up from the note she was writing and stared at Abby in a most disconcerting fashion.

"Then exactly what did you come for? Perhaps you would care to tell me. Since you seem unable to exercise any further self-control you may begin your explanation now."

"I… came to complete a doctorate in professor Petrov's department," Abby answered, doing her best to keep her voice even.

"Professor Petrov would be flattered with his promotion," Sarah Cole said sarcastically. "And that's precisely what it is, isn't it? Flattery."

"I… was trying to be polite," Abby stammered. "Have you read my C.V.?"

"Please tell me exactly what you have done and when you did it." Sarah Cole fixed her with those huge blue eyes.

Abby launched into a carefully rehearsed monologue of the material contained in the dossier on professor Cole's desk. The creature stared at her without saying a word. A short silence followed.

"I must say I'm impressed with your ability to remember your lines Ms. Saunders," Professor Cole said at last, her voice dripping with sarcasm. "Your rehearsal was flawed on two points. You began work in Cornell on the fifteenth of March, not October as you said just now, and you flew to Paris on the nineteenth of July not the twelfth of December. More work is needed before your next recital."

A look of frozen horror appeared on Abby's face. The creature had not even opened the dossier, yet she knew it word perfect, far better it would seem than its owner. This was turning into a catastrophe. Perhaps she had found another member of the demon terrorist group. This creature she felt sure, could tear her apart with her mind, let alone any other way. She could feel sweat running down her arms. Curse this short sleeved cotton T-shirt! The creature could see what was happening too.

"We will see if your knowledge of physics is as rehearsed as your previous history, Ms. Saunders. I will leave aside your recent reading in doctor Petrov's area, and concentrate on the work you did with professor Blaney at Cornell." There was a contemptuous edge to professor Cole's voice which made Abby feel knee high to a gnat.

What followed was fifteen minutes of utter hell. Having demolished Abby's attempt to appear knowledgeable in the complex mathematics behind medical nuclear magnetic imaging, the creature turned to examining the physics of her undergraduate degree. In this Abby was better placed to answer, and felt at the end of another gruelling fifteen minutes that she had at least been able to deal with some of the horrible probing questions put to her. The creature wasn't impressed, and she knew it. Next there were the references. It was clear the creature didn't believe them either, despite Abby's repeated request that professor Cole should write to the email addresses listed on the page and discuss her misgivings with her former supervisors.

"I was actually doing something of the sort when you interrupted me," Sarah Cole said. "I have to tell you, Ms. Saunders, the result was somewhat unexpected."

"That someone said something nice about me?" Abby said defensively.

"Not at all, that professor Blaney's mail server has moved so close to Sydney. I think it must be located less than ten kilometres from this very building. Very convenient, wouldn't you say?"

# THE PETROV EFFECT

"I don't know what you mean," Abby stammered.

"Of course you don't." Sarah's eyes bored into her victim. "Would you care to tell me what you are actually doing here, Ms. Saunders, and in particular, what organisation sent you?"

Abby stared at the creature open mouthed. There was fear in her eyes now, no, more than fear, terror. Something was happening over which she had no control. She was the sacrificial lamb and the slaughter was just around the corner. Time to activate her long delayed exit strategy. First to escape this terrifying woman's clutches. She stood to her feet, wrapping what little remained of her dignity around her.

"I... I've had enough of this interview. I... no longer wish to work in this department. I would be grateful if you would—"

The creature had just thrown her entire dossier into the rubbish bin.

"I will inform doctor Petrov of the outcome of this interview," she said tersely. "He has gone to the university of New South Wales for a series of meetings and will not be back until tomorrow, but I will leave him a note. You may go, Ms. Whoever- you-are."

Abby fled the room, down one flight of stairs, out into Science Road, through the university's City Road gate, and onto the first bus she could find. Half an hour later she was hurrying along Martin Place in the centre of the city. She turned into a doorway and ran up two flights of stairs to another one with the words 'Martinborough Engineering' in gold letters stuck on the glass. Swiping her card through the reader, she entered the room. The office had not been completely set up, and boxes of various items were strewn all over the floor. On a desk near the window sat Harry, a hamburger in one hand and a Coke in the other. He took one glance at Abby's face and put both down on the table.

"What on earth's happened to you?" he demanded.

"I'm out of here," Abby stammered. "It was a disaster. Petrov is on to me, and that demon woman Cole nearly had me telling her I work for the CIA. It's finished. I think I was lucky to reach here alive."

"Steady on," Harry said, standing up. "Tell me what happened."

"The intel on Petrov is a load of crock." Abby flopped down in the nearest chair. "He's probably gay. In any case he has an aversion to female body parts."

"Which bits did you show him?" Harry asked, grinning from ear to ear.

"Shut up, Harry!" Abby shouted. "Does it matter? I walked right into it. Someone set me up. Then I had to go and be interviewed by some monster from another galaxy. She took over my brain. I'm soaked with sweat. Right now she's writing Petrov a note telling him the only genuine thing about me is the shoes I'm wearing."

"A real battle axe, eh?" Harry laughed unfeelingly.

"No," Abby shuddered. "She's the most utterly beautiful woman I've ever seen. I'm terrified of her."

The last statement gave Harry cause for pause. Instinctively he picked up the complicated looking phone from the floor and pushed a number of buttons. "Director Harding, please."

A full minute ticked by.

"Director, we have encountered an immediate and serious problem with Petrov." Harry said at last. "Apparently the brief given to our operative was critically defective. She thinks he's gay. That missing information has probably put her life in danger, and certainly placed the mission in jeopardy. We have to pull her out..." Harry's eyebrows went up. "Pardon? You can't be serious. In that case, I will need specialised help and I want it now, or the whole lot is on your head. I refuse to put her back in the field without a decent brief... I don't care if you do, and it's already gone pear shaped because your people bungled the job... I see... Right."

He turned to Abby who was wiping the sweat from her arms with a tissue and looking as frightened as she felt.

"Apparently the brief from ASIO was over eight hundred pages long, and you've got the cut down version," Harry explained. "Obviously our backroom boys stuffed up. They're sending me the whole thing plus some specialised assistance. We have to take Cole out of the equation."

"She's going out of the equation – a lecture tour in Europe, and Petrov hasn't got her report yet, because he's been out all afternoon. If he gets to read it we're so screwed. I'm not staying around to be butchered by some demon terrorist group for their Sunday entertainment."

"You can't leave, Abby," Harry said very seriously. "If you even look like pulling out I have orders to kill you."

"You wouldn't!" Abby sat bolt upright on her chair, staring fearfully towards the door.

"No, maybe not," Harry said grimly, "but others will, and there's some sick people in the organisation. No, we have to fix the problem. Stick around, kid. Get some food and bring it back here. We'll have the whole story in couple of minutes."

Abby returned with the utmost reluctance to find the printer spewing out reams of paper. Harry was speed reading each page as it flopped onto the tray and throwing it on top of an already large pile. Half an hour later there were no less than three separate piles on the floor, and Harry was adding to each in a selective manner. An hour later he took the largest pile and threw it into the shredder bin.

"Bloody fools," he muttered. "He's not gay, he's a Christian. You know, one of those do-gooder Bible bashing types, or at least that's his cover. No wonder he didn't like the sight of your boobs shoved right up in front of his face. It was your boobs, wasn't it?"

"Mind your own business," Abby snapped defensively. "How do I handle this? He thinks I'm a whore."

"So incredibly perceptive. First things first, we have to retrieve that report. Did this Cole person say she was going to email him or write?"

"A note I think."

"Damn and blast. Emails are so much easier to divert. Have to get the original. Let's hope she typed it, if not Donovan can copy anyone's hand. I'll get him up here. This is going to be a busy night."

"How do I play this one, Harry?" Abby toyed nervously with the sandwich in her hand. "I've never seduced a Christian before."

"Why not pretend to be one yourself?" Harry suggested with a smile.

"I'd rather die." Abby's face blazed with anger at the thought.

"Well, for goodness sake don't go around ridiculing his religion. Don't try to give him the come-on by wearing any of that stuff I've seen you in. Just be a nice girl who is eager to please, keep your eyes open. Warm and friendly. If he shows an interest in other things, well, you know how to encourage him."

Harry threw another pile of paper into the rubbish bin with a good deal more force than necessary. "Why am I saying this? If you only knew how I hate thinking of what you do with your targets." He sighed heavily. "Now go and get some rest. Abby, I mean what I said about leaving. You really wanted this assignment, remember? Don't blow it. You won't last twenty four hours if your scamper."

Abby slammed the door and descended the stairs to Martin Place, her heart still hammering in her chest. Her delicious revenge had morphed into a nightmare.

# CHAPTER 27

David Petrov arrived in his office a little late on Tuesday, only to find a new cleaner busily emptying his waste paper basket. He sat down at his desk reflecting on events of the previous day, the odd business with that applicant, and a totally boring afternoon at the other University. Thank goodness for Sarah. Ms. Saunder's antics would be totally ineffective on her. Glancing into his IN tray he discovered her note, not that he needed it really, he had already made up his mind. In fact he never expected to see the girl again, which was rather a pity in a way, because she was incredibly pretty. No, better not wish for the company of that sort of young woman, pretty or not. He tore open the envelope, took out the note, read the first few words and nearly dropped it on the floor.

> *Dear David,*
> *Thank you for the pleasure of interviewing Ms. Abigail Saunders. I must say you managed to embarrass her no end, and it was quite a while before I was able to get her to say what was obviously distressing her. First allow me to clear that matter up. All her luggage was stolen from her flat on Saturday night, and she has been wearing borrowed clothes ever since. She was so eager for you to read Blaney's excellent reference that she didn't think what leaning over towards you would reveal. She is deeply apologetic, and wishes me to convey that to you, which I have done.*
> *As a student I find her knowledge of Physics on a par with your own, which is meant as a compliment. I believe her to be quite the*

*genuine article, and feel your research would benefit from her assistance. She admits to a certain lack of direction in her former life, but that is fairly common in people of her age. I have confidence she will work hard and be useful to you. I look forward to seeing you in a few months' time. Please pray I might have more patience with fools and fawning men. Sarah.*

David put the letter down in a state of shock. A recommendation like that from Sarah was unheard of. The girl must be brilliant. How wrong he had been, how quick to judge, he reflected. One's past does influence the way one handles the present. He had totally misinterpreted an innocent moment of excitement. How embarrassing for the poor girl, how embarrassing for him. Picking up the phone he dialled her mobile number.

At precisely nine a.m. on Wednesday, a neatly dressed Abigail Saunders walked into his office. She was wearing a comfortable pair of blue jeans, a snug fitting knitted top, and a pair of sensible white joggers. Her long hair was tied back behind her head with a clip, and she carried a small briefcase in one hand.

Reaching his desk she held out the other. "Doctor Petrov, thank you for allowing me the privilege of working with you. I'm sorry about the other business." She coloured her face just the appropriate amount.

"There's no need to mention it, Ms. Saunders," David replied, glowing with spontaneous embarrassment. "I regret I misinterpreted your action rather badly. I believe it is I who should apologise to you."

"Let's forget it, shall we?" Abby smiled beautifully. "Please call me Abby, everyone else does."

"Please call me David for the same reason. Now let me show you around. It's a small walk, I'm afraid."

"You don't do your experiments in this building?" Abby asked, following him out the door.

"No. I take it you know about incoherent scattering? My transmitter was interfering with my colleague's heliostat work and so I moved it."

"Your transmitter? You have a transmitter?" Abby seemed surprised. "I thought you simply detected ionisation in the upper atmosphere caused by gamma ray impact from the sun. I didn't know you actually caused any."

"I don't," David frowned. "The gamma rays ionise the atoms into positive ions and electrons, and I detect the presence of these electrons by seeing how they reflect the large pulse of high frequency energy that I send up into them. It works like radar."

"So you transmit data into the ionosphere?" Abby's voice sounded unexpectedly tense.

"Of course not." David frowned again. "Why would I do that?"

"But the transmitter is capable of sending data, isn't it?" Abby insisted.

David, who was leading the way towards City Road, turned round and stared at the girl. She had the same angelic expression she had worn the instant he set eyes on her, yet the tone in her voice gave the lie to it. Something lurked beneath that fair countenance, a sharper than expected edge, another agenda, some hidden reason why she would not believe his straightforward and truthful answer. Once again his mind returned to the unexpected affirmation of Sarah's note. Perhaps she was just stupid, no, that didn't fit with her wonderful academic record. Perhaps she had some sort of psychological problem, but that didn't fit with the accolades her supervisor at Cornell had given her.

"Ms. Saunders, do you have any knowledge of electronics?" David asked tersely.

"A little, why?"

"I'm perfectly willing to show you the schematic circuit diagram of my transmitter and explain its method of operation in any detail you wish, however I would prefer it if you simply took my word. If we are to work together some level of trust would seem to be a reasonable prerequisite. If you find you cannot believe a thing I say I would suggest you find another supervisor."

"At least you can receive data from satellites, can't you?" That same insistent voice.

"I beg your pardon?" David answered, annoyed. "This isn't some covert satellite communications system. The receiver is set up to record signal level at a given frequency. It has a type and serial number. Would you like to check on the internet?"

"So you do have an internet connection in this laboratory?"

"As a matter of fact I don't," David snapped. "There is a dedicated data line back to the mainframe computer in the basement of the Physics building. It isn't connected to the internet."

"Surely you must—"

"Ms. Saunders," David said, his voice heavy with exasperation, "I think we will abandon this tour of my research laboratory. I would like you to go home – wherever that is – and ask yourself if you really want to work with a man you can't trust to tell you the time of day. Now I have work to do. Please let me—"

"I... I'm sorry," Abby stammered. "Oh, this is terrible. I've got you offside in the first five minutes. Of course I believe you. Please continue with our tour. I promise to be absolutely silent and to believe everything you say from now on."

Once again that angelic smile. Once again the feeling that something not nearly so angelic lurked behind it.

"Fair enough," David said tersely. "If you have any questions please ask them. You led me to hope that you had done some prior reading in this area, seeing as you wanted to take your doctorate in this field, but I detect a basic lack of understanding of the principles of incoherent scattering. I really suggest you spend some time in the Physics library as soon as possible."

"Yes professor." Abby had to use every ounce of self-control to keep the seething rage out of her voice.

David turned and strode off, annoyed and confused. Abby began to follow him, breathing hard. She had almost blown it again. Why had she done that? Why was her anger overwhelming all her training? Why wasn't he just like other ordinary men whose flirting she could return all the way to the bedroom? This Christian front of his seriously depleted her standard arsenal of seductive weaponry, and she wasn't going to make the mistake of pretending to be a Christian herself. Even the thought made her feel sick. She trotted along after David feeling like a puppy following its master, smouldering with rage against the demon terrorist who also happened to be her new physics supervisor into the bargain.

Damn it, he was good.

The tour lasted for the next three hours, with Abby being very silent and very intent, taking in every detail of the experimental arrangement. Didn't understand about incoherent scattering? Hadn't done her homework? If only he knew. Yet, as each piece of equipment was explained to her patiently as if she was a girl just out of high school, Abby's conviction about the demon terrorist took its first serious beating. There was nothing here which looked the slightest bit suspicious. Of course that was to be expected, she told herself.

Damn it, he was good.

In fact there was a transparency about him which she warmed to, despite her hatred for half the human race and physics supervisors in particular. He possessed a frankness and freshness which stirred forgotten memories, pleasant memories, of good and decent things in her past before the evil days came. Although she was hardly aware of it, the first seeds of doubt were being planted in the frigid, frozen soil of her heart.

Afternoon lengthened into evening, for Abby had made it very clear that despite her deplorable lack of knowledge about incoherent scattering, she would actually like to do some. David took her into the Wentworth Café and bought them both some sandwiches, and Abby bought two bottles of iced green tea. Armed with such sustenance they returned to the lab.

"What's that terminal over there?" Abby pointed with her sandwich.

"It monitors traffic on the high speed data line," David said. "The data from our analogue to digital converters gets sent to the mainframe in the Basser Computer complex. It's in the basement of the Physics building. Rather a sore point that. You see, all the data has to be analysed in real time or stored and then analysed later. That takes much longer, as you can appreciate."

Abby nodded. "Yes I can," she said. "There's a lot of processing required."

"When I was forced to move to this building, I was promised a high speed data line to do the job," David explained. "The other staff here take it in turns to use it as well, and while they're using it we can't. If they do, their data gets corrupted with ours, and it halts the program running on the computer at the other end. We came to an agreement with the others I could have exclusive use after six pm, and I don't start experiments until six forty five to be on the safe side."

David sighed. "For a while all went well, then for some inexplicable reason I found that whenever I sent a series of pulses skywards, I would get a whole heap of junk on my dedicated line. I've been round to everyone in the building and nobody wants to own up. I even posted some of the rubbish on the University chat room to see if someone would recognise it. No one did. In the end I managed to buy a fast digital storage unit and pump all our data into that. I take the portable hard drive down to Basser each morning and download the previous evening's experimental data directly into the mainframe. It's a blasted nuisance. We have to wait a whole day before we can see whether our experiments were useful. When the data line was working we could see straight away."

"So you don't use it at all now?" Abby asked thoughtfully.

"I tried it once not so long ago, and the same thing happened," David said with another sigh. "Do you know what I think? There's some experiment set up by one of my colleagues in this building, and my transmission somehow triggers it to send data. Probably there's a loose earth wire or something. There's no data on the line until I actually pulse the ionosphere, so that would explain it."

"Why not try it tonight? We might be lucky," Abby smiled enthusiastically.

"Okay, if you want. Its six forty, so we had better start throwing switches. You man the transmitter control if you like, I'll switch over to the data line and initialise the program on the mainframe. As soon as we hit forty five minutes past the hour start pulsing the ionosphere."

"The same time every night so you can compare the changes occurring?" Abby asked.

"Exactly," David said. "Four, three, two, one, pulse."

Abby hit the 'transmit' key and immediately a flood of data appeared on the screen. "Is that the rubbish?" she asked.

"No." David said, surprised. "That's our data going out to Basser. You'll know when things go wrong, because the computer program sends us an error message. So far so good, yes, we're in luck tonight. Now, here's the results coming back to the laptop."

After a few seconds a graph appeared on David's laptop screen. He looked at it with satisfaction.

Abby's comment rather threw him. "Typical bimodal distribution predicted by a standard Thompson scatter – two delta functions with some Landau damping. What's the little blip right on the transmitter frequency? Reflection off some stationary object?"

At first David had absolutely nothing to say. Here was the woman who not so long ago was asking inane questions, telling him what only a person very familiar with the theory of his experiment would know. Another conundrum. One thing was for certain, she wasn't stupid, but that left some less pleasant alternatives on the list.

He replied, finding it hard to keep the surprise out of his voice.

"You're right, it's a reflection. I have absolutely no idea from what. It's a pain in the neck, because I can hardly publish data with that little peak there. Makes the whole lot look very third rate. I thought it might have something to do with the scaffolding that's growing all over the building but it really doesn't make sense."

"Perhaps it's a satellite," Abby suggested.

"It isn't," David grunted. "One of the reasons I started experimenting so late was the satellite check. I had to make sure none of them were within range of the beam. It took ages to get all that data."

"What happens if one of them actually is in the beam?"

"Well, the transmitter would send its receiver into next week, completely take it off the air, perhaps permanently. I don't want the University to end up with a million dollar bill from some satellite owner."

"Can you change this to an energy – time distribution?" Abby asked, staring at the screen.

"Yes. Wait a minute." David typed some keys on his laptop, and the display changed.

"There," he said, "I've added a time scale along the bottom. What are you doing?"

Abby had pulled a scientific calculator out of her handbag. After touching a few keys she looked up. "It's three hundred and ninety seven kilometres away. Right height for a satellite."

Once again David was silently impressed. He checked her figures on his own calculator. She was absolutely correct. Another tick in the "smart" box.

"You're right on both counts, but it can't be," David said, frowning heavily. "Look at that shelf. See the large folder, the one stuffed full of paper? That's the trajectory of every satellite in the southern hemisphere, and not one of them passes over the beam, not even close."

"It's not passing over the beam, there's no Doppler. It's a geostationary satellite," Abby added.

"True again, but I've checked them too. See the folder next to that one? Every geostationary satellite above the entire planet."

"You could have missed one in all the excitement."

David grunted. "Your first assignment tomorrow is to look through every page and tell me if I have."

He sounded a little annoyed, and Abby, seeing the size of the folders, couldn't really blame him. Alright, she would search through the satellite listings. Not those of course, because the files on the shelf were probably doctored, but through the ones provided by the small team of staff back at Martinborough Engineering who were going to be pouring over them all night while she was asleep. They sent more pulses into the ionosphere over the next three hours, and Abby, despite herself, was fascinated by the picture emerging in the data. The solar wind was changing, the ionosphere becoming higher and higher. It seemed no time at all had passed when they finally shut down the equipment at ten p.m. and prepared to leave the laboratory for the night. It had been one of the most enjoyable evenings Abby could remember. She took copies of the data so that she could work through the calculations on her laptop in the flat.

"I thought your flat was burgled," David asked, surprised.

"It was, but I hid my laptop in the bathroom cupboard under some towels," Abby lied smoothly.

Why did she feel uncomfortable telling that lie? Tired, she was tired, and her day was far from finished. The calculations would be done in the small hours of the morning after she had reported in to Harry at eleven that night. He would be asleep on a stretcher at the back of the office, most likely. Well, when she got there everyone was going to wake up and jump to her music.

❊ ❊ ❊

The first person to jump was Harry himself, roused somewhat unkindly from a deep sleep by the empty Coke can that landed on his stomach, thrown from a table near the door. He sat up slightly dazed and very annoyed. Abby couldn't have cared less. Waking up a sleeping man by sitting on his bed and gently shaking him was prone to complications she could do without.

"What the blazes was that all about?" Harry complained loudly. "Been working back late? Left Petrov whimpering for more, did you?"

"Keep your filthy mind to yourself, Harry. There's work to be done. Get the team in here."

"They've gone for the night. It's almost eleven," Harry yawned, glancing at his watch.

"Then get them back," Abby ordered. "Petrov has a transmitter, a really powerful one, strong enough to knock a satellite out of commission. What's more, I think that's exactly what he is doing, despite what he says about there being no satellites for miles around. Looks kind of bad for doctor Petrov, doesn't it?"

"I've got to admit it, you're quick," Harry muttered. "Why didn't we pick up all this?"

"Probably because Harding asked the wrong question," Abby said. "He's not using a dish to transmit with as you would expect, he's using a very clever tube antenna which has an exceptionally narrow beam. Harry, I want the location of every possible satellite whose footprint lies within that antenna. Get busy. I want that info by morning."

"Slave driver," Harry groaned. "I'd better report this to the boss. He's not happy. You know the guys who filtered all that info from the Australian intel? Most of them got shipped to nasty locations in the Middle East. The head of that section is in retraining. I tell you, Abby, there's some heat in this thing. Alright, I'll have your satellite data by early morning. Call in before you go to work. Anything else?"

"He's very good. There's not a thing which would indicate he's doing anything out of the ordinary." She paused, "Harry, what happens if he isn't?"

"No chance of that," Harry grunted again. "What did you expect to find? That's why Harding has put you there, to dig up stuff which isn't obvious. These people are real pros, Abby, clever pros. They wanted us to look-see and go away empty handed. Just make sure you don't, that's all."

"Or I'll be joining the doomed in retraining?" Abby retorted. "Don't worry, no one's immune from the Deadly Angel. Goodnight, Harry."

She sauntered out the door, down the stairs and out into the grey granite paving of Martin Place Plaza. There was a taxi cruising in George Street, and Abby caught it to her flat in Annandale. Half an hour later she was pouring over the numbers which the scattering experiment had produced, becoming more and more interested as the hours went by. At four a.m. she shut the laptop down and threw herself on the bed. Ten minutes later she was in a deep sleep.

※ ※ ※

At eight a.m. precisely, Abby bounced through the glass door into the busy office of Martinborough Engineering, as fresh as if she had slept for the last twelve hours. Papers and tired people littered the floor and the chairs. Printers buzzed, telephones were ringing, and Harry was on the secure phone sucking up to someone with unusually apologetic language. Every eye turned in her direction. Not one of their owners wished her a good morning. Harry put down the phone, swiped a ream of loose paper off the chair next to him and motioned her to sit down.

"Petrov is right," he yawned. "There isn't a single satellite within reach of the beam – at least that was our conclusion up to ten minutes ago. I rang Harding. By now, let me tell you, his unhappiness has reached monumental proportions. I managed to get the truth out of him though. Petrov's antenna is right under secure military satellite twenty nine, the one that he's been using to wreck all hell with our national security. I still can't find out what he's supposed to have done, but it's like fire and brimstone in Washington. I think Harding is sweating on losing his job."

"Could Petrov have found out that it's there?" Abby frowned heavily.

"Well, obviously he did," Harry muttered, "but how he did beats me. Perhaps we have a mole in the highest level, because this info has top security classification. No way he could have found out without that sort of help."

"Just suppose he really didn't know it was there?" Abby asked, still frowning. "What then?"

"Look, babe," Harry sighed, "the guy's a ruthless bastard with a lot of really twisted people working for him. This transmitter of his explains the way he can override our satellite and force it to send his own data into our network, but what we can't work out is how he reads the stuff we send to the satellite in the first place. That receiver he has must be pretty special."

"Standard off the shelf," Abby said. "Can't do what you suggest it can."

"Then it isn't standard anymore. Look, Abby," Harry let out a long breath, "let me give you some really good advice. Find out how he does it and do it fast. So far Harding is impressed, keep him that way."

"That man's a monster," Abby shuddered. "I want you to search for any receiver in the one to three gigahertz waveband that is capable of receiving data. I want its sensitivity, type number, availability and a picture of it. Can you do that? By this afternoon?"

She looked at the faces in the room and decided this was an excellent time to make an exit. The thought that inspired her question lingered in her mind however. So far all Harry had discovered tallied exactly with what David had told her. Perhaps he was linked to an organisation of extremely dangerous people, but what if he wasn't? She had seen nothing in the transmitter which would have enabled it to send any sort of modulated data into the sky, and she had looked very hard. No, she chastised herself, this was just sentiment. It had to be there, and she was going to be the one to find it.

❊ ❊ ❊

Abby bounced into the David's office at exactly eight fifty to find him halfway through a coffee. A pile of student assignments littered his desk, and another even larger pile occupied a space on the floor near his chair.

He looked up wearily as Abby walked into the room. "Hello, Abby. Sorry I don't sound very cheerful. I've been marking these since seven this morning and they haven't put me in a very good mood."

"Let me help," Abby smiled.

She pulled a chair across to the desk and set to work on the pile. It took them two hours to finish, but her presence had turned a dull and depressing task into a rather enjoyable one. They would laugh together at some of the more ridiculous answers. Abby would accuse David of not teaching properly, then laugh at him as he tried to defend himself. David would finally realise that she was teasing him, and then laugh at himself for being so defensive.

Abby sometimes commented on how good this or that answer was, and David would tell her about that particular student, and how long he had spent with them in the voluntary tutorials he ran on Thursday afternoons. Abby complimented him on the way he cared for his students, and David enjoyed the music in her voice when she did.

Neither of them realised it was the beginning of a bond which would grow through the days that followed, despite the strange circumstances which had brought them together. In truth it was the physics itself which provided the catalyst, for both of them enjoyed it immensely, a common bond between two very different people. In those times Abby forgot she was the Deadly Angel sent to destroy the man, and simply enjoyed his company instead.

She showed him what she had done with the data they had collected, how she had managed to develop clever equations which enabled them to predict the changes in ionospheric height, and when he expressed his genuine delight, she felt her spirit soar in a way it had not done for a long, long time. In her own eyes it seemed to restore a little of her dignity, to be valued for something honourable for a change. She reflected in a quiet moment, when David had to leave the room to give his lecture, that all the accolades she had accumulated over the last two years were for things she was ashamed to remember. And this man was a demon terrorist, the worst the world had known? Surely evil could not cloak itself so admirably. Deep within the woman that small seed of doubt began to grow, all the more surprising considering her hitherto unremitting hatred for men in general and physics supervisors in particular.

# CHAPTER 28

The Café in Regent Street was dimly lit and very private, and the three men around the table were speaking softly into the bargain. Occasionally one of them would look towards the open door at the other end of the room, but nobody who entered or left seemed to cause them any concern. Another excellent Columbian long black arrived at the table. Brian Hill took it from the hand of the waitress whose coal black hair and deep olive skin made him think she had probably come from where the beans had been picked.

He sighed and continued the sorry tale. "I tell you they're up to their usual tricks, only this time we have this blasted American – sorry – Australian Anti-Terrorist lot running the show. Helping us, they are. I'd like to help them right to the bottom of Sydney Harbour."

Noel Clark sipped his excellent mocha, and spoke to the third man who happened to be no less than Robin Naylor, Chief Commissioner of police. "We've been told to prepare dossiers on just about everyone in the Physics department, including professor Cole who is overseas. It's a witch hunt gone mad, I tell you. All the time they're telling us our work is vital to the stability and survival of the Western World. We have six separate surveillance teams in the field, all working their butts off for our little American friends."

"I thought they were concentrating on Petrov." Robin placed his empty cup on the table, wiped his mouth with the back of his hand. "You must have a bug in every room of his house by now. I'm sure you just forgot to ask for the appropriate warrants."

"Well, that's the odd thing," Brian replied. "We've been told to back right off any surveillance on Petrov. Keep away. Why? He's not the prime target any more. We're not to go within a hundred miles of him. Mind you, we haven't exactly stuck to that directive, but the AAT don't know that."

Brian placed his empty coffee cup on the table. "There's another funny thing," he grumbled. "Doctor Petrov has recently acquired an attractive assistant with an American accent, one Abigail Saunders. We know a bit about her from the trash in professor Cole's waste paper basket, or at least we know what Ms. Saunders has told the University and Petrov in her C.V. I'm inclined to disbelieve her, however. In my book we're looking at a CIA operative working under our very noses without our knowledge. Such trust they have."

"Is there anything you would like me to do?" Robin signalled the waitress for another Colombian single origin black. "Is she travelling on a false passport? I can alert some people in immigration who would be interested to know that."

"I would be amazed if the CIA were so damn careless, although in their haste they might have let something slip." Brian forked another piece of black forest cake into his mouth. "No, I've had a little chat with Ross Baker, our mate in MI6 – with whom we get along very well – and he's going to activate a couple of his helpers in Boston, just to check a few details on Ms. Saunders. I imagine the dean of the faculty would be very interested if this woman's C.V. is a pack of lies. Then your mates in immigration could rescind her study visa. That would put the crocodile in the koalas."

Robin smiled, as if recalling a pleasant memory.

"I know professor Cole. She's been very helpful to us in the past – can't say how. Sarah is an incredibly upright and decent woman. I don't want our friends to get their murky hands on her whilst she's lecturing in Europe, and take liberties. She's extraordinarily beautiful, did you know? I would vouch my entire reputation on her complete innocence in this blasted rubbish."

"I know about the good professor Cole," Brian assured him. "So does Ross Baker. She's been helpful to him too, Robin, and he's grateful, very grateful. Holds her in some sort of awe." He began to chuckle to himself.

"What's so funny?" Robin asked.

"Ross has a pet theory. He thinks she's actually an angelic being come down to help the human race. He'd skin me if he knew I'd told anyone. He's very protective of her each time she goes lecturing in the U.K. When I briefed him, he increased his network around her to quite extraordinary proportions. If someone tries the slightest thing on they'll end up looking very stupid or very dead. His own words."

Robin pushed his chair away from the table. "Thanks. Next week, same time, same place? My boys are keeping the streets clean while we're here, so to speak. Any nosey operatives will find themselves in all sorts of embarrassing situations. These are troublesome times, Brian, Noel. I'm glad we can work together."

There was a murmur of agreement amongst the two men as Robin stood to leave. It was an association which had proved very beneficial to both parties in the past.

Noel grinned as he watched Robin walk out the door. "Our mates from AAT have no inkling as to our devious nature, I trust?"

"They're too busy being devious on their own bat to notice." Brian grinned at his second in command. "I'll saunter out of here first, you pay for the coffee and follow in about ten minutes, okay?"

It was a ruse, and Noel knew it. He had been caught with the bill many times before.

# CHAPTER 29

The three week old Presidential blockade of secure traffic on all satellites had turned the Whitehouse Situation room into a microcosm of a full scale war. None of the chiefs were on speaking terms with any of the others, and as far as they knew their commanders were no longer on speaking terms with them. That's if they were still where they were supposed to be, but for all they knew the entire United States navy, army, and air force could have been decimated by aliens. There had been a potentially nasty incident between two destroyers who had independently decided to sail for the same port at the same time in order to pick up new secure orders, only narrowly avoided by the vigilance of one Petty Officer who noticed the other vessel's wake before the collision occurred.

Every single plane had been grounded, and the troops in Afghanistan were communicating by public telephone in spoken code. There had been a predictable reaction from their allies, who had begun to wonder if some sort of coup had occurred back home. The President had received several carefully worded requests to clarify who was in charge of his armed forces. Each one had added to his rapidly escalating rage. Norm Harding was persona non gratia, and Brett Dyer, military advisor to the President, was on the verge of a nervous breakdown. Dianne Collins had nearly come to blows with General Albright when he had suggested – suggested, mind - that she was only there to crow over other people's misery and incapable of doing anything useful.

At the end of the latest weekly briefing, alias screaming match, Harding had left under threat of immediate dismissal if he didn't bring matters to a head within twenty four hours. Peter Lawson had been the next down the chain to be hit with the tsunami from above, and he had in turn passed its somewhat depleted fury on to Harry O'Callaghan, who had politely told him to get lost. Their operative, in spite of the perilous situation, was slowly but surely infiltrating the organisation. Didn't they remember it was because of her intel that they knew Petrov had been knocking out satellite twenty nine with his own transmitter? A little patience, if you please.

Whilst faithfully backing his operative, Harry had been less than gentle with Abby, principally because every time she reported in, he sensed she was less and less inclined to believe Petrov was anything other than innocent, a trend which was disturbing for its very uniqueness. There had been a fiery meeting at the Martin Place offices of Martinborough Engineering that evening, and it wasn't over yet. Abby was standing near the door, frustration edging her voice and anger in her eyes.

"I tell you there's nothing to report on," she said loudly. "I know men, Harry, and I'm telling you this one doesn't fit the profile. He never makes contact with anyone suspicious, and his equipment simply can't do what you think it can. All the time you sit there and tell me to dig deeper, someone else is stuffing up the United States and getting clean away with it. If you were a terrorist organisation, would you advertise yourself like you think Petrov has? Doesn't it make more sense to shift the heat away from your own people so they can get busy with their nasty schemes uninterrupted?"

Harry threw a pen into the rubbish bin. "Abby, this is getting nowhere. You have to look harder. Hold off on the sex for a while until he's desperate, then only make him happy if he lets you into his confidence."

"We haven't had sex at all." Abby's voice was dangerously soft.

"No, of course you haven't," Harry gave a cynical laugh. "All you do is sit together playing with equations. Do you think I'm a complete fool?"

"Why do I have to have done it with him?" Abby demanded angrily.

Harry sighed. "Because that's what you do, Abby. It's what you always do. Don't try to tell me you've been beaten by his Christianity. All that repressed sexual energy, just waiting for the nudge of a pretty woman's wink to get his gear off and dive in. And you're good, Abby. He might have been a bit put off by your boobs in his face, but I'll bet an hour later he wanted a closer look at them."

"You're disgusting," Abby spat at him, fire in her eyes. The explosion was just around the corner.

"And you're worrying me," Harry said sharply. "Why try to hide the obvious? He hasn't started to compromise you, has he, Abby? By all the saints he must be a good lover. Come on, tell Harry what he does – I could use a few good tips."

The shouting match notched up a few more levels after that, Harry making pointed accusations that Petrov had already compromised her integrity with his bedroom expertise. Abby screamed back that he didn't fit the profile at all, and there was no evidence. What good would sleeping with him do under the circumstances? Did Harry actually want her to get into bed with another man just to satisfy his own sexual fantasies? How dare he suggest that Abby was becoming attached to her target.

Seeing the battle of wills completely stymied at every turn, Harry tried another approach.

"Alright," he sighed, "just suppose the good fairy's right and he's innocent. What about the hard drive on his machine? Get me a copy of it and we'll see if it's clean. If it is I'll tell Harding the whole thing is a red herring set up by someone else. I think he's likely to disembowel me, but I'll do it. That satisfy you?"

"Fine," Abby snapped. "Give me the gadget."

Harry went over to a cupboard and fished out a small device about the size of a cigarette packet. Abby stuffed it into her handbag and hurled herself out through the door. As usual Martin Place was as busy as ever even though it was after eleven at night, and loud music was coming from some disco further down George Street. She caught a passing taxi and went home to bed, furious with Harry and a little afraid.

Perhaps she was wrong.

What if the hard drive turned out to be incriminating? That had never worried her before, quite the contrary. Why hadn't she tried to seduce David? Was she losing her touch? Yes, she must be, because it was the very last thing she wanted to do. They had spent so much time together doing good physics, there hadn't been time for anything else. Besides, David wasn't interested in her, although he thought she was a good physicist, and that mattered more to her than trying to get him into her bed. Perhaps her days as an operative must be coming to an end.

The argument had made her feel particularly tired. She hated screaming at Harry. She drew her doona over her shoulders, cuddled down into her pillow and went to sleep.

※ ※ ※

It was a simple matter for Abby to copy the hard disk drive on David's desktop PC while he was delivering his lecture the next morning, but that didn't mean she enjoyed doing it. Normally it would have been the highlight of her assignment, copying her target's secrets and securing his destruction as well as a good bonus payment for her. All she felt as she opened the case, detached the cable to the hard drive and plugged it directly into her small battery powered device, was an acute sense of guilt. She was betraying the man who had begun to restore her self-esteem. No, she couldn't think of it that way. If he was guilty she was doing the world a favour, otherwise she was establishing his innocence.

Either way, it had to be done.

David returned just before lunch and suggested that they go out the back door under the scaffolding, buy some sandwiches in the Wentworth Café, then cross over the City Road Bridge and eat them in the shady grounds of Paul's College next to the oval. It was a suggestion that appealed to the girl, still feeling guilty with the image of his hard disk safely stowed in her handbag, and she offered to buy the sandwiches as well as the usual iced teas.

They reached the soft grass of the oval with these items in hand and sat down. A group of young men passed them on the way to lunch at their College's mess hall. One of them made a loud passing remark about the shape of Abby's legs stretched out on the grass, and what he would like to do with them.

In an instant David was on his feet. Several heated words flowed back and forth between him and the group. By the time he sat down again he had the student's name and number written down on the back of the brown paper bag containing his sandwich, and the said young man was retreating with an apology to Abby and a worried expression on his face. He knew that the Master of Paul's College took an officially dim view of indecent behaviour, and his place in the College was in jeopardy.

Abby had tucked her legs under the skirt she was wearing and tried not to display the conflicting thoughts racing through her head. She was perfectly capable of standing up and attacking the young man, emaciating his manhood until he felt knee high to a grasshopper in front of his mates. Normally she would have enjoyed doing it, but the fact that David had defended her virtue had secretly delighted her too, because he had acted entirely as a gentleman and not out of any sexual rivalry. When the group of young men had disappeared around the corner, she uncurled her legs again and squeezed his arm with both her hands.

"Thank you, David," she said softly. "That meant more to me than you will ever know."

"The hide of him," David muttered. "I'll see to it the Master of his college gets to hear about this."

Abby laughed softly, and without thinking at all, rested her head on his shoulder. "I guess you can't blame him in a way. I do have rather nice legs."

"Yes, you do," David answered after a short pause, "and that's not the only nice thing about you."

"I have others?" She lifted her face towards him, teasing him with her eyes.

"You do," David said quietly. "When you laugh there is real music in your voice, Abby. I… I guess lots of people have told you that."

"Not that I can remember. No one whose opinion I valued, anyway."

"I am totally amazed." David raised a quizzical eyebrow. "But then I don't know a lot about you. Your family come from Boston too?"

As he watched the sun drained out of her eyes, and it shocked him to see the expression which replaced it.

"I have no one I want to call family, David," Abby said bitterly. "I'm sorry, can we not talk about them? It's very … painful, if you must know. I'd rather we just did physics together and not talk about me. I know that sounds completely selfish."

"Sorry. I have no right to pry. Shouldn't have asked." David turned away, feeling a fool.

They finished their sandwiches, but the moment had gone, and David had retreated back into the formality of their relationship. It was better that way, Abby told herself, and instantly regretted the distance which had suddenly opened up between them. She suddenly felt the urge to place her head back on his shoulder, slip her arm around his, and stay there until she felt him respond, but such behaviour was so much part of her seduction routine she couldn't separate her true feelings from it. For a second she had wanted to respond from an altogether different motive, or thought she did. Perhaps it was no different after all. Perhaps the paths of seduction had become her only way of relating to a man, a cold substitute for the real thing. She felt a shudder all the way down her spine, and for no reason she could fathom, suddenly wished she could cry.

They made their way back to the lab. Some large sunspots were producing huge changes in the solar wind, and she couldn't wait to measure them. Confined within the safe constraints of their favourite subject, it wasn't long before they were laughing, calculating and planning together.

✳ ✳ ✳

Harry picked up the drive from the rubbish bin in front of the Physics building where Abby had arranged to leave it, and gave the small device to Norm Harding in person. The man and a team of experts had flown in from Pine Gap on a special flight that very afternoon, as soon as he had heard that Abby had succeeded in her mission to copy Petrov's files. Back on the plane which was stationed off the runway at Richmond RAAF base, Bruce, head of the decryption team, took the small device from Harding's hand and assured him it would be minutes before everything on Petrov's drive would be an open book in their hands.

Two hours later the only thing in Harding's hand was a note from Bruce to say they had not been able to break the encryption.

Harding hit the roof. In a matter of seconds the entire team was assembled in front of him. They weren't happy either.

Bruce attempted a pacifying explanation. "It's a standard private key encryption," he said in a very worried voice, "but the key is a whole 1024 bits long. To make matters worse, it keeps changing."

"Explain yourself." Harding's face was impassive as usual, his voice was anything but.

"Petrov has some way of cuing the changes in his key," Bruce stammered. "Somewhere there must be a gadget which contains all the keys, and he uses them in some sort of sequence. It's not that we can't decode the drive, it's just that it'll take forever. We get one key and the next second it's changed to another one. This guy must he one hell of a smart cookie."

"When can you get me a printout of what's on the drive?" Harding asked.

"If we were granted exclusive access to the Cray supercomputer back home, about six months," Bruce said unhappily.

"*Six months?*" Harding exploded. "I thought you were going to says six hours. Okay, forget it. We've got all the evidence we need. No innocent physicist encrypts his data like that. The time has come to have a little conversation with Petrov himself. He'll be begging to tell me everything he knows before I'm done with him."

❋ ❋ ❋

A tired but happy Abby arrived at Martinborough Engineering that evening. The experiments had gone so well. The solar flares had made such an incredible difference to the electron density and temperature of the ionosphere, that the amount of GNSS positioning error would have become quite significant. No matter, the equations they were developing would allow any navigation unit to correct for them and so avoid potential disasters from occurring. Something worthwhile was being done here, and she was part of it.

The euphoria was destined to be short lived.

Harry, seated at his desk, turned round as she entered, a sour expression on his face. "Well girl, you've done it," he said with a sigh. "Glory and honour will follow. Any job you want is yours. I guess old Harry might well end up working for you soon."

"What's all this nonsense about?" Abby snapped.

"We're pulling you out tomorrow night," Harry sighed again. "By that time Petrov will be hanging up by his own entrails somewhere. You've succeeded, Abby. The disk was encrypted with some algorithm even our clever boys were unable to break."

Abby threw up all over the floor.

Harry jumped off his chair and surveyed with disgust the mess on the carpet and the mess standing on it. "Do you have to do that every time you get— No!" he shouted. "Keep away from me. Go clean yourself up."

He retreated rapidly behind his desk. Abby strode towards him without a sign that she had even heard, leaving a very unpleasant trail of footprints behind her. From the other side of the desk she reached out, grabbed the man by the collar and dragged him forward so hard he nearly fell face down in the remains of his dinner. Her voice was no more than a hoarse croak, but nobody could miss the tenor of pure horror in it.

"You bloody fool. Stop them. He's not a terrorist, I tell you. There must have been something wrong with the data transfer. Look, we've used that computer together – we're writing a paper on it. It's as open as the sky. Harding's boys have made a mistake, and one scapegoat doesn't stop the real demons. You can't make him tell you what he doesn't know."

"Easy, babe," Harry grinned. "Of course we can. Harding's got a team of experts to work with. They'll have Petrov singing in minutes. He's boiling mad, I tell you. I think he's going to enjoy ripping Petrov's organs out one by one, even if he does sing like a bird."

Still holding onto Harry's collar with one hand, she slapped his face hard with the other. Harry, who had had quite enough hysteria for the evening, grabbed her arms, dragged her over the top of his desk and dumped her hard on the floor at his feet. Squatting down, he pushed his knee hard into her stomach and returned the compliment to her face with his left hand. He watched her fury morph into her usual angelic smile without trace of a tear, only this time there was more than a trace of sneer behind it.

"Why Harry," Abby said sweetly. "Is this where you have your way with me? It doesn't work with your knee in my stomach, you know. Do you want some help?"

Harry got off and stood up, leaving Abby lying on the floor, the same horrible smile on her face, goading him by seductively removing the belt from her skirt and dropping it on the floor beside her. He turned away and walked deliberately over to the table with the coffee machine on it.

"Clean up that mess on the floor," he ordered. "Why do you chuck so much? Something wrong with your stomach? I thought you would have liked the idea that another man – especially that one - was going to end his life screaming. What's got into you?"

"Some girls cry, I throw up," Abby said angrily. "You think I like it?" She got up and massaged her stomach where Harry's knee had been. "Is it any wonder I do when you knock me around? When are they going to take him down? Tonight?"

"Tomorrow I think. Best keep away from the lab when it happens. Now clean that mess up before someone else comes in and walks through it."

"Clean it up yourself," Abby retorted, went out and slammed the door behind her.

Harry threw his half empty cup of coffee into the wastepaper basket in fury. At first he thought of running after her, twisting her arm behind her back, marching her up the stairs and shoving her face in the mess on the floor. What was the point? She would be flavour of the month in a couple of days, and it wasn't beyond her to make sure the rest of his life was even more miserable than it was at present. With great reluctance, and a constant string of very unprintable language, he threw a roll of paper towel over the mess and rang the night service. There was no way he was going to demean himself to the level of cleaning it up himself.

Abby walked across Martin Place and along George Street until she found a taxi. She was feeling so nauseous she could barely stand, let alone walk, and she wished that pictures of David in the hands of his torturers would not keep coming into her mind and making it worse. She had to stop them, but how? Her first thought was to go to his house and tell him all, but a swift reflection put paid to that idea. She was likely to end up hanging beside him in the same state. Arriving at her flat in Annandale, she staggered into the kitchen and managed, after a while, to finish a glass of milk and keep it down. She had to eat. There was no point in depriving her brain of the very things it needed to function, and function it must, if she was going to prevent murder. Another man to die horribly at her hand? No, not this one, please God.

God? There was no God, why did she mumble this nonsense to herself? Think, girl, use the brain that God gave you, and stop saying that Name!

# THE PETROV EFFECT

✳ ✳ ✳

David came into his office at the usual time of seven thirty to find Abby already there sitting at his desk. She turned round at the sound of the door opening.

"What's wrong with this computer?" she asked, trying desperately to keep her anxiety out of her voice. "I couldn't sleep last night because I was going through the equations we developed for predicting ionospheric height. We've left out the sunspot constants. I tried accessing the file and I can't. The hard drive must be corrupted. It's a disaster."

"You look awful," David exclaimed. "What's the matter? You're as white as a sheet of paper. No, the drive's not corrupted, its encrypted."

Abby grabbed the waste paper basket and threw up in it. She felt David's arm around her shoulders, steadying her gently, his handkerchief held out towards her hands. She took it and wiped her face, then without thinking, pressed her head against him, feeling his hand on her hair gently stroking, his voice full of concern. She gave a soft groan and pushed herself away, her heart sinking into the depths.

"Why? Why is this drive encrypted, David? What have you got to hide? Tell me."

David was astonished by the desperate tone in her voice. Suddenly he began to laugh. Abby was stunned by such an unexpected response. She felt like shaking him. Didn't he realise his life hung by a thread? No he didn't, but it wasn't funny in any case. Seeing the strange look in her eyes he stopped, and dragging a chair over next to her, sat down and brushed the hair gently off her face.

Take a look at this computer," he chuckled. "Does it look like the others in the department?"

"No its quite different and a bit older," Abby gave a groan. "So what?"

"This is my own computer. I bought it while I was working for a company that specialised in secure computer systems. I invented a little device which encrypts a hard drive in such a way it would take forever to decrypt. It's not really clever, just incredibly annoying."

He took a small device about the size of a bar of chewing gum out of his pocket.

"This little thing contains about a million keys. It communicates with a Bluetooth device located in the printer where nobody would think of looking for it. While I'm around the drive looks normal. When I disappear no one can read it. My supervisor tried to rip the whole thing off as his own idea and I fixed him. I'm afraid the company sacked me for the trouble. I took my computer and its little device with me and here it is."

"So... it's just a ..." Abby gasped. "Oh, oh! I'm feeling awful," she exclaimed suddenly. "I have to go. No I'll be alright, don't follow me." She ran out of the room, leaving a very puzzled David Petrov staring through the open doorway at her retreating figure.

✳ ✳ ✳

Abby ran all the way to City Road and caught the first cab she could find by running out in front of it. Arriving at Martin Place she ran to Martinborough Engineering as though the Devil himself was behind her. There were no less than ten people in the office and one of them was none other than Norman Harding.

"You've got to stop this nonsense," Abby shouted breathlessly. "Hello, Director. Harry, can you get that ASIO file on Petrov? Is there an incident where he gets sacked by the computer company he worked for?"

"What's all this?" Harding was looking at her in a way she didn't much care for. "Petrov is going down this morning, that is unless you have an excellent reason for cancelling my orders?"

"Director, sir, I believe I do," Abby said, breathing hard. "Harry, hurry up with that file! You want to know what's on that hard drive? I can get it for you, the whole lot. If you take him out you will precipitate retaliation which would be disastrous. Please let me do it my way. Harry, have you got that blasted file yet?"

Apparently Harry had, because he was approaching with a large pile of paper in his arms.

"What am I looking for?" he asked.

"There was an incident in which the company Petrov was working for sacked him," Abby replied. "It was because he designed a drive encryption device and they tried to steal his intellectual property."

Some time elapsed before Harry found the incident amongst the reams of extraneous information sent by ASIO. Abby, trying to keep the desperation out of her voice, continued her explanation, whilst Harding sat impassively staring at her without uttering a sound.

"You see, it's the same computer," she said. "Who knows what he's got stored on that drive, but I can get the whole lot without him even suspecting a thing. Surely that's a much better alternative. Don't you think this cell or whatever it is would be expecting us to do the very thing you're contemplating, Director? Do you think it's remotely likely they haven't got some sort of really awful response set up ready to go? That they can't protect their own man? So far they suspect nothing. Why not keep it that way until we have the full picture, then take them all down before they can really wreak havoc?"

There was long silence. Eventually Harding spoke, his voice a measured calm that sent a shudder down Abby's spine. "I am surprised, Ms. Saunders, knowing your penchant for letting us dispose of your male targets in unpleasant ways, that you would have taken the trouble to delay this one's execution. I can assure you it's a simple matter to take the machine to Petrov and get him to activate his small device. Indeed, I believe he would do so with a willingness hitherto unparalleled. You could watch if you doubt me."

Abby swallowed hard. This was not the time to make a mistake. Nonetheless it took every ounce of self-control to keep the anxiety out of her voice.

"When you gave me the mission you told me this terrorist organisation was the most lethal you've ever encountered. I undertook to take the assignment knowing that if they discovered my identity they would take me apart the way you're planning to do with Petrov. You know I practically begged you for the chance to take them down. Don't deprive me of that opportunity, Director. So far I've managed to find out Petrov had a transmitter capable of destroying the satellite he's underneath. This encrypted computer probably contains all the information you want to know, and I'm prepared to give you a copy of it. If you act prematurely I will not be responsible for the consequences, and I have a feeling you don't want to be either. Let me do what you sent me to do. Have I let you down so far? You have an operative in place. Petrov trusts me. If your scheme backfires, what will you do then?"

Harding stared at her as though he was trying to read her mind. Abby stared back, trying to hold an appropriate expression on her face, not too sweet, not too belligerent.

"It would seem you have a point after all, Ms. Saunders," Harding said after a long pause. "For a moment I was prepared to believe the impossible had happened, and you had become emotionally involved with your target. Perhaps I was in haste. I concur we may not be able to control the consequences if we pursue this action, so for the present I will allow you to provide the intel in your own way."

He paused, his voice hardened. "One thing, if I ever suspect that you are being compromised by Petrov, I will personally make sure you leave the world most uncomfortably. I'm prepared to consider the possibility Petrov chose to tell us about his operation because he felt himself untouchable, and that could well extend to his ability with women. I take it that Petrov is a very capable lover?"

"He's skilled, but he likes what I do. Don't they all?" Abby locked eyes with Harry in a very meaningful manner. Harry said nothing. He didn't like Harding any more than Abby did.

# THE PETROV EFFECT

"I want the latest and fastest backup device commercially available at any price, and I want it this afternoon, two of them," Abby ordered with much more command than she felt. "Can anyone do that for me?"

"I'm perfectly sure such devices will be in your hands within the hour, Ms. Saunders," Harding assured her. "Why don't you go and have a decent coffee? There's an excellent barista at the café on the corner of Martin Place and Pitt Street. We will bring them there."

"Thank you, Director." Abby gave him a brief smile.

She left the room with one last meaningful look at Harry, noticing with relief an almost imperceptible vertical movement of his head. She walked slowly down to the café, not for a moment wishing to order a coffee of any sort. Her plan, developed slowly in the early hours of the morning had paid off, although she had not expected the Director to be there in person, a bonus as it happened. Now to persuade David to back up his precious drive whilst his little device was in the vicinity, which wouldn't be too hard. She was sure it wouldn't contain a single incriminating thing, and perhaps she could use that as yet another means of establishing his innocence. She felt terribly tired, and all of a sudden wished David was there with her so he could stroke her hair and offer her head the comfort of his shoulder.

❄ ❄ ❄

The devices arrived an hour and a half later in the hands of a very nervous courier. It had taken longer than expected. Would Ms. Saunders please excuse the unavoidable delay, and could he go back and tell director Harding that each device was exactly what Ms. Saunders had requested? There was fear in his eyes, and for good reason.

Abby smiled at him. "They're perfect, thank you. Go back and tell director Harding that Ms. Saunders had only just finished her excellent coffee and croissant."

"But you're only drinking a glass of water," he said nervously.

"I know, but tell him that anyway, will you?"

"Thank you, Ms. Saunders, I will."

Abby took each small black device out of its cardboard packaging and stowed them in her handbag. Now back to the lab in time for lunch after David had returned from his lecture. Once again he arrived to find her sitting at his computer, only this time he noticed the colour had returned to her face.

"Look what I've brought." She smiled and held out one of the devices in her hand.

"What's that? A portable hard drive of sorts?" He took it from her hand. "I've never seen one so small. Must be worth a packet."

"It was, and it's yours, a present. If the machine is as old as you say, it's likely to have a drive failure just before we go to publish, and we don't want that, do we?"

"You mean you went out and bought one of these for me this morning? When you were feeling so bad? That was really nice of you." David gave her a warm smile.

"Can we see if it works? I think it might be better if we copy the whole thing in its decrypted form."

"Yes," David agreed. "It's a good idea anyway, because you should have access to the files in any case. If you like, you can see all the stuff I've been up to designing the antenna and writing to people to check no one else was duplicating our research. Look, I've got to see a student for a while, so why don't you back the thing up when I've gone? I'll leave this little gadget with you. When I come back I'll take you to lunch."

She could have kissed him. He left the room and Abby connected up the first backup device. The computer hard drive wasn't very large, and the entire backup was finished in less than fifteen minutes. Quickly disconnecting the first backup drive, she placed it her handbag and brought out the other. Fifteen minutes later it had also finished, and ten minutes later David walked back into the room.

"All done." She handed the drive to him with a beautiful smile. "We can do that from time to time as we write the papers."

"Thank you, Abby," David said, his face serious. "Do you know, I thought at first you were some loose woman who had come to campus to escape extradition or something." He smiled, "but you're as clever as you're pretty, and I'm so glad you stayed. I'm glad I was wrong. We get along really well together, don't we?"

She stood up and gave him a friendly punch on the shoulder. "We do. Now, where's the sandwiches? I thought you were buying."

"No, I'm taking you to a little restaurant in Haymarket which makes the most delicious Chinese food. I take it you like Chinese food? I'm sure you'll like this at any rate."

"I love Chinese food," Abby laughed. "Hold on while I visit the bathroom." She walked down the corridor with a small spring in her step. Going into the ladies, she liberated her hair from the clip which turned it into a pony tail, and spent the next five minutes brushing it into shape. David, waiting patiently at a respectful distance outside, noticed the difference immediately.

"You're really beautiful," he complimented her warmly. "I guess a lot of men tell you that."

"What matters is you think so." Abby meant it, and to hear the words from her own lips surprised her. Surely there was no truth in the director's words. No, she would never be attracted to a man that way.

It was a long time before they returned to the laboratory that afternoon, and the glow in Abby's face had nothing to do with the excellent Chinese food. Hard as it was for her to accept, she had finally found a man whose company pleased her. Somehow he managed to make her forget who she was and what she was supposed to be doing, and think only of how very much she wished to continue doing ionospheric experiments with him. There was no doubt at all in her mind now. This was no terrorist, no accomplished seducer of women, and she was going to prove it.

David left Abby to do the experiments that evening because Lydia had invited him to dinner, and she felt pleased she had gained so much of his trust. The experiments went well, and after shutting down at ten pm, Abby made her usual pilgrimage to Martin Place and handed Harry the drive as promised.

# CHAPTER 30

Lydia met David at the door with her usual love hug and ushered him into the dining room. Geoff was already seated at the table, his hands occupied in the task of carving a very respectable leg of lamb. All was as it should be.

David settled down in his usual chair and the meal began.

"We thank you Lord for this good food, for your generous provision at all times, and especially for your grace in sending the Lord Jesus to die on a cross for us," Lydia said while they all held hands.

The food was hot and delicious, the conversation swift and enjoyable.

"How is that new assistant measuring up, David?" Geoff put down his knife and fork and leaned back in his chair.

"Abby is doing well," David laughed. "Initially I wondered whether she was going to be suitable, but we are doing good work together. I think she's rather nice, although we only talk about the project. Any other subject is pretty well taboo for some reason."

"Be careful, David." Lydia's face reflected a concern he was surprised to see. "Don't confuse being her supervisor with being her friend. Apart from the physics you study together you may have practically nothing in common. Is she a Christian?"

"No," David said sadly, "and for some reason I detect a real animosity towards anything remotely connected with God."

"All the more reason to be doubly careful," Lydia said. "Look, a letter arrived for you yesterday, from Sarah Cole. I thought it strange she didn't just email you."

"From Sarah?" David sat bolt upright in his chair. "How did it come?"

"A visiting professor from Cambridge hand-delivered it. I'm ashamed to say I can't remember his name," Lydia said, frowning. "It was all so quick. There was a knock at the door, and there he was with an envelope. I did offer him a cup of tea but he said he had to go. Now, would you like ice cream with your strudel?"

After the meal, when they were all seated comfortably in the lounge room, Lydia took a letter off the mantelpiece and handed it to him. "Here it is David," she said. "What's this all about?"

"I have absolutely no idea," David replied, frowning heavily. He ripped open the envelope. Inside was a hand written note.

> Dear David,
> After my lecture today I happened to browse through our faculty's web site and was astounded to learn that you had taken the woman known as Abigail Saunders on as your assistant. The note which I left on your desk has obviously been replaced by another crafted with some skill, for you are familiar with my handwriting. This alone will give you some insight into the seriousness of the situation facing you. Although I did not make a copy, I can remember exactly what I wrote, and here it is.
>
> David, have nothing to do with this woman who calls herself Abigail Saunders. As far as I can tell there is hardly anything genuine about her. She has some knowledge of undergraduate level physics, probably from Boston, but her employment history at Cornell is fictitious. She has recently read four papers – which I could name – on coherent scattering in the ionosphere, and

*planned to use these as a basis for her declared interest in your field. I am sure this is far from her real intent.*

*As to her character, your assessment was completely correct. If this were her only flaw I would not be so worried, but I fear there is more to Ms. Whoever than that. While she was sitting in front of me I pinged the mail server of a colleague in Cornell and received a reasonable value. I then pinged the mail server of the address which appeared in her C.V., supposedly from the same university, and obtained a completely impossible time, forcing me to conclude somebody within ten kilometres radius of the Physics building has gone to the trouble of intercepting all mail to that address for the purposes of falsifying any correspondence. This infrastructure is not simply the work of an amoral young woman in search of a study visa, but an indication that some larger and more sinister organisation lies behind her. Once again, have absolutely nothing to do with her.*

*Such was my original message.*

*I have not been able to confirm my darker suspicions concerning this young woman, but I am now in the process of doing so via a gentleman who has some connections with such matters, a Mr. Ross Baker. As yet I have not had any reply from him. Should I be able to confirm my suspicions I will write to the dean of the faculty and inform him of the situation. In the meantime place no trust in her whatsoever, but do nothing to make her suspect you are privy to her deception. Such is the nature of the dark forces surrounding you I deem it would be dangerous to take any other course of action at present. I cannot hazard a guess as to why you have been made the subject of their attentions, but I am doing what I can to find out. It is for this very reason I have used such a circuitous route to inform you of the above.*
*Take great care, David.*
*My prayers are with you,*
*Sarah.*

David put the letter down and shut his eyes, conflicting emotions doing battle within his head. So he had been right all along. Why did he feel so wretched? So he should get rid of her. Why did her want her to stay?

Lydia read the expression on his face with more accuracy than he would have thought possible. "This assistant of yours, this Abby, is not quite what you thought she was, is she? Why did Professor Cole take such measures to let you know, David? What have you learned?"

"It would appear my assistant may not be qualified to complete her studies with us," he sighed heavily. "Please don't worry, Lydia, Geoff. This is the first experience I've had with this sort of thing. I will have to speak to the dean. Such a pity, she's very intelligent. I will be sorry to lose her."

"I should think it's for the best if I read between the lines, David," Geoff said softly. "There will be other students. Perhaps God has acted to remove her before she was able to do any damage to your faith."

"I think my trust in God is firm enough, Geoff," David assured him. "Thanks for the warning. I'm not looking forward to discussing this with the dean though."

He loved them far too much to worry them about his real concerns. He turned the conversation by asking how the Woman's Bible study went last night, and followed that by some very genuine enquires as to how Geoff's practice was going. Was he working too many hours? He knew he had little hope of throwing dust in Lydia's eyes. An hour later he left and drove his Kombi van back to the flat in Glebe.

❈ ❈ ❈

The silence of Abby's apartment was shattered by a terrified scream, then another. A light came on in the bedroom, followed by every single light in the house, one after the other. A bleary eyed Abby appeared in the kitchen wrapped in a dressing gown. It had been another encounter with Henry Makin and his red hot needle, and even now Abby thought she could feel the wound it had made as her tormentor thrust it through her side. Turning on the television so there was some sound to add to the light, she returned to the bedroom, dragged her doona off the bed and headed for to the couch in front of the blaring set. Some charlatan was telling the world they would secure God's favour if they sent their money to the address crawling along the bottom of the screen. How she hated religion. No matter, even this was better than what Makin offered her if she fell asleep again. The curtains were bright with the morning sun and the television was blaring with some mindless morning show when Abby finally came to consciousness. She stood up and massaged the muscles which had not appreciated their sojourn on the couch, and hobbled into the bathroom for a shower.

# CHAPTER 31

As fate would have it, Norman Harding arrived at Sydney International at precisely the same time as Abby stepped into the shower. With all secure communications frozen, he had been told by phone to return to Washington for a briefing with the President, a meeting which Harding was dreading. All had gone well up until the instant he sat down in the departure lounge at Gate 64. Suddenly he was aware of the voice booming over the public address system.

"Would a Mr. Norman Harding please report to immigration immediately. Would a Mr. Norman Harding of Washington DC please report to immigration immediately."

Publicly broadcasting the name of the director of the CIA, especially as he wasn't supposed to be in the country, was disastrous. Gritting his teeth he went back towards immigration and reported in, noticing the large contingent of police and customs officers who were standing around like an unwelcome reception committee. Trying his best to be inconspicuous Harding approached the counter. An officious looking female with "Australian Customs" emblazoned on her jacket asked him for his passport.

She examined it briefly then handed it to another officer.

"Mr. Harding," she said, "could you please explain how it is that you can be leaving Australia without a record of entry?"

Harding handed her a card from his pocket. "Please call this number. Do it now. I do not wish to miss my flight."

"And who is Mr. Brian Hill?" The customs officer asked.

"Just call him now," Harding said, showing almost superhuman restraint.

He noticed the police had formed a tighter cordon around him. Curse their hides, he muttered silently.

"Mr. Hill does not appear to be at this number, sir," the customs officer said. "I would ask you to accompany these officers. It's a very serious matter to travel on a false passport. There are heavy penalties."

Harding missed his flight.

It took two hours to find Brian Hill, and the latter gentleman insisted on coming to the airport so that a positive identification could be made.

"You can't be too careful with all these terrorists around" were his parting words.

Harding caught a cab back to the city in a completely foul mood. This relationship with ASIO was souring by the minute.

# CHAPTER 32

The Café in Regent Street was dimly lit and very private. Two men were seated at their usual table, awaiting the arrival of the third. The coffee was up to its usual standard as was the almond and blueberry muffin which Noel was consuming along with his usual mocha.

Robin Naylor pocketed his rather special mobile phone and glanced at his watch. "Shouldn't be long now, I've just had word from the airport. I regret to say our much beloved Norman Harding has missed his flight."

"Such a shame," Noel murmured, his mouth full of muffin.

At that instant the familiar form of Brian Hill darkened the lighted doorway, a smile still lingering on his face. He nodded to another man on the footpath and stepped inside the café. "George is on the job I see. Thanks Robin."

"Pleasure," Naylor smiled. "All went well at the airport?"

"I think we nearly gave him a heart attack," Hill chuckled. "Better luck next time. Now Noel, have you ordered for me?"

"Don't be daft. As if you would drink a cold black."

Noel summoned the waitress, the same one with the long black hair and eyes to match. He ordered a Colombian black and another muffin for himself – or Brian, whoever got in first.

Brian grunted his appreciation, grimaced, and turned to Naylor. "Now Robin, we have things to report. I've heard from Ross. The American girl keeping Petrov company in the lab is bad news squared. She's known among the traps as the Deadly Angel, and has a reputation for vice as long as your arm. Quite notorious in Boston, where she practiced her trade on her supervising professor."

"She's an assassin?" Robin looked genuinely shocked.

"Of sorts. Not the kind who actually murders her target, but the one who seduces all the information out of him, and then has him taken out by the nearest wet team. A true paragon of virtue."

"We have to get rid of her," Robin said urgently. "Is she travelling on a false passport?"

"No, unfortunately, but we've managed to put her pot well and truly on the stove," Hill grimaced. "Ross contacted the Vice Chancellor at Boston, an old guy who should have been retired a decade ago. He's made it his life's mission to ruin this woman's reputation wherever she goes, and he sent the dean of Science at Sydney a dossier on her which would have made him blush. I believe there's a meeting with Petrov going on right now. Only a matter of time before she is out of the picture."

"I wonder what the CIA will do next?" Naylor muttered, a worried expression on his face. "That is surely a matter of concern. With their operative neutralised they may be driven to more extreme measures."

"We've thought of that and stepped up our surveillance," Hill replied, "as much as we can without alerting Harding. None of his boys have gone anywhere near him, probably relying on the work of their operative. There's another nasty aspect of all this."

"You mean it gets worse?" Robin slowly returned his coffee cup to its saucer.

"We have some intel – I can't reveal the source – that this woman's last target was an industrialist called Henry Makin, apparently a fine public spirited individual. She was engaged to him, apparently, then he disappeared. Never found the body. You don't have to be guilty of anything to be destroyed by the D.A."

"The man's in great danger," Robin exclaimed. "How do we protect him?" His voice was edged with concern. Murder was very definitely within his brief, and he didn't want to be the only one left holding the mess.

"If this latest attempt fails we're thinking of removing her on a more permanent basis," Hill replied quietly.

"You're not expecting me to condone murder," Robin cautioned.

"No," Hill smiled reassuringly. "Perhaps she just disappears for a while until her own masters come to believe she's betrayed them." Hill cut a slice of muffin with his fork. "They do take care of their own, you know. With any luck we can catch them doing her in, and then we've got the whole lousy bag of them. We're working on that. Probably no need to worry. Petrov won't want to be associated with a woman of Saunders' reputation."

The coffee arrived, and Brian stirred a sugar into its depths. He had already polished off the muffin.

# CHAPTER 33

David walked into his office at seven thirty that morning to find the phone ringing. The dean wanted to see him urgently at his office in the Carslaw building. It was a long meeting, and truly distressing, for the content which the dean could add to Sarah's note was shocking in the extreme. He read the original letter from the Vice Chancellor at Boston and felt physically ill. A promiscuous, violent woman, a liar and a fraud. Why did his heart ache so much?

He handed it back to the dean and slumped back in his chair. "What happens now?"

"I will convene a meeting tomorrow morning," the dean sighed. "There's no way the faculty can condone her continuance. Leaving aside her moral character – or rather the complete absence of it - we cannot allow this faculty's reputation to be tarnished. Imagine the reaction if such news became public. I'm so sorry for you, David, your first student. Take heart, man, not all of them will be like Ms. Saunders. I will readvertise the position as soon as I can next week."

"Thank you Dean, you have been most kind," David said sadly. "I will let the woman know."

He didn't feel grateful, however. How could he have been so taken in? For a moment he thought to ask the dean if he would care to break the whole sorry story to her himself. No, this was his affair, and he had to face it, had to act, had to execute justice. He felt like an executioner as he prepared himself to do it.

He returned to the Physics building to find Abby sitting at his desk with a cup of coffee in her hand and another beside her. She turned at the sound of his entry and lifted her lovely blue eyes up towards him.

David felt ill.

"Abby, who do you work for?" David asked, his eyes reflecting the turmoil in his heart.

"I beg your pardon?" she laughed. "Oh, and hello, David. I brought you a coffee."

"Thank you. Who do you work for?"

The look on his face brought a frown to hers.

"I told you," Abby replied. "I work part-time at Martinborough Engineering and Construction as a consultant."

"The name George McReadie mean anything to you?"

He watched the light drain out of her face, her expression frozen momentarily in disbelief, then fear, then anger. Initially she couldn't speak at all, then she sprang to her feet so rapidly David took a step backwards thinking she was about to hit him.

"How dare you pry into my private affairs," she said, her voice trembling with rage. "How dare you!"

"I've just returned from a meeting with the dean. He has received a report from the Vice Chancellor at Boston Univ—"

Abby threw her coffee cup into the rubbish bin, her eyes blazing with wrath. "So, you're throwing me out are you? I'm glad to go. Go on, collect your brownie points from God for disposing of the trash." She glared at him, her eyes blazing with fire. "Now are we done? Get out of my way."

David shut the door behind him and stood in front of it, blocking Abby's path. He saw her pause in her stride, her eyes narrow. A wave of fear swept over the rage in her face and disappeared. He stood his ground against the door, wondering what would happen next.

"Abby, please sit down. I swear I had nothing to do with this," he pleaded. "Please listen to me before you race out of here."

The girl sat down, tense as a leopard about to spring, never taking her eyes off him, still waiting for a chance to bolt through the door if he gave her the chance. Yes, he was sure of it now, she was angry as all hell, but she was also afraid. Afraid of him? Surely not.

"Do you have a copy of your original thesis?"

Silence from Abby.

"Can't you see I'm trying to help you?" David said, exasperated. "Do you have a copy of your thesis, the one McReadie said was rubbish?"

"I might have." She spat the words.

"May I see it, please? Can you get it to me before I go home tonight?"

"Can I go now? Do I have to listen to any more of this rubbish?"

"You can go." He sighed heavily. "The dean wants to see us both in his office tomorrow morning at nine twenty. If you don't turn up then you will be expelled from the University automatically. Abby, I can't help you unless you trust me. Please let me see the work you did for McReadie."

"Can I go now?" she snapped at him.

He opened the door and stepped away from it. "You can go. Good-bye, Abby. I'm sorry it has to be this way, but it's your choice. I always believed if something was good it was worth fighting for, but apparently you don't care."

"There's not a dime's worth of good things in my life," Abby hissed as she passed.

She ran through the doorway and disappeared, leaving a troubled and unhappy David Petrov behind her.

In truth he had read her face extremely well. The long fingers of that foul man had found her again. No matter where she went, McReadie's filthy curse followed her, destroyed her all over again, wrenched the pain barely buried in her heart right to the surface, and made her relive the humiliation, the hate, the ostracism. How she hated men. Petrov was just as bad, gloating over her misery, his religious little world purified from her presence. Once again a wave of fear passed over her. What would Harding say now that she had blown her assignment? Another loathsome man, but he terrified her.

There was no question of her next move. See Harry, tell him what had happened and activate her exit strategy immediately. Perhaps it was already too late. An empty cab was travelling down City road and she dived for it, telling the driver there was an extra fifty dollars if he could get to Martin Place within five minutes. After three of those five minutes she bitterly regretted her incentive. Leaving the world from a taxi was not the exit strategy she had planned. Arriving at her destination she thrust seventy dollars into the driver's outstretched hand and bolted out the door. A large group of British tourists was strolling down Martin Place, unfavourably comparing its architecture with their own back home. Abby joined them, forcing herself to move slowly until she could see the stairway leading up to Martinborough Engineering on her left. Leaving her wandering cover, she ran rapidly to the entrance and flew up the steps.

"Harry, they're going to boot me out," She yelled. "They've heard from Boston. It's over, Harry."

She paused, because Harry was staring beyond her in a very meaningful way towards someone standing at the side of the doorway behind the door.

"Good morning, Ms. Saunders," Harding greeted her evenly. "I take it you are here to report progress?"

Abby wheeled around to find Director Harding's impassive face staring at her.

"Director! I had no idea," she stammered.

"Me neither, Ms. Saunders. I should be high over the Pacific right now instead of skulking in this hole. I take it there is some sort of problem?"

Abby told him exactly what sort of problem there was.

"There is no question of pulling you out, Ms. Saunders," Harding continued evenly. "It's quite obvious this terrorist cell has managed to obtain intel from some source in Washington, perhaps from within our own ranks, sadly. They must also be aware of the sorry state of our secure communications network, and no doubt they are planning a major offensive."

He paused to collect his own thoughts. "The hard drive you copied was completely clean – or cleaned rather, especially for our benefit. Their next move was to blow your cover. You have managed to get in their way, Ms. Saunders, and now they want you out of it."

He gave a wry smile. "Let's disappoint them. No, you must remain the fly in their ointment. Go to this meeting with the dean, fight the accusations. Stay close, complicate their plans."

"It's all very well to order Abby to stay," Harry protested. "If the cell has blown her cover it must mean they're on to her. We have to pull her out."

"Exactly what they want us to do," Harding countered, "which is why she's going to stay. Have a tracer sewn into her panties. If they try to take her anywhere, we can follow. With any luck we might manage to get hold of a couple of their own operatives to interrogate."

He turned to Abby, "be careful where you drop those panties, Ms. Saunders. We wouldn't want to think you were in Petrov's bed when you were in fact in danger somewhere else."

"Just how is she going to maintain her candidature with some lurid pack of lies from Boston being passed around the dean's office?" Harry demanded. "I still say we should pull her out."

"I wonder which member of this terrorist cell wanted her out of the way?" Harding mused softly to himself. "Perhaps Petrov saw straight through her and has simply been enjoying the sex." His focus returned to Harry.

"I'm surprised the solution hasn't occurred to a womaniser like you, O'Callaghan," Harding said with a wry smile. "We let the Deadly Angel work her magic on the dean. In hindsight she should have done that first, just to ensure his cooperation if something like this happened."

From out of nowhere Abby heard her own brother's cynical laughter. 'So you tried to do McReadie. Appalling taste. You should have done the dean first.' The crushing reality of that nightmare evening rose from the darkness of her mind with soul-damming clarity. Exactly the same thing was happening now. Her doctoral success depended on her willingness to prostitute herself, not on her academic ability. She felt her heart racing, her breathing fast and shallow.

"What are you suggesting?" she snapped angrily, fixing Harding with a furious stare.

"Of course we need to do some homework on the dean first," Harding said, not really answering her. "A man in his position is likely to have enjoyed such opportunities with students before, in exchange for favours. Just in case he hasn't, we need to organise things differently. Yes, a private interview with Ms. Saunders, a small tranquiliser dart stuck into his palm, and then we send in one of our team to take the oh-so-revealing pictures. I'm sure Ms. Saunders knows exactly how to stage the scene."

"A common whore, is that what you think I am?" Abby hissed through her teeth. She saw Harry flinch.

"No," Harding said evenly. "You're an agent with a great deal of sexual expertise. I recall you pleading with me to take on this mission." His voice hardened slightly. "Right now our country needs that expertise, Ms. Saunders, and by God they're going to get it."

"The dean was appalled by my reputation," Abby protested angrily. "What makes you think he would want to be alone with me for five seconds?"

"She has a point," Harry interrupted before Harding could reply. He could see the rage building in Abby's face and knew the explosion was just around the corner.

"It's up to Ms. Saunders to make sure the dean will see her," Harding said. "Apparently when it comes to persuading men to drop their pants she is without peer."

Abby hardly heard him. In her mind she was still back in Boston, all her academic ability demeaned as worthless, subject to satisfying another man's perverted lust. Now Harding was commanding her to do the same thing.

"And if I refuse?" Abby countered in a dangerously soft voice, her eyes like fire.

"That would be most unwise," Harding said smoothly. "You would jeopardise the entire operation, and your life would end in a decidedly unpleasant manner, Ms. Saunders."

"Better than being your brainless whore," Abby shouted in fury. Marching towards the door, she wrenched it open. "I'd rather die," she screamed at Harding. "Seduce him yourself." The door slammed with such force the glass panels on either side wobbled.

Harding's face registered no emotion whatsoever. He turned towards Harry. "You have ten minutes, O'Callaghan," he said evenly. "If you have not managed to modify Ms. Saunder's attitude in that time, I will have her disembowelled. You're welcome to watch. You had better pull something clever out of the hat for a change."

Harry swore under his breath and belted out the door. By the time he reached the street, Abby had nearly travelled the entire length of Martin Place. Harry raced towards her, finally catching up just as she turned down George Street.

"You're a dammed fool," he panted breathlessly, gripping her arm like a vice.

"Let go my arm or I'll make a scene you really don't want to have," Abby snarled into his face.

Harry let go. "Please," he pleaded. "Harding has given me ten minutes, then you go into the meat processor. Give me a break, let me go back and tell Harding you've changed your mind."

"You can go back and tell Harding I'll handle things in my own way," Abby growled. "If I need his help I'll ask for it. Tell him to treat me like an intelligent woman not a brainless whore."

"You'll fight to stay with Petrov?" Harry asked amazed. "You're not going to bail out?"

"Let's say I'm going to give Petrov and the dean a chance to do the right thing. If they won't do it, then there's always another way out, isn't there?" Her face contorted in a horrible smile.

"Do the right thing?" Harry objected. "The man's a bloody terrorist. What makes you think he's going to do the right thing? Have you taken leave of your senses? This is Harding we're dealing with, Abby. If you're thinking of activating your exit strategy, you won't make it."

Abby glanced at her watch. "Five minutes gone," she sneered. "Better go and give Harding the message."

She turned her back on Harry and strode off down George Street. With another oath, Harry raced back to Martinborough Engineering with the news. He hoped Harding had stuck to his word.

❋ ❋ ❋

Marking assignments from students who had apparently done them in the bus on the way to university that morning, is the bane of any lecturer's life. David's morbid concentration and preoccupied heart may have accounted for his failure to hear the door open behind him, the soft footfalls approaching. The first indication he had of anyone else in the room was a large discoloured volume landing smack bang on top of the papers on his desk. He sprang up in surprise.

"Enjoy," Abby sneered angrily. "I'll see you at the crucifixion tomorrow morning."

"Abby—"

But she had turned, and seconds later disappeared through the doorway.

Abby strode out of the Physics building, her mind a turmoil of fear and rage. She knew she ought to have come back to David in tears, begging him to read her thesis, saying how sorry she was, using every feminine skill she possessed to make herself indispensable to him. But her mission had vanished. She was still back in Boston, about to have her intellectual credibility destroyed in exactly the same way it had been before. McReadie had been so kind, so nice, right up to the time he betrayed his true motivation, and now doctor 'Christian' Petrov was about to deal her the same hand.

Christians hated whores, didn't they? Despite all that had gone before in their relationship, this was how he would judge her, how he had already judged her, and there was no stopping it. Just as McReadie had done he would throw her out, ignoring her worth, destroying her, yes, leaving her to the mercies of Harding, who regarded her life of less value than a sheet of toilet paper. Even though her fear threatened to choke her, she could not bring herself to grovel before another Physics supervisor who was once again going to destroy her life.

Once more she would be forced to defend her own intellectual worth before some dean, another man. How she hated them. This the last turn of the screw, the same scenario repeated with so much higher stakes. Then it had been her reputation, now her life, all on a pack of lies.

Buy her own intellectual credibility with Harding's disgusting schemes? What a demeaning insult. She had been offered that route once before. If she had spread her legs on McReadie's desk, she would be enjoying the fruits of her doctorate right now. No, she would face her judges defiant and alone.

If she could have seen the sorrow in David's heart that very instant it might have given her cause for pause, but in her mind he was wearing McReadie's face, and that was all that mattered, that was all she would see when they met tomorrow for the sacrifice of Abigail Saunders on the altar of their obnoxious piety.

What would happen then?

Harding would try to have her murdered and replaced with someone else, but he would never find her alive. Why not end it all now? Because she wanted to be there to spit in the dean's face when he kicked her out, to tell Petrov what she really thought of him, what she thought of Christians, what she thought of God. The rage and hatred in her heart would be justified, at the price of her life. Damn them to hell. Damn them all to hell.

With her thoughts teetering on insanity, she arrived at her apartment. Throwing open the fridge, she wrenched a bottle of French Riesling out of the door, and transferred its contents to her stomach in all of five minutes. The rage began to dissipate a little, but fear took its place.

Harding would remember that her sexual expertise had failed to salvage her mission. No doubt he would devise what he considered an appropriately perverted end to her life. She felt around her back for her bra strap. Yes, the pill was still there. Better to die at her own hand than by the hand of Harding's sadistic fiends. Another bottle of Riesling followed the first on the same journey, and now Abby was sleepy, very sleepy. She lay down on the comfortable sofa in front of the television and went to sleep.

Makin was waiting.

# CHAPTER 34

The Dean's office could have doubled as a funeral parlour, its heavy dark furniture and sombre grey carpet sucking almost all the light out of the meagre glimmer which came through the high and dirty window in the opposite wall. The present occupants of the room did nothing to dispel the funereal atmosphere either. The Dean, serious, his voice intoned with a sepulchral resonance, some clerk from the Vice Chancellor's office suitably chosen to enhance the solemnity of the occasion, and Abby Saunders, dressed in some fabric which, in contrast to the bright colours she usually wore, would have made the grim reaper feel at home. Finally David Petrov, wearing a dark suit, came through the door carrying a black briefcase.

The dean peered at Abby over the rims of his half-frame glasses.

"Ms. Saunders, it gives me no pleasure to convene this meeting. As doctor Petrov will have informed you, I have received correspondence from the Vice Chancellor at Boston University. I have since made other enquiries at Cornell. Leaving aside the allegations of promiscuity – what you do with your personal sexual life is no concern of mine – I have reason to believe that you falsified your academic record which formed the basis of your studies at this University. Your previous attempt at a doctorate was an abysmal failure, your subsequent postgraduate experiences at Cornell a pack of lies." He paused.

"Under these circumstances I feel we can do no other than discontinue your candidature, that is unless doctor Petrov, your supervisor, has any objections. Speaking to him yesterday I cannot think that he does."

"As a matter of fact I do." David cleared his throat.

There was a stunned silence. The Dean stared at him as though he had grown an extra head, Abby returned from Boston and fixed him with a pair of uncomprehending eyes.

"Not only that," David continued, "I believe it is incumbent on this University to redress the injustice under which Ms. Saunders has suffered for so many years."

Utter silence.

"This, Dean," David said, extracting a discoloured volume from his briefcase, "is a copy of her thesis. Before you say it could be another fabrication, allow me to show you the stains on the cover, bloodstains from where she defended herself against McReadie when he attempted to rape her."

Utter silence.

"I have read this thesis, and far from being an abysmal failure, it is quite excellent. When McReadie publicly declared it worthless he was lying. That he would lie about three years of solid, careful work and dedication produced by his own research student, speaks volumes about his character – or lack of it. I am far more inclined to believe that this young woman has been made the scapegoat in the cover-up which the University no doubt engineered. If you doubt my assessment of her work, you are perfectly at liberty to submit her thesis to professor Jacklin who works in this area, for his own assessment. I have no doubt he will concur."

He glanced across at Abby and found no hint of gratitude in her eyes, which surprised him, then at the Dean who looked as astonished as he felt.

It was he who broke the silence. "This is unexpected, David. Are you quite sure? What about her fictitious academic record at Cornell? I still believe she should be shown the door."

"I cannot condone her deception either, Dean. I ask you to consider. If the University of Boston has gone to the trouble of destroying this woman's chances of academic success in such a faraway location, can you imagine how actively they have performed the same service when she was in the United States? I believe if you ask her she will confirm this."

"Ms. Saunders?" The dean turned towards Abby.

"Every university in America and several on the continent," Abby growled bitterly. "Every job, every single job, every chance. How do you think it feels to be branded a fool and a slut? No, you have no idea," she spat. "You're just another man like all the other men who have ruined my life. What's the point of—"

"Abby!" David exclaimed, glaring at her. "That is no way to speak to the Dean. Whatever other men have done to you, he is not to be included in their number. I do not condone your deception either. It neither adds to your character nor rights a previous wrong. Can't you see that?"

Abby lowered her smouldering eyes and said nothing. This was the justice she was so certain she would never obtain, but her mind refused to process or accept it. All she could feel was the devouring rage which mastered her, a rage which refused to be assuaged by the genuine kindness she had been shown.

The sepulchral tones in the Dean's voice had disappeared. "Young lady, you are not assisting your own case. Are you sure you want to be saddled with this woman, David? Even if what you say is true, I hardly think her character will enhance the tone of this university, and especially your own reputation. I can hardly believe professor Cole should have been so deceived."

"It does seem very odd," David agreed. "Nonetheless, I'm arguing as her supervisor only on purely academic grounds. She has the ability, she has been denied the award of a doctorate which she well and truly deserved. I know you to be a fair minded man. My recommendation is still the same."

There was another long pause.

The clerical assistant from the Vice Chancellor's office now made his one and only contribution. "There can be no question of a fee refund. My department is quite adamant. All private overseas candidates have signed an agreement to that effect."

The dean said nothing for a considerable time. At last, closing the folder that was open on his desk he turned to Abby.

"Very well," he said. "On the recommendation of doctor Petrov, and provided the assessment from professor Jaklin is satisfactory, you may continue your doctorate studies. I warn you that this University takes a dim view of falsified qualifications, Ms. Saunders, and I hope you will take this opportunity to obtain some genuine ones which will serve you well. I think we can get on with our usual business now, can't we?"

"Why, thank you, Dean," Abby's voice dripped with sarcasm. "I promise to be such a good little girl."

David glanced across at her, angry and disappointed.

"Thank you, Dean," he said, apologetically. "I'm grateful, far more grateful than my student would appear to be. Nonetheless, I feel justice has been done. I'm sorry we've taken up your valuable time."

He picked up his briefcase and strode out, far too angry for further conversation.

Outside that mahogany tomb the sun was shining and a cool autumn breeze was blowing up from the sea. Its refreshing touch on his face helped calm the angry indignation he felt, but enough of it remained to make him wait for a certain Abigail Saunders who emerged on the scene a few moments later, her head high, still mastered by the unjustified rage in her heart.

David reached out and snatched her wrist, far from gently. "Not so fast. I want to speak to you someplace without a lot of company."

She turned towards him, the same sarcastic smile on her face. Lifting her other arm, she held it out seductively in front of him.

"Why, David," she purred, "do you want to bruise my other wrist as well? Some men do like to hurt their women before they get on."

He flung the captured wrist away from him. "You're disgusting."

"Listen to yourself," she screamed as he turned away from her. "I said, listen!" The fire in her eyes matched the rage in her voice.

"Not here." David hissed, and set off at a cracking pace towards the grassy slope near Paul's College, not really caring if she followed or not. She did. Reaching a semi-secluded spot under the shade of a Morton Bay fig he turned towards the furious woman, ready to tell her exactly how he felt, but Abby got in first.

"Think you're some bright knight in shining armour?" she screamed, her voice trembling with rage. "You sanctimonious hypocrite. Redress the injustice done? By giving me the honour of working with you? How dare you believe for a second you could redress what's been done to me!"

"As bad as that?" he shouted back, striving to master his escalating fury. "No wonder you can't tell when people are decent towards you – you've forgotten what gratitude is. Did McReadie do that to you too? I doubt it. Years of gnawing on your own wounds did that, biting at every hand held out to you. You were grossly discourteous towards the dean who showed you every consideration."

 "As bad as that?" Abby's eyes narrowed, and her nails bit into her hands as she clenched her fists in rage. "As bad as that?" she screamed again. "Your sanctimonious tiny mind can't conceive of what has happened to me. First McReadie tries it on, then I get kicked out of my degree. Next, my father throws me out of home. I was such an embarrassment. My own mother screams to all her socialite world that her daughter – who happened to be a virgin - is a promiscuous slut. I crossed the continent and tried to continue my studies. Thirty universities, all enthusiastic until they heard from Boston, two hundred and thirty job applications, same thing."

Her breath was coming in short, sharp gasps, and she could feel her whole body trembling. "Two hundred and sixty rejections – all from men, oh, with such flattering descriptions of my character – loose woman, whore, slut, promiscuous she-devil. So inventive, each one another knife through my heart!"

She thrust her arms out in front in a demeaning gesture. "Then like the great guru Petrov says I started gnawing at my own wounds a bit, sinful, pathetic little shit that I was. Of course you would have just said a prayer, wouldn't you? But I took drugs instead, and it worked. When you can't feel the wounds there's nothing to gnaw on, is there? But drugs are such expensive things, aren't they? Do you know how a young woman pays for drugs, Petrov? Come on, use your imagination."

Her story had shocked him. Underneath the heated fury in her face he began to see something else, an abused woman robbed of her self-worth as she had been robbed of her academic achievement, denigrated and cruelly rejected, denied the slightest comfort of love or grace.

"Well?" she shouted.

"I… I suppose—"

"Whore, Petrov," she screamed. "I became a whore. You want to know why I hate men? Men who rejected me on lies, men who emptied their lust into my young body and hurt me while they did it? Now you know. I *am* disgusting. Far too disgusting for the likes of Mr. Perfect Petrov. Unforgiven and unforgivable, heading straight for hell. Don't you want to go and find some stones somewhere?"

She was screaming at him, her whole body shaking, her tearless eyes wide and staring, her mouth set in a hard, bitter line. For a whole ten seconds there was silence, to be broken only by David's softly spoken words.

"My father was a drug addict who wanted me aborted. My mother was a prostitute. I loved her very much and forgave her."

Those softly spoken words seared through Abby's mind like a knife. She stared at him, unable to speak. A dull pain gripped her around the heart and made her breathing difficult. Time seemed to stand completely still. All she could see was his sad face, his eyes holding her with a tenderness she had never known in any man ever before. Suddenly one enormous tear squeezed out of her right eye, ran unbidden down her cheek, and splashed cold on the back of her hand. Abby felt her body flinch with shock. It was as though some unseen fingers had reached into her mind, grasped hold of all the pain and anger which had up to that moment controlled her, and wrenched them out of her head. All that remained were those words reverberating over and over, 'my mother was a prostitute ... I loved her... I forgave her'...

How long she stayed suspended in this state she could not afterwards tell, but eventually the rest of the world returned, slowly, at a distance. Only that sad, lovely face was close. As a woman waking from a nightmare she stumbled towards him.

"Please tell me about your mother," she pleaded softly.

Kneeling down at his feet, she reached up and took hold of his hands in her own, pulling them towards her. "Please," she begged again, "Tell me about your mother. I want to know... how you could forgive her."

Silently he sat down beside her, stunned at the extraordinary transformation which had taken place. Her voice was so changed David could have believed a completely different woman had taken up residence in her body.

"Please." Her eyes were begging him, the moisture from that single tear still lingering.

He did, beginning with the things Lydia had told him about her, and ending the terrible night that she died. "She asked God to forgive her, Abby, and I'm sure He did," he said sadly. "Then sometime later she died in her sister's arms."

"I can't cry." Abby choked on the words.

"Why are you telling me this?"

"Because I really, really want to, but it won't come."

There was a sort of desperate sadness in her face, a forlorn helplessness that defied description. Not knowing what to say, he stretched out his arm and wrapped it around her waist, pulling her closer. Suddenly she flipped herself into his lap, her arms wrapped around his shoulders as though he was the last tree trunk in a tidal wave, her head buried in his neck. He could feel her heart thumping in her breast, her body trembling. Only for a few seconds, then she rolled herself off onto the grass beside him.

"I didn't want you to think..." she stammered.

"I didn't. Are you still on drugs?"

"No... and no to the other question you're about to ask."

"You certainly pulled the wool over professor Cole."

It was a trick statement, and David was never sure why he said it right then. Perhaps he wanted just a little more assurance that the change in her was not another front, not another deception.

"I didn't deceive her at all," Abby confessed quietly. "She saw right through me in five minutes. She wrote you a note which told you the truth about me, but I stole it and got someone I know to imitate her handwriting." She shuddered. "She's the most terrifying creature I've ever met."

There was a long pause.

"I... don't hate you, David... I... I... *can't* hate you." Her voice was so quiet, almost frightened. David had to strain to hear the words.

He put his arm around her waist again and pulled her gently towards him. "I'm glad. Perhaps this is the beginning of a friendship. What do you think?"

"Yes, a friendship." She turned her face towards him, her eyes large and serious. "The only one I have."

She rested her head against his shoulder, and for a very long time neither of them needed to say anything at all.

❄ ❄ ❄

There was a different atmosphere in the lab that evening, not nearly so many words, but so much more communication. Something had happened to the relationship between them, and neither appreciated just how profound had been the change. It would be completely incorrect to say that Abby found herself falling in love with him, because she simply had no way to tell. She had so often used the language and devices created to express genuine love for exactly the opposite purpose, that they had become bereft of all significance and meaning. All she was aware of, was a growing certainty that this man was someone she needed, someone in whose presence she felt the first beginnings of a new dignity, the first stirrings of feelings in a long dead heart. With these beginnings came endings as well. She no longer felt the hatred, the desire to belittle, to seduce, to overpower, only to stay, to grow, to come back to life.

That night in her apartment she had time to further reflect on the strange happenings of the day. She had phoned Harry to say that all was well, listened with disgust as he attributed her success to her sexual expertise, and hung up in his ear before he finished fantasising. Her mind went back to that moment under the fig tree when time had stopped, when all the sordid reality of terrorists and seduction and Harding and the CIA had totally disappeared from her world, and in their blessed absence she had felt alive for the first time in so many years.

Why had she screamed all those lies about being a whore? Was it just to make David feel terrible? At the time it might have been, yet now she perceived a deeper truth beneath her angry words. Her drug addiction had brought her to the very brink of prostitution, but then her life had suddenly changed direction... or had it? She hated it when people like Harding treated her like a whore. Yet deep inside she realised it was the way she regarded herself, and her private self-loathing lay behind her public intolerance. Yes, of course she had lied, but her lies had nothing whatsoever to do with her employer. To tell David the truth was to lose him, and deep down in her heart she carried the conviction that to be separated from him now meant falling back into the abyss.

Then there was that tear.

That tear, just one. Even now she could feel its cold splash on the back of her hand. Why had that happened? Yet when she had wanted to cry so badly, not a single tear could she summon to her eyes, even though they ached from trying. So this man, this extraordinary, gentle man was a terrorist? How utterly preposterous. That was the CIA all over, paranoid, suspicious, devoid of all trust, and as a consequence blinded to the obvious truth.

How would the story end? One day surely they would find the real culprit and David would be free. Then she would be free, because in all the uncertainties of the world this alone she knew, that she was leaving forever the life she had led. Would David be the one to walk this new road with her? She could hope for that, but if not she would try the road alone, not looking back. In the meantime she would luxuriate in the joy of studying with him, biding her time, keeping up the pretence with her masters until the situation changed and she could be free of them. She wondered if Harry would notice the change in her. No, she could deceive him. Harding was a different matter, a dangerous enemy who had to be placated with great care. Day at a time, Abby, day at a time. She cleaned her teeth, undressed, threw herself on the bed and dragged the doona over her. Minutes later she was sound asleep. There was no appointment with Henry Makin that night.

※ ※ ※

For his part David was equally uncertain of his own feelings, but for a completely different reason. He knew Abby well enough and not at all. Well enough to know she was a very troubled young woman. His words had brought about a transformation which had endured – at least to the end of the day.

But what would tomorrow bring?

There still remained the unanswered question as to who or what lay behind Abby, and her explanation of the forged note, whilst doing much to grow his trust in her honesty, had by no means dispelled all doubt. Over all hung the one great unanswered question. Why was she there at all? He wanted to believe it was simply her attempt to escape and get on with her life, but Sarah had other ideas, and when Sarah said something, only a complete fool would not take her very seriously.

Yet he found it almost impossible to believe Abby could be duplicitous to that extent. If that were true, everything she had said to him was a cold, calculated lie. In any case, if some powerful organisation had indeed sent her to investigate him, wasn't it better they learn the truth? He had done nothing wrong. But then Abby would be nothing more than an actress, each empty word a cruel deception, their friendship a farce. Surely not. His heart rebelled at the thought.

Even so, she was damaged goods in practically every other way. Lydia would throw up her hands in horror if she knew. Geoff would tell him to have nothing to do with her. Sarah would call him a fool, and he was, damn it, he was. Why did his heart feel so relieved when she had been allowed to stay? Why had he shared such personal and private details of his own life with her? Why did he want to see joy in her eyes and hear the musical laughter in her voice? Oh, but he did, and he had found himself constantly trying to make her smile, make her laugh. Even the touch of her hand was pleasant. He thought of her head against his shoulder, so eloquent in silence, and wished he could feel it there right now.

On the other hand she hated Christianity. He should have let her go. He had made a dangerously foolish decision, and in his head he knew it, a decision which could even be construed as sinful, as poking his nose right into temptation. Yet once again his heart rebelled at that conclusion. At least she had never made the slightest attempt to seduce him again. That would be the test, the point at which he would cut all ties and build oceans of distance between them. Should he let Sarah know what had happened? Yes, he ought to, and no, not tonight.

❄ ❄ ❄

Abby bounced into his office the next morning with two cups of coffee in her hands, laughter in her voice, and a beautiful smile in her eyes. She sat down in the chair next to him and dumped the extra coffee right on top of the papers he was trying to mark.

"Enough," she laughed. "Time for a coffee break. Do you like this dress?"

She stood up, twirled around and sat down.

"Yes, I do," David said, smiling appreciatively. "It suits you, and the matching top. Brings out the colour of your lovely blue eyes."

"Why thank you, kind sir. How are the students doing this morning? How many hours have you been here already? Why not give me half and I'll do them when I get home?"

So continued a very pleasant conversation, and if anything it seemed to David the transformation begun beneath the fig tree had been steadily working during the night.  He could not remember her looking so radiant, her eyes sparkling, her voice musical and happy, the spring in her step which made the long dress with yellow flowers spin around her feet as she walked.

They spent the morning writing the paper they were planning, and if David had ever doubted her intelligence before, by morning tea he had reached the conclusion that she was a good deal smarter than him. Her mind was razor sharp, darting here and there, pulling data together, calculating final values, changing the constants in their predictive equations and formulating reasons which explained the changes.

By the time they reached lunch it was David who was the student, listening with rapt attention as his teacher explained her latest ideas. They went out the back of the building, under the scaffolding which was still in place, then over to the Wentworth Café to collect their lunch. They carried their sandwiches and iced tea back to their tree in the grounds of Paul's college which, by unspoken understanding, had become a very special place. They ate and drank and laughed, and Abby forgot all about the CIA, and David forgot all about her sordid past in the mutual delight of each other's companionship. Abby told him funny stories about the Brahmin class in Boston which she had completely forgotten, and David told her some funny stories about his students, and Abby told him he needed a haircut, and David told her that she had nice toes, and Abby pulled his shoe off to make a comparison.

All that week you could not have found a happier couple of friends. Whether gathering data in the evenings or writing up in the mornings, or marking student assignments, they seemed to find joy in whatever task lay to hand. Even a casual observer would have noticed an unspoken resonance between them, a blending of purpose and function without the need for many spoken words. The weekend came with regret. David asked Abby if she would go out with him on Saturday night, and Abby had refused with much more regret than she expressed. She was going to see a girl she had travelled with ages ago. It was a complete untruth, but going out to dinner with her target had always been her way of beginning a seduction, and so she deliberately refrained from doing it, as much for her sake as for his.

# CHAPTER 35

The following week would have continued in much the same enjoyable manner, but the tornado which had begun this whole affair had by no means blown out its fury, and in the last sorry chapter, CIA operative Abigail Saunders was to play a sad and crucial role. It all began with a phone call to the Sydney hotel where Norman Harding was staying. For a whole week he had dismissed the bleating coming from the Whitehouse to return stateside and report.

"The contract you negotiated has run into difficulties, please come back to the office," he was told.

"The director is due to hold a crucial sales meeting in forty eight hours. Your presence is required," he was told.

"Sales figures indicate a deplorable failure in your area. You are required to present your report within twenty four hours or face instant dismissal," he was told.

Harding had ignored them all. It was for that reason he was loathe to pick up the phone when it rang in his room. Placing his finger on the hook so that he could hang up instantly, he answered the call.

"This is George Russell, Mr. Fredricksen. I'm calling from a box in Alice Springs. I believe I may have the solution to the sales problems we've been having."

"I am relieved to hear it," Harding continued evenly. "Pray continue."

"In order to check the prospectus I will need one of our satellite companies, number twenty nine, to be reactivated for business," Russell said. "They can only do that from Paradise Gardens."

"And what about our friends at Noosa? Can't they do the job from there?" Harding said, using the same coded sales talk.

"Apparently not, Mr. Fredricksen, and it requires your authorisation," Russell assured him. "I have a message to give the company which is time dependent. Can you help?"

"I cannot ring Paradise Gardens from this phone," Harding answered, frowning. "I will have to go there. You had better be right, Russell. Pick me up this evening at the Alice. I think the flight gets in at four thirty."

He hung up instantly and dragged on his coat. The flight to Alice Springs left in a couple of hours and he hadn't had lunch. He rang the airport and booked his seat.

❈ ❈ ❈

It was hot, very hot. Harding walked slowly across the tarmac at the Alice to find George Russell waiting for him with a car. With no more than a curt nod he slid into the front seat and shut the door. It was cool inside the vehicle, thank goodness. Only when they were clear of the town did Harding enquire as to why Russell had the hide to drag him all the way out here into this God forsaken desert.

"Director," Russell said nervously, "I would ask you to trust me for just a few hours more. There is a possibility that I'm wrong, and one test is required to put my theory to the proof. If it turns out that I am correct, I can safely say our problems are over."

"I'm truly amazed, George. Just exactly what do you want to send via satellite twenty nine and to whom?" Harding asked evenly.

"I don't want to send it anywhere, Director, just to the satellite. All the others have been deactivated with the Presidential Silence, and I know you're not supposed to activate any of them, but it's just that I can't perform this test with them all down."

"I take your point, George. Okay, so we activate twenty nine. Do you want to send the message from Pine Gap?"

"No, Director," Russell continued, "it must be sent from Nuralungunya, from the same console used to launch the missiles. I'll need your permission to do that too, Sir."

"That may not be so easy to organise," Harding said, frowning. "The chiefs might not like it either."

"I'm really begging you not to tell them Sir, not to tell anyone," Russell said anxiously. "I think it would be in the best interests of everyone if no one else had any idea what was going on."

"Does everyone include me, George?"

"Especially you, Sir. There's one – actually two – more requests. The second only if my theory is correct. Do we have an operative close to Petrov?"

"Her slippers are parked under his bed most of the time."

"Could you contact her and ask her to make sure Petrov is doing his experiments at six forty five p.m. precisely? Then I want her to monitor the digital line Petrov uses to transfer his data to the computer in another building. Could you do that?"

"It depends. What is this message you want to send? As soon as any encrypted data goes out there, Dianne and her team of desperados will have it in their hot and sweaty little hands."

"It's not encrypted, Sir, plain ASCII, plain language," Russell explained.

"Once again you amaze me, George. And what is the actual content of this message?"

"Doris, I'm bringing the pumpkins back home." Russell stammered a little.

"I beg your pardon? Have you lost your mind?" Harding's normally impassive face registered an expression of sheer disbelief.

"You want me to open up the entire secure facility at Nuralungunya so you can tell Doris you're bringing pumpkins? Is this what you're saying, or is the heat getting to my brain?"

"Sir, I want to see if exactly that message appears on Petrov's screen. I have every reason to believe it will. I need someone there so that they can check that it has."

"Very well, George, we will play it your way," Harding sighed heavily. "I take it you have found out how Petrov can intercept the signals we send to the satellite? That in itself would be worth knowing."

"I prefer to refrain from any comment until the test is performed," Russell said nervously.

"Six forty five, tonight? Turn the car around, George. I have to get to a public call box."

❋ ❋ ❋

Harry had called Abby in to Martin Place to give her the instructions. She wasn't in a very receptive mood. The man was innocent, how was some message going to appear on his screen? Was this some filthy attempt to frame him? He had no idea how the other garbage appeared on their dedicated line, only that it was a damned nuisance when it did. Would Harry please tell her what was going on and stop patronising her?

# THE PETROV EFFECT

Harry couldn't answer her for the simple reason he didn't know. He kept emphasising that his instructions came directly from Harding, and if Abby had any sense she would follow them to the letter, even if she didn't want to. The fact that she objected so strongly added weight to his belief that she had been emotionally compromised by Petrov's skill as a lover. Never had sex? She didn't expect him to actually believe that, did she? How else could he have blinded her eyes to the truth?

The slanging match began to heat up after that until Harry, who had quite enough, told her he was reporting her non-compliance to Harding and let him sort her out. It was a trump card he would never think of playing, of course, but Abby's natural distrust of anything male – with one single exception – told her she had reached her negotiating limit.

"We normally start our ionospheric experiments at six forty five," she said, "so that isn't a problem, but how do you expect me to pass this phantom message on to you? I can't just pick up the phone and say, hello Harry, here it is."

"I'll meet you in the Ladies toilet any time after six forty five," Harry replied. "The cubicle which has a piece of toilet paper on the floor outside it. Write down the message and pass it under the door. No words."

Abby grunted her reluctant compliance, and hurled herself through the office door.

# CHAPTER 36

A bby went home a worried woman. Just what game was her employer playing? She trusted Harding less than a mad rattlesnake. What was he trying to do? Was David in danger? She had always insisted David was innocent – to Harry.

Suddenly a terrible thought struck her with some force.

The picture of David which Harding had received from her was completely different to the one she had given Harry, and unwittingly, for no other purpose than ensuring her own safety, she had jeopardised David's. Surely Harding would not act on a complete lack of evidence? What if he had begun to manufacture his own? No, the CIA wouldn't want to destroy an innocent man?

Then another sobering thought.

They had selected the Deadly Angel to target him, the same woman whom they knew hated men, the same woman who had already sent an innocent man to a horrible death. Was this what she was meant to do to David? She must tell Harding the truth without delay, tell him herself, but how to contact him? There were no secure communications available for some reason. Why? Somehow David's experiments had upset the satellite in the path of the beam, and that had caused every other secure system to be shut down. But why? After several sleepless hours under her doona Abby was still no closer to an answer.

The sleepless night had taken its toll, and in the morning Abby found she was still muzzy headed, even after her second cup of coffee. She walked into David's office and sat down in her usual place, opened his computer and began work on their joint paper. The clarity with which she had worked on it the day before was lacking, however, and its absence annoyed her greatly. David had been so impressed with her ability. Today he was going be very under impressed. A short time later the gentleman himself walked into the room, threw his notes down on top of the filing cabinet near the door, and thumped the unfortunate piece of furniture hard with his fist.

"They're impossible," he groaned, exasperated. "I spent six hours preparing that lecture, and I might as well have spent six minutes. I'm going to sit down and write a really foul assignment for next week, and pity help them if they don't do it. Sorry Abby. I shouldn't have poured all that over you."

"It's really okay," she said, smiling her understanding. "Look, David, I've had an awful night, couldn't sleep, and I feel like a limp dishrag this morning. Can we go for a coffee? I've already had two and they haven't worked at all. I don't want to drag the chain today, but I can't even understand the changes we made to this thing yesterday."

She gave him another tired smile, and David returned it with a frustrated one. Abby stood up, squeezed his arm, and without saying another word they headed out for the Wentworth Café. Half an hour later found them sitting in the sun on the grass outside Paul's College. It was too cold to be under the shade of the fig tree that morning. Abby stretched herself out on the grass, shut her eyes and lifted her arm across her forehead. David sat close beside her, his body unconsciously touching hers. Taking advantage of her lack of vision, he allowed his eyes to travel slowly upwards from her toes, pausing at each highlight to admire her truly lovely figure. Her breasts, softly rounded under a blue cardigan, rose and fell gently as she breathed, her nose twitched a little, her lips, soft and full, were held in a slight beguiling smile. For an insane moment he wanted to lean over and touch them with his own, caress that pretty face, lie down beside her and feel the warmth of her body against him. He banished the thought from his mind and deliberately turned away, but in doing so felt her hand reach out and touch his own.

"You're such a gentleman, David," Abby said softly.

He could feel the blood surging up into his face. Somehow she knew what he had been thinking. How was that possible? His thoughts were interrupted by the sound of soft laughter beside him, and he turned back to find her body shaking, her arm now over her mouth, her eyes shining.

"How did you know?" he asked, marinating in embarrassment.

"I felt you turn away, don't ask me how, and I saw your face had gone pink. It's alright, David. I don't mind you looking at me, and I'm glad the sight pleases you."

"I shouldn't have been staring, but I find it hard to take my eyes off you sometimes. It's not just the sight of you either, it's ... hard to explain. I like being with you, more than I should."

"More than you should?" A frown crossed her smooth brow.

"I'm a Christian, Abby, and I know you're not exactly fond of God. That creates a problem for me, for us. We have two fundamentally different ways of thinking, and that difference puts us on two different paths. I don't want to end up by hurting you like the other men in your past."

"I like the path I'm on, David, at least since we became friends," she said seriously. "I thought you liked it too. Not exactly fond of God? Why should I be? He didn't lift a finger to stop all the dreadful things which happened in my life. Can you explain that to me? Sometimes I don't believe he exists at all, because if He does He doesn't like me, and I don't like Him."

"I can't explain it to you, Abby," David replied gently. "All I know is that God is real. You ask me why I believe in him? He explains my world, the universe around me. The purely physical description is incomplete, and adding the metaphysical makes it so much better. The other reason is I'm convinced there was a man called Jesus who claimed to be God in human flesh. He rose from the dead like he said he would, and anyone who can do that is worth listening to."

"David, can you do me a favour and change the subject?" Abby said gently, frowning. "Perhaps one day I will come to see life your way, but I can't yet. Perhaps that's why you're here, to show me something that so far I've been unable to see. I need a few more nice things to happen before I can forgive God for wrecking my life. I know life hasn't been easy for you either. In some way our lives have been opposites, but now we've found one another. We've become friends, haven't we?"

"Yes we have. Very close friends in such a short space of time."

"You have to remember what I was, David," Abby said earnestly. "Your life was hard, but there was love in it, and because of that you know what love is. My life has never had any love in it, and as a result I have to learn what love is, because I don't know what it is. I can't give what I don't comprehend to anyone, even God. Can you understand a little? But I'm learning what friendship is, and I like it very much." Her blue eyes were large and entreating.

"I like it very much too, Abby." He smiled at her, reached out and ran his hand softly over her hair. "We had better get back to the paper. Do you know, I think by the end of the week it will be quite suitable for publication? Petrov and Saunders – has a nice ring to it, doesn't it?"

She raised her arm and let him pull her up onto her feet. Dusting herself down she turned quickly and gave him a soft kiss on the cheek. "It has a very nice ring to it, David, and that's not just on top of a paper."

It was a happy couple who returned to David's office that morning. Abby found her muzzy head had cleared, and David found her quick mind stimulated his own, so the progress they made was rapid indeed. By the end of the week the task would be complete.

It was the only paper Petrov and Saunders would ever publish.

The evening was a different story. Abby was dreading the impending collision of the two worlds she had so far successfully managed to keep separate in her life. Now she had to spy on him, and she hated doing it. David could sense the change in her, and put it down to her lack of sleep. In one way it was fortunate she had told him of it in the morning, for it gave her the excuse she needed. At exactly six forty five they pulsed the ionosphere, and immediately their stream of data went out to Basser via the dedicated line. The terminal beeped, and the laptop screen flashed with the message

'Data corrupt – processing terminated'

"Damn it," David exclaimed. They had been trouble free for so long, now this. He turned his head to the screen monitoring the dedicated line and stared open mouthed in disbelief. "What the blazes is going on?" he muttered at length.

Abby came over from the transmitter triggering console and stared at it herself. The data read:

0E6DFC5A8DCE59B5FEAC0A0A0AFFFFFF0000
DC06C4A7D0C632B4AB9F20ACB748B10476A82900
Doris, I'm bringing the pumpkins back home.
00FFFF000000 0A 0A 0A 00 00 00 00

"It's someone in the building," Abby shouted. "I've got to go to the toilet. I'll check to see if there are any lights in the offices on this floor. You check the ones below."

She belted out of the door. As soon as she was in the corridor Abby allowed the rage she felt to appear on her face. Running down its length without bothering to check a single office, she burst into the Ladies toilet, saw the piece of toilet paper on the floor outside the middle cubicle and hammered on the door with both her fists. "Come on out of there Harry," she demanded.

The door flew open. Two powerful hands reached out and grabbed her wrists in a vice like grip. "What part of no talking didn't you understand?" Harry hissed into her face.

314

"There's no one else in the whole damn building," Abby exclaimed angrily. "What is this nonsense, Harry? I'm sick of being fed bullshit. What's going on? Tell me!"

"What was the message?" He squeezed her wrists so that they hurt.

"Go on, Harry," she goaded, "bruise them both and blow my cover. What do you want me to tell David? There was a pervert in the 'loo?"

"What was the blasted message?" Harry insisted, squeezing harder. "I'm telling you, Abby, I'm getting really pissed off with your calf love for this bloody terrorist."

"Let go my wrists or you'll never know," Abby threatened loudly.

"Alright." He flung her wrists away, and Abby began to massage each of them with her other hand.

"Doris, I'm bringing the pumpkins back home," she muttered reluctantly.

"Don't try to be smart with me." Harry grabbed her wrist again, pulled her towards him and slapped her across the face. The hand he had forgotten to capture treated him exactly the same way with a good deal more force than strictly necessary. They stood there glaring at one another, until Harry let her other wrist go and stepped away.

"Alright," he sighed angrily, "you want to play silly buggers with me, go ahead, but Harding won't think it's so funny, and then you won't either."

"That was the message." Abby continued massaging her wrists, glowering at him. "Why don't you go up and see for yourself? David is racing around the building searching for some other occupant who might have sent it on our dedicated line. Go on, check it out if you don't believe me." Her eyes blazed. "Now what's this garbage all about Harry? What's Harding doing? Trying to set David up? He's innocent, I tell you. He has no idea what's going on. He's as much a terrorist as I am. Why can't you get it through your thick head?"

"I haven't a clue as to what's going on," Harry muttered.

"Now for goodness sake get him back in the lab so I can move out of here. I'm sorry about your face, and you'd better make it up before you go back to lover boy."

Suddenly he found himself pushed violently backwards, Abby's hands gripping his t-shirt near his neck. He felt his back thump against the tiled wall, her face nearly touching his.

"We... are ... not... lovers!" She spat the words into his face.

He pushed her off roughly, grabbing her wrists again and throwing them off his clothing.

"Well go back to whatever you do with one another," he said angrily. "Look, I'm as much in the dark as you are. Harding tells me what he wants me to know, nothing else. Now get out of here before there's a showdown you really don't want to have."

Abby went slowly out the door, pulling her cardigan sleeves over the marks Harry had made, her heart still racing and her body trembling with rage. Had Harding finally lost his tenuous hold on sanity? When she got back to the lab David was already there, quite out of breath, and to hide her anger she pretended to be the same.

"Nothing," he panted. "Not a single office was occupied. This garbage must be coming from outside the building, but if that's the case, how is it possible for our transmitter to trigger it?"

"Could it have something to do with our phantom satellite?" Abby said, pretending breathlessness.

"That's an idea," David said thoughtfully, "but how could the satellite interface with us? Besides, this nonsense isn't coming from our receiver, it's coming down the dedicated line. Look, I can prove it. I've backed this set of data up on our local storage, just in case the line went funny. Wait, I'll disconnect the dedicated line and connect our storage unit to the screen, then we can see exactly what came down from our receiver."

David made the change, and Abby watched as the stream of hexadecimal numbers scrolled down the display, numbers without the slightest reference to pumpkins going home or Doris.

She nodded her complete agreement. "What else could be mucked around by the transmitter?"

"Nothing," David said, scratching his head. "Its beam is very narrow, has to be for reasons we both know. I think you're right about that reflection being a satellite, and if that's the case it's probably some military one, or at least one that isn't supposed to be there. But if we knocked its systems into next week how could it transmit to anyone? And besides, Doris doesn't sound like someone who uses military satellites to find out if the pumpkins are coming home."

Abby suddenly burst into fits of laughter. "Perhaps pumpkins are code for nuclear missiles, and Doris is some covert operator who has paid millions of dollars for them."

"Or perhaps Doris is some covert operator who has a passion for pumpkins."

If Harry had been anywhere in the vicinity he would have no doubt been somewhat puzzled by the gales of laughter coming from the lab, as two serious scientists constructed more and more hilarious scenarios to explain the mysterious message.

❄ ❄ ❄

A certain Norman Harding however, receiving the news from a telephone in his hotel in Alice Springs, didn't think the message was funny at all. He phoned another number. George Russel picked up.

"You were perfectly correct, George," he said. "Message received as expected. Now perhaps you can reveal all."

"Can I meet you for a drink somewhere?" Russell asked him. "Your hotel has a good bar."

"In five minutes, George."

The two men selected a table well away from the crowd of tourists who were telling each other and everyone else just how much they had enjoyed the golden sunset reflected off the walls of King's Canyon, and how much they had not enjoyed the bus trip back when the air conditioning had broken down.

George lifted his beer to his lips, took a long drink and put it down. "I know this is a strange request, Director," he said a trifle nervously. "There's a street in Sydney called Redfern avenue. Somewhere along its length there's a manhole cover. Under that there's a pit – probably quite a long one, with a cable running its length."

"Your omniscience is becoming a trifle disturbing, George," Harding murmured. "I seek enlightenment as to where this interesting information is about to lead."

"The cable is the main optical feed that transfers phone and data to everything west of the city. It's a big cable. I would like someone to go down that manhole and see if they can find one of these."

He took a photo out of his pocket. Harding studied the small grey box with the odd connectors on it and handed it back. "What exactly is that, George?"

"It's an optical line splitter. Allows data from one optic cable to be fed into two others and vice versa."

"And this explains what has just happened – how?" Harding's eyebrows were raised.

"Director, would you allow me to answer that question when we have confirmed the existence of such an item?" Russell asked. "If it's not there I will look the complete fool I am, and we'll have to go back to the drawing board."

"That's unkind of you, George," Harding murmured again, "but I must admit your last unlikely prediction was deadly accurate. Tell me, if this box is where you think it is, do we have our answer? Has Petrov set this whole thing up by himself, or are there others involved with him?"

"I don't believe he's set anything up, Director. I think the man is completely innocent of any deliberate attempt to subvert our communications."

"That opinion is not shared by many others, George."

"I am aware of that, Director. Now, can you organise someone to look for this splitter?"

"Consider it done, George," Harding nodded. "Our recently formed Australian Anti-Terrorist unit will be on the job tomorrow morning. I will meet you somewhere with the information, somewhere private. Do you know Alice Spring?"

"This is Alice Springs, Director. Our hotel is—"

"No, George. The town is named after a spring, Alice Spring. It's near the old Telegraph station. Can you find it? I'll see you there at six o'clock tomorrow afternoon. Thanks for the beer, George."

Harding strolled back to his room, leaving his communications expert to order another beer. George was nearly sure they would find the box he had described, and he was completely certain his boss would hate the truth when he heard it. Harding had invested a great deal of money and time on his terrorist hypothesis, not to mention his own personal reputation. How would he react to being so totally wrong? George shuddered. Perhaps he would simply refuse to believe it, and more unnecessary mayhem would ensue.

Suddenly he remembered the arrangement he had agreed to with Peter Lawson, and decided to send him an encrypted copy of his report. He flipped out his mobile phone to check the name and address of the company. *Lawson said backup was important, and he was right,* George thought to himself. He would visit the local post office and shove the lot in an express courier bag, using the agreed sender name of doctor Samuel Townsend. With Lawson in the know, Harding could not afford to ignore the truth. By the time Lawson received the message the existence of the device would have been confirmed in any case.

He sighed. That such a brouhaha could have been initiated from this remote and tiny hiccup would be preposterous indeed, were it not the truth.

Back in his hotel room Harding rang the AAT number in Canberra. He had thought carefully on how to frame his request. This deadly terrorist cell which had been corrupting satellite communications, had also been active in monitoring certain telephone traffic for their own subversive purposes. To do this they had installed a device – Harding described the device in great detail – on the main western optic fibre line from Sydney. This device compromised the security of the nation, and he was sharing this intel with the AAT as a gesture of helpful goodwill. Could the AAT organise to confirm the existence of this device, and could they do so immediately? He gave them his hotel number to report back to. No, this wasn't a secure line, and it was west of the city, and yes, it was possible that the terrorists has already intercepted their conversation so the AAT had better be quick.

※ ※ ※

The next afternoon at precisely six p.m., Harding strolled from his car through the car park, past the quaint wooden buildings of the Old Telegraph Station, across the dry red-brown ground behind them and up to the banks of Alice Spring. The afternoon sun painted the rocks on the other side in reddish gold, their glory reflected in the brown waters of the Spring. George Russell was already there. Harding joined him.

"The item you predicted was exactly where you said it would be, George," he said evenly. "Now, would you do the director of the CIA the courtesy of explaining just what this brouhaha is all about?"

The worried expression on George's face betrayed the complete lack of excitement or satisfaction at hearing his predictions confirmed. He stared out at the still waters in silence for some time.

"I asked myself," he began, as if addressing nobody in particular, "why did Nuralungunya have a telephone line?"

"A telephone line?" Harding queried.

"You recall when Claydon first made contact when all hell broke loose. He called on a public telephone line from Nuralungunya."

"Indeed he did. Lucky there was one in existence or we would be sheltering in a bunker right now, George, instead of admiring this tranquil scene."

"Err, quite. Now as I was saying," George continued, "I thought, why does a secure facility, whose location is known only to a few in the Australian government, a top security area, have an open telephone line when all its communications are via ultra-secure fire-walled encrypted lines to satellites? It took me a long while to find out, but eventually I located the original contracts which set up the place, contracts which we drew up and which the Australian government, always willing to please big brother agreed to."

He paused, weighing his words carefully. "I guess we didn't want to tell them we planned to set up an entire satellite communications system. It was a bit touch and go in those early years. Pine Gap wasn't exactly the flavour of the month with the general Australian public. Anyway, the original contract specified half a dozen telephone lines and three high speed secure, dedicated data lines, two to Pine Gap and one to Sydney."

"What on Earth for?" Some of Harding's evenness was missing in his voice.

"The one to Sydney went out to the Overseas Satellite facility at Belrose. The Australian Government set up a dedicated secure channel that went out over their large Pacific dish, to be picked up by our satellites in the Pacific, then relayed to the U.S."

Russell took a deep breath. "The point is, that channel was never shut down, it's just been unused for years. Then I took a closer look at the communications software attached to the supreme command centre at Nuralungunya, and it works like this. Ultra-top secret comms are sent out via Pine Gap then via satellite twenty nine on to our Pacific satellites and so on – we already knew that."

Russell took another deep breath. "What we didn't know, is how the software behaves if there is an unresolvable error on that pathway. The software searches for another channel then sends via that. In this case the other channel was the optic fibre cable to Belrose. When Petrov activated his transmitter he took out satellite twenty nine. It sent back – via Pine Gap – an unrecoverable error message, so the software switched to the optic fibre line. Our top security data went out via Belrose into our network."

He paused, watching Harding's face. "The next bit is tricky. I knew that somehow Petrov's data line had become attached to our own secure feed, but how? I searched back through the Sydney papers and I came across this incident in nineteen ninety when a company, Wild Bore Services, cut the main optic data line to the West in two places. It caused a furore, and they repaired it as fast as they could – too fast. The technicians must have miscounted their connections, and to make up for the mismatch, they installed a splitter, normally something which would not have made the slightest difference, because optic fibres can carry an enormous bandwidth of data. But in this case, and by a most unfortunate coincidence, the line they patched into was our very own secure one from Nuralungunya. That's why I wanted confirmation. It's a long shot, but it happened. The only thing Petrov did was to locate his transmitter directly under satellite twenty nine."

"I take it you have disconnected this secure optic line, George?" Harding asked quietly.

"I called in at Nuralungunya before I came here. The line has been deactivated. I did it personally. Somehow Petrov will have to be told he's interfering with our satellite, and when he shifts his transmitter all our secure network can come back on line."

"Thank you, George. A nice piece of work," he said, smiling. Suddenly he pointed towards the Spring. "Look at that, you don't often see a Darta bird so far south."

"Where?"

"On the opposite bank of the Spring, see?"

"I still can't see—"

He didn't say anymore because Harding had shot him twice in the back of the head. Unscrewing the silencer, he scanned around to make sure he was alone, pocketed the gun and walked briskly back to his car. "Sorry, George," he muttered to himself, "you did a fine job. I hope that didn't hurt too much. Your widow will get every benefit, I promise you." With those cynical sentiments he started the engine and drove back to Pine Gap as quickly as the speed limit would allow.

Just as George had missed the non-existent Darta bird, Harding had missed the very real pair of dark Koori eyes which had watched him in terrified stillness from the shadows a little further downstream. Whitefella blood had been spilt on blackfella lands. Blackfella lands had been desecrated. He must speak to the elders about this, they would know what to do.

# CHAPTER 37

Retuning to Pine Gap, Harding put himself on the first plane out of there, which happened to be the very next morning. He slept fitfully on the long trip to Washington, and was thankful neither Dianne or the President knew of his return. There was unfinished business to attend to first. He burst into Peter Lawson's office and shut the door. Lawson looked up from his desk, his startled face showing all the signs of exhaustion and stress, the result of daily facing the music from the Oval Office in the absence of his superior.

He addressed his unexpected visitor with less than the usual courtesy. "What the hell brings you back here, Norman?"

"The end of this messy business, Peter." Harding flung himself into a chair. "We have urgent matters to attend to in order to clean up the very last problem. Secure communications will be a reality in twenty four hours. I'm going to brief the President shortly, but first, I want you to organise a few things in Australia."

"Thank goodness we've got some of our people there."

"Not for this operation, Peter."

"Why ever not?" Lawson barked.

"For a start Saunders is compromised, and O'Callaghan is unreliable. Our friends in ASIO have been giving us a bloody hard time, and the AAT is having a bad case of divided loyalties. Now let me give you the brief. This is a black op, Peter, between you and me and the operatives you send. No one else."

It took all of five minutes for Harding to brief his second in command. Peter made two phone calls and lay back in his chair, his eyes shut. "So, you say this terrorist cell has been all but neutralised," he sighed. "I'd love to know how they did it."

"Classified, I'm afraid, highest level," Harding said seriously. "All that matters is we finish this business so the good old U.S of A can go back to playing the games it loves to play. Oh, and could you phone the President for me? Tell him I'm on my way."

❉ ❉ ❉

Harding entered the Situation Room at the Whitehouse to find Trudy Wilson, Brett Dyer, and naturally, Dianne Collins from the NSA already present. Every hostile eye turned towards him as he came through the door.

The President was the last to arrive and the first to speak. "So, Harding, here at last, despite my many directives that you return to report. I take it your presence is the harbinger of better news."

"Indeed it is, Mr. President," Harding said evenly. "I can now assure you all our secure network can be reactivated with the exception of satellite twenty nine, and that can be reactivated in the very near future."

"You can give me total assurance on this, Harding?" The President growled. "Do you realise the state of our armed forces at present? No, you don't, because you haven't had the courtesy of even returning a phone call."

Harding's face had resumed its impassive expression. He looked over at Dianne, her smouldering eyes riveted on to his. "I can categorically give you that assurance, Mr. President, and you may throw my entire department in jail if I happen to be wrong."

"Such confidence, Norman," Dianne sneered. "And how are you able to make such a sweeping, authoritative statement? Do tell. The NSA have not been nearly so productive of a solution."

"Above your pay grade, Dianne," Harding answered in an infuriatingly level voice. "I'm afraid above the pay grade of anyone else in the room except you, Mr. President. I'm happy to brief you concerning this cell's methods, but as they are very technical, I would rather you take my statement on trust. When our secure comms are back on line you may run any test you wish, Dianne. I'm telling you the problem has all but been solved, and in a few days' time it will pass on into history. I'm sorry for my absence, Mr. President, but it was a necessary one. Unlike my colleague in the NSA I have actually been very busy."

If looks could kill Harding would have been lying cold on the floor. The President rubbed his chin thoughtfully. "You say you have solved the problem, Harding. Does this mean this terrorist cell has been neutralised?"

"Completely, Mr. President. The operation was a little more complex than we thought. Regrettably it has cost the life of a valuable man, our communications expert George Russell. I learned from the Chief Minister of the Northern Territory only hours ago that his body has been found near Alice Springs, shot in the head. Revenge, I'm afraid, a parting shot from our enemies. George was instrumental in unravelling their methods. I would like you to consider his family for some sort of honour."

"I will do that." The President gave an enormous sigh and stood up. "If that is all, Dianne, gentlemen, I bid you good morning. Thank you, Norman. It has been a hard road for you. I regret the insinuations made against you from within this room. I will see to it that you and yours are suitably rewarded. This country owes you a great debt."

He walked out of the room, a much happier man than the one who had walked in.

# CHAPTER 38

Almost done, what a great job." David gave Abby a quick hug. They were together in the Edwards building, which was unusual for the morning. David did not have lectures that day, and he wanted to add the data from the last three experiments directly to the tables in their paper. The data was on the laptop in the lab, and so it had been easier to do the work from there. He smiled at Abby again. "Petrov and Saunders are about to have their names in print. I'm sure the editor will let this through without alteration. What's more, with the stuff you've already done, I wouldn't mind betting by the end of the year you will be able to resubmit. Professor Jacklin is enthusiastic and wants you resubmit your original thesis right now, but I think it might be better to add this extra material, especially as there has to be a least two more papers coming. Might as well take credit for them too."

"Thank you, David." Her eyes were shining. "I've never been so happy in my life. Doctor Saunders. I love the sound of that."

"What are you going to do next?"

It was an innocent enough question, but its implications took the smile from her face with a suddenness which surprised David no end.

Aware that he had upset her unwittingly he tried to make amends. "I hope you're not thinking of going back to the States," he said.

"Two years here with some recommendations, and you can become a permanent resident. There are quite a few jobs around, and maybe Martinborough Engineering will want to take you on full time."

It didn't work. Abby's face clouded even further. "I don't want to think about the future, David. I'm so very happy with the present. I don't suppose anyone will want a tutor attached to the Physics department?"

"It would be up to professor Cole, and there's some bridge building to be done in that area, I fear."

"She's terrifying." Abby gave an involuntary shudder. "She looks about eighteen, and there's not a catwalk in the word that wouldn't kill to have her stroll down it. I've never seen such a beautiful creature. And she's a genius, isn't she? I've read some of her papers – it's just not natural. I thought she was going to sit there and turn my brain into jello. I felt like I was in the presence of an alien from another world."

"She is all of that," David said smiling, "but she's also a really beautiful person inside, Abby. You can't fool her and it's dangerous to try, but she's not the monster you think she is. Life has been hard for her too. Can you imagine what she gets from every man who sees her? You're not alone in feeling angry with half the human race."

"Yet she's nice to you." Abby wrinkled her nose.

"We're both Christians."

"Really? I'm amazed."

And she was, really amazed. How could such an incandescent mind be a believer at the same time? Professor Cole was still having an impact on her life, whether she wished it or no. She shuddered again at the thought of actually meeting her, of confessing she had stolen her letter. Even worse, that David and the She-Devil had become friends. There was no way that scenario was going to play out with her having a job in the Physics department.

Abby glanced at her watch. "Lunch time. Shall we duck out and visit the Wentworth Café?"

"Great idea," David said, tossing the papers in his hand towards the desk. "We'll have to go round the back. There's some electrical work being done in the foyer and they've closed the front door."

They left the lab and went down the corridor. At the end were the stairs leading down to the rear entrance. Two floors down, and Abby, who was leading, pulled the door and held it open for David. The door had not even closed behind them when an odd noise from above made her look up at the scaffolding they had passed beneath on the way out.

It was moving, peeling off the building like a skin.

She stood watching it, rooted to the spot in terror, unable to move, unable to cry out. All of a sudden she felt hands grab her by the waist and shove her violently against the nearly closed door, throwing it open. Into the stairway she tumbled. Hitting herself against the railing and falling headlong over the bottom steps, she landed in a crumpled heap on the concrete. From outside the now closed door came the loud sounds of twisting, falling metal. Half dazed from her fall, Abby picked herself up and opened the door, but the exit was completely blocked with ruined scaffolding piled high across it.

With a scream she flew back up the steps and pelted along the corridor shouting at the top of her voice. "Help! Help! Help!"

Behind her she could hear office doors being flung open, pounding feet following. She raced out the front door dodging around the signs which said 'no entry', around the building to the back entrance. The scaffolding had peeled off a good half of the building on that side, and now lay in an jumbled mess across the courtyard, burying all under it, burying David.

"Doctor Petrov!" She screamed and pointed to the heap of metal outside the door. "Oh, dear God. He's under there. Dear God!"

The crowd who had followed her was growing. Someone grabbed hold of a bent length of pipe and tried to wrench if free, but it was bolted to the rest of the jumble, and his attempt only made the pile groan and settle a little more.

Abby wrenched his arm away. "Stop, stop!" She screamed. "You'll crush him even more. Oh dear God. He's dead."

She was wringing her hands in grief, not knowing what to do, who to turn to. Out of the corner of her eye she saw some men in yellow uniforms running to the scene with spanners in their hands. They sprang to work loosening the clamps which held the pipe sections together, then pulling them away very carefully. Abby grabbed hold of each loosened length and dragged it over to the other side of the courtyard, desperate to do something. Now more men were arriving, and amidst the sound of soft cursing they set to work. Another man with a large grinding wheel had begun to cut some of the bolts which were bent so badly they could not be undone. Others were lifting the long lengths of galvanised steel planking as soon as it became free, and over all the cacophony she heard the mournful wail of an ambulance.

"It's impossible," the man undoing the bolts next to her said to his mate. "The whole bloody thing's come loose. Look, you can still see the pipe sections sticking out of the windows. How in the name of God can this have happened?"

"Poor bastard's had it," muttered the other one. "Shit, this is going to rebound right back in our face."

Abby thought she was going to throw up on the spot.

They were about halfway in by now. A small portable crane which bore the sign "University Maintenance Section" had moved into position, and was lifting larger pieces clear as they were cut or unbolted.

Suddenly a shout rang out from the crane driver. "Over there! Careful. Don't move that planking, it's right over him."

Fighting her way to the front, Abby could see David's head , partly covered by the galvanised planking.

There was another shout. "It's a bloody miracle. He's got a chance. See? The planking's caught on that pot."

Sure enough, the first piece of metal to knock David to the ground had been a large plank which had slid off the scaffold and come to rest with one end on the paved courtyard, and the other on top of the pot. It was a large pot, and whatever tree had been planted in it was reduced to matchwood, but the pot, although cracked and crumbling, had provided a small triangular space, and in that space lay David. There was blood all over his head and he wasn't moving. Abby stared at him grief-stricken to the heart. Her legs were trembling, but she commanded them to support her as she came forward, helping to shift the remainder of the metal which rested on the planking, carefully, carefully. Now they could get to his side, ambulance officers slid a metal carrier underneath him, and lifted him onto a stretcher. Abby pushed the crowd away and followed on their heels to the ambulance.

"I'm coming with him," she said to the two paramedics.

There was a look on her face which silenced all argument. She stepped into the back of the ambulance and sat down on the seat besides the stretcher as the back door closed and the vehicle moved off rapidly with its siren blaring.

The paramedic on the other side of the stretcher removed his stethoscope and nodded to the stricken young woman. "He's breathing, but his blood pressure's a bit low. Keep you hope up, lass. There's still a chance he's going to be okay."

Abby nodded soundlessly, never taking her eyes of David's face. This was no accident, and she knew it. Someone had tried to kill him, kill her too. Perhaps they had succeeded with him. The paramedic was washing the blood away now, revealing a nasty cut just above his right temple, and another on the top of his head. Now some tape was being applied, the bleeding had stopped. David looked very pale, and his hand, which Abby had never let go of, was cold.

After what seemed a long time they arrived at Prince Alfred hospital emergency, and David was wheeled into casualty. Abby was told she had to wait, and wait she did, feeling cold and utterly wretched. One of the nurses came over with a hot cup of tea, and Abby took it gratefully. Somehow she managed to drink the whole lot without throwing up, although her stomach told her she might any moment. "No!" She told it, "you're not doing that here. David will need you soon, and the last thing he wants is a girl being sick all over him."

It felt like hours, but in fact it was just over one, when a white coated doctor came into the waiting room and spoke to her. "Ms., are you the woman who came with the scaffolding victim? We've run a heap of tests, and as far as we can see it's mild concussion, nothing more. We thought he might have had a cranial aneurism, but scans show there's no bleeding in the cranial cavity. He was very lucky. Lot of bruising, and we've sedated him, but he's asking for you. Not too long now."

Swallowing hard to prevent herself from throwing up all over the place, Abby followed the doctor through the emergency ward to a bed which had been enclosed in a curtain. He pushed the curtain aside. David was lying on the bed with his eyes open, a rather dazed and sleepy look on his face.

Abby ran to his side and took hold of his hand. "Why?" she said softly, "David, you could have died. Why did you do it?"

She felt his fingers tighten around her own.

His voice was soft and a little dreamy. "Didn't want you to die. You froze. No time to get out of the way."

There was a chair beside the bed, and Abby sank into it, her legs finally delivering an ultimatum. Holding his hand in both of her own, she bent her head down and pressed it against her forehead, against her lips.

"Oh, David," she stammered, "I'm not worth it. Not worth anything. Not worth your life."

She turned her sorrowful face up towards him, tears the only thing absent from its plaintive grief.

Slowly he raised his hand and tenderly stroked her face. "You're worth it to me."

"Oh, David." Her voice choked, and once again she lowered her head on top of his hand, holding it, keeping it against her face, kissing his fingers again and again. When she finally lifted her head he had gone to sleep, and the doctor was standing over her, holding the curtain open.

"He should rest now, Ms."

"Of course. Thank you, Doctor. He's going to be all right?"

"As far as we can tell he will be on his feet tomorrow," he said, reassuringly. "We're going to keep him here for twenty four hours under observation, just to be on the safe side. He's a lucky man. Lucky to have such a caring girlfriend."

Abby smiled at him and left the ward. On reaching the exit she walked a few paces and threw up in the garden. Lucky to have such a caring girlfriend? If only he knew. She was a curse. She had nearly cost him his life. Wiping her face with her handkerchief, she set out to find some transportation back into the city. A showdown with Harry was looming, a showdown like no other, and even as she thought about it she could feel the rage building in her heart. By the time she had reached Martin Place it had assumed murderous proportions. *This is it*, she thought, *now Abby, time to go on stage.*

Deliberately arranging her face into a beaming smile, she swiped her card and came into the room. There was no one else there save Harry and the faint smell of Bushmills Whisky. Half-filled boxes were strung alongside one wall, and some of the engineering posters had been taken down. Harry was shovelling more papers into another box as she bounced past the reception counter.

"Afternoon Harry," she said brightly. "I see you're being a good boy and tidying up the room. Mind if I sit down at your desk, it's got the most comfortable chair."

"Backside hurting, is it?" Harry mumbled something and threw some more papers in the box.

"You've been on the Bushmills, haven't you, Harry, or you wouldn't be so sweet."

"The boys and I went out for lunch in the pub down George Street," Harry said. "They're still at it. I drew the short straw. Now what brings you here so early? Petrov feeling a little fragile today is he?"

"As a matter of fact he is."

With her right hand she had been quietly rummaging in Harry's desk draws, and now she had found what she was looking for. She knew he always kept one close. Her fingers screwed the silencer on behind her back. She felt for the magazine and quietly pushed it home.

"Suffering from sexual exhaustion," Harry said without turning round. "You should go easy on him, Abby, especially as you're out of here on Monday."

There was click. Harry turned round suddenly. He knew that sound. Abby was standing next to his chair, holding a very steady Beretta in her hand, every trace of friendliness wiped from her face and replaced by an expression Harry didn't much care for.

"Is there a termination order on David? On me?" she asked in a voice like ice.

"What the hell do you think you're doing?" Harry exclaimed, astonished. "Put that down now."

"I'm going to count to three, then I'll pull this trigger. So help me, Harry, I mean it. David is in hospital, and if it wasn't for him I'd be in the morgue. When did you get the contract to kill us?"

The colour drained from Harry's face. The woman was in earnest. There was a look of cold murder in her eyes, and not for a moment did he think she was bluffing. "I don't know anything about a contract," he said, trying to keep his voice level. "Lawson phoned this morning and told us the operation had been completed, and we were to move out Monday. I swear to God—"

"One."

"Honestly, Abby, I don't know any more. Have I ever done the dirty on you? You know damn well I haven't. I've—"

"Two."

"Aargh, for God's sake go and pull the bloody trigger. As if I give a shit anymore."

He sat down on a chair watching her, pure resignation all over his face. Oddly enough it was this last expression which convinced Abby he was telling the truth.

She lowered the Beretta. "There's a contract on us, has to be. Half the scaffolding fell off the building on top of us. He saved me, Harry, and it nearly cost him his life."

"Bloody hell!" There was nothing false about the shock on Harry's face. After a pause he continued. "Abby I don't know anything about it. All I know is Lawson phoned and said we were pulling out Monday, dammed if I know why - and until then it was business as usual with you and Petrov. He said you were to stay close to him, keep up the observation. Said something about you doing a great job, glory and honour and all that rubbish."

"He's lying." Abby snapped. "Where's Harding?"

"Heaven knows. Look, I haven't a clue what's going on. Isn't it vaguely possible you're wrong and the scaffolding just wasn't assembled correctly? There's some shonky tradesmen around."

For a second a seed of doubt crossed Abby's mind. Only for a second, then she remembered the comments of the workmen who were cutting the bolts.

"Why are we pulling out?" she demanded. "Have they found their terrorist? No, they think it's David and they're taking me out with him."

"I swear none of our boys were involved. When did this happen?"

"Lunch time."

"We were all down the pub in George Street, all celebrating our impending return. All of us. Go ask if you want to."

"Then who, Harry? It wasn't an accident." The murderous expression was still on her face.

Harry got out of the chair and walked slowly towards her, holding out his hand for the gun, but instead of handing it to him she tossed it back on his desk within easy reach, too easy.

Harry halted in his tracks. "I don't know, but I tell you what Abby, I'm going to find out. Can you trust me with that? I don't like it when someone tries to take out my operative, especially when it's you, and I swear I'll find out. Believe me?"

"Maybe I do, maybe I don't," Abby said, her voice still like ice.

Harry threw up his hands in disgust, turned round and sat down in the chair again. "When haven't I been on your side?"

"When you said you'd tell Harding I'd been uncooperative. Seems to me like you did, and he's decided to take out the garbage."

"Yeah, I know I said that, but honest to God you know I'd never do it." He sighed heavily. "You were being a bloody stubborn bitch and I had to shake you, or Harding would have taken you apart. Don't you get that?"

"If it isn't Harding, then who tried to kill us?"

"Ever thought it could be the terrorist cell you say doesn't exist? Perhaps they weren't happy with you bouncing on Petrov's—"

He stopped instantly, because quick as a flash the Beretta was back in Abby's hand.

"There's no terrorist cell," she hissed. "David isn't a terrorist. Got that? Something else. We've ... never... had... sex."

Three coffee mugs on the sink behind Harry exploded into shards. Harry jumped up from the chair, and there was fear in his eyes. Three bullets had passed very close to his left ear. What would this crazy woman do next?

"Alright! Enough!" he shouted. "When did you learn to shoot like that? Okay, I believe you. I guess with your record when you say a man's innocent he's innocent. Put the bloody gun down before someone gets hurt. What if the guys come back and find you pointing that thing at me? Frank is packing too, remember, and he hates your guts."

She opened the top draw of Harry's desk and slid the weapon in there, silencer and all. "So if it isn't this ghost cell which exists only in Harding's imagination, then who's trying to kill us? Is ASIO fed up with the way we've been running a covert operation under their noses?"

"Not their style. I don't know, Abby, but I'm going to find out. Come on, you've got to trust someone. You damn well know how I feel about you. I'll find out, trust me."

"Just remember I don't feel the same way, Harry," Abby said coldly. "Find out, and do it fast before we all end up dead." Her voice hardened. "I tell you this, Harry. If anyone tries to hurt David I'll kill them. The boys are coming back. Tell them you found a better way to wash up."

"As if they'll believe me," Harry muttered. "What are you going to do?"

"Stay alive."

The door had opened now and the others were coming in. No one had noticed the pieces of porcelain strewn all over the floor, the rather obvious dents in the stainless steel plate behind the sink. But they noticed Abby all right, and they read that same murderous look on her face. So she and Harry had been having a lover's quarrel, had they? About time Harry got the message, the bitch didn't even have a heart.

"Hello boys, good-bye boys." Abby left the room. Harry, she knew, had got the message at last.

❋ ❋ ❋

She was back in the hospital in an hour, but David was still asleep. Despite the staff telling her to go home, she tucked her legs up on a comfortable chair in the waiting room and proceeded to flip through the collection of old magazines which had been left for that purpose on a low table. Half an hour later she finished skimming the last one, wondering just what sort of people went to the trouble of buying the mindless rubbish in the first place. The café bar on the other side of the room eventually provided a remote approximation to a coffee. Abby could only stomach half before throwing the rest into the waste bin thoughtfully provided close to the machine. She noticed other people had done the same. Her stomach was making all sorts of gurgling noises. She knew the others in the waiting room could hear them too. They had silly smiles on their faces, and tittered softly as they turned their heads away.

Leaving the waiting room she found a café a little further down the corridor which offered better fare at exorbitant prices. No matter, her tummy felt better for it, and in half an hour she had returned to the waiting room to resume her vigil. Around eight that night David woke up, and a nurse escorted her to his bed. She had come prepared with some goodies David liked, which she was sure would not be on the hospital menu. As soon as she pulled the curtain back his eyes lit up with delight. Soon they were sharing Violet Crumble bars together, and talking softly. David was holding her hand, and Abby was caressing his face. Even the most obtuse observer could have seen that far more than friendship was quietly being shared between them.

Around nine o'clock Abby left and let him go to sleep again. She caught a taxi back to Annandale which dropped her a block away from her apartment. Using all the skill she had acquired in her training, Abby slowly approached the darkened flat from the alleyway behind, retrieved the back door key which she had hidden underneath an unsuspecting plant pot, and let herself in the rear door. She picked up a hammer from its resting place on the laundry wall, and without turning on the light, she crept from room to room, using only the faint illumination from the street light on the other side of the road. The place was empty, and there was no surveillance across the street. Closing all the curtains she turned on the light and made herself some supper. Violet Crumble bars are not very sustaining. Taking a carving knife from the set in the kitchen, she went into the bedroom and placed it under her pillow. If someone tried it on that night they were going to get more than they bargained for.

# CHAPTER 39

Geoff Burkitt arrived at Prince Alfred Hospital the next morning to take David home. Somehow he had managed to persuade the staff that he, doctor Burkitt, was perfectly able to take care of his own son. David had gone with them willingly, but he insisted on phoning Abby first to tell her what had happened, not wishing her to come and find an empty bed. Lydia met him at the door, a worried expression on her face, and threw her arms round him. It hurt him to feel her silently sobbing against his shirt, hurt him much more than his recent experience, but in a different way. Geoff left them together and went to make tea and warm up the scones which his wife had baked in anticipation of their arrival at some ridiculous hour in the morning when she couldn't sleep. They had seen the report of the accident on the television the previous evening, but it was the phone call from the E.R. registrar to Geoff an hour earlier which had told them of David's condition. Lydia released him from her arms and turned away least he see the tears in her eyes. See them? He didn't need to see them.

Blowing her nose on her apron she turned around and faced him, the annoyance in her voice trying to cover the anxiety she felt. "I suppose this wonderful assistant of yours was nowhere to be seen when this happened?"

"Not exactly," David said quietly. "She was right in front of me. I heard a bang, turned round, and saw all the scaffolding collapsing on top of us. She was frozen to the spot. I threw her into the doorway. Don't remember anything after that."

Lydia hugged him ferociously, pinning his arms down to his sides. She was openly weeping now and made no attempt to hide it. "I'm so proud of you. And you fell inside the door? Is that what happened?"

"Ah, well, not exactly," David explained with great reluctance. "The scaffolding came down but I was standing near one of those courtyard miniature trees in a big pot. I was knocked to the ground, but the pot stopped me being crushed."

"Merciful God in Heaven!" Lydia looked as though she was going to faint, and David, shocked to see this hitherto unknown reaction, guided her to the nearest armchair and knelt down beside her.

"It's alright, dearest Lydia," he said, trying to keep the anxiety out of his voice. "God took care of me. Please don't look so distraught. I'm here, I'm not hurt. Oh, Lydia."

He leant over and folded the sobbing woman in his arms, gently rocking her from side to side and rubbing her shoulders. Geoff, coming into the room laden with tea and hot scones, put his burden down on the table and came to stand beside the two of them.

"I take it there's more to this story than we already know," he said seriously. "It's alright, Lydia my love, he's still with us. God took care of him. We should be thankful."

In response Lydia stood up and wrapped her arms around them both.

"Dear Lord," she prayed, "thank you, thank you for saving the boy we love. We know this is your hand at work. Please keep him safe, please don't let anything happen to him. You know what he means to both of us."

Then, as if she was feeling guilty for being a bad host, Lydia detached herself and began furiously buttering scones, whilst Geoff poured out the tea. Always a doctor, he added a little more sugar to David's cup. Lydia wasted no time in telling her husband the extra details she had learned, and to see the shock in his face sent another pang through David's heart. In truth he felt weary beyond measure, but whether it was his concussion, or seeing his family so distressed he couldn't tell. Perhaps both were to blame. After they had eaten, Geoff insisted David lie down and sleep, something he was only too willing to do, and went back to comfort his beloved who was cleaning up in the lounge room.

"It wasn't an accident." Lydia banged the last saucer down on the pile.

"You don't know that, my love. Whatever makes you think someone is out to harm our son? Besides, that other woman was with him. It's a miracle they didn't both die." He picked up the tray. "My, he's a brave boy. I'd like the University to give him a medal."

"He's all too fond of that wretched woman!" Lydia said angrily. "That note professor Cole sent – it was all about her. She's no good, Geoff. Somehow I can feel it. There's an evil around her, and now it's reaching out for David. How I wish she was back in America where she belongs."

"We mustn't jump to conclusions, Lydia. Besides, if God is able to protect our boy in circumstances when he should have been killed, doesn't it give you confidence He will continue to protect him, no matter what this evil woman of yours can do?" He put the tray down. "Last time I checked it was God running the show, not her."

He smiled and gathered his beloved into his arms. "It's a time to trust, Lydia, not give way to fear. Look at the lessons God has taught us in our long lives. Has He ever let us down?"

Arm and arm they walked out into the sunshine of the garden.

✳ ✳ ✳

Abby had a wretched morning. David had gone to the Burkitt's, and his absence ripped a hole in her heart. The last thing she wanted was to go back to the lab. When the dean rang to find out if she would come and make a statement, she gave it to him over the phone, saying she was still far too shaken up to go back to work. By lunch time she had discovered that wandering around her flat and looking out of windows for suspicious people was a good way to scare herself silly, and decided to return to the University. Not only would she go back, she would go to the Edwards building and see how the investigation was progressing.

She arrived to find the front door sealed with police tape. A sign across the entrance told the building's usual occupants that a police investigation was in progress, and would they please get lost, or words to that effect. A small group of men standing away from the building were taking note of her presence, so she decided to make a quick exit and return to the Physics building to work on their paper. Not much remained to be done, and if she worked carefully she could email it to the referee this very afternoon. That would be something nice to tell David when he returned to work tomorrow, at least she hoped he would. Several times she thought of visiting him, but something told her that she would be far from welcome, especially if Lydia had gleaned a whiff of her background. A less suitable friend for her son would be hard to conceive. The task took longer than expected, and evening shadows darkened the room as she finally added the paper as an attachment to the all-important email.

The phone rang.

It was Harry, and his voice sounded wrong.

"Martinborough engineering, Ms. Saunders. Would you be able to do an earlier shift this evening? We have just received an urgent project which involves a new contract and we wondered if you could assist us?"

"I'll be there directly. At the office?"

"No, there is a management briefing down at the café in Martin Place. Can you make it in half an hour?"

Abby said she would, tore out of the building and caught the first taxi she could find. Harry's voice had never sounded like that before, a mixture of anger and apprehension. The café was busy with office workers having a coffee before the long commute back home, and Harry was sitting at a table far away from the street. Even from her place at the door his face confirmed the tone of his voice. She hurried across the room and sat down next to him.

"Abby, keep away from Petrov. Don't go within a mile of him," he said quietly.

"What's happened?" Abby asked, her voice heavy with apprehension.

"Patrick."

"*Patrick?* How do you know?" Abby stammered, aghast.

"He called in to have lunch with me," Harry said under his breath. "We go back a long way, Abby, both born in Belfast, both got caught up with stuff you don't want to know about. Just a friendly visit. He said he was staying with relatives, having a holiday. Patrick never takes a holiday. You can't save Petrov, Abby, just get out of the way and let it happen. Tell him you're ill, and you'll be back to work Tuesday. We'll be sipping champagne on our way to Washington by then."

"Why Patrick?" Abby could feel goose bumps spreading down her arms.

"Because they want the big show, they want to kick ASIO up the arse, launch the new Australian branch of the CIA, who knows? Point is you can't stop it. He's got a perfect score, and you know it."

"So perfect he's killed hundreds of innocent people, women, kids, old folk, just minding their own business," Abby said angrily.

"So he's a sick bastard. Aren't you listening? They'll probably have the red carpet rolled out for us back home. Another day, another target. Don't lose the rage, Abby, it's kept you alive." He reached out for Abby's hand, but the girl was already on her feet.

"See you in hell, Harry."

There was a rubbish bin in Martin Place not far from the café, and Abby made it there just in time.

# CHAPTER 40

On Friday, the day after his refreshing sleep at home, David returned to work just before lunch. Abby had left him a note on his desk saying the receipt of their paper had been acknowledged by the referee, and she was out getting sandwiches and coffee. He went over to the filing cabinet to stow the last sheets of data which were scattered on his desk, and was busily engaged in this task when Abby came into the room. Before he could turn around her arms had found him, hugging him tightly around the shoulders, her head buried in his neck. David, a little surprised at this spontaneous display of affection, was about to respond in kind, when Abby disengaged herself and stood away. David flinched from the shock. Her face was taught and drawn as though she had not slept at all the previous night, her eyes the windows of a tormented heart.

"What on earth is the matter?" he gasped.

"Can we go someplace where there aren't a lot of people?"

He followed her out of the room all the way to their special spot near the Moreton Bay fig. Abby had brought their lunch, but made no attempt to sit down and eat it. She turned to face him and took a great breath.

"I work for the CIA. I came here to seduce you because they think you're a dangerous terrorist. I've told them again and again you're not, but they don't believe it, and now they're going to kill you."

David felt as though he had been struck a physical blow. He stood there staring at her, trying to come to grips with her words.

Finally he spoke, his voice unsteady, soft. "All this time, all the things we've done and said to one another, all a lie, a dirty, horrible lie."

"No!" Abby protested. "It began that way but—"

"I stand by you, I stop you from being thrown out. You must have enjoyed that, a fool playing right into your hands. Then I save your life. How ironic. Another man added to your filthy list of victims. How many other innocent men have you slaughtered, Abby? How much more innocent blood cries out from the ground for justice?"

Abby stared at him in silence, the self-loathing in her heart mirrored on her face.

"I thought I saw laughter in your eyes and warmth in your heart, but they were nothing but a cruel mockery," David said softly. "Your heart is dead, Abby, and something horrible has taken its place. Who was it thrust the final needle through, turned it into stone?

"Please don't use that expression."

"I pity you," he said sadly. "Once you were alive, now you're dead and already in hell. No wonder you don't know what love is, no wonder you can't feel, can't cry."

He paused, staring into her stricken face. There was no response, no argument.

"Will it be quick or do your charming employers want me to suffer first? I suppose you would enjoy that."

"It will be quick." Her voice was barely audible. All her world was crumbling, crashing down, and beneath her the abyss was opening its willing arms.

"I pardon you for shedding my blood, Abby," David said softly. "One painful moment, and I will be standing with my Lord in joy forever. No, that will not be a bad thing. But you will bring sorrow and grief to my beloved Lydia who has already known so much, and for that you're despicable in my eyes. So you've completed your mission? So good of you to let me know. A little more hate to express, a little more fear to spread into your victim's heart. Go now, Abby. Walk away. I want to spend some time talking to God my Father, and I know you hate Him even more than you hate everything else."

Abby stared at him, stricken, unable to say a word. David sat down on the grass and buried his head in his hands, ignoring her. Despicable in his eyes, despicable in her own. She turned and walked away, not looking back. There was no turning back now. She had reached the point where every aspect of living was worse than dying. Makin was waiting. She could feel the burning thrust of his needle through her body even now. Every thrust, every piercing pain so thoroughly deserved.

Beyond forgiveness.

David was right, she was already in hell. What could be worse than knowing you had destroyed the man you had come to love? Love? No, she didn't know the meaning of the word. It must have been the same perverted desire for power. Nothing good, nothing decent ever came out of her, only death and lies. She wanted to scream, to run back, to prostrate herself at his feet and beg for the forgiveness she knew she would never obtain. Despite the grief which plunged her into despair, her face remained dry.

A dead heart sheds no tears.

Reaching the Woman's Sport Centre on the other side of the oval, she went into the ladies toilet and removed her top, her bra, and using a nail file managed to extract the thin red capsule which she carried in the lining. Placing it in her mouth, she dressed and went out, heading towards Parramatta road. Once there, she caught the first bus to the city. She was going insane, her mind slowly disintegrating. All night long she had been tortured by the emotional forces raging within her. Tell David the truth, or run away and let him die still believing the lie. No, she couldn't live with that, even though she knew he would hate her. It was all she deserved. At least he would know the truth at last. Somehow this seemed better to her than allowing him to die believing that she was a lovely young woman, when she was nothing more than the foul angel of death, the enemy of all decency and love.

Her natural desire for life had been replaced by a longing for death and the justice of eternal pain. Yes, justice. Justice for the anguish her life had brought to others, the only thing she deserved. It was waiting for her, she knew. Running her tongue around her mouth she could feel the capsule wedged between her gums. Judgement was hovering close, but she would decide the time of its beginning.

What place would she choose from which to exit the world and plunge into hell? Harry, that was it. She would find Harry, the man who had ripped every shred of decency out of her, the man who was always hanging out for sex. Well, today he was going to get his wish. She would wait until just the right time, then bite on the capsule and die underneath him. She hoped it would destroy his enjoyment of that moment with every other woman forever.

The bus had reached Town Hall, was passing St. Andrew's Cathedral. A crowd of people were gathering for the lunch time service. Suddenly her insane mind rebelled. Destroying Harry's sexual pleasure was far too small an accomplishment for her last act of hate in the flesh. An eternity of screaming needed something greater to herald its beginning. She began to giggle softy. No more rational thought remained. Somewhere in the maelstrom of her disintegrating mind came David's last words. "I know you hate God more than anything else." The words suddenly became pregnant with purpose.

She would hurt God.

Even if He didn't exist, she would hurt him. She giggled like a child. How could she hurt God? By hurting his gullible followers, causing them pain, damaging their cause. Much better. God had crushed her like a gnat, but this gnat had a sting, and He was going to feel it. She pressed the button, got off at the Queen Victoria Building, and went back to the cathedral. By the time she had reached the front door, the congregation had already begun to sing. An older woman handed her a sheet and gave her a smile.

"Nice to see you. There's plenty of room down the front," she said in a friendly voice.

Returning the smile with eyes which blazed unnaturally bright, Abby took the sheet from her hand. "Do you see that man up there?" She pointed towards the front of the cathedral to the man who was leading the service from the pulpit. "I'm his mistress. He got me pregnant, and then he blackmailed me into having the child destroyed. Do you know why I'm here today? I'm going to tell everybody just what he did, then I'm going to take my own life. It's going to be really entertaining. Stick around and watch. Better still, call the TV stations. This is going to make the six o'clock news."

An expression of shocked horror appeared on the woman's face, and Abby smiled to see it. Her insane revenge against God had begun. Sauntering right down the aisle, she found an empty pew at the front and sat down in the middle of it.

The older woman signalled to one of the church wardens who happened to be standing at the back of the congregation. Seeing the expression on her face, he came over immediately.

"See that young woman walking down the aisle?" The older woman pointed with her arm. "I think she's on drugs." She shuddered. "Her eyes were terrible to look at. She threatened to make a scene then take her life. I believe she's insane enough to go through with it. What can we do? Call the police?"

The other man thought for a while before answering. "Premature," he said. "We would cause a dreadful disturbance if we did, and then the woman could deny everything. No, we go and sit near her. The first sign of trouble, we act as discretely as possible. I'll tell the other wardens to be ready." He moved off down another aisle.

A short time later Abby noticed the older woman had taken up residence at one end of the pew, and some man at the other. No matter. The congregation had finished their hymn, now there were some announcements.

Abby felt the capsule with her tongue.

Another hymn, blast them. The woman at the end of the pew was watching her like a hawk. At last the man she had seen before came up to the pulpit to speak. *Not yet. Wait until he's reached the climax of his talk, the point when he expects his audience to be completely captivated,* Abby thought. Then all hell would break loose.

The man began. "Today we are due to look at the next passage in our journey through Luke's historical account of the life of Jesus." He paused, frowning. "I can't say this happens very often, but as I began to prepare, I could not overcome the conviction that today I had to speak about something else. So, if you will pardon what is most probably a whim, I want to speak about God's forgiveness."

A tear splashed down on the back of Abby's hand, then another. It gave her such a shock she felt her body jump as though someone had prodded her in the back with a needle, and she nearly cried out.

The man continued. "Our text comes from the Apostle John's first letter, chapter one verse eight. 'If we claim to be without sin, we deceive ourselves and the truth is not in us. If we confess our sins, he is faithful and just and will forgive us our sins and purify us from all unrighteousness.'"

Tears began to stream down Abby's cheeks. Just as she had not been able to summon a single one before, now she couldn't command them to stop. It was as though a dam had been breached, its swollen waters cascading freely down her face, running down her neck, soaking her top in silence. The man continued speaking, and in that instant Abby knew exactly why the topic had changed that morning. God, the God who was

351

really there, had something to say to her, and He was commanding her attention through her tears.

She listened as God explained the reason why He had sent His only Son to the cross, that because of Jesus all His anger against her had been burned away. There was forgiveness offered, waiting only for her to reach out her hand and receive it in trust. Every word the man spoke burned into her heart. Before her eyes she saw the Christ hanging by the nails, heard Him cry "Father, forgive them for they know not what they do."

She began to sob, quietly at first, then louder and louder, her whole body shaking, and all the time the tears kept flowing as from some inexhaustible supply. People were staring at her now, nudging one another, whispering. The hymn began, but the enthusiasm of the congregation was diminished somewhat. It's hard to sing joyfully to the accompaniment of non-stop sobbing. Now the service had finished, and the congregation were filing out, casting meaningful glances at the mess in the front pew.

The woman she had first spoken to was coming towards her. "Can I help you, young lady?" she asked.

Abby turned round. "The man who spoke. I need to talk to him," she demanded brokenly.

"Peter is a busy man, young lady," the older woman frowned. "If there is—"

Abby opened her mouth and shoved the capsule on to the end of her tongue.

"See that?" she stammered loudly. "One bite and I'm dead, and I swear I'll do it if you don't get him for me. I swear I will."

The older woman stood her ground. A hard, determined expression grew on her face, as if she was dealing with a naughty child. "Give that thing to me or I'll leave you to die anyway you want to," she said without raising her voice.

The time of decision had come. A new life, a new pathway stood before her, but to tread it she must forsake the old, close the door which led to safe oblivion. Safe? Only hell lay in that direction. She spat the capsule into her palm and splattered it into the older woman's hand. There was fear in her eyes now. What would the woman do? Did she realise what had happened? Pray God she did. Without a word the woman left, and Abby sank down onto the pew, covering her soaking face with her soaking hands.

A man's voice startled her. "What can I do for you, young lady? Are you on drugs?"

"I want to know if God can forgive me," Abby stammered, staring up into his face.

"Didn't you hear a word I said?" he answered, a little annoyed. "Of course God can forgive you."

"How can you say that? You don't know what I've done," Abby choked.

"What *have* you done?" The older woman said suddenly, and there was a strange expression on her face.

"You want to know?" Abby stammered. "You really want to know?"

She told them, and they listened in silence. It was a long confession. Beginning with her life in Boston, she told them of her drug addiction and her subsequent forced recruitment into a large "American organisation which deals with security." Her description of the things she did after that was deliberately vague, not wishing to place either of her hearers in danger. Vague it might have been, but Peter and the older woman missed nothing of her self-loathing, the way she had caused the death of an innocent man because of the hatred that had driven her.

"And now another innocent man is going to die," she sobbed at last. "I've tried and tried to save him, but it hasn't worked. Can God forgive that?

"Perhaps you should go to the police," the older woman said sternly. "I suppose that might cost you your life though. No doubt that's far too high a price to pay for saving someone else."

Abby stared at the woman, tears flooding down her cheeks. "Yes, they'd kill me," she said in a broken voice. "You don't understand. It wouldn't prevent anything, and more innocent people would die. Oh God, I know I don't deserve to live. I don't deserve your forgiveness. Please tell me there's a chance. I'm terrified of dying. Oh, dear God, help me!"

She covered her face with her hands, her body shaking with sobs. Peter frowned towards the older woman. "I don't think that sort of comment is helping," he said softly.

The woman pressed her lips together, and for a whole minute nobody spoke.

Finally Abby lifted her head, and stared up into Peter's face with wide, frightened eyes. "Well?" she stammered at last.

"God's forgiveness is not a light matter, young lady," Peter said gravely. "It was purchased at an indescribable cost. The things you have told us are truly horrific. I can in some small way understand that you have been very much the victim in your life, but you have deliberately done terrible things as well."

"You think I don't know that?" Abby stammered bitterly.

A long conversation followed, and in the end Abby covered her face with her hands and begged her Lord to forgive her, accepting His unspeakably gracious gift. All the time the tears were flowing out between her fingers, and her voice was often broken by sobbing.

Peter reached out his hand and touched her shoulder. "Young lady, what's your name?"

"Abby."

Neither of them saw the horrified expression on the older woman's face.

354

"Abby," Peter said gently, "let me show you this verse in Paul's letter to the Romans, chapter eight. 'There is now not even one bit of condemnation left for those in Christ Jesus...'"

They talked on for quite a while after that. Peter offered her counselling, and Abby asked if she could take the Bible she had been reading from. Peter said "yes" and marked some verses for her. In the end Abby threw her arms around him, grabbed her Bible and ran out of the building, leaving the two of them staring after her.

Peter picked up a sodden tissue from the floor and tried to wipe the wet pew with it. "I've never seen anyone cry like that in my life," he sighed, shaking his head. "Do you suppose she was actually on drugs? What do you think of that story she told? What do you – Lydia! Whatever is the matter?"

✻ ✻ ✻

There were golden leaves on the Planus trees of the cathedral courtyard, children laughing and a busker was playing the guitar, playing it well. Abby felt a cool breeze on her face and her soaking top, and it was nothing but totally refreshing. There were colours in her world, fresh, poignant colours, as if they had sprung into existence for her pleasure right then and there. She felt a bounce in her step and a peculiar lightness in her heart, an inexpressible joy just to be alive. Alive. Yes, she was alive, and deep down she knew it. Sorrow and difficulty might be lurking around the corner, but right now this was her time of joy, and she crossed the courtyard as though she was holding the very hand of God and delighting in His company. Moving down the hill she came to Darling Harbour and bought an ice cream. It was cold, creamy, delicious, sweet and satisfying. Going further she came to a long pool, its smooth surface broken only when the water tumbled over to a lower level. In the distance she could see fountains playing, and above her on the flyover to the Western Distributor, traffic was rumbling softly.

Choosing a sunny spot on the soft grass she sat down, tucked her legs under her dress, and opened her Bible. Luke's narrative, Peter had said, and she was soon absorbed in it. About chapter nine she looked up and saw a young man approaching her from beside the long pool. Smiling at him, she held up the book so he could see it was a Bible, and watched him reverse his direction so suddenly he overbalanced and tipped into the water. She laughed, a musical laughter totally devoid of malice, and several people who had seen what she did laughed with her. She returned to chapter nine. The evening shadows lengthened to the last verses of Matthew's gospel, and Abby closed the book.

Now came the last darkness before the dawn.

Spreading her hands over her face she prayed. "God, you and I have been strangers until today, but I want you to know I'm yours. You've won me forever. You've made me alive, and I was so, so dead. And as for forgiving me, well you know I can't find words to thank you for that. Read my heart and you'll know. Now comes the hard part, God. I have no right to ask you this, and believe you me I will understand if you say no, but..."

It was quite a long prayer, and Abby made no attempt to hide what she was doing, holding her hands over her face so she could concentrate. There were no tears this time, and there didn't need to be. Soon there might be more, but they would come when she bade them, because her heart could feel again, and whether it was joy or pain it was a blessing.

※ ※ ※

She caught a bus to Glebe point road and came to David's house, praying he would be there. Reaching the place she opened the fly screen, and rang the bell. Closing it again she stepped back, standing in the street. Time seemed to pass with infinite slowness, but finally the door opened, and Abby could see David standing on the other side of the fly screen, his face silhouetted by the light in the hall.

She took a deep breath. "David, I know you despise me, and you have every reason to. I... I just wanted to tell you something important. I don't need to come in, but please listen, just for a minute."

The fly screen opened. David came out, his face carrying an expression she couldn't read. She stood there in the street, staring up at him, her eyes wide and pleading.

"I don't like speaking to people in the street," he said softly. "Please come in."

He held the door wide, and Abby, her heart racing, her legs feeling light and unsteady, came inside. He closed the door, locking it carefully. Following her down the hall into the living room, he found her standing right in the middle under the light. There were tears in her eyes, running down her cheeks. David froze, staring.

In a small voice she began, not really knowing what to say, convinced she was not going be believed, praying she would be.

"When I left you I went to kill myself," she stammered. "I wanted to hurt God because I blamed Him for everything that happened to me, and I found Him all right. But He told me He loved me and wanted to forgive me, and… and I took the offer, David. God ripped out the dead thing that had been my heart and put a new one inside me."

She stared into his face, interpreting the strange expression as total disbelief. She felt tears burning her eyes, running down her face.

She tried to keep her voice steady. "I've lied so many times, how could I ever expect you to believe me? I… I just wanted to try. It's not your fault, David, it's not your fault you don't believe me, and now—"

"But I do believe you."

She stopped open-mouthed and stared at him. His face was blurred through all the water, but she could see his eyes were kind. "You… do? Why?"

"It was in the cathedral," David said softly. "You came to destroy Peter's reputation, and you sat at the front. Something happened while he was speaking and you began to cry, very loudly. I know exactly what happened, you see. I believe you completely."

Her face was a mixture of wonder and joy. "How? Oh God, you're amazing. How?"

"There was an older woman, wasn't there? Now you've met Lydia, my wonderful Lydia."

"Oh," Abby choked.

The implications of that meeting were not slow to dawn, and she shut her eyes, not knowing what to say or how to say it. God had answered her prayer, but in such a strange manner. What had Lydia said to him? Surely he must really hate her now.

Suddenly she felt arms around her, a hand pushing her head gently forward into a warm shoulder, lips softly caressing her hair, warm breath on her head. She gave a mighty sob and clung to him, clung as though no force on Earth could wrench her arms away, her tears soaking his shirt, her body shaking as he held her close. She could have stayed there forever, holding him, telling him she loved him, because now she knew with certainty that she did.

Using every molecule of her will, she gently pushed herself away from his embrace, and standing at a small distance said the rest of what she had come to say.

"I'm going to save you... us, David. I've been praying a lot this afternoon, and God has shown me what to do. It's going to be a different life, David, and I know Lydia is going to be broken-hearted, but it won't be for long, and one day you'll be able to bring all the joy back into her face, I promise you. I know that's not perfect, but it's the best I can do to make up for what I've done. Do you believe me, David?"

He was looking into her face with such tenderness. Abby fought hard not to spring back into his arms.

"Yes, Abby. I believe you," he said slowly. "If nothing else, your tears have told me the truth."

"I can't stay, David," she stammered. "I have a lot to do. Can you trust me just a little more? It won't be for very long, and you'll know I'm speaking the truth. Can I have the van for the weekend?"

# THE PETROV EFFECT

It was an unexpected request. Truth be known he would have much rather she stayed in the comfort of his arms than organise transport.

"Of course," he said, surprised. "I don't need the van this weekend. Abby, when will I see you again? Are you safe?"

He fished the keys out of his pocket and handed them to her.

"God is taking care of me, David, just like He's taking care of you. Monday night in the lab. I'll see you there. Don't do anything unusual, and I beg you not to say anything to Lydia. I hope one day she can forgive me. Now I have to go. Pray for me David. Dear David."

She came over, kissed him softly on the cheek and she was gone, running along the corridor and unlocking the door. David watched her drive away down the street and wished, and wished he had said some more words to her.

# CHAPTER 41

There was no one in the office at Martin Place when Abby arrived, but this she expected. Harry would be having his dinner at some pub or other, and would return later because she knew he slept in the office rest room. She sat down at his desk and began to go over her plans, praying all the time that God would make them work. About half past nine Harry came in, smelling slightly of his favourite Bushmills, relaxed but not inebriated.

He came around the reception desk surprised to see her. "Abby! What the blazes are you doing here, girl?"

He was studying her face. Something was different, incredibly different. The usual cynicism, the usual hard, defiant air she always assumed in his presence was totally missing, and in its place there was something which Harry struggled before he could put a name to. Peace, yes, that was it, peace. He cast his mind back over their acquaintance and remembered he had once seen a shimmer of that expression before, when she had first come under his training. But this was no shimmer, this was the real thing, fully grown, foreign and profoundly disturbing at the same time.

"What's happened to you?" he asked roughly. "Are you on drugs again?"

# THE PETROV EFFECT

The laugh and the smile complimented one another, not a trace of malice in either, and for an insane moment Harry wondered if this was really the same woman, or someone else who had been made up to look like her.

"No, Harry," Abby said gently. "I'm sorry to tell you all the work you've done to turn me into a monster has been undone in a split second by God." She held up her hand in a pre-emptive gesture. "No, don't swear at me. I can tell from the look on your face that you can see it, can't you? I'm a different person."

"No one changes like that," Harry grunted. "Was it a good fix?"

"I'm not going to try and convince you, Harry." The same gentle voice. "I've come to ask your help, beg your help. I'm going to save him, Harry, and this is what I want you to do."

What craziness was this? He sat down on the desk in front of her while Abby explained her plan, his frown deepening with every word she spoke, although he held his peace until the end. He found it difficult to look into her face. What was it about her that made him feel so uncomfortable, as though he ought to go somewhere and wash? This scheme was madness, surely, and how would it end?

As though she had read his mind she told him. "The bomb will go off and I'll go to heaven, Harry. That's how it will end."

She was looking up at him with wide, speaking eyes which seemed to hold a new and greater power over him, as if some other living being was challenging his authority to command his own operative. Well, he would not surrender without a fight. His eyes caught a glimpse of the dents in the stainless steel splash guard on the sink, reminding him of what had caused them. That was the answer, wipe that peaceful serenity off her face and the being which had taken up residence in her skin would be exorcised, once and for all.

"Stockholm's syndrome," he laughed harshly. "You've become his willing sex slave. Go on, admit it. You're just hanging out for when he…"

361

What followed was the filthiest description of the sexual act his mind could conjure, all the while looking at her face. He knew his words were hurting her, yet the same serenity prevailed, occasionally supplemented by a tear, which only served to deepen its radiant beauty. From sexual depravity he turned to fear. The bomb would rip her apart piece by piece, and the detail which followed was gross, inhuman and disgusting. Yet with every word the sense of peace and assurance on her face became deeper and deeper. Now there wasn't a single tear, and it seemed to Harry that the only purpose his foul words were achieving, was to make her more radiant and himself more covered in the dark disgrace of shame.

Moreover his arsenal was now seriously depleted. Neither depravity nor fear had made the slightest difference. His frustration gave way to blind rage, throwing whatever came within reach of his hands. He called her every foul name under the sun. She was on crack, she was a whore and would always be a whore, a psychotic bitch whose heart was long dead and always would be, on and on and on. Every time he glanced at her face it wore that same expression of serene peace, neither sanctimonious nor condescending, an angel waiting for him to finish his raving, waiting with infinite patience, bearing him no malice.

In the end he turned towards her with a sneer. "This favour you want should make you a very thankful whore, and a whore knows how to be thankful."

Even as he looked at her serene, sad face he knew he had lost. The creature inhabiting this woman had won, and in elevating her, it had damned him into the depths. The memory of his own foul words burned in his ears like fire. She was sanctified, he condemned. She turned her radiant face towards him, her voice soft and tinged with sadness.

"A whore's wages, is that what it comes down to, Harry?" she said, softly. "I'm not like that anymore, but if this is the price I must pay for David's life, then I'm willing to pay it. But then that's all I will ever be to you Harry, just another prostitute. I would much rather we finish as friends."

362

In an admission of defeat he wiped the sweat from his face with his sleeve, dragged a chair over by her side and sat down.

"Look, Abby," he persuaded, "I don't know what's taken possession of your mind, but something has. Think, girl. You're asking me to help you throw your life away—"

"I'm not throwing my life away, Harry, I'm giving it to someone else. I'm not afraid to die, Harry. One moment I will be standing on this Earth, and the next I'll be in heaven forever. I've got a lot of catching up to do with God, and I'm really looking forward to it."

"You're barking mad." It was all he could say.

Abby continued, that same quiet, controlled voice. "But you can make sure I'm not throwing my life away, Harry. I need you to make it work. I need access to the databases that only you have. You know what else I need. We don't have a lot of time, Harry. What's it to be? Do I get undressed now?"

"No, you don't have to do that." His voice was soft and muffled. "I'd rather us end as friends, and, well, I don't know how to put it, this thing that's happened to you, damn it, it's like you're suddenly clean and I'm all covered in shit."

"God can forgive you the same way as He forgave me, Harry."

"Not now, girl," he muttered, "this is too much to take in. Somehow I've just turned down the sex I've wanted for years. I think you've put a hex on me. Anyway, I get it. Petrov's innocent, and I guess Patrick deserves what's coming to him. Turn on the computer there, Abby, and we'll need the colour printer. Let's get to work."

❋ ❋ ❋

The arrangements were not completed that evening nor the next day, which was Saturday. Around lunch time Abby ducked out of Martin Place to a store in the Haymarket which sold electronic components, and bought a radio controlled switch, a small box with a couple of relays which could be activated from an even smaller device which fitted on the end of a keychain in her pocket. Back to Martin Place, and then to some other special locations in various parts of the inner city to pick up documents.

On Sunday morning she drove the van to a parking station in North Sydney. Selecting an upper floor where she could see anyone approaching before they saw her, she set to work. It took less than an hour. With her hand in the pocket of her jeans, she pressed the button on the small key ring device, and was rewarded by seeing the ignition lights come on, hearing the starter motor whirr and the engine fire. She pressed it again. The ignition shut off and the engine died. So far so good. Now to cover her handiwork in the engine bay.

Back at Martin Place she took the new briefcase she had bought and added a number of documents to it. That done, she sat down at her desk, drew a sheet of paper out of the printer tray and began to write. An hour later there was a lot of screwed-up paper on the floor and exactly two lines of writing on the latest sheet from the printer. Why was it so hard to express the things you felt so deeply? It took a total of two and a half hours before she was satisfied. She gathered up all the other attempts and fed them one by one into the office shredder, a special machine which ensured that they couldn't be reassembled. Adding the letter to the briefcase, she piled two items on top of it, a passport and an airline ticket, first class to Heathrow.

Now all was done the hard part commenced, the waiting. Harry had gone and by this time was no doubt drowning his sorrows in an excess of his favourite beverage. She wished him well in doing it. They had parted friends, and in Harry's case with sorrow.

Over the last twenty four hours he had come to understand the cause of his rage the previous night. It had little to do with his loss of control over her. Something had come and taken her out of his world altogether, and it wasn't Petrov, although he was sure she was in love with him. Knowing the former state of her heart, that alone gave him cause for pause. She had gone, and deep down inside he felt bereft, regretting more than ever what he had done to her over the years, even to the point where he could feel a shard of gratitude towards whatever had undone it so effectively.

Surely there was nothing in this God thing, and yet his denial had been shaken by the evidence before his eyes. One thing was certain, the CIA and he were soon to part company forever. He still had some good mates back home in Belfast, mates who would protect him against any reprisals. Perhaps he could pick up his old trade, yes, he would feel at home back there. Maybe in time there would be some nice Irish lass... No, she wouldn't be Abby. No other girl could fit into those shoes.

✳ ✳ ✳

David, despite Abby's assurances of safety, had not slept well at all. His mind was a turmoil of conflicting emotions. His life was about to change forever, his beloved Lydia would think he had abandoned her, his satisfying and pleasant career at the University was about to end. Sarah Cole, the woman he esteemed so highly, to whom he owed so much, was going to write him off as a complete fool, all because of Abby Saunders. She had turned his life upside down, wrenched almost everything out of his hand. He remembered the day she had told him of her deception, how he had despised her in his anger, never wanting to see her again, begging God for the strength to forgive her. Then the anxious call from Lydia, worried and perplexed, his false assurances which he was sure she saw straight through.

Not many hours afterwards his nemesis had turned up at his door. He could still see the astonishing tears in her eyes, and recalled the way they had wrenched his heart. Despite everything he would have walked barefoot over broken glass to comfort her. He could feel the warmth of her body in his arms and longed for the time he could hold her again. Helplessly in love, yes, and that love had overturned and destroyed every thread of rationality he had ever possessed, turned his future from comfortable predictability to existential chaos.

But he was certain of one thing.

God had changed her, changed her so powerfully, so suddenly, so completely. In the whole morass of confusion and doubt, this alone stood a steadying pillar, a searchlight of hope in the swirling uncertainty. If God had done this, then He was totally in control of whatever tomorrow would bring. With this comforting certainty he fell asleep in the early hours of the morning.

He planned to spend most of the weekend with Lydia and Geoff, not knowing when he would see them again. Taking the train to Petersham, he composed his face into what he hoped was a carefree smile, and knocked on the door. Lydia opened it and instantly flung her arms around his shoulders, dragging him inside, her tears flowing freely. Behind her in the hall Geoff stood, his face drawn with worry.

"David, you have to go away," Lydia stammered, holding onto to him as if she was drowning.
"Geoff and I have arranged to go on a long holiday in the country, and you're going to come with us. I've put some comfortable pillows in the boot, and you can travel in there until we're—"

"Dearest Lydia," David comforted, holding her close. "There's no need to go anywhere. I'm not in any danger."

Lydia rounded on him angrily. "Of course you are. Do you think I'm stupid? It's that wretched Saunders woman. I know what she was hinting at. It's the CIA, isn't it, and you're their latest victim, God alone knows why!"

David's mind was churning. He remembered Abby's assurances that all would be well, to tell no one that she had a rescue plan in mind. What could he say without further endangering the very people he loved the most?

"Lydia, please listen," he begged. "If, as you say, the CIA are after me, then there is nothing you or I could do. We have to trust that God is able to protect me. He's more powerful than the CIA, or whoever you think wishes me harm."

For answer Lydia flung her arms around him and clung even harder. David felt utterly wretched. He pressed Lydia against him and began to rub her back. "Look at the way He changed Abby," he said in his most comforting voice. "If He can do something like that to someone like her, then we have nothing to fear."

Lydia broke free from his embrace, tears still flowing down her cheeks. "If she has changed," she snapped. "I wouldn't put it past the woman to have made the whole thing up."

"You know that's not true."

"I don't know what's true anymore," Lydia said angrily. "Come with us. We can leave now. If nothing's going to happen to you it won't matter, and if you're in danger you can escape."

"It would do no good," David said with a long sigh. "Lydia, Geoff, can't you see? If you're right, and my life is in danger, I'm certainly not going to put yours in danger too. Trying to run away from the CIA is beyond our power. But it isn't beyond God's power. I admit I'm worried, but the only thing we can do is trust our Lord."

In the background he could see Geoff nodding. For an instant he thought to tell them about Abby's promise, but decided it would do no good at all. She had given him no details, and all he would do was increase Lydia's distrust. Their reaction could well jeopardise Abby's plans. "Come on," he coaxed, "this is no way to spend a lovely weekend together. I'm starving. I've been hanging out all week for some of your scones, Lydia, and I can't wait another moment."

Taking Lydia's hand he headed down the hall towards the kitchen, following Geoff's lead. The rest of the weekend was truly dreadful. Lydia said no more about any escape plans, but she wouldn't let him out of her sight either, even following him down the corridor when he went to the toilet and waiting outside until he had finished. They spoke little, for the haunted look in her eyes, the haggard appearance of her face, told him far more eloquently than words could have ever conveyed, that despite his empty assurances she was preparing to lose him forever. He tried to keep the conversation light, but it was hardly worth the effort. Lydia was saying good-bye to him, the way she had said good-bye to her father in Kiev, her mother, her sister, and the grief in her face nearly broke his heart.

There was no anger, no blame, just the outpouring of a mother's love and sorrow. A dozen, a hundred times he told her that there was nothing to worry about, that he would be all right, that God would take care of him, but he could have saved his breath. Truly distressing was the way she had clung to him at their parting, sobbing hopelessly with her shaking arms around his neck. Of all the sad, inconsolable times of his life this was the worst, his heart torn into pieces in the war of conflicting emotions which raged within.

❀ ❀ ❀

Monday was the longest day of his life. He arrived late to his office in the Physics building, and gave a deplorable lecture with his mind totally occupied elsewhere. Returning to his desk, he read an email from the referee telling him their paper had gone forward to publication, and another about changed security measures. He deleted the rest unread. Lunchtime came and went with nothing more than an apple and a coffee, and the afternoon dragged on. Every second seemed like an hour. He went over to the Edwards building early, liberated only that morning from the miles of yellow police tape across every entrance. The builder's skip stood emptied next to the grassy slope, and a pile of galvanised steel planking was being loaded on to a truck nearby. He wondered if the contractors had been blamed for the incident, and hoped they hadn't.

Reaching the lab he began to tidy up, not wishing to leave a mess behind. He typed instructions on how to use the transmitter, how to set up the receiver, how to connect the data line, the storage unit, and anything else he could think of. He laminated them and stuck them on the various pieces of equipment, so that anyone taking up his research would know what to do. He tried to make it look as though the preparation was simply an expression of his thoroughness, not preparation for a deliberately planned departure. Small chance he had of success. Sarah Cole would see through it in seconds. He wondered what she would think of him, shuddered, and felt as guilty as all hell.

It was a useful activity nonetheless, and evening came before he had completed it. He went out the front door for sandwiches and iced tea, came back and ate them slowly, apprehension rising in his heart. Now it was seven o'clock, and no sign of Abby. Had something horrible happened to her? If that was the case something horrible was about to happen to him. He covered his face with his hands and prayed. He had repeated that act several times when he heard the door of the lab click open. He sprang to his feet, turned round, and there was Abby running towards him with a briefcase in her hand. She dropped the briefcase on the floor and sprang into his arms. They clung together for a long time without saying a single word. Finally, using all the self-control she possessed, Abby pushed herself gently away, turned and picked up the briefcase from the floor.

David caught hold of her other hand. His voice was soft and urgent. "Abby, there's something I've wanted to say to you. Can you put that thing down?"

She put the briefcase down on the floor, turned round and touched his cheek gently with her outstretched hand.

"I know what you want to say, David. Now is not the time nor the place. Please don't be upset or cross with me. I understand, David, dearest David."

She was holding his face with both hands now, her eyes gentle and sad. "I have important things to say, David, and you must listen, must do exactly as I tell you." She walked over to the brief case. "Don't open this now. Inside is your passport. Your new name is doctor David Thomas. All you have to do is write Thomas in your usual handwriting. I hope you like the name."

David stared at her and said nothing.

"There's an air ticket to Heathrow, and all the other things you need. I've left my stuff in the car. In a minute or two I'm going to the ladies to put my face on, and then I'm going out to check all is clear. I want you to give me five minutes, turn off the lights and go out by the back way down the fire stairs. I'll bring the car around."

She paused, holding him by both shoulders, her face very intense, very serious.

369

"David, I want you to solemnly promise me. You must get on the flight to Heathrow. You must go straight to the airport and get on it. Promise me?"

"Of course, but you'll be with me," he said, anxiously.

"I might have to join you at the last minute," she assured him. "I think the coast is clear, but if it isn't I'll have to lay down some cover to keep them off our tracks for a little while. It might be a close call, so don't worry, just get on the plane. Will you do that for me, David? Get on the plane?"

Her hands were on his cheeks, her eyes pleading.

"Yes, Abby, I promise. I really hope we can go together. How close is this danger? Let me come with you. Two are better than one when it comes to nasty people. I'm not without the ability to throw my weight around."

She smiled at him, reached up and gently kissed his cheek. "You've very strong. You threw me quite a way through that door, and I didn't stop very gently either. No, David, I'm trained at this sort of thing, and if there are problems I can deal with them. Please, five minutes, turn out the light and then go out the back way. If the car is there get in, if not, then take a taxi to the airport. Don't forget the briefcase. Will you do that?"

"Yes, I will."

She threw her arms around him again, holding him ferociously. Suddenly she reached up, kissed his cheek, and before he could respond in any way, broke free and ran out of the room. David looked at his watch. The minutes ticked by slowly, and he could feel his heart racing. Four and a half, five. He picked up the briefcase, took a quick and approving look around the lab, turned out the light, shut the door, and headed down the corridor towards the rear exit.

❊ ❊ ❊

Abby had not gone near the bathroom at all. Leaving the lab she had belted down the steps, through the front door and out to the van. It wasn't locked. Passing through the lighted entrance she had checked her watch, thirty five minutes since she had parked it there, plenty of time for Patrick to do his thing. She knew about Patrick's methods. He always hung around to make sure of his handiwork, so he was somewhere out there watching, waiting. Now to winkle him out of his hidey hole, make him approach her. When he was close, she would put her hand in her pocket, press the button and say hello to her Lord. Patrick, she thought, would not be enjoying the same privilege. She had left the car unlocked deliberately to make it easier for him, and now she slid the rear door wide, deliberately searching for anything out of the usual. There was no way Patrick would let her raise the alarm, and he wouldn't shoot her from a distance and leave her body lying. No, he would come over, dispose of her somehow, but instead she would dispose of him.

She peered carefully into the back of the van. Nothing. The black rubber of the floor pan was completely bare. She opened the front door and searched beneath the dashboard. Nothing. Surely she could not have been wrong. Monday had to be the day, this had to be the time. Once again she examined the back of the van. Suddenly something struck her as unusual. The floor pan was not at the right height. Surely she was imagining things. No, she was looking at a false floor, some good twenty centimetres higher than it should have been. Dropping to her knees she grabbed hold of the rubber mat, lifted it and gasped. The whole floor was covered with rectangular boxes, fitted carefully into one another. It was a bomb, alright, but what a bomb. She crouched down and peered at the road underneath the van. It was dark, she couldn't see. She put her hand under the tray. Solid. The entire space under the van was filled with the same packages. A massive car bomb, far bigger than was required to destroy the van and everyone in it. What was going on here?

Suddenly she felt the cold muzzle of a gun pressed into her neck. Damn. How careless. Never mind, her plan had worked. Now to put her hand…

"You keep your pretty little hands away from your pockets, Lassie," Patrick's Irish brogue was soft and even gentle. "Knowing the Deadly Angel you've probably got a nasty surprise for Patrick down there. No going for the shoulder bag either. That's it, up with the hands, keep them coming, now on to your feet, that's the girl, slow, slow. Normally I don't like killing women in cold blood, but in your case I'm doing half the human race a favour."

"I want to blow my nose," Abby objected. "Surely you can let a girl do that before you kill her."

"To be sure I can't. Keep them up, I said, or it's a bullet in your pretty neck. Now, where are the keys? Does your lover have them?"

"Yes. I gave them to him. The van's not locked."

"Good. Now take this piece of paper and write a note to him on the front seat, slowly now, there's a pen inside, don't grip it funny, or the first bullet goes through your backside. That's the girl."

"What do I write?" Abby stammered.

"David, I'm at the gates. Pick me up quick."

"He'll never believe this," Abby protested desperately. "You're wasting your time."

"Here comes the bullet." He pressed the gun hard into her backside.

"Alright." There was unfeigned fear in her voice. Patrick heard it and smiled.

"So good of you to cooperate. Leave it right there on the front seat. Now stand up, that's it. See you in hell, my beauty."

He struck her on the back of the head with the pistol and caught her as she crumpled into his arms. Carrying her limp body, he crossed the car park and heaved her into the builder's skip.

"Put the trash in the trash," he mused to himself. "You're safe now, gents. No more Deadly Angel to rip your hearts out. Thank old Patrick for that."

He went back over to the van, picked up the note, and stuck it in front of the dashboard.

It was the nail that did it, the nail attached to a piece of window frame which had deeply penetrated Abby's thigh when she landed on top of it in the nearly empty skip. The pain had brought her back to consciousness. Dizzy, sick and disorientated she had lain there, her thigh and her head throbbing, trying to work out where she was, what had happened. Slowly and with much pain, she managed to extricate the nail from her thigh by kneeling up a little. Her head was swimming, and she gripped the edge of the skip to stop herself from falling back on the nail. Now she could lift her head above the rim. There was Patrick, standing near the open driver's door. She felt in her pocket for the remote, pulled it out, and pressed the button. She saw Patrick start, stare unbelieving at the dashboard which had sprung to life. He turned towards her, a look of total resignation on his face. The engine started. A wave of light and heat struck her and she remembered no more.

❊ ❊ ❊

David, briefcase in hand, had reached the fire escape at the far end of the building. Opening the fire door he had sprinted only halfway down one flight of stairs when the world exploded. The force of the blast knocked him down the remainder of the flight and he fell heavily onto the landing below, dazed and shaken. Smoke was creeping under the fire door to his left, and the staircase above was cracked and ruined. In some places the concrete steps were hanging only by the reinforcing inside them, and the handrail was twisted and bent. Above his head a single emergency light burned, dangling by its wires. Staggering to his feet he managed to negotiate the remainder of the stairwell, sometimes jumping between gaps, coughing from the gradually thickening smoke. The outside door was bent but mercifully yielded to his shoving, and he staggered out into the courtyard beyond, coughing and unable to see very far in the smoke and dust. Running out onto the road, he came round to the front of the building. Building? There was hardly any building left. Running further away he could see more detail. The dust was settling a little, and in several places gas was burning, casting weird dancing shadows amidst the debris. Only a third of the building was still standing, its walls cracked and leaning dangerously. The rest had been reduced to rubble. Over where the car park had been there was a huge crater, the builder's skip upside down in the grass, dented heavily by the flying masonry. An unearthly silence, broken only by the soft sputtering of burning gas and the occasional crack from a shower of electrical sparks, had taken the place of the horrendous tumult of sound. David stared at the ruin, struggling to comprehend what had taken place. A bomb, a car bomb... His was the only car there...

"Abby!" His voice choked on the word. "Dear God, Abby!"

He sank to his knees, his legs were shaking so badly. Perhaps she wasn't in the car when it happened, perhaps she was far away, leading their enemies on a wild goose chase. His mind told him she was gone forever, his heart refused to believe it. Now he could hear sirens, and in the distance people were running towards the disaster, waving torches in their hands. He scrambled to his feet. All Abby's work would be undone if they saw him. Gripping the briefcase in his hand he ran towards City Road, choosing the darkest and most circuitous route where no security cameras had a hope of seeing him.

Twenty minutes later he was sitting in a taxi heading for Kingsford Smith International airport, the briefcase clutched to his chest. Fifteen minutes after that he was striding into Terminal one. Balancing the briefcase on one knee, he clicked the locks and opened it. On top of a pile of papers was a passport with an airline ticket stuck inside it, and underneath a folded piece of paper with the word "David" written across it in Abby's hand. He withdrew the passport with his ticket and quickly shut the case, went to the first class check in counter, and handed them over to the young woman there. She gave him a smile and a boarding pass, telling him he should make his way through immigration and go straight to the departure gate as first class passengers could now board the aircraft.

He thanked her and set off, his eyes scrutinising every other young woman with blonde hair in the terminal for the one his heart ached to see. Once he thought he had found her, wandering through Duty Free shopping, and started to run in her direction, but the stranger had turned at the sound of his footsteps and given him a most unfriendly look. It wasn't far to gate forty seven, and the general boarding call had already been given when he arrived. The stewardess glanced at his boarding pass and passport and ushered him through the first class entrance on to the plane. Would he like to stow his briefcase or did he have work to do? He had work to do, thank you, he would keep it by his feet until take-off.

He sounded as tense as he felt, for now there were less than ten minutes before the aircraft left the gate, and still no Abby had bounced though the door and run to his side in delight. Five minutes, his heart was beating like a hammer, she was cutting it very fine. Four, surely the next person through the door would be her. Three, yes, he could see some blonde hair behind the stewardess, no, it wasn't her, two, one. The door shut leaving him alone, cutting off all hope. He shut his eyes and ran his hand over them. No, surely not, she couldn't be dead, this was not how everything should end, not without Abby.

The stewardess came over to him, a worried expression on her face, and asked him to fasten his seat belt. Half an hour later they were in the air, and still the briefcase remained unopened at his feet. He was afraid to open it now, afraid to read the note she had written him, unwilling to accept what her words might say. On the other hand, perhaps there was another plan, not revealed to him before. Perhaps he was to meet her in London, perhaps... He lifted the briefcase onto his lap, opened it, took out the note, unfolded it and began to read.

> *Dearest David,*
> *If you are reading this on the plane then you will know that God has wonderfully answered my prayers. You are safe and I am with my Lord in heaven.*

He couldn't read any more. Tears streamed down his face. He took a handkerchief out of his pocket in a futile attempt to hide them, not realising that the other first class passengers, most of them tapping furiously on their laptops, couldn't have cared less. An anxious stewardess came over to his side.

"Are you all right, Sir? Is there anything I can do? A drink perhaps? We have—"

"No, thank you. I... I... I've just learned that a friend of mine has died... We were... close."

There was real concern on the young woman's face. "I'm so sorry to hear that, Sir. I will leave you alone, but if there is the slightest thing I can do, please press this button, or just wave at me."

She left, no knowing what else to say. Indeed there was nothing else to say. Summoning all his courage, David opened the note out and began to read again.

> Please don't grieve over me, David. You're the one who has to stay living on our dusty planet for a while, wearied with its brokenness, while I'm having a party with the angels and all that. I don't think I'll be able to see you from here, because if I did I know I would be unhappy, and I don't think there is any unhappiness left for me anymore. That's what you have to bear for a little while, but I'll be waiting for you! It's not the end, David. You'll see me again, and it will be such a joyful reunion, because He will be there with both of us, God, I mean.
>
> Before I go I want to tell you I love you.
>
> I think it's the way I've felt for ages, but I couldn't put a name to it because, as you said, my heart was dead and ruined. Then God ripped out the old dead thing inside me and made me alive again, and I knew. Even God agrees with me! I read that greater love has no one than he who lays down his life for his friend, or something like that, and this is what I have done for you, David. It's a love gift, and I gave it with joy in my heart, please believe that.
>
> I love you, love you, love you.
>
> I am so sorry about your wonderful Lydia, but you will see her again in a year or so and when you do, please ask her to forgive me.
>
> Whatever I possessed I have given to you, David, a small token of comfort for all the trouble and change I have caused you. Please accept it. Most of it comes from my father as an inheritance which I didn't deserve, and I could never bring myself to spend a dime of it. In your hands it will be used to do good and generous things, but

*most of all I want you to be comfortable and have everything you need.*

*There's some other documents in the case as well, and these clearly show what the CIA was doing in Australia and that it was they who planted the bomb. Keep them in a very safe place and only use them if it becomes ABSOLUTELY necessary.*

*It's good-bye for a while now, dearest David. May God take care of you each day my love.*

*Abby.*

With an unsteady hand he folded the note carefully. Bringing it slowly to his lips he kissed it several times and placed it tenderly in his pocket. Next he extracted the sheet of paper which lay in the briefcase beneath. It was a bank statement, Barclay's Bank, his new name on the top left, an account number on the top right, and an account balance underneath that. He stared at the number unbelievingly, then using his finger, counted from the left towards the decimal point. Ten million, nine hundred and twenty thousand, one hundred and fifty five pounds seventy pence.

His head flopped back onto the comfortable rest behind it, eyes closed. His grip on reality had suddenly become very tenuous indeed. A good ten minutes passed before he could open his eyes and return his attention to the remaining items in the briefcase. Below the bank statement lay a pile of photocopied documents in a folder with a piece of paper stuck in the front of them, also in Abby's hand: ONLY IN ABSOLUTE EMERGENCY. He returned the bank statement to its place and shut the case, placing it at the foot of his seat. His heart had taken enough battering for a while. He waved at the stewardess whose eyes had hardly left him.

"I'd like... I'd like... a hot chocolate, please," he said in an unsteady voice.

# CHAPTER 42

The morning saw a large team of police investigators, state emergency workers, and civil engineers clambering over the ruins of the Edwards building. From further back two men surveyed the scene in the shadow of a large Planus tree which was still standing, although many of its leaves and a number of its smaller branches were scattered on the ground. Not far away lay a builder's skip, turned over and embedded in the slope, its base dented out of shape by the flying masonry which littered the ground for quite some distance around. One of the men was stirring the carpet of leaves absentmindedly with his shoe. Turning to the other man he shook his head slowly.

"These are strange days, Robin."

"They are indeed, Brian. And how is the director of you-know-what this morning?"

"About to be thrown to the crocks for lunch," Brian sighed heavily. "AAT is the flavour of the month with the P.M. He's been on the phone almost nonstop since the story broke last night. Why hadn't I taken more action against this ghastly terrorist cell which the AAT had briefed me about? What had I dug up on them? Could I guarantee the next bomb wasn't going off under Parliament House? We've become a political embarrassment. The press are screaming for answers, and the only people who are talking to them are the AAT. Our name is being buried in horse manure even as we speak."

Naylor nodded sadly. "I've confirmed two victims already, and I hope there's no more. We found a piece of jawbone on the grass right over near the Mechanical Engineering building – or rather a student found it – and it's Petrov's. He had dental records, thank heaven, a perfect match. The other is Saunders – found a blood soaked handbag with an American licence. No trace of a body yet, but you wouldn't expect to find much."

"I feel very guilty about that end of the business." Hill shook his head. "We should have kept a closer eye on him, but it doesn't explain what happened here. Some sophisticated terrorists they must have been. Just look at the blast wave. It demolishes an entire building on one side, and on the other, relatively minor damage. That's not your average terrorist bomb."

"Why such force?" Naylor muttered. "If they wanted to kill Petrov and the girl then a normal car bomb would have done the trick. More questions than answers." He glanced up suddenly. "Hello, what's this?"

The morning sun was glinting on something metallic stuck in the trunk of the Planus tree. Robin Naylor went over and with a little effort pulled it out.

"Looks like the remains of Petrov's iPod, or the girl's. What do you think?" He handed it to Brian Hill.

Brian began to examine the small object. Out of his pocket he produced a steel key ring and snapped it against the metallic square which protruded from its underside. A smile began to spread all over his face.

"Robin, my friend," he chuckled, "there really is a God."

"That's no news to me, Brian, but I'd never thought to hear it coming from your lips."

"This, Mr. Naylor, is what we in the spy trade call an intelligent alarm. Very new, very sophisticated. You programme this tiny chip" – he pointed to a small black thing on the tiny circuit board – "with the sound you want the alarm to respond to. It's very specific, a particular person's voice, shower running, toilet flushing, window opening, or a car engine starting. When that sound is received the alarm sends a signal, in this case to the device attached to the bomb detonator."

"Ingenious," Robin grunted. "So small. I've never heard of this."

"Not many people have, Robin, and until a week or so ago I hadn't either. We have these regular show-and-tells of useful goodies. This little device comes from a British manufacturer, and we ordered a dozen of them. Shouldn't be telling you this."

"Why are you telling me this?"

"Because each of them has a unique serial number. Our good friend Ross Baker of MI6 has got someone on the inside of the company. One phone call and we'll know who bought this one." He took his mobile phone out of his pocket and spent the next five minutes making the call, holding the small device in his hand. Returning both to his pocket, he gave Robin a grin. "This day is beginning to look better by the minute. Ross is giving it top priority. Had to get the poor blighter out of bed. We'll have the answer soon. Care to adjourn to our favourite café? Coffee's on me."

The two men strolled back to Brian's car, and drove off. As they went through the door to the café Brian's phone rang. Robin ordered two Columbian blacks, and sat down at their usual table. Shortly afterwards Brian joined him, a large grin all over his face.

"The device was one of fifty bought by our American friends," he said. "What a surprise."

"Well, well, well, so the plot begins to sicken, doesn't it?" Robin grimaced. "They don't mind taking out their agent as well as their target, but why the grand demonstration?"

Brian grunted. "To set their AAT on a rock solid footing. As I said, who will guarantee the next bomb doesn't go off under the Opera House? We can't, but the AAT can - for a damn good reason – the CIA planted the bloody thing."

Robin Naylor took his coffee from the hand of their usual waitress. A smile began to spread across his face as well.

"This is really your day, Brian. Hmm, yes, I think I can add a further point of interest. I had a phone call on Sunday from the Chief Minister, Northern Territory. Strange incident. A Pitjantjatjara man witnessed a murder out at Alice Spring last week. It was on Indigenous land and he didn't want his people to be blamed, so he reported it straight away. The police came and grabbed the body. Professional hit, no doubt about it. He described the assassin quite well. I have a good memory for faces. I'm sure it was our good friend Mr. Norman Harding. I need a photo we could wire to Alice Springs to confirm. You must have thousands."

"As you know we had a camera mounted across the plaza from their covert nest in Martin Place."

"Thank you," Robin continued, the smile still lingering. "This morning I had a phone call from one Dianne Collins, Director of the NSA. Most unusual. One of their countrymen, a Mr. Harry O'Callaghan, was on holidays here and has gone missing. Could I trace him, please?" He drew a photograph out of his pocket and handed it to Brian. "Ever seen him before?"

"He features in a great deal of footage from the same camera," Brian said, smiling. "So, the CIA is taking out their garbage. When we've finished our coffees we could call past my office for the photo you require – even send it to Alice Springs if you want to. You've really brightened up an otherwise total disaster of a day."

Brian Hill was feeling quite elated. A little more piecing together and he would pay the P.M. a visit and brighten up his day as well. They might not know what had sparked this brouhaha with the CIA, but they knew enough to ensure the AAT was about to pass into history.

# CHAPTER 43

D avid Thomas went somewhat nervously through immigration at Heathrow, receiving nothing more than a stamp in his passport. He caught the train to Paddington and made his way to the comfortable guest house whose name appeared on the piece of paper which he had found in the lid of the briefcase. Yes, the room was booked for a week, doctor Thomas, and would he sign the register, please? He signed it by writing D. Thomas in his normal hand, silently remarking on how well it matched the signature in his passport. He took the key and went upstairs to his room. It was comfortable if not luxurious. He used the bathroom first, then set about planning his day, knowing that the best treatment for jetlag was to go to bed in the evening and not the morning.

Truth be told, the time shift hadn't hit him at all, his grip on reality was still far too tenuous, his heart far too sad to concentrate on such mundane matters as weariness. It ached as he thought about Lydia and Geoff who would be in agony of spirit right now, grieving his reported death. It ached even more for Abby, which surprised him. How he wished he had told her that he loved her, and now it was too late. She had died without knowing his heart belonged to her. Perhaps she had worked it out. He hoped very much that she had.

He needed clothes and toiletries, so now it was time to test the reality of that ridiculous bank statement. He walked slowly back towards

Paddington station, then around a little further until he came to a sizeable branch of Barclays Bank. He hesitated at the entrance. Suppose all this was a fantasy, some sort of con job? Pushing open the door he went it, identified himself by passport to the young woman on the enquiry counter - who looked a bit like Abby but wasn't nearly as pretty - and was told to wait. An eternity seemed to pass. Had they called the police? Was he waiting until they arrived to arrest him for travelling on false documents? Fraud? A gentleman's voice to his left startled him so much he nearly jumped off the chair.

"I'm so sorry to have startled you, Doctor," the gentleman apologised. "Please come into my office. Is there anything we can do to assist? I understand you have only recently returned from Australia and transferred your entire assets to our bank. We are most gratified, Doctor, and let me assure you that you have made the right choice. Barclay's can offer you the best service you will find in Britain. Now, can I get you some refreshment?"

He left the bank an hour later, an ATM card, two thousand pounds and a safety deposit key in his pocket. His grip on reality was growing stronger. Catching the train into London he spent a busy morning buying a suitcase and filling it with necessities, nice necessities. He returned to Paddington wearing the ones which wouldn't fit in the case, a fashionable tailored pair of black trousers, dark navy blue shirt and a rather expensive tie. He was beginning to feel tired, but the retail therapy had done much to temporarily lift his spirits.

There had been several unfortunate incidents when he was sure he had seen Abby in the crowd and called out to her before he could recall the words. His mind told him it couldn't be. His heart saw her every time. On the last occasion, the woman – whose name just happened to be Abby – had treated him to a short but colourful lecture on what she thought of 'foreign jerks who were always trying to crack onto decent English girls.' No doubt any competent psychiatrist could have explained what was happening to him and given him a technical name for his condition. All David knew was a burning ache in his heart which intensified after each predictable disappointment.

Returning to his room, he had picked up the briefcase and caught the train to Windsor, where he purchased another safe deposit box in a small bank not far down the street from a lopsided tea house which looked as though it had been constructed by an ancient builder who had enjoyed his whiskey far too much. In this deposit box he had placed the folder of documents. Returning to Paddington, now quite weary, he had placed the key to this safe deposit box in the other one he owned at Barclay's bank. A double layer of security, the best he could do.

Feeling hungry as well as tired, he turned in to a friendly looking Indian restaurant on his way back to the Guest House. Taking a magazine off the stand near the door, he went to sit at a table at the back of the room. He opened it to an article on the expanding universe of all things, and settled down to read. The waiter came and took his order, brought him a large glass of lemon lime and bitters, and left him to finish his reading while he waited for his meal. The end of the article came first. David glanced up.

There, across the room, her back towards him, reading the menu on the wall, was Abby. Instantly he was on his feet, his knee catching the table with such force the lemon, lime and bitters sailed over its edge, and emptied most of its contents all over a young man and his girlfriend sitting on the table next to him.

"Abby!" He called out loudly.

The girl turned round, stared in his direction and swore at him. So did the two young people on the next table, now trying to blot their clothes dry with a couple of serviettes. The waiter arrived with his dinner, and while he didn't actually swear at him, conveyed much the same sentiments by the steely look of intense disapproval in his face. David apologised to the soaking diners, and not waiting to see if his apology was accepted, turned back to his dinner and his article, not reading one and not tasting the other. How long would this sort of thing continue? He was tired, so perhaps it would stop when he felt more refreshed. Then he thought that feeling refreshed might only sharpen the pain in his heart. He had to begin the process of moving on, reminding himself she was dead, he would only see her again in heaven. Poor Lydia and Geoff. How long would it be before it was safe to send them word that he lived?

He left the restaurant at seven thirty that night feeling totally miserable. On his way back to the Guest House he passed a small park bordered on three sides by other terraced Guest Houses like his own. In the park were two lovers sitting on a seat. She was on his lap, her arms around his neck. They were kissing passionately without regard to anyone else who might be passing. David found himself staring at them, wishing so very much that his own lips were pressed against Abby's, that it was her warm body cradled in his lap, her eager arms around his neck. He had to turn away, so great was the empty ache in his heart.

"Dear God," he prayed, "help me stop this. Help me face reality."

He arrived at his room even more tired and dispirited than he had been that morning. After making a semi-serious attempt at stowing his newly acquired wardrobe in the cupboard, he threw his dressing gown over a chair, cleaned his teeth, jumped into bed and sank down between the sheets, thinking he would probably never get to sleep. Five minutes later he was breathing slowly and softly. The impossible oblivion of sleep had come.

❋ ❋ ❋

He was awakened by someone knocking at the door. He glanced sleepily at the alarm clock by his bed. Seven thirty. Who could be knocking at his door at his hour? Suddenly a wave of fear passed over him. He was discovered. The CIA were outside the door waiting to take him out somewhere and dispose of him. Better find out, nothing was worse than not knowing. He glanced at his dressing gown. No, he thought, a dressing gown hampered movement. Seconds later he reached the door and flung it open.

To his surprise a young woman stood there, wearing a cream leather coat and gloves to match, holding a newspaper in her hand. She could have been Abby, right height, wrong hair colour. Not that you could see a great deal of it under the wide-brimmed floppy hat she wore. Much of her face was hidden behind ridiculously large round sunglasses, but David's refreshing sleep and yesterday's fiascos had cured him of making yet another false identification.

She smiled at him and handed him the paper, all without saying a single word. He took the paper from her, said "thank you," and was about to close the door. Suddenly he noticed the picture on the front page. He turned away and went over to the lighted window. She had handed him a copy of the Sydney Morning Herald, and there in huge letters he read:

TERRORISM COMES TO OZ
HORRIFIC SCENE AT SYDNEY UNIVERSITY
TWO SCIENTISTS DEAD.

Underneath was a large picture of the demolished Edwards building, and under that a picture of himself and one of Abby next to it. This then was the final confirmation. They had found her bloodstained handbag, her driver's licence, enough to identify her as the other victim. Vaguely in the background he heard the sound of the door closing behind him. A picture of her, the only one he would ever have. He would treasure it forever. He reached out his hand and touched it tenderly with his fingers, tears welling in his eyes, and groaned softly into an empty room.

"Oh Abby, my beautiful, darling Abby."

"Yes?"

He whirled round at the sound of the voice. The door was shut, which he had expected, but now the woman was inside the room. She had shed the huge glasses, hat and gloves, and was standing there watching him. A large bruise discoloured the smooth skin above her right eye, another on her forehead, and her hair was dark brown rather than golden. For a full ten seconds he stood staring, his mind refusing to believe the testimony of his own eyes. Then, with a choking cry he launched himself towards her.

"ABBY!"

She grabbed hold of his wrists and brought his arms down to his sides. "You can't hug me, David," she said softly. "Inside all this Armarni I'm a badly battered woman."

"How?" he stammered in confusion. "No one... no one could have survived..."

"I never meant to survive, David, but Patrick hit me over the head and threw me in the builder's skip. When the bomb went off it turned over and got buried in the grass like a little fall-out shelter. Took me hours to dig myself out with a piece of window frame. My nails are ruined."

Tears were streaming down his face as he stood there, disbelieving for joy the sight before him, her lovely blue eyes alive and inviting. She came close, close. He shut his eyes as she reached up to his face, wiping his eyelids and his cheeks with soft, caring fingers. Closer now, she lowered her head onto his shoulder and felt his arms wrap gently around her.

An overwhelming sense of peace enveloped her. This was God's doing, and well she knew it. She had given her life to Him first, and then offered it for the man she loved. God had taken the gift, blessed it, and handed it back to her. He had brought her to her heart's desire, to this supremely beautiful moment, and in her heart she sang His praises. Never in her life had she felt this way, the unshakable conviction she had come home at last. She was in the arms of the man who loved her, whom she really loved, and everything was new and wonderful, fresh and clean.

His voice was soft and broken by the emotion surging through it, his breath warm on her neck. "Abby," he choked, "I've just ached and ached for you. Oh Abby, I love you. I love you!"

She raised her face towards his, and as though this was the first time she had ever done it, touched her lips against his own. It was the softest of kisses, shy and innocent, but it triggered a totally unexpected response. Perhaps it was the shock of seeing her return from the dead, the joy of feeling her alive and warm in his arms, the scent of her familiar perfume wafting around him. Suddenly he was holding her tightly, kissing her passionately. Abby, abandoning herself to the outpouring of his desire, returned kiss for kiss, her arms wrapped tightly around his neck, her fingers threading themselves through his hair. It wasn't until the symphony of complaint from every bruise had reached the point where it could no longer be ignored, that Abby relinquished his neck, snuggled her head down against his shoulder, and wrapped her arms around his back. She could feel his heart pounding fast against her breast, her own racing against his.

She gave a small chuckle. "My, my, for a stuffy old physicist you really do come on, doctor Thomas."

"Doctor Thomas? Oh... Oh! I've just had a rather bizarre thought."

She removed her arms and stood close to him, her eyes full of his smiling face. "What's that?"

"Here I am, passionately kissing a beautiful young woman in my bedroom – in my pyjamas, in fact – and I don't even know her name."

Abby laughed, stepped back, and held out her hand in mock greeting. "Susan Abigail Fenwick. Pleased to meet you, Doctor Thomas."

"Fenwick?"

"Do you like it?"

"Well..."

"I hate it," Abby said, wrinkling her nose. "I'm going to change it."

"Again?" David said, surprised. "What to this time?"

"Thomas," she murmured, snuggling back into his neck. "Abby Thomas. What do you think?"

"That," he replied softly, "is an absolutely perfect choice."

# CHAPTER 44

A week after this happy reunion had taken place, the Prime Minister of Australia had a surprise visit from the director of ASIO, which had turned out to be unexpectedly pleasant. One week after that, the P.M. had embarked on an unscheduled trip to the States, ostensibly to discuss trade with the President. That meeting had not been so pleasant for the latter gentleman, but it had produced the desired effect. The P.M. on his return, had been delighted to announce that the United States, as an expression of their appreciation of the warm and friendly relationship they had with their allies, as well as their utter abhorrence of terrorism, had contributed four hundred million dollars towards the establishment of a new and ultra-modern research facility at the University of Sydney. Less well known to the public was the sudden disappearance of the AAT, and even less well known was that, following the sudden and untimely death of Norman Harding, Peter Lawson had taken over the directorship of the CIA.

✳ ✳ ✳

The same day as the P.M. made this happy announcement, but not at the same time, Abby lay asleep in the room she had rented down the hall from the one occupied by doctor David Thomas. The infection in her thigh had spread and necessitated the attention of the house doctor, who, surveying the bruised condition of her body, had politely enquired as to what had happened to her. "Car accident," she had replied, the answer bearing some semblance to the truth. She was awakened by a knock at the door, and glancing at her bedside clock, saw it was nine thirty. Never mind, she felt so much better after another long, refreshing sleep. She smiled, jumped out of bed, and threw her dressing gown around her body, tying the cord around her waist. This would be David bringing her breakfast as he had done every morning since her arrival, and she flew to the door and flung it open. The excitement and joy on her face morphed into sheer terror, and she backed away, unable drag her eyes from the figure in the doorway.

"How did you find me?" Her voice was barely a croak.

The figure walked slowly into the room.

"A friend of mine, Ross Baker, alerted me when David passed through Heathrow under another name, and he soon discovered this location. Do not fear, Miss Saunders, Ross knows all about the deplorable activities of the CIA. He is somewhat dedicated to ensuring David will have a completely trouble-free life in his new country, especially after I had a word with him. Indeed, I feel any academic post is completely open to him if he would care to apply."

She produced a folded sheet of paper from her pocket.

"I believe you wrote him this note." She held it up. "I must say it profoundly altered the counsel I was about to give him. Now, Miss Saunders, please sit down on the bed if you wish, for I perceive you are still in some pain, and begin at the beginning. The truth, please."

Sarah Cole fixed her with her beautiful blue eyes, but this time Abby detected something else in them, something which she would never have thought to see, a certain tenderness, a willingness to understand. The fear in her own eyes lessened a little, although her heart was still hammering in her chest. Sitting down on the bed she began the life story of Abigail Saunders, leaving nothing out. Throughout the recitation, often accompanied by tears, Sarah remained silent. Abby was once again gripped by the conviction that this beautiful creature could see deep into her heart, and would know instantly if she uttered the slightest untruth. Just as before, she could not will herself to look away from those huge blue eyes. When all was done she felt both exhausted yet relieved. The moment she had dreaded in her dreams had come and gone, and Professor Cole had not turned her brain into jello. In fact she was smiling at her, and the beauty and light in that face sent warmth into Abby's racing heart.

"You have been rescued by the grace and love of God, Miss Saunders. Never forget it," Sarah said softly.

"You can see into my heart, can't you?" Abby replied. "Can't you hear it singing for Him?"

"Yes, Miss Saunders, I believe you. Know also that in David you have won a treasure. See that you treat him as such."

Abby stared deep into those captivating eyes. "Look for yourself. Don't you know I love him more than all my life?"

"I believe you do," Sarah said gently. "You have been singularly blessed Miss—"

"Can you… would you… please… call me Abby?"

There was a pause. Sarah looked closely at the woman for a long time, then smiled.

"Yes," she said, "I can."

❋ ❋ ❋

Two weeks after that, Sarah Cole returned to Australia, and paid an unexpected visit to Lydia and Geoff, officially to offer her condolences on the loss of their son. In a matter of minutes the shouts of excitement and squeals of laughter amidst the music of joyful tears, would have told anyone who happened to be passing that her visit had been extraordinarily effective.

**End**

# ABOUT THE AUTHOR

Mac Cusiter was born at Lewisham, a suburb of Sydney. His boyhood interest in science culminated in his graduating from Sydney University with a doctorate in physical organic chemistry. He began his professional life as a Chemistry teacher at Sydney Institute, and retired as head of the science department. He has been a youth leader for much of his life, and is at present a lay pastor at Christ Church Northern Beaches.
He lives with his wife Val in Sydney's northern suburbs.

## Also by the author

## THE BREACH

*Doctor Daniel Van Dekker is a worried man. Political engineering destroyed Australia's world class Institute for Nuclear Research. As chief scientist he had failed to protect the institute he loved. Furious with his political masters and angry with himself, Dekker pressured the government to allow him to conduct experiments into nuclear fusion, holding out the promise of cheap energy and intellectual property rights worth a fortune. To this his political masters agreed, their hidden agenda to ensure Dekker's failure and subsequent humiliation. But Dekker also had a hidden agenda. Instead of investigating nuclear fusion he planned to perform high energy collision experiments with the aim of discovering new fundamental particles. If he was successful, Australia's reputation in nuclear research would be restored.*
*But Dekker's experiment went horribly wrong.*
*With only two scientists on his team, doctor Mark Chambers, a particle physicist and a committed Christian, and doctor Candice LeBlanc, a power engineer who hates religion of any sort, Dekker must solve the problem he has created.*
*He has just had to flee the country to save his life.*

## STORM DANCING

*By half past eight the wind had died, and the torrential rain had lessened slightly.*
*Brian started the engine, and they began to move forward slowly. Not far ahead lay Toongabbie Creek Bridge, buried under a swirling torrent of foaming water.*
*Suddenly Brian slewed the car to a stop. He stared out the window, as if his eyes were playing tricks on him. "What the blazes is that?" he yelled. Caught in the glare of the headlights was a teenage girl, her face turned upward into the rain, her eyes shut. She was moving along the footpath in a bizarre twirling motion, her hands outstretched as if she was engaged in some strange dance. Suddenly she froze, her head jerked upright, and a pair of large, terrified eyes turned into the glaring light. Her mouth opened in a scream they could hear inside the car, and twirling around frantically, she tripped over her own feet and rolled out of sight down the embankment towards the surging, swollen water. So began the avalanche which would change the life of an ordinary suburban family forever.*

# THE PETROV EFFECT

## STRANGE ICE

*He turned south to face the blizzard and screwed up his eyes into slits. The mountain path was fast disappearing under the swirling snow and ice. He quickened his pace. Blinded momentarily, he stopped, wiped his eyes and staggered to regain his balance. The snow under his foot moved. Not only did it move, it made a noise. Dropping to his knees he began to scrape the snow off the path to see what he had trodden on.*
*It was a woman.*
*An ecological menace was about to be unleased on the world.*


## LORD CAULEY'S DEMON

*Alicia froze, staring at the apparition. The apparition stared back at her with large blue eyes. Her heart began beating so hard she felt it was about to leap out of her chest. Her limbs had turned to water, and she was shaking so much it was a wonder she didn't fall over on the uneven ground and go sliding off the path into oblivion...*

*Lord Cauley Island is inhabited by a demon, and everyone is terrified of it. Tim Raines has come to the island seeking to find some experiential reality to his Christian faith. But how to tell truth from fiction, reality from legend? Tim's life is about to be turned upside down. Soon he will learn the real purpose of his coming to the island – from a teenage girl who can't even say a word.*

www.ingramcontent.com/pod-product-compliance
Lightning Source LLC
Chambersburg PA
CBHW071645260626
47170CB00001B/235